D0742687

The Gatherer

BY THE SAME AUTHOR

The Widow of Ratchets
Inheritance

The GATHERER

OWEN BROOKES

Holt, Rinehart and Winston
New York

Copyright © 1982 by Owen Brookes
All rights reserved, including the right to reproduce
this book or portions thereof in any form.
Published by Holt, Rinehart and Winston,
383 Madison Avenue, New York, New York 10017.
Published simultaneously in Canada by Holt, Rinehart
and Winston of Canada, Limited.

Library of Congress Cataloging in Publication Data
Brookes, Owen.
The gatherer.
I. Title.
PR6052.R5815G3 1982 823'.914 81-23735 AACR2
ISBN: 0-03-059531-2

First Edition

Designer: Amy Hill
Printed in the United States of America
1 3 5 7 9 10 8 6 4 2

To
Dan and Barb
with love

The Gatherer

"You must be mad," Evie said, and to reinforce her statement, or perhaps declare her angry disbelief, she stubbed out a half-smoked, lipstick-stained cigarette in the glass ashtray on the littered supper table. At once her long, blood-colored nails picked at the open pack of cigarettes. Pursing her lips, she held the king-sized cigarette in place and flicked angrily at the small gold lighter.

Sue, her sister, younger by twelve years, did not reply. She began to clear the table, drawing the soiled dishes toward her and stacking them methodically. She had vowed that she would not quarrel with Evie. There had been too many quarrels with her family. They had exhausted her. More importantly, she saw her determination as proof that this was one decision she had reached by herself and meant to keep. In the past, she admitted, there had always been an element of approval seeking when she told Evie or her mother of plans made, decisions taken. Not this time. It was entirely hers, a declaration of freedom. She could not be moved, would not even consider a compromise.

"You realize what will happen, don't you?" Evie asked. She waved her painted hand in front of her face to disperse the smoke, coughed, and said, "I'm talking to you," as Sue carried the stacked plates through into the tiny kitchen.

"I can hear you," Sue replied, placing the dishes on the draining board and snapping on the electric percolator.

"But you can't look me in the face," Evie challenged.

"Yes, I can."

Sue leaned, her arms folded over her chest, against the open archway that connected her small living room with the smaller kitchen, and looked straight at her sister. For the first time ever she felt in control, superior to Evie. She looked at her not with concern for what she would say next, but dispassionately, as though she had never seen her objectively before.

Evie had a pronounced lantern jaw. It gave her cheeks a sunken, hollow appearance and exaggerated the largeness of her eyes. She was not beautiful but striking, commanding even. Hard. But she only *looked* hard, Sue realized.

"You'd never have done this if mother was alive," Evie said, pushing her fingers through her thin, bleached-blond hair.

"Yes, I would," Sue countered. "It would have made no difference whatsoever. Except—" she paused and added, for honesty's sake "—I would probably have asked you to tell her."

"See?" Evie said, tapping ash fiercely from her cigarette.

Sue didn't.

"You wouldn't have been able to tell her yourself because you know it's wrong."

"Wrong?" Sue laughed, quite naturally, for the word was absurd and Evie knew it, had allowed herself to slip into the language of their mother's topsy-turvy view of morality. "That's rich coming from you. You know it's not *wrong*. Remember your weekends with . . . what's his name?"

"All right," Evie snapped. "Not wrong. But stupid. Bloody suicide. And don't you go throwing my past in my face, our kid," she said, lapsing into the accent and idiom of working-class Birmingham that both sisters had learned to control if not entirely eradicate. "What I had with Donald was a business arrangement. No strings. A good time. You're putting your life on the line."

"Oh, don't be so melodramatic," Sue said, smiling, and went back into the kitchen to fetch the coffee.

"What do you know about this chap, anyway?" Evie shouted.

She wanted to say "everything" but she had vowed, along with her determination not to row, to be sensible, unromantic, and honest.

"Enough. All I can expect to know of another human being, given the circumstances," she said, carrying the percolator to the table where mugs and cream were already set out.

"Nothing, you mean."

Sue knelt at the tiled table and poured coffee. Evie lit another cigarette and blew a funnel of smoke toward the ceiling.

"Cream?" Sue asked.

"No. Got to watch my figure. And so had you if you reckon on keeping this chap interested for more than a few weeks."

Sue ducked her head, biting off the retort that rose to her lips. It would sound prissy to say that Gavin saw more in her than her body. She placed the mug in front of Evie and turned it so that the handle faced her.

"Just look at your nails!" Evie exclaimed. "You look as though you could grow flowers under them. And haven't you got some polish?"

"It's only charcoal," Sue said, looking at her short nails, several of which were stained with the charcoal she'd been using earlier.

"We do a lovely line in false ones, you know. I could get you some." Evie's voice always warmed when she spoke of cosmetics, the endless paraphernalia of female adornment that was her job and, Sue sometimes suspected, her only true and abiding interest.

"No, thanks. I couldn't draw or paint with false fingernails."

"Oh, you're hopeless, you are. Hopeless," Evie complained, spreading her own fingers and inspecting them with appreciation. "Still, I don't know what to say to you. I really don't," she said, letting her hand fall into her lap.

"Well, if you don't know, I can't tell you," Sue responded, consciously repeating a childhood chant of their mother's.

"Oh, you!" Evie recognized the reference, the appeal to common ground, with an awkward shift of her body.

"I know what I'd like you to say. I'd like you to wish me luck, share my happiness."

"Well, I would. . . . I want to. . . . You know that. I'd love to be able to. But I can't. I can't wish you well when I see you putting your head in a noose."

"How do you know?" Sue pleaded. "You haven't given me a chance to tell you anything about it."

"You'll be dependent on him, won't you?"

"Only for a roof over my head."

"Oh? And what are you going to live on, then? Love?"

"I told you last time I saw you."

"That contract thing . . ."

"Commission," Sue corrected.

"Whatever. That job for that publisher in London? How long do you think that'll last?"

"There'll be others. I know there will. I'm going to write to lots of people. Anyway, I've been asked to do four illustrations for *Woman* this week. And I've saved."

"And what about that teaching job? I suppose you'll be giving that up."

Sue ignored this remark. The only thing she'd ever done that impressed her family was to teach one day a week at her old art school, and how she had longed to give that up.

"Besides," she went on, "I shan't need much, being in the country."

"The country!" Evie shrieked, as though it were an obscene word. "Oh, I see. He's going to hide you away, is he? Very nice, I'm sure."

"It's not like that," Sue said, twisting her hands in her lap. If only she didn't feel so guilty. If only it were possible to explain to Evie that all men, all relationships weren't like the ones she knew. But to try would be to patronize her, to lay claim to something better and finer, and that wouldn't be fair.

"Where in the country?" Evie asked, trying to sound conversational.

"Northamptonshire."

"Oh."

Sue opened her mouth, wanting to explain about the cottage, the plans they'd made, but before she could speak, Evie went on, in a pitying tone.

"I suppose you think he's going to marry you?"

"You know he's already married. You know that's out of the question."

"*I* do. But do *you*? That's my point."

"Of course. Besides, I'm not sure I want to get married, even if it were possible."

"Oh, come off it."

"Well, why don't you, then," Sue flared, "if you're so taken with it?"

Evie did not answer. From her smart clutch bag she took a plastic container of sweeteners and tapped two into her coffee.

"Sorry," Sue said, feeling suddenly tired and defeated. She reached for her own coffee. "I love him. It feels right, being with him. I promise you I'm not rushing into anything. I've thought about it. Yes, I've even thought, as seriously as I can, that it may go wrong. All I can say is I'm prepared to take that chance. I want to. And if it doesn't work out, well, what have I lost? I'm young enough to start again. I can work. . . ."

"He's old enough to be your father," Evie snapped. "When he's had the best years of your life—"

"That's an exaggeration, and the point is he isn't my father. Besides, he's what makes these the best years of my life, if that's what they are. Him, and being able to work in the way I want."

"You've no security. You're young now, yes, but how long does it last? You're old before you know it. You wake up one morning and say, Christ, whatever happened to the years? You think it won't happen to you, but it will."

"But I've got emotional security. That's what matters to me."

"Oh, don't be so stupid, Sue. You've got nothing without a ring on your finger. *I* know."

Evie suddenly looked vulnerable, pained. Beneath the careful mask of her makeup, her face seemed small, tired, a little frightened.

"I'm sorry," Sue said and wished that, without giving offense or embarrassing her, she could have touched her sister, hugged her, comforted her.

"It's because of the mistakes I made that I'm trying to make you see sense," she said, avoiding Sue's eyes.

"I know." She wanted to deny that there was any basis for

comparison but knew that that would only hurt Evie more. Instead, she said, "But I have to make my own mistakes. You can understand that."

"No. I can't. I won't. Ever since Mam died—before, really—I've felt, well, responsible for you. I know I haven't been a good example. But you did so well for yourself. Just look at this place. *I* never had a place like this when I was your age. I don't want to see you throw it all away."

"And I want you to see that I'm not. I've got a chance to build up a good career for myself, a reputation. . . ."

"Oh, yes. Some reputation. An old man's darling," Evie said, her voice like acid.

"I meant professionally," Sue said, cold.

"I know what you meant. I'm not stupid. But what's everyone going to think? Those people in London, for instance."

"I shouldn't think they'd be very interested. Anyway, it's none of their business. I'm not going to advertise this, you know. It's my private life. And that's the way I want to keep it."

"In other words, mind your own business, Evie."

"I didn't mean that."

"Well, you can't say I didn't try."

"Don't be angry, Evie, please."

"When will you be leaving, then?" She tried to sound indifferent but didn't quite succeed.

"I don't know yet. After Christmas. As soon as the cottage is ready."

"I can't see you in the country," Evie said, shaking her head.

"You will. I want you to come and visit. We won't lose touch. There'll be a telephone. You can come for the weekend."

"We'll see." Evie stood up, looked around the room for her coat.

"Don't go," Sue said.

"Since I can't help, I won't hinder. Besides, I've got to be in Nuneaton by nine tomorrow," she added, softening her tone a little.

Sighing, Sue got up and fetched Evie's fashionable camel-colored coat and helped her on with it.

"I'll see you next week," she said, pleading a little.

"Yes. I'll give you a ring. And thanks for the very nice supper." She offered her cheek, which Sue kissed lightly, her fists clenched to prevent herself embracing her sister as she wanted to do. They were an undemonstrative family, formal and scant in displays of affection.

"Drive carefully," Sue said.

"And you, think over what I've said," Evie called, going down the stairs cautiously on her high heels.

Alone, Sue drifted aimlessly about the small room, coming to a stop at last by her drawing board, tucked away now in a corner to make space for the dining table. She stared at the first two completed drawings for her first book, pleased but with a sharply critical eye. She could not make up her mind whether the meeting with Evie had gone as badly or better than she expected. She found a nub of disappointment in herself. She had wanted an opportunity to tell Evie all about the details of their plan. She had thought her sister would be interested, curious no matter how much she disapproved in general. But the bald statement of intent had been sufficient for Evie, sufficient to set her off. And Sue knew she would return to the attack. This had only been an opening skirmish. Evie would marshal her big guns, and next week. . . . Sue turned sharply away from her drawings. Meanwhile, she longed to confide in someone, to share the most important thing that had ever happened to her. She wanted a sympathetic ear, someone to question her and rejoice with her. For the first time in her life she saw how lonely she was, had always been, and that made her ache for the sound of Gavin's voice, the touch of his hand. Twenty-three years in one city, she thought bitterly, growing up, going to school, art school, working, and she had not one close friend to show for it.

Slowly, her mind elsewhere, she finished clearing the table, carried the coffee mugs into the kitchen, and started washing up. She supposed that her family's distrust of physical contact and displays of emotion were at the root of it. It had made her shy and awkward with people. Only with Gavin had she ever felt abandoned, open, totally free to be herself. That proved that he was right for her, special, didn't it? For Gavin had not had to teach her these things; he had found them, ready and waiting in her.

She had had friends, of course. School friends, other girls at art school, but they had all drifted away into marriages, careers in London. To be honest, Sue had to admit that she had made little effort to maintain these friendships. As a girl, she had hated taking friends home, not, as her mother had sometimes accused her, because she was ashamed of the mean, pebble-dashed house in Weoley Castle, but because she could not bear her and Evie's snide remarks about posh girls from Edgbaston and Bristol Road, about how Sue herself was a cut above the rest of the family now. And when she finally got out on her own, her life had centered on Mike. There had been no time for girl friends. No wonder Mike had found it stifling, too intense.

She pulled the plug from the sink and watched the soapy water swirl into a gurgling vortex and drain away. She stripped off yellow plastic gloves and draped them over the back of the sink. Why was it that Mike, whom she had believed she loved passionately and completely, had made her tight and nervous, ungiving, whereas Gavin had only to smile at her and she felt open and entirely confident? Perhaps she'd understand one day. Perhaps it would always remain a mystery. But now it didn't matter since she had found Gavin, and therefore herself.

Kneeling in the sitting room, she opened a drawer in the small bureau and drew out a folder. Inside was a photocopy of Gavin's hand-drawn plans for the cottage, together with a photograph of it. He had not wanted her to see it until all the conversion work was done. He wanted it to be perfect for her. But, with one of those curious touches of formality that always delighted her, he had sent her this copy of the plans for her comment and approval. She had then asked for a photograph since the plans meant little to her. The cottage, as shown in the photograph, was not in the least like the English person's romantic ideal. It was not stone and thatch, not covered in rambling roses, not gabled and arched so that it looked like the gingerbread house of the fairy story, with sugar-frosting chimneys. It was simple and stark, as Gavin himself had confessed, entirely devoid of any distinguishing architectural feature. It wasn't even old, having been built after the Second World War to house a farm laborer. It was brick and slate, two stories, with a chimney at either end. The front door was placed bang in the center, bounded symmetrically with a sash window on either side, echoed smaller on the upper floor. There was a scrubby strip of unkempt garden before it, unfenced and unhedged. When Sue had first seen the photograph, she had laughed with delight. It reminded her of the first house she had ever drawn, the sort of house every child draws: idealized, simple, and touchingly innocent.

"I didn't know people ever built houses like this," she had told Gavin.

"No architect would," he confirmed gravely.

"But don't you see? This was built by someone who remembered what it was like to be a child, someone who thought back and said, 'What does a house need and look like?' "

"It's certainly functional," he said drily. Laughing, she had thrown her arms around him and kissed him. "But I'll make it perfect for you. I've always wanted to do something like this, and now I have a reason."

"You couldn't do it for yourself?" she had asked, leaning back in his arms to study his face.

"Oh, no. I had to wait for you. Why were you so long in coming?"

"Why were you?"

She closed the folder and slipped it back into the drawer. No, she had no doubts whatsoever. She would be able to work without distractions, in peace and quiet, and every weekend he could manage, even during the week sometimes, Gavin would be with her. She felt bad about his wife, of course. But there always had to be a shadow in every sunlit scene. She was taking nothing from Myra Trope that she had not already lost. Gavin had been honest, completely honest. It was no one's fault that Myra was ill. Gavin would do everything he could for her and he would never leave her entirely. But he had a right to a proper life, a life Myra could not give him. Any compassionate person must see that. And she would never presume or interfere. She would never claim him when Myra needed him. They had made their vows to Myra, not in person, but solemnly and with the fixed intention never to hurt her.

It was this sort of thing she wanted to say to someone, to Evie. Not because she needed approval, support, but to demonstrate that she had thought of everything, was as responsible as she was happy.

She stared longingly at the telephone. She had never had, never wanted Gavin's home number, but sometimes, after Myra had gone painfully to bed, it was possible for him to ring her and whisper a few words of love and encouragement. She wanted so much to hear him now that she thought she could will the telephone to ring. She stood up, moved toward the gleaming black instrument, and, like magic, it rang. She picked up the receiver at once, her voice breathless and warm.

"Hello?"

"I've been thinking," Evie said. "Since you're so set on going to live with this chap, shouldn't I meet him?"

Disappointment confused her, robbed her of the ability to think. She stared blankly at the wall, wondering why it could not have been him.

"Oh, I thought . . . I mean . . . Yes. I don't—"

"Oh, very well, if you're set on keeping us apart."

"It's not that. . . ."

"I suppose you're ashamed of me."

"Evie, stop it. Please. You took me by surprise, that's all." She took a deep breath. "Yes. It would be a good idea. Maybe then you would not worry about me. But it's difficult for him to get away. I'll speak to him as soon as I can. All right?"

"Well, you'll let me know, then?"

"Yes."

"I'd better get my beauty sleep. Take care now."

"Good night, Evie," she said quietly and listened to the line purr emptily.

If anything had dominated or blighted Gavin Trope's adult life it was most certainly not the events of one January morning. He himself would have said that ambition and illness had been the determining influences on his life and that the Gatherer was just a spooky story that had temporarily inflamed and warped a child's overheated imagination. That evacuee child bore such a tenuous relationship to the man he had become that he felt no kinship with him but regarded him as someone he had briefly known rather than as an important link in the inevitable chain from cradle to tomb. Indeed it was not until he stood on the brink of middle age that he thought about that sickly child at all, and before that a very great deal had happened to him.

First he lost his mother, not, as might have been expected, in the Blitz, but shortly after the war, in a safe and quiet Sussex town where she had fled to live out her widowhood in peace and raise her only son. That was his first experience of real illness, and, though it had been swift, many years had to pass before he could see that as a blessing. He carried from the experience a knowledge of pain that turned quickly to resentment and anger. Both his guardian and his headmaster thought for a time that these feelings might tilt him toward medicine, but Gavin knew better. To imagine that you could alleviate suffering by being a daily witness to it was pure romanticism, and he was determined to stamp out all that was romantic in his nature. An orphan, he reasoned, with only a very small income in trust, could not afford to be anything but hardheaded and practical. On his mother's death the war pension she had received to compensate her for the loss of her husband, a casualty of one of the first major offensives of the war, ceased. And he had no wish to be any more dependent than necessary on his uncle and guardian, who had never approved of Gavin's father. There was enough to pay his school fees and to see him, if he were frugal, through university. After that, he would make his own way.

A geographer by taste, he had read architecture at Cambridge because it seemed to have a practical application. The devastations of the war would mean a boom in restoring and rebuilding, providing perfect openings for a young man with only his wits and drive to see him through. The geographer in him, however, soon prompted him toward the relatively new and then fashionable science of town planning, a field in which the scope was wide and clear for anyone who got in on the ground floor. Such architectural dreams as he had could wait until he had reached the top of his profession. Then, perhaps even in retirement, he could build or restore one perfect building and rest satisfied. What good were dreams, he argued, if you lacked the money to build them?

By a series of carefully planned and judiciously timed moves, Gavin Trope advanced in his profession until, at the age of forty, there was only one rung above him, unless he should overcome a lifelong reluctance and decide to go into politics. He had earned a reputation for hardheadedness and competence. His contemporaries marveled that he was a man who never failed to get any job for which he applied. He was regarded as formidable opposition, so much so that word that he had applied for a given post frequently caused the timorous to withdraw. Gavin knew that this success was due not to luck or some Midaslike ability but to the careful gaining of qualifications and experience, to timing. He and his career were perfectly synchronized to the bureaucratic clock, which some of his more talented and impatient colleagues tended to ignore. In this world, he believed, you followed the map, mounted step by step. There were no valid shortcuts, no magical ladders that carried you six places ahead without a writhing snake to spiral you down again to your rightful place in line. By the careful, systematic application of this conformist philosophy, Gavin Trope became director of planning at Higham Furze, one of several towns scattered through the Midlands and northeast of England designated by the government as grant-aided development areas, new towns that would incorporate the old—expansion with preservation.

In 1958, being reasonably secure, twenty-seven years old, and a man with prospects, Gavin Trope had married. It was part of his plan, a necessary part, and having reached the decision he selected his bride and mate with care and attention to detail. She must be attractive but not dangerously so. She must be domesticated, a good hostess, but adaptable. Certainly she must not be cut out for a career of her own. Her breeding capacity, since he could not figure out a way to check this without embarrassment, he was content to leave to chance. He was, in any case, ambivalent about children. They completed the conventional domestic picture he was in the process of building for himself, but they had no material role to play in his plan. If they came along, well and good. If not . . . and here he shrugged mentally.

The most striking thing about Myra Brent was her grooming. She used it skillfully, from the top of her neat, gleaming hair to the tips of her good, highly polished shoes. Grooming overcame the slight gawkiness of her body and provided a façade behind which to hide the diffidence and shyness of her nature. Gavin found her in the drawing department of his then job. She was competent, but no more than that, a plodder who had gained the necessary qualifications but who would never develop flair. Gavin soon discovered that she also had no real liking for her job. On the one hand, she knew there was more to life than marriage, motherhood, and domesticity. On the other, she had been insufficiently educated and encouraged to strike out with determination on a career of her own. By the time Gavin met her and began to court her assiduously, Myra was twenty-eight, knew that she was in a dead-end job, and feared that her chances of marriage were dangerously slim. Gavin was the sort of man she would have chosen for herself in terms of background and prospects, but that mattered little since she fell deeply and devoutly in love with him.

The marriage was deemed a success by friends, colleagues, and Myra's family. It was often described as "old-fashioned," by which imprecise term was meant that husband and wife each shouldered his and her separate responsibilities and did not interfere in the other's allotted sphere of influence. Gavin earned the bread, while Myra sliced it, buttered it, served it. Gavin completely agreed with the public assessment of their unruffled marriage, and, if Myra occasionally stared at herself with a hint of desperation in the mirror and asked "What is it all for?" her image returned no answers. The vague restlessness, a feeling of dying by inches was, she told herself, all in the mind and would undoubtedly be cured by babies. And they did try to make babies. It was simply a question of time and patience.

Gavin was working on one of the last and largest new town

projects to be undertaken in Britain for many years when Myra, then aged thirty-two, began to vomit and complain of splitting headaches. Pregnancy was considered; also migraines, food poisoning, and a whole range of allergies. The attacks became more and more frequent, and Myra complained of a numbness in her toes, a prickling sensation in the tips of her fingers. At the height of these attacks her head would loll as though her neck had become too weak to support it. At Gavin's insistence, she was admitted to a respected research hospital in Cambridge, and twenty-four hours later multiple sclerosis was diagnosed.

On the morning Gavin heard the news he began to love Myra as he had never loved her before. Had it been some other illness, something curable or swift, perhaps that love would have grown and supported them both. For a time, as the disease went into temporary remission and Myra was able to lead a more or less normal life, this seemed to be the case. A new and unaccustomed warmth characterized his manner toward her. She was happy and full of hope. Even the decision not to have children did not pain her as once it would have done. And for a year or so Gavin was able to forget that the disease must and would return. When it did, with a violence that even the doctors had not anticipated, Gavin found only anger in himself, and his love turned to a bleak and frightened pity.

Myra emerged from the hospital in a wheelchair, her body bloated and sickly, with her power to grip seriously impaired. Another remission restored the power of her arms so that she was able to lift her useless, puffy legs in and out of the chair. He did not mention the slight hesitation and slurring in her speech, of which she seemed ignorant. He helped her as best he could, but she knew that their belated honeymoon was over, that somewhere, deep within himself, he shrank from her.

Until the advent of Myra's illness, Gavin had planned to stay on at the new town and to become, in five years or so, its director. Her semiparalysis, and the knowledge that it could only get worse, changed his plans. He could not bear the commiseration and concern of his colleagues, the bluff, embarrassed encouragement, the whispering behind his back. His marriage, once admired, had become a pathetic object of sympathy. He knew that he was thought to be "wonderful," but felt like a hypocrite for all he could find in himself was anger and pity. Consulting no one, he applied for and got the job at Higham Furze. He went there alone and selected, almost at random, an ugly detached bungalow on the outskirts of the old town and had ramps put in so that his wife could maneuver without his help. The ramps depressed him, as did all the specially designed gadgets that would allow Myra to pretend at competence, at a normal life. He longed for steep stairs and a primitive kitchen, coal fires and a garden that did not have to be paved over.

It seemed, once Myra was installed in the bungalow, that their relationship had reached a climax, and would continue thus until the illness finally depleted her strength or he reached retirement age. There was nothing else, nothing at all, to which they could look forward. But two things happened at Higham Furze that were to change everything and fill Gavin's life with purpose.

He was in his office one day, poring over plans and making copious notes that he would present to the next planning meeting, when he received a phone call from a man named Tom Carpenter. Mr. Carpenter, it transpired, was a junior partner in a local law firm who had been retained by Messrs. Button and Co., solicitors, of Nene in the neighboring county of Northamptonshire. Cryptically, and in phraseology that brought a smile to Gavin's face, he urged a meeting, as soon as possible, at which Mr. Trope would "learn something to his advantage." He kept the appointment and found Mr. Carpenter absurdly young and handsome. It appeared that Messrs. Button and Co. had, with the aid of various hired colleagues, been trying to trace Gavin for more than two years in order to inform him that, under the terms of the will of the late Arthur Seton Pownall of Gatherings Farm, Hemming, Northamptonshire, he was the legal owner of a cottage. Carpenter had finally succeeded in finding him and was very pleased with himself indeed.

"I don't understand."

It was all explained to him again and, while Mr. Carpenter jubilantly telephoned Messrs. Button and Co., the recesses of memory began to open and admit light. The deeds and the keys to the cottage and all other relevant material would be forwarded to Mr. Carpenter's office. There would be documents to sign, of course, and Mr. Carpenter would telephone in a day or two. Holding out his hand, Mr. Carpenter begged leave to be the first to congratulate Mr. Trope, who nodded and went away bemused.

As it happened, he had time on his hands just then, for Myra was again in the hospital for a routine checkup, more physiotherapy, and a course of drugs in which no one had much faith and which would certainly make her vomit and feel weak and querulous. Yet Gavin was glad of the empty bungalow, the time to think and remember.

He had never known Grandpa Pownall's name and, had he thought about him at all, would have considered him dead years ago. George Pownall must be an old man now, Lucas in his mid-forties, Hettie grown up. But then, searching his memory to piece together a picture of this forgotten stranger, Arthur Seton Pownall, he realized that the man must have been much younger than he—a child at the time, judging and seeing entirely from a child's perspective—had imagined him. He'd been known as Grandpa by right of relationship, not weight of years. With an almost physical sensation he remembered the old man's agility and strength, remembered his arms about him, and saw the wicked twinkle in his eye as he worked by lamplight in the old stables, fashioning scarecrows. Still, apart from that physical sensation, a sort of body memory, he felt no connection with that old man, with that time. It was dead and buried as surely as the old man who, for some quirk, some unimagined reason, had left him a cottage.

He could not remember the cottage. Images of the village, the farmhouse, the road, and the great flat fields came to him like old, yellowed snapshots, but of the cottage he could remember nothing. Then he remembered them saying the old man had a screw loose, was touched in the head. *That was why we wasn't sure we should take in evacuees, you see. Well, we couldn't say straight out, could we? After all, he's harmless.* Gavin stiffened in his chair at the sound, so clearly recalled, of Mary Pownall's voice. He saw her plump face, framed by tight, dark curls, hanging over him, talking to him, as though he were a child again. And George, too. *He tells these stories, see, and then, well, he, like, he believes in 'em. He don't mean no harm. They're only stories, see?* That was when he was ill, had a fever from being out in the cold when he shouldn't have been. Just after Christmas, years and years ago. He remembered the illness as a time of unpleasant heat and severe, shivering cold. Of voices and faces, talking at him, explaining. Even Lucas. *You don't want to take no notice of Grandpa. He's touched in the head. Other day, I caught him talking to the scarecrows. Crazy, that's what he is.* And then he woke up and there was sunlight in the room and his mother was sitting by him, holding his hand, smiling, but with tears in her eyes. *You see? We sent for your mum, we were that worried about you. Now, you don't want to go worrying her with no daft old stories, do you?* And he'd gotten better, well enough to go out walking with his hand tucked tight in his mother's until she had to go back to her war work in London. He had gotten stronger and better and went to school again with Lucas and Ashton. To school, where Mr. Roberts taught them and thwacked their wooden desks with his blackboard pointer when he thought they weren't paying attention.

What happened to Miss Peterson?

Don't you remember? Well, poor soul, she went a bit funny. Ran off. Don't you remember at all? We only heard later as how she'd had a telegram, one of those every woman fears who's got a man at the front. Her fiancé was killed overseas. Poor soul. I always liked Miss Peterson. So did you, didn't you, Gavin?

A blush spread across Gavin's cheeks as he sat in the bungalow, ransacking memory. He had an image of a small boy ensconced in a warm parlor, with music, and the flowery scent of a woman. He remembered smooth arms and soft breasts, his first awesome knowledge of a woman's breasts. He blushed because he realized he had been a little, or perhaps dangerously, in love with Miss Peterson.

It's not right, not proper. A grown woman like that, spending all her time with a boy. What's she up to, that's what I want to know?

Whose voice was that? George's? He could not place it now, or where in that long-ago time the words had been said and overheard.

Not right. Good-looking woman she is. Must have urges. What's she want him down there for all the time? I tell you she's up to no good. I've seen the look on her face, the way she looks at menfolk. And he's our responsibility. If anything should come out, it's us would get the blame.

His cheeks burned again, this time with shame and fear, as they had many years ago when he was a child, a vague, small, shadowy figure who appeared in the snapshots of his memory, along with all the others.

Did she touch you? Did she? Down there?

Gavin got up from his chair and poured himself a stiff whiskey. He gulped half of it down and, as it burned his throat, it seemed to cauterize, seal off the things he had already forgotten once.

That night his sleep was troubled by dreams that left him feeling guilty and shamed, but he could not recall anything precisely except the unpleasant image of a woman's breasts, raked and torn, bleeding. He put it down to too much whiskey, anxiety about Myra. Because she was in the hospital he did not tell her about his unexpected legacy. Indeed he considered declining it altogether, but that, on reflection, seemed ungrateful. However, when he received the expected summons from Tom Carpenter, he went armed with questions. Since it had taken so long to find him, was the bequest still legal? Had the surviving family, George Pownall in particular, not contested the will? And if not, why not? Mr. Carpenter assured him that the bequest was valid, that no challenge to any detail of the will had been made, and that he knew nothing of the motives behind this. Why did Mr. Trope raise such a question?

"Because," he replied, uncapping his pen to sign the necessary papers, "I don't understand why the old man should have remembered me, let alone wished to leave me something in his will."

"If I were you," Tom Carpenter smiled, "I would accept graciously."

Gavin took the deeds and keys back to his office. Without looking at them he locked them into the bottom drawer of his desk and, that night, after visiting Myra, he sat down and composed a short, formal note to George Pownall. He made no personal reference to Grandpa Pownall but expressed his astonishment and gratitude. "I have no plans for the property as yet. You will understand that it is all such a surprise to me that I must consider very carefully before deciding how best to use this unexpected legacy. Unless, of course, you should require the cottage for any reason? I would be happy to rent it to you or accept any reasonable offer to buy."

He added this final sentence because he felt the family might, justifiably, resent the bequest. He received no reply to his letter and, as the time of Myra's return from the hospital drew near, he put the whole matter out of his mind. At first, Myra was weak and exhausted, but, as the days stretched one into another, he noticed a slight improvement in her speech, and physically she became more dexterous and able. The pride and pleasure this improvement gave her—apparent in her shining eyes and ready smile—made him rage within. It was ridiculous, this cat-and-mouse game with inevitable death. He understood at last why the speed of his mother's illness had been considered a blessing.

The other event that was to change his life was still in the future. At the time of the legacy and Myra's improvement, Sue Jackman was still unknown to him.

She had felt lost, even a bit panic-stricken, in the large, open-plan office. Not being used to interviews, she was naturally nervous to begin with, and when she found the place deserted, the inevitable doubts crept into her mind. Perhaps she had come on the wrong day, at the wrong time. Her portfolio felt defeatingly heavy, leaning against her leg. The only thing she could be certain of was the name on the door of the one private office, also empty: C. H. Minchip, Publicity. She wondered if she could find her way back to reception. And what then? Even if it were the wrong day, he'd have to see her. She couldn't face the journey back to Birmingham with nothing gained or lost.

"Can I help you?"

She turned, relieved, in the direction of the voice. It was

lunchtime, and someone had turned out the lights in the big office, so she could make out only a gray figure coming briskly toward her through the rows of drawing boards and desks.

"You look lost," he said, stopping a few feet from her. He did not smile, but there was no hint of that impatience in his voice that often characterizes people who are familiar with a strange and bewildering building.

He was a little taller than she, and she thought him distinguished-looking rather than handsome. There were comfortable crow's-feet beneath his eyes, which steadily regarded her. She looked down. Beneath the careful gray suit, the matching gray-and-white-striped shirt, worn with a plain silver tie, his body looked lean and fit.

"You're not Mr. Minchip, by any chance?" she said, meeting his eyes.

"No. I imagine he's at lunch."

"I have an appointment," she said quickly. "He said one-fifteen because of the trains. I've come from Birmingham, and the service isn't very frequent."

"Then we must find him for you," the man said, moving toward her. "I expect he's gone to get a sandwich."

"Thank you," she said, following him into the private office.

Before picking up the internal telephone, he glanced at Minchip's open desk diary.

"Sue Jackman, is it?"

"That's right. I've come about . . ." She stopped talking as he looked up at her with alert, interested eyes. After all, she had no reason to justify her presence.

"Well, you've definitely got an appointment," he said and picked up the receiver.

"I know."

He smiled at this, and the effect was to soften his rather gaunt face.

"Oh, Linda, can you find Charlie for me?" he said into the telephone. "He's probably in the cafeteria. Tell him there's a young lady waiting for him. Miss Jackman. Thank you." He put the receiver down and looked at her again.

She was staring around the office, looking puzzled.

"Won't you come sit down?"

"Oh, yes, thanks."

"Is something wrong?"

"No. It's just . . . I didn't expect anything so big. Do you work here?"

"Yes." He smiled as though she had said something amusing.

"It seems odd they should want free-lance people—that's me—" she explained, "when there seem to be so many . . ."

"Ah, no. Let me explain," he said, gently taking the portfolio from her. "This," he went on, indicating the small, screened-off cubbyhole of an office, "is the entire publicity department. Out there is the draftsmen's studio. Charlie . . . Mr. Minchip badly needs help, but we have to build something before we can publicize it."

"Oh, I see."

"Ah, there he is now. Excuse me."

She turned in her chair when he hurried out, wanting to thank him again. She liked his voice, low and precise, as she heard him talking to Minchip, who came bustling in a moment later, full of apologies, and balancing a tray of coffee and sandwiches.

"I thought you might be hungry," he explained.

"That's very kind of you."

Minchip walked behind her to close the door.

"Who was that man?" she asked.

"Gavin Trope, the director."

He left at 5:30 sharp that night, having promised Myra that he would be home early and would help her with dinner. He had to join the rush-hour traffic he usually missed. The project headquarters stood in a sea of mud onto which they would expand in due course. For the present, there was only the one narrow road for vehicles, and jams were inevitable. The cars inched forward, a few impatient drivers needlessly sounding their horns. He looked out across the muddy site and did not immediately recognize her. She was picking her way through the mud and puddles, teetering along planks where she could find them. It was the big, square portfolio banging against her calf that he recognized first. He could not help smiling. He sounded the horn a couple of times and wound down the window. She glanced in his direction, looking confused.

"Miss Jackman," he called. "I think you'd better get in before you disappear into the mud." He leaned across and opened the door for her when she veered in his direction. The car behind tooted impatiently. "Here, let me." She was flushed and out of breath as, together, they maneuvered the awkward portfolio into the back of the car. She looked down at her muddied feet. "Don't worry about that," he said. "I just hope you haven't ruined your shoes."

"I thought it would be quicker to cut across there," she explained, slamming the car door. "It was quite firm at first."

"Yes. The soil is mostly clay on this side and the rain just lies, I'm afraid. You're probably anxious to catch the six o'clock to Birmingham, I imagine."

She turned her head sharply toward him as the car slid smoothly forward, making up the space gained by the delay.

He smiled then, looking at the car ahead. She didn't understand his smile.

"Charlie should have put you in a taxi or arranged a lift. Have you been with him all afternoon?"

"Yes. He showed me round, told me all about the long-term plans, radio advertising and everything. It's very exciting."

"You're a copywriter?"

"No, graphic designer; though I want to be an illustrator, really; only it's difficult to get a start."

"And will you be designing for us?"

"Mm." She smiled happily, obviously pleased. "Mr. Minchip's given me lots of work."

"Good."

At last the blunt nose of the car faced the main road. The indicator lights clicked quietly in the silence as Gavin waited for a gap in the oncoming traffic. She twisted around, put her hand on the portfolio.

"Thank you ever so much," she said. "I can manage now."

"Nonsense. I'll run you to the station."
"Oh no, really, I know my way now."
"But it's no trouble." At that moment a space appeared in the traffic, and Gavin swung the car onto the road.
"Well, if you're sure it's not out of your way, . . ." she said hesitantly.
"Not at all."
It was, two miles, and in quite the opposite direction, but he did not think about that until he was driving home, late, to Myra.

Later they were to confess that they did not know who had been the more surprised when he telephoned. He at his own audacity and entirely uncharacteristic behavior, or she because she accepted his invitation spontaneously. None of it had been planned. Laughing, he later blamed it all on his natural parsimoniousness, adding that it was as well she should learn all his faults before he became too desperately in love with her.

He had tickets for a regional opera company that was playing a short season in Birmingham. Myra, who had been looking forward to it, began to nod her head and complain of numbness in her left hand. They both knew that it would be painful and embarrassing for her to go, but she insisted that he must. He saw so little opera now, and she knew how much he enjoyed it. He invited several colleagues, but none was free that night. He had just about resigned himself to going alone, when Charlie Minchip brought him some artwork for their first brochure. It was good—clean, bright, economical. She had done it, of course, and he remembered her so clearly that he felt disoriented. The memory of her made him smile and feel warm. He made an excuse to hang onto the artwork and copied down her address and telephone number, feeling like a guilty boy. The next surprise was that he dialed the number at all. After that it seemed unstoppable, a chain reaction of surprises—that she answered, remembered him, and agreed to go with him.
"Though I don't know much about opera," she warned him.
"As long as you won't be bored . . ."
"Oh, no. It's just that I'm ignorant."

And after the opera he did not want to go home. It wasn't the ordinary, daily reluctance to return to Myra's pain and helpless frustration, but a sense of having to wrench himself away from something warm and right. He could pretend the car had broken down, that he had to spend the night in Birmingham. But Mrs. Ferris, a neighbor, would not be able to stay with Myra, at least not without considerable inconvenience to herself and her family. Besides, he'd never lied to Myra, never done anything like this. Even if he did lie and put others to unjustifiable trouble, what would he gain?

"What's wrong?" she asked, touching his sleeve. "You look as though you've seen a ghost."

"I think I have," he said, his throat dry. "The ghost of my menopausal self."

"Do you believe in that, then, the male menopause?"

"I didn't," he confessed, turning his troubled face toward her, "until I met you."

And then he told her, in order to lay that ghost to rest forever, what he had been imagining and scheming. She listened attentively, her eyes exploring his face.

"But you can't," she said, when he had finished. "I see that you can't."

"Of course not. And now I must apologize and take you home."

They drove in silence to her door. She made no attempt to get out of the car but sat rolling her program into a tube on her lap.

"If you're still going to apologize," she said in a voice that did not sound like her own, "let it be for leaving me, not for wanting to stay. All right?"

"You don't mean that," he said, thinking that she was trying to be kind, that she pitied him.

"I don't say what I don't mean. Not intentionally, anyway. And I've never said anything like that before. I don't want you to go, and since you don't want to, I thought we should be straight with each other."

For a long time he did not trust himself to speak. "If I could see you again, perhaps take you to dinner . . . ?"

"Yes."

"I'm sure you're very busy."

"No. There isn't anyone else," she said bluntly. "I'll go out with you or you can come here, anytime."

"But why?" he almost cried, turning toward her.

"I don't know," she said quietly, "any more than you do."

He put his hand on her shoulder, leaned toward her.

"No," she said. "Please don't kiss me. It would only make me cry."

Before he could stop her she was out of the car and standing on the pavement. She bent down, her face framed by the doorway.

"If you still feel the same tomorrow or the next day, whenever, call me."

"Sue . . ."

She closed the door and hurried toward the house in which she had her flat.

The next day, early, he set about finding a trained nurse to stay with Myra, and then he telephoned Sue.

"I was frightened," he told her, lying on his stomach, tracing the smooth valley between her breasts. "For you, of course, but also that I wouldn't be able to—God, if you only knew how much I've thought about it, wanted you. And I was scared it would be all wrong, for you, that I'd fail you. You see I . . . please, let me tell you this. Myra can . . . I mean it's possible, sometimes, for us to make love." He paused. "I realize this can't be very pleasant for you but I want you to know, I need to tell you. Sometimes we have, over the years, and you see she can only respond in a limited way. God knows she tries, she wants to, but I . . . I feel so lonely. Sometimes I hate myself. It's inevitable, I suppose, the feeling that I'm using her. But worse than that is the feeling of loneliness. I wanted to tell you. And something else, now, so that you know what you're getting into. There haven't been others, all these years. That's why I was so scared of not being able to. I thought about it, I even thought of paying for it, but that seemed so unfair and bleak somehow. And as I said, Myra and I . . . we could. That's been all. I have no practice to offer you, my darling. Can you be patient with me? Was it all right for you?"

She twined her arms about his neck, drew his head down to her throat.

"Yes," she whispered. "Yes and yes, only you must stop apologizing to me."

She held him very tight then until they were both ready to move, as one.

"And when, exactly, did this idea of you two living together come up?" Evie asked, fixing Gavin with narrowed eyes.

"Well, we won't actually be living together. I shall remain in Higham Furze, with my wife." Gavin twisted awkwardly in his chair. Why was honesty, which he valued, so horribly embarrassing? "This way I shall be able to see more of Sue, weekends. It's a much easier journey to the cottage than here, Birmingham." He gave up, glanced at Sue for help, Evie's original question forgotten.

"About a year ago," Sue said. "We talked about it and then, well, it took that long to get all the alterations done."

"You be quiet, you," Evie said, teasing. "Let the man speak for himself." Evie beamed at Gavin, who returned a pallid smile. "So, you just upped and bought this place, did you?"

"No. I already owned it. It was left to me by someone I knew a long time ago. I didn't know what to do with it. To tell you the truth, it was a bit of a white elephant until—" he glanced tenderly at Sue "—I realized that it would be perfect for us, the perfect solution. The cottage gets used, and Sue and I can be together more often." He hadn't told the full truth, how he felt the cottage had been *meant* for Sue. Until she came into his life it had seemed a perverse gift, without meaning. Then he understood that it could be a means to his happiness.

"You've no intention of leaving your wife, then?" Evie said bluntly.

"Evie! I've told you," Sue said, blushing. Gavin took her hand and held it.

"No," he said, meeting Evie's narrowed eyes, with the very green and slightly greasy-looking lids. "My wife is an invalid. The disease she has is incurable. Under the circumstances, I can't leave her. Sue understands."

She squeezed his hand, to reassure him.

"Well," Evie said, sitting back in her chair, "you're dead honest. I'll say that much for you. And what does she say about it, your wife?"

In Sue's, Gavin's hand trembled a little and became tense.

"I think she understands. She's dependent on me. She knows that I won't fail her. I won't pretend to you that she likes the arrangement, but she has tried to be understanding, has been very good and brave about it. She's a very generous woman."

"I'll say. A damn sight more than I'd have been." Evie lit a cigarette, puffed at it, looked at them sitting close together, still holding hands. "I don't know," she said, shaking her head with its piled-up curls.

And truly she did not. He wasn't at all what she'd expected. Good-looking, not fat and gray and sort of clammy-looking, as she'd imagined. A bit quiet for her tastes. Didn't look as though he had much go about him, but then that would probably suit Sue. He was nicely spoken, well dressed. He didn't look or behave like a man who'd string a young girl along, but then appearances were deceptive. And still waters run deep, she reminded herself. As for Sue, there was no denying the change, the transformation in her. That slightly confused look, as if part of her were always off somewhere else, dreaming, had gone. She looked complete, confident, like someone who'd gotten what she wanted and knew it. That hurt, of course, a bit. She was no longer dependent on her, didn't need her big sister. It put an end to something that had been a factor, an important one, in Evie's life ever since she was twelve. Sue had grown up, she realized. That's what it was. And it made her feel a hundred and ten.

"I can see it would be a waste of breath to ask if you're sure," she said, looking at her sister.

Sue nodded and smiled.

"If it helps," Gavin said, feeling like an intimidated adolescent, "I will take very good care of her."

"She's old enough to look after herself," Evie replied, grinning. "But just in case, make sure you do, or you'll have me to answer to."

"A daunting prospect," Gavin said, smiling faintly.

"All right, then. I wish you luck."

Sue went to Evie and, for a moment, the older woman accepted her embrace. Then she thrust her away, fussing with her hair, an uncomfortable flush on her cheeks.

"Don't be so soft, Suzanne," she said.

"And I want to endorse what Sue said. You'll always be welcome at the cottage. I hope very much you will come and stay."

"Careful. I might take a liking to it and move in permanently. That'd cramp your style."

They all laughed, Sue and Gavin uneasily.

"So, when are you off?" Evie asked, rising to fetch the brandy bottle.

"Just as soon as I can get everything organized. I've found a place to store my furniture. It shouldn't take more than a week, ten days at the most."

"You're not taking your things with you?"

"No. Gavin's furnished the cottage completely."

"Oh, well, I suppose you know your own mind. Personally, I like my own bits and pieces round me."

"They are hers," Gavin said quietly. "It all is."

Evie's eyes flickered with interest, but she said nothing. Maybe Sue had fallen on her feet after all, she thought, pouring the brandy. Most certainly she had fallen.

Everything about that day had been wrong.

First, the light that fell unimpeded through the gable windows of the attic room. Possibly, the strange light had woken him, for he was aware of the unaccustomed silence in the house below. No smell of frying bacon and homemade bread, the crisping edges of eggs sizzling in lard. Nothing but the intense light, as though reflected off snow.

The whitewashed ceiling between the open rafters above him seemed to dazzle. He turned his sleep-tousled head toward the windows, his eyes involuntarily narrowing, squinting against the light. That must be it: snow. With a lurch of excitement, he sat up in the creaking, narrow trundle bed, pushing the covers down to his bare feet. He glanced automatically at the other two, similar beds that stood in a row beside his, giving the room the appearance of an improvised dormitory. Neither Lucas nor Ashton stirred. Excited, wanting now to be the first to see the snow and break the news, he swung his feet to the floor. The cold hit him, settled about him like a gripping hand. The unheated, drafty attic room was always cold, but never like this. The very air seemed made of ice. He heard his teeth chatter and clamped them together for fear of waking the others. His feet, once they left the strip of threadbare, fraying carpet beside his bed, cringed from the smooth and icy boards. He ran to the window, his breath clouding before him.

He approached the window diagonally so that at first it showed him only the gray slate roof of the peculiarly shaped wing that gave the house its lumpy appearance. For a moment he thought his eyes were playing tricks on him. Where was the snow? Whipped by the wind, it must have missed this protected slope. He faced the window full on and looked down at the neglected flower garden, which was brown and muddy as usual. Only the clump of Christmas roses gleamed white against the washed-out, monochrome earth. No snow then. But the light. He lifted his small face, which Mrs. Pownall told him daily was sickly looking, and immediately had to squint again. The sky was a uniform silver, as though washed and burnished, like a great metal bowl or salver inverted over the flat, dreary landscape, the drearier house.

His dreams of slides and toboggans vanished with a pang of disappointment. He turned away from the window, the dazzling light, his arms clasped about his thin chest, conscious of the cold biting into his bones. His shoulders shook as he walked back toward the beds. Lucas, as usual, was just a lump beneath the motley bedclothes. Not even his dark hair showed. Ashton snuffled into his pillow, his nose still clogged by a winter cold. Perhaps it was very early, he thought. Perhaps that was what was wrong. Usually, he never woke before Mrs. Pownall called them all, chiding, saying breakfast was on the table and they'd be late for school. That must be it. This must be the dawn, through which he normally slept.

He considered a moment, shaking with the cold, climbing back into bed. In his excitement he had left the covers turned back so that the heat his body had imparted during the night had evaporated. He felt wide awake and still, despite the disappointment of the snow, curiously excited. Quickly, letting his teeth chatter now, he pulled off the thick winter pajamas and put on his chilly clothes, which seemed to lock the cold against his skin rather than insulate its natural warmth. Shivering, he sat to pull on his long gray socks. He wore boots here, like the Pownall boys, and the sturdy leather still felt harsh and unyielding to his "townie's" feet. The boots clumped and clattered on the boarded floor. Reaching for the loose latch on the wooden door, his numb fingers became clumsy. The latch rattled loudly, but when he looked back, the two boys slept on, undisturbed.

The stairs from the attic led straight down in a single, steep flight at the end of a short, narrow corridor. He trod carefully, gripping the handrail, for the metal tips on his boots had a tendency to slip on the smooth, worn boards. At the foot of the stairs he paused, head twisted a little toward the door of Mr. and Mrs. Pownall's room. On a normal morning, Hettie, the baby of the family, could often be heard chattering to herself and rattling on the wooden bars of her crib. Today he heard nothing, not even the whine of the wind or the creaking of the old house. His steps muffled by strips of patterned red carpet, he moved along the first floor and down the main staircase to the square, tiled hall. Here it felt warmer, but only a little. He turned back along beside the staircase, toward the kitchen door, and lifted its heavy latch.

Warmth struck him, but no smell of food, no bubble of the porridge pot. Unlike the attic, the kitchen was naturally dark, its small windows shadowed by farm buildings and the side wing of the house. The wide ledges were blocked with geraniums that, miraculously, always flowered, from palest pink to richest magenta. The first thing that caught his attention was the large brown teapot on the table, which reflected the light from the fire. Then, behind it, slowly coming into view as he lifted his head to identify who had entered the room, Gavin saw the lined and leathery face of Grandpa Pownall.

"What you doing up?"

Gavin did not answer at once. He pushed the door shut by leaning his weight against it and wondered why he felt relief. Just to know that someone else was up, he supposed, that this morning was not, after all, totally strange. He walked around the vast wooden table and stood by its corner. Of all the Pownalls, it was Grandpa he liked best.

The old man, tall and gaunt as the scarecrows he made in the old stable block outside, was sitting on an ancient milking stool drawn close to the fire. His back curved as he leaned forward, elbows on his knees, to feed bundles of dried twigs into the already blazing fire. At his feet on the raised hearth stood a shallow bowl of milk, its white surface marred by specks of black that Gavin took to be wood ash.

"I don't know, really," he said, remembering the old man's question. "I just woke. I thought it had been snowing."

"Likely it will by noon," the old man said, his eyes fixed on the fire.

"Really? Do you think so?"

"Usually does on . . ." Grandpa Pownall stopped, turned his brown, leathered face to the small boy. "You shouldn't be up," he said, his eyes seeming to focus on something behind and beyond Gavin. "No school today."

"No school? Why not? Miss Peterson said nothing yesterday." His excitement was mixed with a nameless anxiety.

"Likely she sent a message last night," the old man said, turning his eyes back to the fire and extending his large, bony hands to the warmth. He was famed for his vagueness on all things domestic and practical, any routine concerning the house or children.

"Is she ill? She looked all right yesterday."

"How should I know? All I know is there's no call for you to be up and about. There's no breakfast yet."

"I don't mind."

Gavin squatted down, his bare knees thrust toward the fire, arms clasped about his shins.

"Couldn't sleep, could you?" Grandpa Pownall asked after a long pause, during which the twigs he fed into the fire crackled and popped and sent bright red sparks dancing up the wide chimney. Some caught in the mottled layer of soot that clung to the back of the grate and glowed for a moment like winter stars in a velvet night sky. "Likely you knew this were a special day."

The man cocked his head at him, a twinkle that was not caused by the firelight enlivening his pale blue eyes.

"Special? Why is it special? Like Christmas, you mean?"

The light in old Mr. Pownall's eyes increased. His mouth

moved, forming words. Gavin watched him intently, certain that an explanation of this strange morning was forthcoming, his heart tense and ready to skip with excitement. Then the old man's mouth closed, pursed even, and the light faded from his eyes. He turned back to the fire, hunching his shoulders, and when he spoke his voice was gruff, as though he had grown impatient with the expectant boy.

"It's special, isn't it, to get a day off school? What more do you want?"

Gavin nodded solemnly, let his chin rest against the thick, gray wool of his sweater. "You've got ash in the milk," Gavin said. "It's spoiled."

"Plenty more where that came from. Cows haven't run dry." The old man ended on a sigh and slowly straightened up again, his hands pressed against his knees. He looked tired, perhaps even exhausted. "Mary won't be down to get breakfast for a while. You'd best go wash yourself or whatever it is you boys do."

Gavin, recognizing the dismissive tone in his voice, stood up.

"Can I go out?"

"Aye, but just into the yard, mind."

"I'll wash first," Gavin said, to placate and strike a bargain with the old man.

Grandpa Pownall swiveled on his three-legged stool, watching the small boy go into the steamy scullery. He'd taken a liking to the boy, the little evacuee from London, who talked so funny and knew nothing about the countryside, only about two-story buses and gas lamps in the street and trains that traveled under the ground. The old man could not explain his liking. It just happened, just came upon him, and, though he acknowledged it disloyal, he had grown to favor Gavin over his own grandchildren. Perhaps it was because he could teach the boy. Lucas and Ashton were country born and bred, steeped in its ways from the first cries they made on earth. But this little man with his solemn ways and his mild eyes . . . Grandpa Pownall chuckled to himself, recalling in vaguest outline the long afternoons when Gavin had sat watching him make the scarecrows, listening intently to all the stories and legends that were to his grandsons a part of life. He wanted to tell him more. He wanted it so much that he struck his knee with the flat, calloused palm of his left hand. He wanted to make the lad one of them. That's what George, his son, had said last night, backed up as always by Mary. He'd denied it then, telling them not to be so fanciful, but he admitted it now, sitting before the fire after his nightlong vigil. It was too late now, he realized, since all was done and ready: the feather ash dispersed in the fresh milk, the Sign burned and drifting on the outside air as smoke. And, as his desire to speak, to have his irrational way melted, he nodded his head, agreeing silently with something Mary had said. How it wouldn't be fair on the boy since, sooner or later, they'd have to send him back to London or to some safer place his mother might have found.

Gavin, emerging from the scullery, two spots of color on his thin cheeks where he had scrubbed them, saw this nod. He thought the old man was asleep, for so he nodded after Mrs. Pownall's enormous Sunday lunches. He stepped lightly across the flags, holding his breath, and opened the back door quietly. He slipped out into the dazzling silver morning, his breath caught by the gripping cold.

The cold almost drove him back, but after a second the novelty of being on his own, in the early morning, and the wish not to disturb Grandpa Pownall prevailed. It was not ever being alone that he missed most. Being an only child and, for a year now, fatherless, he had made a friend and ally of solitude, which was something the Pownalls neither understood nor knew how to cope with. Then it struck him, as he trod around the frozen edges of the yard, avoiding the waves of mud and ice-sheeted puddles of its main area. He had been alone last night. The strangeness, the wrongness of the day had begun last night. He had been sent up to bed before Lucas and Ashton—not as a punishment, not because he had done anything wrong. Their father had taken the two boys into the cold parlor and Mrs. Pownall had told him to go on up, he looked that tired. He must have fallen asleep before they came up to the attic room, and sleep had temporarily washed the memory from his mind. Suddenly it didn't seem so odd that Grandpa Pownall should be nodding off before breakfast, that

Lucas and Ashton and Mr. and Mrs. Pownall should all be sleeping like logs. Once again he wished for a watch of his own, not, this time, in order to feel grown-up and to be able to show off to the other boys, but simply to tell the time. Screwing up his eyes, he looked at the sky. His stomach rumbled. It wasn't really early at all. He'd woken at the usual time, and his stomach wanted the breakfast he now felt certain was due. Why hadn't they let him stay up?

He reached the road, full of potholes and wide enough only for a single tractor, which bounded the farmyard and house on two sides. Ahead of him the fields stretched unfenced, flat and uniform to the horizon where a few stark trees reached their bleak limbs to the silvered sky. He shuddered. It was a very odd morning indeed, made oddest of all by the sudden cancellation of school. Had Miss Peterson sent a message after he'd gone up to bed, and then had Lucas and Ashton been allowed to stay up late precisely because there was no school? If so, it wasn't fair. But surely he'd have heard a car, seen its lights sweeping the windows as it turned into the yard? Though it might have been someone on a bicycle or on foot. He turned instinctively toward the village, although it could not be seen from where he stood, only the arrow-straight road passing between the limitless fields and the gray winter mesh of bare branches that was Gatherings Copse. Just beyond that lay the schoolhouse and Miss Peterson.

Gavin glanced apprehensively at the house. Its windows remained blank. Smoke curled toward the village from only one chimney. It was as sleeping and still as when he had awoken. Suppressing his doubts, the knowledge of disobedience, he set off at a trot along the straight, glistening road.

For all that the Pownalls were kind and did their best to make him welcome—treating him as one of their own, expecting him to obey the same rules as Ashton and Lucas and to adjust to their undemonstrative, bluff ways—Miss Peterson was special. She and the postman who brought his weekly letter from his mother in London were his sole links with the outside world. Miss Peterson had brought him here, him and three other children, girls, who had been placed in homes in the village. Two came from Miss Peterson's old school, and she had brought them to meet him and the third girl at Birmingham's Snow Hill station. The teacher herself had wanted to escape the bombing that had razed her previous school to the ground. She had transformed herself from a metropolitan into a village schoolmistress and with determined cheerfulness had set about making herself and her handful of charges, urban and rustic alike, happy and comfortable. When the three other evacuees had left, their parents having found safer homes for themselves or having placed the children with rural grandparents, Miss Peterson and Gavin had drawn closer together. They shared a knowledge of and a love for the city. They felt, Miss Peterson more than Gavin, since she lacked the warmth of a village family to wrap around her, like outsiders. She had confided as much to him, admitted her loneliness, which he had helped to ameliorate by taking Sunday tea with her and visiting her some evenings. Then they would talk about the sights and wonders of London. He would crank her ancient gramophone and listen to the precious records she had brought with her, the *Eroica* of Beethoven, Mozart's sparkling *Abduction from the Seraglio*, and lambent Italian and French arias by Caruso, Lily Pons, and Conchita Supervia. It was their little island of urbanism, keeping the flat and inhospitable countryside at bay.

It was for this that he ran that strange morning to the schoolhouse. Only severe illness or disaster would cause Miss Peterson to close the school on a weekday in term time. He had to know what it was, even though he might be punished, even though Lucas would accuse him of being a teacher's pet. He didn't mind that anyway. He was proud to be Miss Peterson's friend, for that was how she put it. When the war was over they were going to write to each other, and Miss Peterson would come to London and they would go to concerts together. They had sworn this and if anything should have happened to Miss Peterson . . .

He slowed as he approached Gatherings Copse. He had a stitch in his side and the icy air pained his panting lungs. He bent over, trying to touch his toes. As he straightened up, his eye was caught by a streak of darker gray against the shining sky. It was like the smoke trail of an airplane shot from the wartime sky. For a moment he thought that was what it must be, but then he realized that it was too small a trail. His eyes followed it and before he had located its source, he knew it. It was the smoke from the farm chimney. It rose up, gray and steady, but did not disperse. Like a misty ribbon it bent and hung in the sky, arcing across toward the schoolhouse. Gavin knew that what he saw was impossible. Even on a windless day—and it was certainly windless—smoke broke up, scattered. This hung together like a veil, a banner stretched across the sky. As he stared at it, his chest heaving, his mouth open in disbelief, he remembered Grandpa Pownall feeding needless twigs into the blazing fire, doing it with a deliberate concentration of purpose, the black ash scattering on the surface of the milk.

He felt afraid then and, almost simultaneously, foolish. What was there to be afraid of? This was just the sort of phenomenon Miss Peterson was good at explaining and in such a simple way that he always grasped it at once, more quickly than Lucas or Ashton and the other village boys. He set off again, still too winded to run. He didn't look at the smoke anymore, nor would he let himself think about the silence. The copse was a playground for flocks of tiny birds that swooped and whirled about the bare branches as the children plodded each morning to school. At dusk the crows roosted there, calling to each other and flapping their great wings. Even in the mornings, the presence of the children, chattering, chasing each other, disturbed the birds as they worm-hunted in the bare fields, and they rose, crying, to seek indignant shelter in the copse. Where were the birds? He looked around him, up, saw the smoke again, hanging overhead, exactly like a sinister gray rainbow.

Miss Peterson had told him never to be afraid. All fear, apart from that occasioned by facing the naked barrel of a German gun, was unnecessary and sprang from a morbid turn of mind. When you did face the barrel of a German gun, fear vanished and you became brave as the British Lion. So Miss Peterson said. That was after he had had the bad dreams, the ones about the scarecrows. Mrs. Pownall had been cross about them and told him he ought to have more control and not go waking the household with his childish screams in the middle of the night. She had been even crosser with Grandpa Pownall, who had told Gavin the stories about scarecrows that could walk in the dark. He did so as they sat together, and Gavin watched him fashion the increasingly lifelike creatures from wood and straw and sacking. Miss Peterson had sensed that something was wrong, and, with relief, he had told her of the dreams and their source. Patiently, she had coaxed from him the story Grandpa Pownall had told him, partly, as she said, because she was interested in such country lore and meant to profit by her stay in remote parts by studying it, but mostly so that he should see, in the sunny warmth of her cozy sitting room, that there was nothing to be afraid of. Why, she had laughed her tinkling laugh, scarecrows didn't even frighten the crows. And to prove her point she had led him into the school yard and shown him the fat black crows feasting on the summer grain in the shadow of the silly, insubstantial stick man.

"What is there to be afraid of, Gavin?"

"Nothing, Miss Peterson."

"That's my good boy."

But her remembered words sounded hollow in his head as he passed the copse and saw the dour stone schoolhouse, unlit and shuttered. The windows looked like sheets of metal as they reflected the sky. His heart beat a strange and complicated rhythm as he pushed against the sticking gate that led to the living quarters. Suppose Miss Peterson had gone? What would he do then? The gate gave at last, scraping against the concrete path. He did not know whether to take the drawn curtains at the parlor window as a good or a discouraging sign. He stood on the step, pressed close to the blue-painted door and lifted the old horseshoe knocker. It creaked for lack of oil, then banged against the door. He knocked many times, not counting, then stepped back, his chest heaving with tension and exertion. He could hear nothing but the rasp of his own breath and his heart's blood drumming in his ears. After a wait that seemed interminable but that in fact was only a few seconds long, he flung himself at the door, beating it with his fists and crying out her name in broken syllables. The sharp, jutting edge of the old-fashioned letter flap dug into his stomach, stilling his frenzy. He squatted down at once and pushed the flap inward. It rolled on a pivotal hinge and remained open.

"Miss Peterson," he called, his lips close to the aperture. "Please, Miss Peterson. It's me, Gavin Trope. It's me, Miss Peterson. Are you all right?"

If she were ill she would be upstairs. He must give her time to get up, descend the stairs. He brought his eyes to the oblong gap in the door. The room, into which it opened directly, was curtained, dim, so that he could make out only the vague shape of familiar pieces of furniture. They looked forlorn, forgotten.

"Please, Miss Peterson, let me in. *Please.*"

It seemed futile. He stood up and, his emotions turning suddenly to anger, he kicked out at the door, which shivered with the impact. The toe of his boot left a black mark against the blue paint. He backed away from the door, not knowing what to do or how to stem the tears that rose hot to his eyes. Then he saw the curtains move, tweaked back, and her face, a white shape behind the glass.

"Miss Peterson," he whispered.

He hurried back to the door, heard her scrabbling at the bolts like a mouse scuttering in old plaster. The sounds stopped.

"Gavin?" Her voice was very high-pitched and odd-sounding.

"Yes, Miss Peterson?"

"Are you alone?"

"Yes, Miss Peterson." No longer sure of anything, he glanced over his shoulder. Across the strip of road the fields stretched black and empty. "Let me in, Miss Peterson, please."

"Swear to me . . . swear on your mother's life . . . you're alone." Her voice swooped out of control, like a parody of one of the opera singers to whom she had introduced him.

"I swear, Miss Peterson, honest." He heard the sound of her nails against the wood, searching blindly for the bolts and then, at last, the click of the key turning in the stout lock. Gavin moved forward anxiously. The door opened a few inches. Her arm shot out, seized his wrist tightly, and dragged him inside with such force that he caught his breath in surprise. He stumbled into the shadowed room, collided with the back of a chintz-covered chair.

He heard the door close, the lock turn, the bolts rasp home.

Fearfully, he turned to her. She was leaning her right shoulder against the door, her face turned toward him. He had never seen her or ever imagined that she could look like this. Her brown hair was loose, spilling in waves and demi-ringlets over her shoulders. It was very fine, beautiful hair, and, released from the tight bun into which she always coiled it, it gave her a wild, disturbing look. Her face was blanched, and the skin looked waxy, as though drawn too tight across the bones of her cheeks. In this colorless face, her eyes were unnaturally dark, like holes bored into her skull.

"Miss Peterson, are you all right?"

His small voice seemed to soothe her and make her aware of how she must look. Her left hand, which had appeared to be frozen to the topmost bolt she had just closed, dropped to her side. She straightened up, turned fully to face him.

"Yes. Yes, Gavin."

Conscious of his eyes searching her face, she tried to smile. Her hands fluttered up to her hair, lifting it from her shoulders so that it hung down her back.

"I thought perhaps you were ill," he said. "Grandpa Pownall said there was no school today."

"No. Not today. I . . . No, I'm not ill." She walked past him into the room. Turning, following her with his eyes, he saw her soft-topped suitcase on the table, all her pretty things spilling from it. She glanced at him and then, hurriedly, as though embarrassed for him to see, began cramming slips and stockings, blouses and a nightdress into the case. "As you see, I have to go away."

"Why, Miss Peterson?"

Her hands became still, buried in the jumbled clothes.

"Because . . . Oh, I should never have let you in."

She spun around, tottered the short distance to him, and seized him by the arm.

"You must go. Come along now, quickly. As you see, I'm perfectly well. You must go now. Run along. Quickly." She bundled and pushed him toward the door.

Gavin twisted away from her.

"Why, Miss Peterson? What for? What have I done?"

She became still then, her hands twisting at her sides. She saw him, a small, bewildered boy, huddled where she had pushed him.

"Oh, Gavin . . ." She scooped him into her arms, pressing his head against the softness of her breasts. Her familiar, flowery perfume reassured him. He leaned against her, trusting, as her hand alternately ruffled and smoothed his hair. "Not you, Gavin. Oh, my dear . . . you're my true friend. You always will be, yes?" He nodded against her. "That's my good boy. Only I must go, quickly. And you can't help me."

"Why, Miss Peterson?" He tried to lift his head, to look at her face, but she clasped his head tightly.

"You wouldn't understand. I can't tell you. You must just—"

There was a sound then, a sort of rattling, like pieces of dead wood clattering together in the wind. Her whole body tensed. Her carefully manicured and polished nails dug involuntarily into the soft flesh of his cheek.

"What's that?" he whispered, pulling against the tightness and pain of her embrace. "Please, Miss Peterson . . . You're hurting me."

She caught her breath sharply as the sound came again, closer. It was toward the back of the house somewhere. He tugged free of her. Her arms fell listlessly to her sides.

"Miss Peterson?" He rubbed the smarting places where her nails had indented his skin.

"Sh!"

He stared across the dim room at the back window. It was too dark for him to be sure, but he thought he saw a shadow fall across the curtained window. A sound like a branch, scraping and tapping at the window, made her gasp and bite her lower lip.

"What is it?" Gavin moved forward, toward the window.

"No." She caught his shoulder, spinning him around. "No. You mustn't."

"There's someone there."

"All right," she said, her voice warming. "You be calm now. You can help me, after all. Go and stand by the door. Go on. Quickly."

Puzzled, he did as she said. She went to the table and quickly fastened the suitcase, heedless of the scraps of material that stuck out from the lid. Walking on tiptoe, she carried the case to where he stood.

"I'm going to leave with you. I want you to open the door when I say. You must follow me out. Then I want you to go straight home."

"What's going to happen?"

"Nothing. Don't ask questions. You must do as I say." She shook him a little, frightening him. "I'm going to cut through the copse. It will be safe there." Her eyes rolled a little as she paused, perhaps imagining the gray copse. "And you . . . you must go straight home, as fast as your legs can carry you. Do you understand?"

"Yes, Miss Peterson."

Her fear was like a scent in the room, robbing him of clear thought or voluntary action. She took her coat from a peg on the wall and shrugged it on. Unbelted, it flapped about her as she stooped to pick up the suitcase.

The rattling, scratching sound at the window again made her flinch.

There was a rambling rose at the back of the house, Gavin remembered. He thought one of the thorny sprays must have worked loose and was now scraping against the window.

"Quickly now," she said. "Draw the bolts."

He wanted to tell her about the rose, but her manner made her strange and forbidding. He stood on tiptoe and slid the upper bolt back.

"Quietly," she hissed.

He eased the second bolt back without noise, then turned the key. She stood close to the door, staring at it.

"Now!"

He snatched the door wide open and she ran out, the suitcase bumping against her legs. Gavin hesitated just a moment, then ran after her, afraid to be left alone.

He had a brief impression of her legs kicking out awkwardly to the side as she ran, but it was the smell that impressed him most.

The strangely behaved smoke that he had noticed earlier seemed to have settled over and around the house. The air was gray with it and the smell, known but unplaced, clogged his throat. Black soot wavered in the air, settled on his face and hands. At the gate she turned and looked back at him, waving him to hurry, hurry. Still puzzled by the smell and awed by the smoke, he ran to her, leaving the door of the schoolhouse open.

She did not wait for him but set off along the road toward the copse. He caught her up easily and jogged beside her. He started to speak but she shook her head fiercely. She was unused to running. The suitcase swung bruisingly against her leg and her breath sounded short and painful. The air was clearer on the road and, looking up, he saw the smoke funneling across the sky. No more issued from the distant chimney of the farmhouse. They ran in awkward silence until they reached the edge of the copse. A few yards along there was a natural opening, a path worn across the verge by village boys who sometimes played there. Miss Peterson slowed down, pushing the loose hair out of her face. Gavin fitted his pace to hers, staring at her anxiously.

"Go . . . go now," she panted, moving toward the copse.

"When will I see you again?" he called, feeling bereft at this sudden and unexplained departure.

Pausing at the edge of the trees, she turned her chalk face to him. "Go now, Gavin. Don't tell anyone you've seen me, that I've gone away. Go, as quick as you can."

Like a startled animal she plunged into the copse without a wave or a kind word. He saw the suitcase catch against the gray trunk of a tree and twist from her hand. It fell, the lid springing open, her clothes spilling. Immediately he started forward but quickly stopped. She wasn't bothering with the suitcase. She ran on, panicked, without direction, her arms flaying against twigs and dead briars that tugged and pulled at her clothes and skin.

He could not leave her things lying there. Even if she did not care about them now, he knew that one day she would. He ran into the copse and, kneeling by the suitcase, began to cram the spilled, feminine clothing back into it. He would take it home with him to the Pownalls' and keep it in a safe place. Then, when she wrote to him, he would tell her about the case, and she would come and fetch it and everything would be all right again.

Where he knelt, only just inside the copse, the trees were sparse and denuded by winter. He could see through the bars and latticework of their slim trunks and twining branches into the big field that stretched between copse and schoolhouse and away behind it. What he saw when he looked there seemed like a trick of the imagination, a nightmare.

It moved across the field, approaching the top end of the copse, like a huge man with two stiff legs. He stared at it, openmouthed, forgetting to breathe. It crossed his line of vision, split and fragmented by the intervening trees. He thought perhaps the trees moved, swayed by some tempest wind to lend this staggering, clumsy figure an illusion of movement. But there was no breath of wind. To his left, deep in the thick heart of the copse, he heard a shrill and startled cry.

Miss Peterson.

Gavin scrambled to his feet. The thing, the swinging, walking thing, its ragged black coat flapping around its swaying, creaking body, changed direction. He saw it lumber around, attracted by the cry, one leg arcing through the air. It passed from his view, but at once he heard it entering, crashing through the thicker top end of the copse.

Forgetting Miss Peterson's case, he turned on his heel and ran in roughly the direction she had taken. He had no breath to call and knew, in any case, that he dare not. Since the creature was sensitive to human cries, he would draw it more surely upon them. The thing to do, his young and terrified brain reasoned as he plunged and slipped through the thickening undergrowth, was to lie low, the two of them huddled together, scarcely even breathing, until it had passed or snapped its terrible stick legs. To that end he ran, for he had to find Miss Peterson and make her understand.

His foot slipped and he half fell onto the ground, his hands disappearing into years of soft, dark leaf mold. Above the sound of his own breathing, he heard the crack of broken wood. The sound was too loud to have been made by Miss Peterson. With a quick flutter of his heart he hoped that perhaps she had already forced her way through the copse and was off across the fields in her ungainly run. What caused the noise seemed to him unstoppable, a giant from a fairy story, sweeping all obstacles away, crushing them with its terrible swinging legs.

The earth beneath his hands trembled with the reverberations, the shock waves, of those oncoming, stomping feet. He pushed himself upright, as though burned, and started forward again. A twig slashed his face, making his eye water. The creature was ahead of him and a little to the right. His skin prickled as though touched by some cold and loathsome thing, as he realized that their paths must cross. He stopped, his arm wrapped around a silver-barked sapling. He wanted to go back then, to run away from the horrible, marching figure. Probably he would have done so had he not heard her cry out again. She was very close, just up ahead somewhere, and he did not understand why he could not see her. With a crashing, crunching, snapping sound, the creature came on, drawn by her startled, birdlike cry.

Gavin pushed away from the sapling, ran as fast as his legs and the impeding vegetation and soft earth would allow. In a few seconds he understood why he had been able to hear but not to see Miss Peterson. The ground shelved steeply away before him. The dead leaves made a russet, rustling carpet that swept down into a hollow like the bed of a dried-up pond. It was a perfect basin, hidden, surrounded by trees, but quite clear of them on its own floor. He paused on the lip of the steep decline down into this clearing. Even as he looked, the dried and curled leaves leapt in the air, danced, while the earth shook with the oncoming tread. His ears were filled by the sound of snapping wood and clumsy, pounding feet, moving in the rhythm of a double limp.

Miss Peterson lay where she had slipped, spread-eagled against the opposite bank of the hollow. The terrified boy saw at a glance that the bank was too steep for her. In attempting to climb it she had lost her footing and slipped back. Her feet scrabbled uselessly in the dry leaves and the soft, slippery loam beneath them. He saw her hands clutching at dead leaves. Leaves stuck like crushed, dead ornaments to her coat, her hair. Her head was turned toward the noise, and he saw her mouth split open in a scream that was lost in that same din.

He followed the direction of her gaze, willing it not to be so, willing it to be anything but what he saw. It seemed a part of the wood come to life. Black, skeletal, still, it teetered on the edge of the hollow. The gnarled stick arms stood out from the ragged black sleeves like the crosspiece of a crucifix. The two legs were splayed apart, rooted in the earth. But its head moved. The rotting sacking face, through which wisps of graying straw stuck, swung from side to side, then became still as Miss Peterson cried out again.

Gavin saw that he could not run down the slope. It was too steep and would cause him to fall. He sat down and pushed against the carpet of leaves. He began to slide down, twigs snagging his long socks, tearing the backs of his knees.

The creature had no such difficulty. One leg swung up and out in a half-circle and planted itself, with a force that made the ground tremble, halfway down the slope. The other leg activated with the creak of pliant wood strained almost to breaking point. In two awkward, ugly strides it had gained the floor of the hollow.

Gavin pushed himself up, his feet slipping from beneath him. He threw himself backward but his foot caught in the concealed root of a tree. A sickening pain bit through his ankle, which twisted to the right. He pitched forward, a cry escaping him, and lay with his face pressed into the leaves, still some feet short of the floor of the hollow.

The pain and the impact of his fall drove the breath from his body. His ears drummed to the thump, thump of the creature's steps on the soft earth. In comparison, Miss Peterson's vain struggles to climb the bank sounded like the fluttering of a butterfly's wings against glass. He pressed his hands hard onto the shaking earth and forced himself up. His arms trembled so much that he thought they might give way and even this slight movement pained his ankle, making him feel sick. He got his right knee under him and straightened his back, but his left leg remained trapped at the ankle and splayed out behind him.

Miss Peterson had managed to twist herself around and get firm ground beneath her feet so that her back now rested against the bank she had been unable to climb. Her face was a white oval, with a black hole for a mouth. Her eyes rolled white in her whiter face. Leaves decorated her hair like some spirit or goddess of autumn he had seen in art books. All this Gavin saw at a glance as the thing planted its footless stumps before her. Its coat hung limp about the stick body, the plaited straw hair drifted from its sacking head. Then, with a creaking sound that made the boy's blood run cold, the stiff arms bent. They bent with incredible, terrible slowness, and he saw the bunches of twigs that served it as obscene hands come together, reaching for Miss Peterson.

Her scream rang out, jarring the still and silent air. For a moment, the thing blotted out his view as it seemed to stoop stiffly toward the helpless woman. Her screams became a sob, and when the creature straightened, he saw the scratches, the torn and bloodied flesh of her white cheeks. The twig hands had scraped with unbelievable force down the woman's face. Blood ran down onto her dress, revealing that these were no light, superficial scratches. Her flesh hung open in gouged and ragged lines, and he could even see the white gleam of bone through the spoiled, scraped-off flesh.

The thing lunged again, raking her. She could only whimper this time. As it straightened again, according to its own, stiff rhythm, the appalled and now sobbing boy saw the clothing scraped from her chest in two ragged furrows. He glimpsed her milky breasts torn and bleeding before the dreadful wooden arms closed again and the twig hands sought her bloodied throat.

Gavin pitched forward again. All the strength left his body. His eyes refused to see any more. He slumped, his face buried in the leaves, and gave himself up to black unconsciousness.

The Pownalls' old farm dog, Towser, found him. He came woofing and scampering through the leaves to lick the boy's pale and frozen cheek until he stirred and rolled his head from side to side in a vain attempt to elude the lashing pink tongue. Next came George Pownall, his boots slithering in the leaves, muttering and cursing under his breath. He whistled the dog off and knelt by the whimpering boy. As he lay there, feeling Mr. Pownall's strong but sensitive hands exploring his leg, he heard another voice calling. He raised his head a little and saw, near where Miss Peterson lay, a jumble of broken sticks and twigs, enmeshed with tatters of black cloth, wisps of straw, and rags of damp-rotted sacking.

George Pownall eased Gavin's already swollen ankle free of the treacherous root. Cautioning him to put no weight on that foot, he lifted him beneath the arms and, grunting with the effort, dragged him carefully up the slope.

"He's all right, is he?"

"No thanks to you. How the hell do I know?" George Pownall's voice was a hoarse shout. Grandpa Pownall reached out to help the hopping, unsteady boy up. "Now look what you've done," George went on, his voice dropping to a confidential hiss. "You meant for this to happen, didn't you, you old devil?"

"Maybe I did, maybe I didn't. Come on now, my little man. Grandpa'll take you home."

The boy fell against the rough tweed of the old man's coat. It smelled of smoke and wood shavings, and he clung to it for comfort and consolation.

"What you going to do now?" George demanded of his father.

"I'm going to take this little man off home. He's half-clemmed with the cold."

Stooping, with a surprising strength and agility, Grandpa Pownall swung the boy up in his arms and cradled him like a baby. Gavin rested his head against the old man's shoulder and closed his eyes. Tears squeezed from beneath the lids. In no time at all, Grandpa Pownall picked his way with familiar ease through the copse. When they reached the road, he hefted the boy and told him to hang on tight to his neck. Gavin opened his eyes then and looked at the sky. The strange light had gone. It was a sky of lead now, not silver, and it seemed a little warmer.

"Miss Peterson . . ." he groaned, shifting in the arms that held him.

"Don't you fret about her now. It's all over with. The important thing is, you've seen it for yourself now, haven't you?"

"I don't know," he whispered. "What I saw—"

"Was the Gatherer. Mind how I told you about him way back before Christmas?"

"Miss Peterson," Gavin said solemnly, "said it was just a story "

"That shows what a foolish woman she was. You know better now, don't you? And you're better off without her."

Gavin did not answer but hid his face against the man's shoulder.

"You listen to me now. You listen good. You must never tell anyone what you saw. Never a word, mind."

Gavin shook his head halfheartedly.

"If you do, if you breathe one word, old Gatherer'll come for you. Do you understand that?"

Gavin heard again the terrible creaking and splitting of wood, saw the blind face twisting in search of its prey.

"No," he screamed. "No. Don't let him, please."

"Hush now, hush. That was only a warning. There's nothing to be afeared of, little man. You say nothing and the Gatherer'll mind his place and time."

"All right," Gavin said, shudders of fear wracking his cold body.

"That's not important anyway," the old man said as he trudged on toward the farm. "Important thing is, what you've seen this morning, what you know and won't ever speak of, makes you one of us. You belong here now. You're one of us. There's no call for you ever to go away."

The fierceness with which he said this, the way his thin arms clamped bone-tight about the boy, sent a sick shiver through Gavin. He moved his head so that he could see the man's perpetually tanned and wrinkled face. The blue eyes were smoked over, the lips stretched in a private smile. Before the child could speak and say that he wanted his mother, the first small flakes of snow began to fall. They struck icy against his skin and melted into alien tears. The old man looked up as the snow increased.

"There, what did I tell you? You wanted snow and you're going to get it, sure enough."

The flakes grew in size and increased until they were like white feathers, drifting. As he thought this, Gavin remembered what the smell was, the smell in the smoke around the schoolhouse. It was the scent of burning feathers.

They watched the young woman arrive as they had watched all the comings and goings of the last year, the workmen as well as the man who came to inspect their work and give instructions. The seasons could be measured by the variations of the man's clothing, from overcoat to jacket, shirt-sleeves to sweaters. And now again it was bitterly cold with a dust of snow on the ground, as the young woman got out of her van and stood, shading her eyes against the glare. They watched her impassively. Only when she had gone inside did they share the news, like village gossips.

Ta-ta-t'-tap. Ta-ta-t'-tap.

A dry sound, whispering on the bleak winter air.

Few people, Sue thought, ever got a chance to start a really new life. It was a big thought, a momentous occasion, and she sat for a while behind the wheel of her beat-up old van, considering it. She wanted to fix and remember this moment, for it would never come again. Parked outside her flat, the van loaded with those possessions she planned to take with her, she felt herself outside time, poised between one life and another. She looked up at the windows of her flat and felt neither regret nor relief. It had been a neutral place. Neutral: that word seemed to sum up the life she had led there. Everything lay ahead of her now, would begin when she started the van. It was early, the streetlights still on, the lamps softened to fuzzy orange suns by an incipient mist. She had been unable to sleep, was starting out earlier than she had planned. Yet still she waited, spinning the moment out, wanting to find its essence and unique texture. Cold and silence. The mist. Lights behind curtained windows denoting the early risers. The sense of something wiped out, like a soft eraser drawn across a piece of heavy paper, removing the tentative lines and cross-hatchings of her life so far. Ahead of her were bold strokes, bright colors.

Behind her she heard the purr of an electric motor, the clink of milk bottles, glass against glass, glass against stone. The milkman began to whistle as he swung back into his cart and started up again. Time to leave, she thought, reaching for the ignition key. The cold engine spluttered and coughed, as she nursed it into life, revved it gently to warm it, and drew smoothly away from the curb before the milk cart reached what used to be her door.

She wondered how Gavin was beginning this special day, but almost at once shrank from the ready images that came of him. Even in imagination, she never wanted to enter his other life, the bungalow he shared with Myra. However promising and golden the day appeared to her, she knew that it must be a black one for Myra Trope. There was only pain to be gotten from imagining how Gavin would balance his excitement and anticipation with regret and concern. He must be, she would make him be, the lover who came from nowhere, who existed only when they were together. This had to be a condition of her new life, and she had better get used to it straight away.

To distract her thoughts, Sue switched on the radio she had had fitted to the secondhand van. Debussy, liquid and slightly sweet, played softly as she drove through the seemingly endless industrial suburbs of Birmingham. The commuter rush had not yet started, and she was glad that she had set off so early. It meant, too, that she would have longer to explore the cottage by herself. Gavin would not arrive until dusk at the earliest. He had wanted to be there to welcome her, but she had insisted: she wanted to take possession of her new home in privacy, to familiarize herself with the territory before he arrived.

By noon Sue had reached the village of Brooking. She parked by the village green and got out, easing her cramped legs. Gavin had told her the village was beautiful, and she had imagined something folksy and rustic. In reality, the houses bordering the green had an elegance and spaciousness of design that recalled the Georgian style. All were built of warm, brown-gray stone and were either reed-thatched or roofed with a local weather-roughened slate. She decided, on impulse, to stop awhile. It was the last place of any size before she reached her destination, and suddenly she wanted to delay the moment of arrival, like a child postponing a birthday treat. It took her only ten minutes to walk around the village and to identify the choice of two routes she could take to Hemming and the cottage. During that time, the sun came out, dazzling bright and low in the sky.

The village boasted a shop and a public house. Sue went into the former and selected a few items to add to the box of groceries already stowed in her van. The range of goods was small but surprisingly good, including a number of items that confirmed the impression she had already formed of Brooking as essentially a retreat now for upper-middle class, senior management people, with a couple of gentlemen farmers thrown in to maintain the link with the village's land roots. The advantage of this was that she could shop here easily and adequately, thus keeping the longer trips to Nene to a minimum. Afterward, prompted by her stomach, Sue decided to have lunch in the village pub.

She was the only occupant of the lounge bar, which felt slightly damp and chilly. The landlady apologized and, while she bustled about switching on electric heaters and subdued lighting, explained that they got very little lunchtime trade. And there was no hot food, the woman added, but she would be glad to make fresh sandwiches. Seated close to a heater, Sue selected cheese and onion sandwiches and half a pint of beer. From the other bar, the public, came the rumble of male voices. Sue felt shut out, isolated; for the first time, doubts entered her mind. She was, after all, a city person. Would she adjust as easily as she had anticipated to an essentially solitary life? Perhaps not as easily, she told herself; but she would do it. The mistake had been in the stopping. It made sense to eat here, leaving the afternoon free for settling in and preparing dinner for Gavin's arrival, but this hiatus in her journey left her too much time to think. It was the cold emptiness of the bar, she decided. A bar should be warm and crowded, noisy with voices. Outside the sun continued to blaze, melting the few patches of snow that had survived the morning.

"Here you are," the woman said, reappearing. "Sorry to be so long." She placed a plate of sandwiches, neatly arranged on a red paper napkin, in front of Sue. "Just passing through, are you?"

"I'm going to Hemming."

"Good job you stopped here, then. There's nothing there," the woman said. "Never was, really, but now—"

Sue wondered what else the landlady would have said had one of the customers from the other bar not shouted for her. Nothing that she did not already know, probably, for Gavin had described the decline of the village and had warned her that it could look forlorn and unwelcoming in its empty decay. In such things Gavin was punctilious. She had told him that she did not mind, would not care, and she meant to keep that promise. The only society she wanted or needed was his. That and space and peace in which to work. She ate the sandwiches hungrily, enjoying their freshness, and told herself to snap out of this mood of uncertainty and doubt.

She paid for her meal and hurried back to the van, anxious now to reach the cottage, see it at last. Because of this she took the shorter route, what Gavin had told her was called the "back road" to Hemming. It took her straight up the main village street, past a couple of ugly, square, brick houses and the yard of a prosperous-looking farm where the breaths of penned Friesian cattle misted on the air. A sign announced wormlike bends for the next mile, and she changed down a gear. The road began to rise and twist, a serpent between hedged fields that stretched as far as the dazzled eye could see. She reached up to adjust the sunshade. The radio, which she had flipped on out of habit, played something triumphal, unknown, with a blare of brass, and the music heightened her mood. She seemed to be ascending directly toward the sun. The higher she twisted and climbed, the more evident the snow became. It lay like a frosting on one face of the tilled ridges, turning the fields to a striped pattern of brown-black and white. Stretches of the road ahead were coated with a white carpet through which the incisive tracks of a tractor were clearly marked. Soon she saw that tractor, gleaming red, way off to the left, cutting deep furrows in the earth. The road ahead was virgin, at least for that day, stressing the isolation of Hemming.

It was not isolation that Sue felt, however, as the road, after one last, dramatic twist, disgorged her onto the edge of a limitless plain. She slowed down, adjusted the sunshade even lower, and stared around her. Ahead, beyond the stark tree, she could make out buildings, small and sharp as a child's model. All around her the ribs of snow augmented the light to the garish dazzle of an op-art painting. As though timed to coincide with this rushing moment, the music erupted into a climax, silvery and magisterial. Reaching to turn up the suddenly fitting sound, she recognized the last trump of Verdi's *Requiem*, gorgeous and terrible.

The magnificence of the music and the immensity of the space outside the van made her want to shout with exaltation. Her heart raced. The "Dies Irae" rushed on into its choral conclusion, just as she approached the village of Hemming. Deserted and forlorn as it was, it could not lessen her excitement. It was not a village at all but a cluster of buildings, most in disrepair and disuse, strung along the side of the straight narrow road. Sue slowed down, her eyes suddenly relieved by the interposition of a small wood between her and the sun. The light seemed, by contrast, exaggeratedly gray. She passed untended gardens, blank windows, and then, miraculously, it seemed, she saw a thread of smoke rising from a solitary chimney. Not entirely deserted then, she thought, glimpsing rags of washing on a stretched line. To her right stood the schoolhouse, barred and blinded, an incongruous tuft of grass growing from its sagging roof. A tumble of stones indicated where the old porch had crumbled away. Then she was approaching the gray copse, sunlight striping through it to create the effect of a Venetian blind. Strips of light and shadow obscured her windshield, patterned her flushed face as she strained to see the cottage. At the far end of the copse stood two rusted, dilapidated Dutch barns, their great bellies open, making a tunneled perspective of the view.

Beyond the barns, dropped down carelessly, was the cottage, just as she had seen it, dreamed of it, imagined it. The fresh white of its paintwork stood out, welcoming, and the sun added a dazzling aura around its sharp, uncompromising lines. She swung the car over to the right and coasted to a silent stop before the cottage. The untidy garden of beige grass stood in semi-shadow. The fence that separated it from the surrounding field leaned half-rotten to the ground. Sue got out of the van, gasping against the cold raspy air, and stared around her as though lost. Far off, where the road took a right angle, she saw the red bulk of an ugly farmhouse with its wisp of wavering smoke. But that was not her nearest neighbor, for on the other side of the road, in the great, flat, snow-decorated field, she saw three scarecrows, policing the land between them.

They saw the young woman arrive, and watched her stand, sunstruck, outside her new home. Ashton saw her, no more than a moving spot, from the distance of his tractor and grinned his slack, moist smile. Mary Pownall, her eyes dimmed by age, saw her only in imagination since she had to rely upon Hettie with her binocular glasses at the attic window.

"She's younger than I would've thought," Hettie said. "As far as I can see."

"What's she up to, then?" the old woman asked querulously.

"Looking. Just standing, looking."

"Funny," the old woman said for the hundredth time, "he never came to see us, not even to pass the time of day."

"She's going in now," Hettie said. "Going round the back."

Lucas, hidden among the straggle of farm buildings, staring down the road, saw her, too. He gathered saliva in his mouth and spat it out onto the newly thawed mud at his feet. His strong hands bunched into fists in his pockets as he turned away, his small store of curiosity easily satisfied.

Old George Pownall did not see her. He sat in the warmth of

the stable block, fashioning scarecrows, the wood he handled tap-tapping on the worn brick floor.

Sue picked her way along the almost overgrown path, followed it along the shadowed front of the cottage and around to the back. There the fence had been mended, cleanly separating the strip of garden from the Pownalls' field, which reached away to a line of smoky-vague trees. The glare was too much for her. She let her eyes rest on the tussocky grass, where a little snow still lay, melting. No gardener, she wondered if it was too late to put in spring bulbs. She wanted this domesticated strip of earth to become a blaze of daffodils, sweet-scented narcissi, and stiff-stalked tulips in all their endlessly variegated colors. She would ask Gavin. He would know. She would make the spring planting of the garden a priority.

The back door, also painted white, rested under a frilly porch. She opened it with the heavy old key Gavin had given her. A blast of dry warmth from the central heating met her, and the lingering smell of new paint and wood shavings. Gavin had sliced a strip from the width of the house to make a narrow, galleylike kitchen, with storerooms and pantries at either end. Her boot heels clicked against the floor of glossy brown tiles. A double wooden draining board surrounded the stainless-steel sink beneath one of the windows. The tall refrigerator and large electric stove were dark brown. Everything fitted together to save space and for ease of access and use. She stared around her at the rows of cupboards, all with stripped pine doors and small brass handles. The kitchen gleamed and shone in the sunlight, warm and welcoming. She loved it, wanted to touch each pristine surface and lay her cheek against the smooth wood and the gleaming paintwork. This, then, was the home he had made for her.

An old, latched door led into the main room, two rooms combined into a single open space. The floor was new, of blond wood veined in pink, coated with some laminate that gave it a permanent shine without obscuring the natural colors of the wood. At one end, there was an open stone fireplace and, at the other, a tiled Scandinavian wood stove. Sue exclaimed aloud at the formal pattern of the tiles. They were dark brown and bore alternately the stylized image of a marigold and that of a bright yellow sunflower. They were cool and beautiful to her fingertips. These same colors were picked up in the rugs, the two settees. An expensive black record player, with two enormous speakers, was built into a complex of shelves. A heavy curtain, hung on wooden rings from a wooden pole, masked the front door. A vast pottery dish, filled with moist pebbles, awaited the ferns and other potted plants Gavin had promised to bring with him.

Sue walked the length of the room, touching, smiling. She pulled the cord of a beige blind that completely blanked out the window and let it rattle up again. The room was perfect. It reached out to her with Gavin's love.

Against the kitchen wall a new staircase, oak, open-tread, rose to the upper floor. Holding her breath, almost fearful, she climbed it. She stood in a narrow, pink-carpeted corridor. What downstairs was the kitchen was here a shining white bathroom, the remaining space being taken up with fitted cupboards. She moved to the first door on her left and pushed it open.

The bedroom occupied a little more than half the available space. Carpeted in dark brown, it was painted white, these colors being repeated in the geometric design of the comforter that covered the ornate brass bedstead. There were drawers and built-in cupboards, which she slid open, a velvet-covered rocking chair set to catch the light from the window. Tentatively, feeling a little like a child again, Sue sat on the bed, testing its softness. Then, with a laugh, she kicked her legs in the air and let herself bounce on it, claiming it for herself, for love. She wanted to make love in every perfect room of this house, she thought, and the idea excited her, made her loins feel loose and moist. She wanted the house dedicated to love by the joyous performance of the act. Twisting her head toward the window, smoothing the fresh-smelling cotton of the comforter, she whispered his name, longed for him to be there with her to share this bed, this house. And then she thought, pushing herself up, that the room was a little austere, a touch too masculine. But she would soon alter that, she promised herself, as she stood and straightened the bed.

She still had not seen "her" room, as Gavin always referred to it. She hurried there now, anticipation putting a healthy flush in her cheeks. Her drawing board, which he had planed and mounted himself, stood at right angles to the window, to catch the maximum light. Next to it was a plain pottery vase in which he had placed a crowded bunch of dried strawflowers. Tears of love and happiness rushed to her eyes as she stared down at them, her fingers feeling the sharp prick of their dried, curled petals, orange and burnt yellow, darkest magenta and the silvery pink of finest porcelain. Anchored beneath the vase was a sheet of paper. She pulled it free and read:

> Welcome, my darling Sue. May your happiness here be as everlasting as these flowers. G.

Oh, God, she loved him. She loved him so much that it hurt, and his absence seemed like a gritty dust that lay over everything, dulling all that was bright and polished in her world. She leaned against the drawing board, fighting the pain of loving him and saw, on the wall opposite, beautifully framed, the very first drawing she had ever made for Charlie Minchip, the one that had enabled them to meet. She closed her eyes against that poignant drawing, against the delicate pink-sprigged wallpaper of this room he had created for her, where she might be free to work. She allowed the tears to fall for a moment or two before she looked out of the window and saw the van standing at the roadside, in the elongated shadow of the house. It prompted her into action. She must unload, take a chicken from the freezer, start a fire. The list grew in her head as she made herself leave her lovely, special room. She wanted everything to be ready when he arrived so that she could tell him how much she appreciated it all and how very deeply she loved him.

Downstairs, she swept the curtain from the front door with a dry rattle of wooden hoops clacking eerily together, and opened the door to the cold.

Two hours later, the brief life of the winter sun was almost over. The darkening land looked cold and already wrapped in sleep. In contrast, the uncurtained windows of the cottage were all cheerful with light. Her unpacking finished, Sue hesitated for a moment in the living room, debating whether to start the *coq au vin* before having her bath or afterward. It was then, for the first time, that she became aware of the silence. In Birmingham there was always some noise, the distant rumble of traffic, a neighbor's muffled TV set. Here, on this windless evening, the silence was total, a kind of noise in itself to which she found herself listening. The contradiction of silence as sound did not bother her. In fact, it seemed apt.

Ta-ta-t'-tap. Ta-ta-t'-tap.

After the silence, the noise startled her. She had no idea what caused it, but turned instinctively to look over her shoulder, her heart thudding. As she did so, something caught her eye at one of the windows, and she walked quickly toward the front door.

Ta-ta-t'-tap.

This time the dry, rhythmic noise seemed to come from the back of the house, and she whirled around, heading for the kitchen. There she saw a face pressed against the window and heard, almost simultaneously, a voice calling:

"Oo-oo."

The face moved away from the window and Sue, laughing at herself for being so easily scared, went to open the back door.

"I didn't want to startle you," the owner of the face said with a grin. She was a small, slightly overweight woman, wrapped in an old duffel coat. Her very round face was brightly flushed from the cold and framed by a halo of almost silver curls. "I just wondered if you wanted any eggs or anything?" Her speech had a naturally questioning lilt, more noticeable than the flat *u*'s of her rural accent.

"That's very kind of you." Sue felt slightly flustered.

"I ought to introduce myself," the woman said. She craned her neck, inspecting the kitchen as she spoke. "I'm Hettie Pownall from Gatherings Farm up the road." Her pale eyes switched to Sue and saw that the name obviously meant nothing to her. "Your neighbor," she said.

"Oh, of course. The farm up the road. Look, won't you come in?"

"My, hasn't he done it up grand," she exclaimed. Her face seemed to shine with pleasure.

"I think so."

"Oh, yes. Mind you, all them dials and things," she said, referring to the electric stove, "would get me all confused." She laughed cheerfully at herself. "Still, I mustn't hold you up. You'll be busy, I dare say, settling in. What about eggs, then? Fifty pence a dozen 'cause they're rather small just now, with the new pullets coming into lay. And we could let you have milk, too."

"That sounds marvelous," Sue said, trying to think what she needed. "I did bring some eggs with me but it would be nice to have some fresh ones. Perhaps I could have a dozen tomorrow and a pint of milk?"

"Right you are. Then perhaps you'd like to place a regular order, when you know what you'll be needing?"

"Yes. I will. Thank you. But it won't be very large, I'm afraid, since I shall mostly be on my own."

"Oh?" The woman's eyes roamed greedily toward the open door of the living room. "Mr. Trope won't be living here then?"

"No, not exactly. He'll be here at weekends."

"Still, you'll be here permanent?" she asked sharply.

"Oh, yes."

The woman nodded, looked around her again.

"Lovely he's made it."

"Yes," agreed Sue, deciding that she must take a firm line. "I'd love to show you round, but just now . . ."

"I know. You must be up to your eyes. Mr. Trope coming tonight, is he?"

"Yes. And I've got a hundred things to do. Look, why don't you come and have tea one day next week, when I'm settled in? I can show you round then."

"Oh, I'd be ever so pleased. My old dad'll never believe what he's done to this place."

"We could talk about the eggs and milk then."

"Right you are. I shall be glad of a bit of company, too, I don't mind admitting," she said with an open, happy smile.

"Well, we'll fix something," Sue said, moving toward the door.

"A dozen eggs tomorrow and one pint. They'll be here nice and early."

"Thank you very much."

Sue held the door for her and Hettie Pownall stepped out.

"It's been nice meeting you, Mrs. Trope, and I hope you'll be very happy here."

Sue, caught off guard by the name, did not know what to say. Nobody had ever called her that before, or assumed that she might be married. The woman was still scrutinizing her.

"You're younger than I expected," she said frankly.

"Look, I'm not Mrs. Trope. My name's Jackman, Sue Jackman. We might as well get things straight."

She hated herself for feeling so awkward and embarrassed, feared that she must sound apologetic. Hettie Pownall stared at her, her eyes narrowed. Was it imagination, Sue wondered, or did the woman look genuinely shocked?

"Yes, well," she said. "I'll be seeing you then."

"Yes. Thank you. Good night."

Sue closed the door quickly. She hoped the woman wasn't going to be a nuisance. Naturally she was curious. Naturally she wanted to see inside the beautiful house. And it didn't matter a damn what she thought. Country people were always said to be behind the times. The gossip, even if Hettie Pownall had anyone to gossip with, could not harm her. She was proud to be living with Gavin, in his cottage, and she was pretty well pleased with Sue Jackman, too. She had no cause to apologize to anybody.

They lay, twined together, before the fire. The room smelled of apple wood and wine. It had been dedicated, as Sue had wanted. Gavin stirred, raised his body a little from Sue's, and looked down at her with wonder. The firelight gilded her flesh. He reached out and wound a tress of hair around his finger, let it spring loose again, then stroked it, smoothed it into place. She smiled but did not open her eyes. Gavin looked at the room, at the leavings of their meal, their clothes pooled on the floor, at the potted plants he had brought and arranged on the bed of pebbles. It did not seem possible that they had inhabited the cottage for only a few hours. Gavin liked that. He could happily go with the illusion that they had lived there for years, perhaps forever. A log shifted on the fire, flared, crackling. That and the beating of their hearts was the only sound. The silence cocooned them, made them safe. If there was a world outside, it was possible to forget it. Here, with the blinds drawn, they were entirely shut off, their happiness sealing doors and windows so that nothing and no one could intrude.

Sue opened her eyes, looked at him, then followed the direction of his gaze.

"I was just thinking," he said, "it looks as though we have lived here forever."

"Is it that untidy already?" she asked teasingly.

"Who cares?"

"Come on. Get up." She pushed gently against him.

"Is it all right? Really all right?" he asked, touching her chin with his finger.

"It's really wonderful. How many more times must I tell you?"

"Sorry." He sat up.

"Don't be," she said. "I can never tell you *how* wonderful."

Sue began to dress. He watched, admiring, because of Myra, probably more than other men would have done, her health and vigor, the free and unconsidered movements of her joints and limbs. The bend of her knee was erotic, the suppleness of her young, straight back enchanting. He had never confided these thoughts to her, nor would he ever, but they brought him an intense pleasure, and awoke a sense of wonder and of awe.

"Gavin?"

"Mm?"

He turned to the fire, began tossing logs on to it.

"Can I ask you something?"

"Of course."

His back made her nervous, somehow exaggerated her sense, which she had never experienced with him before, of being about to enter forbidden territory.

"Why didn't you tell them about me, the people up at the farm?" she blurted out.

He held a log loosely in his hand, hesitated, hefted it, then leaned forward to place it at the apex of the fire.

"Why should I have?" It was his neutral voice. He recognized it. The voice he used in committees, never with Sue.

"I don't know. I don't expect it matters. Only a woman came here this afternoon."

He turned and watched her, his eyes searching her face for every nuance as she related her interview with Hettie Pownall.

"I told them nothing," he said when she had finished. He stood up and began to dress. "I haven't spoken to them."

"Not at all?"

"No."

"But why not? After all, if it wasn't for them—"

"The cottage has nothing to do with them," he interrupted.

"But surely, since you knew them, used to live with them . . . ?" She sounded as she felt, bewildered.

"I saw no reason. They must think what they like. They're not the sort of people I would want to be friends with."

"Oh?" Sue wanted to laugh, but his manner was too strange, too cold. "Are there such people? Do you draw up lists?"

For a moment, hurt and anger showed on his face.

"I meant simply that we have nothing in common with them. Nothing at all. There is no basis for friendship."

"But they are our only neighbors," she pointed out. "They're bound to be curious."

"I didn't come here, and I didn't think you did, for the neighbors." There was ice in his voice. He was a stranger. As though to underline this, he turned away from her, pulling on his sweater.

"Well," she said, "I told her, Hettie Pownall, the truth about our living arrangements. I thought that would be best. I hope you don't object?"

"You must do as you think best, of course. Only, Sue—" he reached for her and, for the first time, she held back "—I don't want to know them. I don't want them dropping in or in any way interfering with our lives."

"But it's different for me," she said, "being here all the time."

"I realize that. Only don't tell them too much. Keep a civilized distance."

"Why?" she asked, letting herself move into the comfort of his arms. "Are they so very dreadful?"

"No, of course not."

"Were they unkind to you when you were a little boy?"

"Not at all. It's just as I say. We have nothing in common. Besides—" he smiled then, hugging her close "—don't you realize that I want to keep you entirely to myself?"

Gavin walked down an endless road. It flowed like a narrow gray ribbon beneath him, without end. Trees crowded around him, rattling their bare branches together. He walked among the trees, pushing the snagging branches away. He came to a clearing where a woman sat, enthroned in a chintz-covered chair. Her clothing was modest and precise. Garlands of leaves and autumn berries hung in her hair, wreathed her hidden feet. She had very fine hair, curling over her shoulders. The woman smiled at him, a gracious and very sweet smile. Her hands moved down the buttons of her pale blouse. When all were undone, she pulled the blouse from the waistband of her skirt and opened it wide. Dry-mouthed, he stepped forward. Her breasts hung in fleshy tatters, misshapen, oozing blood. And behind him, towering over him, was something monstrous and very terrible.

"Gavin, wake up, please. Gavin, wake up."

He stared into Sue's distraught face as though he had never seen it before. This frightened her more than his previous cries, the wild thrashing of his arms.

"Gavin? Please."

He turned his head on the pillow, disoriented, caught in his dream, not recognizing the dim, lamp-lit room. Slowly, he remembered.

"Sue?"

He reached for her, pulled her relieved face down against his shoulder.

"You were dreaming."

"Yes. I frightened you? I'm sorry."

"It's all right." She snuggled close to him. "It must have been a very bad dream."

"I don't really remember." He reached across her to snap out the light.

"Do you dream like that often?"

"No. Never. Hardly ever. It's this place." As soon as he heard the words he regretted them. He stretched in the bed, hoping she would think that he was settling in for sleep.

"This place? Why?"

He could feel the slight bristle of alarm in her and stroked her upper arm comfortingly.

"It's nothing. Go to sleep."

"No. You must tell me. If you tell me, the dream will go away."

"There's nothing to tell," he protested.

"Was it about your childhood, when you were living here?" He remained silent. It seemed to her a stubborn, secret silence. Sue sat up, pushing her hair back. "Gavin, you ought to tell me. If there's something about this place that—"

"Sh," he said, putting his arm around her. "Don't jump to conclusions. Lie down and I'll tell you all about it."

She obeyed, pressing close to his still tense body.

"It's embarrassing," he said. "Not dreadful or sinister."

"You needn't be embarrassed with me."

"I know. All right, then." She felt his chest rise against her protective hand as he drew a breath and released it in a long sigh. "When I was evacuated here—long before you were born, I may say—there was a schoolteacher, a Miss Peterson. She had sort of been evacuated, too. At least her school had been bombed, and I suppose with the extra children here . . . anyway, we came here together, Miss Peterson and I, and we became very close."

"You'd known her before?"

"No. She just met four of us children in Birmingham and brought us on here. She was a city person, like me. She didn't like the country. I missed the city. She introduced me to opera—I never told you that, did I?"

"No."

"She used to play me her records and explain the music to me. She was a very good teacher and a very lonely woman."

"It's sweet," Sue said, smiling in the darkness.

"Yes, it was. And completely innocent. Only . . . this is where it gets embarrassing."

"What? Were you in love with her?" Sue laughed at him. "Did you bring her flowers, wish that you lived with her?"

"She showed me her breasts," he said in a bleak voice.

Sue did not know what to say. She could not picture it, could not fit this information into the charming image of a schoolboy's crush.

"You're shocked," he said.

"No. Why? Should I be?"

"I'm not sure. You know, I've never told anyone this, never. I . . . perhaps *I* find it shocking."

"Did you, at the time?"

"No. I don't think so. It was so sudden, so strange. We were sitting there, on either side of the fireplace. Every so often I had to wind the gramophone. We were listening to Lily Pons, I think. I'm really not sure." His voice faded as though he were trying to recall everything, precisely.

"And then?" Sue prompted, afraid that by realizing it all in his head, he would forget to tell her.

"She opened her blouse and showed me her breasts. It was all very matter-of-fact, ordinary."

"Just like that?" Sue tried to make her voice neutral.

"Yes."

"She wasn't wearing anything beneath the blouse?"

"No. She couldn't have been. Funny, I never thought of that."

"And what did you do?"

"Nothing."

He saw the breasts, torn and shredded, bloody, and screwed his eyes tight shut to obliterate the memory.

"What about her?"

"Nothing." This was not true. He realized it as soon as he had said it. He saw her lift the full white breasts in her hands, squeezing them, caressing them, rolling the hard, large nipples between finger and thumb, smiling. "When the record came to an end," he said, after a long pause, "she fastened her blouse and handed me the next record as though nothing at all had happened."

Sue lay against him, thinking. "It upset you?" she suggested.

"No, I don't think so."

"How old were you?"

"Oh, ten, something like that."

"And she?"

"Late twenties, thirty maybe."

"And . . . did it excite you?"

He tried to remember. He saw her again, opening the blouse on the ragged tatters of her torn breasts.

"No," he said fiercely.

"And you dreamed about it?"

"About her, yes. Something—"

"Why did it frighten you so?"

"I really don't know. Darling, dreams aren't rational."

"But you think coming here, being here reminded you?"

"Subconsciously. I haven't thought of Miss Peterson for years."

"What happened to her?"

"She went away. I really don't remember. I was ill at the time, some kind of fever or something. When I went back to school, she had gone."

"How odd."

"It's nothing. I told you it was nothing. Now go to sleep." He kissed the top of her head.

"But why? Was she trying to seduce you?"

"A ten-year-old boy? I scarcely think so."

"Well, you must admit it was a pretty odd—"

"That's why I never told anyone. I knew people would think it meant more than it did," he said, obviously wanting to close the topic.

"Not if it didn't mean anything to you," Sue said carefully.

"Of course it didn't. Now I'm going to sleep." He kissed her lightly and turned over.

Then why did he dream of it, why cry out in such a horrified way? Sue lay, wide-eyed, wondering about it all. It had not shocked her, but there was something vaguely unpleasant about the story. If a man had exposed himself to her at that age? She dismissed that thought as irrelevant. What bothered her was the instinctive sense that Gavin had not told her everything, certainly not enough to justify the nightmare. Had there been more, then? She turned onto her side and began to drift toward sleep, so safe and warm, far beyond the reach of Miss Peterson and her eccentric ways.

Ta-ta-t'-tap.

A branch somewhere, knocking against a window, she thought. Ignore it. Go to sleep. She could not quite relinquish consciousness, had to listen for the sound. It did not come again, but she heard the wind gust, beating against the house. In the morning, she thought drowsily, she must check for a loose branch and tie it back. In a high wind such a noise could make for a sleepless night. Not now, though. Not now. She put her arm around Gavin's waist and yawned, then drifted to sleep.

The wind rose during the night, became ferocious, whipping snow from the skies to send it whirling and dancing across the flat land. When Sue awoke the wind had abated, although the snow continued to fall. Gavin slept peacefully, his arm crooked over his face. She crept cautiously out of bed, wrapped herself in a warm robe, and descended the stairs to the kitchen, where the snow danced past the window like confetti. She felt a distinctly childlike excitement that prompted her to open the back door. There, under the shelter of the porch, was a shallow wicker basket containing fresh brown eggs and beside it a tin container of milk. And Evie had said it was impossible to get anything delivered in the country! This was service.

Sue clutched her robe about her and stood for a moment, watching the snow, which reminded her of a flapping lace curtain. The faded grass in the backyard and the rich brown soil of the field beyond were only speckled with white, but if it continued all day . . . she smiled to herself. Supposing they got snowed in and Gavin could not leave on Sunday night? It was wrong of her to hope for such things, of course, but dreams were still possible.

She picked up the milk and eggs, shouldered the door closed against the cold. She decided to make boiled eggs for breakfast, with hot buttered toast cut into fingers. She would set a tray and carry it up to Gavin, eat with him herself. She felt light and happy moving around the kitchen. While she waited for the water to boil, she carried the egg basket to the refrigerator and transferred the cold brown shells to the plastic storage slots. At the bottom of the basket was something odd. At first she thought it was a wisp of straw or a chicken's feather but, looked at more closely, it was obviously an artifact of some kind. She set the basket aside for a moment while she carefully lowered the eggs into the boiling water and set the automatic timer, then she lifted the little object from the basket and held it between her fingers.

It was a little manikin of some kind, made of twigs, skillfully bound together. The impression was that its skeletal body wore a sort of cloak, a single black, green-sheened feather—a crow's feather, she thought. It was a charming little thing, but Sue could not think what it was or why it had been left there. And then, of course, she realized that it must have found its way into the basket by accident.

The timer went off, distracting her. She quickly prepared the tray of eggs, toast, strong tea, and a jug of fresh milk. Just before lifting it from the counter, she added the manikin thing. It might amuse Gavin. He might even know what it was.

He stirred awake, yawning, as she came into the bedroom.

"Good morning. It's snowing." She set the tray down and let the blind up. "You know something? Snow is entirely different in the country." She came to the bed and kissed his sleepy face. "In Birmingham I used to dread it. Here, it's gorgeous."

He pushed himself up, smiling at her.

"You've made breakfast?"

"Mm-hm. Fresh boiled eggs and lots of toast. I thought we could plan what we have to do today while we eat." She sat on the side of the bed and lifted the tray onto his lap. "Here we go. Start before the eggs—"

"What's that?" He flinched from the tray as though scalded.

"Oh, that. I don't know. I wondered if you . . ." She paused, looking at his face. It was gray, drained of all color, as though he were sick. Deep lines scored his cheek on either side of his nose. "Gavin? What's the matter? It's only a couple of twigs and a feather." She picked the offending thing up, twirled it between her fingers.

With a monumental effort, he forced a pale smile.

"Of course. It startled me. I thought it was . . . I don't know."

"I'm sorry. I shouldn't have plunked it on the tray like that." She put it on the night table beside the bed.

"It doesn't look very hygienic," he commented.

"I'll throw it away. Eat your breakfast."

His hand shook a little as he sliced the top cleanly from his egg.

"Poor darling. It did scare you."

"I wasn't properly awake. It's nothing. Really."

"No more bad dreams?"

"None."

"Good. I could get to be quite jealous of your Miss Peterson. I bet she had enormous, gorgeous breasts," she teased.

"I don't remember. Now, what about today?"

She forgot all about the manikin as they ate and planned. The eggs were delicious—another bonus, she thought, of country life. They agreed that there was no need to shop. Gavin had stocked the freezer to capacity. If the weather broke, he would make a start on the sagging fence. If not, there was some carpentry he wanted to finish, and he'd brought seed catalogues with him so that they could plan the garden together.

"Or," he concluded, "we could just make love."

Sue laughed and kissed him.

"Later. Right now there are other fires to be started."

"I'll do that."

"No. You have your bath. I've got to learn how to start that stove. You can do the open fire later."

"It's a pact," he said, smiling. Sue removed the tray and went out. A moment later he heard her humming as she went down the stairs.

He leaned across the bed and picked up the twig-and-feather monstrosity. He felt cold and sick inside. He hoped that she had forgotten it, prayed that she would. Quickly, he got out of bed and dropped it into a drawer, pulling some underwear over it. He was shaking a little, but underneath his fear was anger and determination. He'd put a stop to this at once. This very day, somehow, he would have a confrontation, nip it all in the bud. Of course he knew what the manikin was, or pretended to be. It was for fear of this, fear of being forced to confront something like this, that he had stayed far away from the Pownalls. That was no longer possible, obviously, but he would pay them only one visit.

He was no longer a boy to be terrified with tales and legends, to be plagued by superstition. And none of this, ever, must come to Sue's knowledge. For all she would laugh and dismiss it as the nonsense it was, being alone here—he could not risk it. For she was more precious than life itself to him. He was resolved even to go to the police if necessary. And he would tell the Pownalls that to their stupid, country-bumpkin faces.

It felt eerie to be walking along the road he had so recently dreamed about and the snow, falling gently now, reminded him of that other time, best forgotten. He regretted not bringing the car, but his excuse to Sue had been that he wanted to walk and stretch his legs. The car might have made his arrival more impressive, though. He hunched his shoulders and walked on, leaving a trail of solitary footprints in the light snow. Ahead was the farm with its curl of smoke. It still had that squashed, lumpy look about it, and, as he drew closer, he could see that the garden was still a haphazardly attended place. But there were changes. Some of the old stone and tile outbuildings were half demolished. They looked as though an angry giant had smashed down once with his fist and then wandered off, bored with his work of destruction, or his anger spent. In the remains of one barn were a number of automobiles. He saw that the stone had been chopped away to make a wider entrance for them. They were brightly painted; some had numbers stenciled on their sides, and the hoods of two of them were raised, as though someone had been tinkering with them. He was staring at them, wondering who in this remote and backward place could have taken up drag- or stock-car racing, when he heard a step behind him. Quickly he turned around, feeling nervous and guilty.

Lucas had not changed; he had simply grown and weathered a little. The same lean face, the same rather sullen dark eyes, even the cowlick of dark hair still flopped unruly across the narrow forehead.

"Lucas," he said.

"Gavin."

Neither man offered to shake hands. They regarded each other suspiciously, each seeking an advantage, weighing up the mutually assumed opposition.

"I want to talk to you," Gavin said.

"Oh, yes? We've been wondering when you'd stop by." Lucas paused, glanced up at the sky and then toward the house. "You'd best come inside, then," he said and set off across the muddy yard without waiting for Gavin's reaction.

The kitchen, too, was unchanged. The geraniums blooming on the crowded window sill could have been the very ones Gavin remembered from so long ago. Sitting at the table, picking apart what appeared to be a crankshaft and grinning up at him was a man he did not immediately recognize as Ashton. There was something wrong about him, something lopsided and foolish about his grin. Gavin nodded and turned to meet the speculative gaze of a woman much younger than Lucas, who held three small children against her skirts like a brood of sheltering chicks. She had the strong black hair and olive coloring of a gypsy.

"This is Shirley, my missus," Lucas said.

"How d'you do?" She nodded at him but did not smile. The children avoided his eyes.

"Your father isn't home?" Gavin asked Lucas.

"Out back. I thought it was me you wanted," he said, a hint of challenge in his voice.

"Yes, you'll do." Gavin pulled the twig-and-feather manikin from his pocket. "I want to know the meaning of this."

Ashton chuckled to himself, reached out an oily hand for it, and grasped it delightedly, twisting it before his eyes.

"You know as well as I do," Lucas said, his face impassive.

"Yes, I think I do. But what do you mean by it?"

"It's like, I suppose you'd say, a warning."

"To me?"

"If the cap fits," Ashton said and giggled.

His brother watched him, waiting until Ashton's senseless laughter had wasted itself on the dry, warm air before continuing. "To you and yours."

"I thought—I had thought you might have grown out of that nonsense," Gavin said. "But since you haven't, I want to make something quite clear. It is nonsense, and I will have no part of it. If you do anything like this again, I shall go straight to the police."

At this, Ashton dropped the manikin and turned his slack face toward Gavin. His features tightened, took on a studied expression of meanness.

"What for? What would you tell them?" Lucas asked, his tone reasonable, his voice quiet.

"You know damn well what I could tell them, but I'm not so stupid as to think they would believe me. I shall complain that you are harassing me."

"And your fancy woman?" Shirley asked, her head lifted pugnaciously toward him.

"That's my business. What I do, who I live with has nothing to do with you—any of you—and I'm warning you. If you don't leave us completely alone, I shall take steps." He looked directly at Lucas. "I could make things pretty unpleasant for you."

"Seems to me you're doing a lot of threatening."

"You started it. All I want is for this to stop now. I've kept my mouth shut for over thirty years. I want and intend to keep it shut still. But I'm warning you. . . ."

Lucas reached out and took the manikin from the table.

"Seems like we're all square then: a warning for a warning."

"Just so long as you understand."

"This," Lucas said, waving the thing between them, "wouldn't have been necessary if you'd told us your plans."

"Why on earth should I? What has it got to do with you?"

"You don't know why the old man left you the cottage?"

"I gave you a chance to have it back."

Lucas shook his head impatiently, as though Gavin was missing the point entirely.

"It's yours, legal and proper."

"Then kindly let me do as I like in it, without interference."

"We had thought you'd be living there permanent now," Shirley said.

"With your missus," Lucas added.

"One day, possibly, I will. For the moment I shall be a frequent visitor and I will not tolerate any harassment of Miss Jackman."

At her name, Ashton sniggered. Gavin suddenly wanted to hit him, but he kept his hands bunched in his pockets and waited for Lucas to reply.

"We're not concerned with her," Lucas said. "It's just that we wanted to remind you. It's like the old man said, you're one of us, always will be. He left you the cottage so you'd live in it and be here, like he wanted, like you have to be."

"But I'm afraid that's not possible," Gavin said, preparing to play his trump card. "The cottage no longer belongs to me. I've signed it over, lock, stock, and barrel, to Miss Jackman. There was nothing," he added, enjoying the surprise and consternation on their faces, "in your grandfather's will to prevent me."

Ashton stared at his brother, obviously not understanding. Shirley and Lucas exchanged a private look.

"You shouldn't have done that," she said.

"It's really none of your business. And it's perfectly legal. You're welcome to check."

"And what does she know of this?" Lucas still held the manikin and now he raised it, thrusting it toward Gavin.

"Nothing. And she never will know. Not from me."

"Well, then." Lucas snapped the twigs with a dry crack between his strong fingers and let the pieces fall onto the table.

"I'm glad we understand each other," Gavin said, and turned toward the door.

"The old couple'd like to see you," Lucas said, "when you're next in these parts."

"Yes," Gavin said noncommittally. "Well, let's see how it goes, shall we?" He nodded at Shirley and let himself out into the yard.

The snow had stopped falling. A pale sun was turning it to slush, making it slippery underfoot so that Gavin could not walk as quickly as he would have liked. On the whole he was pleased with the interview. Lucas wasn't stupid. He must know that Gavin had meant what he had said about the police. And they wouldn't want that, probably for petty reasons Gavin could only guess at. That motley collection of cars, for example; he doubted that they were licensed and taxed. But what he really banked on was their being completely blocked by his having signed the cottage over to Sue. Every word of that was true. He hoped they would check, if they knew how to. He felt a little guilty about it, though. He would have preferred to have done it from an entirely pure motive, just to give Sue security. But he had to protect himself, too, and by the time Sue learned of it, there would be no danger.

Coming toward him along the straight, flat road was a woman on a bicycle. He was walking into the sun and could not see her clearly, but the very ordinariness of the sight, the fact that there was another person in this desolate landscape, helped to reduce his fears. He walked on with more confidence and was not particularly surprised when the woman slowed and veered her bicycle toward him.

"Afternoon, Mr. Trope."

"Afternoon," he said, frowning a little at her open, apple-cheeked face. Seeing his confusion, she laughed pleasantly.

"You don't remember me at all, do you? Well, to speak the truth, I wouldn't have known you from Adam."

Her smile was infectious. Gavin wracked his memory.

"You must be Hettie," he said, pleased.

"That's right." She put out her hand in a dirty, knitted mitten and he shook it briefly. "I've just been by your place," she said. "Your friend's asked me to tea. She's going to show me round. Oh, you have made it lovely."

Gavin's smile faded as the old apprehension came creeping back into his mind. "I suppose you brought it," he said in a cold voice, noticing the egg basket attached to her handlebars.

"The eggs? Oh, yes. I do most of the deliveries. Keeps me out of mischief."

"I wasn't referring to the eggs," he said.

"Then I don't know what you're on about, unless you mean the milk. Nothing wrong with it, was there? Fresh this morning."

"No," he said, "there was nothing wrong with the milk."

"Well, then?"

"It doesn't matter." It suddenly seemed possible that she did not know, and if she didn't then he would feel easier about her visiting Sue.

"Well, nice to meet you at last, but I must be getting on. Cows won't milk themselves."

"No," he said. "Good-bye."

"Be seeing you," she shouted cheerily as, wobbling, she got the bicycle balanced and began to pedal doggedly away.

Gavin hurried on toward the cottage, wondering how she could not know. The whole family were schooled in it. Admittedly Hettie had been too young when he was there, but surely, as she grew up, she would be a party to it, like the boys? After all, Lucas's wife knew. Yet there was something wholesome, something naturally sensible about Hettie Pownall that made him dare to hope that perhaps she dismissed it, would have no part of it.

Sue was standing at the cottage window, watching for him, he thought. He felt so glad to see her that he waved and ran toward the front door. All the tension seemed to drain out of him. He heard the curtain rattle back on its wooden hoops, and then she opened the door, was laughing in his arms. He kissed her and hugged her tight.

"It was lovely to see you watching for me," he told her. "It felt like a proper homecoming."

Sue laughed and pulled him inside, into the warm.

"Sorry to deflate your ego, darling, but I was looking at those scarecrows. I could have sworn there were only three yesterday, but look, there are four there now."

He looked at the field and saw that there were indeed four scarecrows where there had only been three. And he thought they seemed closer to the house.

"Shut the door," he said in a thick voice. "You're letting all the heat escape."

Sunday night came quickly, too quickly. Sue clung to Gavin, but she did not plead with him to stay, not even for a little longer.

"You're sure you'll be all right?" he asked anxiously.

"Of course. What could possibly happen to me here?"

"Nothing, of course." He held her tightly. "I shall miss you so much."

"I know. I love you."

She went out with him and stood at the side of the road until the red taillights of his car disappeared around the right-angled bend by the farm.

It was a clear night with a certain promise of frost. Gavin did not look at the farm as he passed. The road stretched clear and straight for miles ahead of him, with no hint of other traffic. A more fanciful man might have considered that the road seemed to lead into the impenetrably black, star-punctured sky. Gavin knew that it did not. At the far edge of the great plain across which he traveled, the landscape changed dramatically. The road would begin to descend gradually, passing between the remains of an ancient forest. At sight of it, he was reminded that the second Pownall son had been named for the place—Ashton Wold. He was just thinking of that when he found his way blocked by a scarecrow.

He was not traveling fast. His lights picked it out, leaving him ample time and room to slow down, brake, and stop. It stood as though planted in the very center of the road. The headlights showed it clearly. He wanted not to look at it but he was frozen, could look only at it, as he was intended to do. It was a female scarecrow. At first glance this was suggested by a rag of skirt that reached partway down its stick legs. A blouse hung open on crudely suggested breasts of sacking, which, he saw with a mingled feeling of disgust and fascination, were rent and dribbling straw. Fearfully, he looked up to its face. Something lank and soft surrounded the head to suggest hair that curled over the straight shoulders. The face itself, sacking stretched taut over something unidentifiable, had a look of Miss Peterson.

He closed his eyes then and let his body slump against the steering wheel. He was going mad, was allowing his imagination to dance out of control. The recent dream and the similar one he had experienced when he first learned that he had inherited the cottage he had tried to ignore. But now he knew that he must take steps. No matter how repugnant it might be to him, he must deal with this segment of his past that he could no longer control. He *would* deal with it. He *would* take steps, first thing in the morning. But now there was nothing there but an inanimate construction of poles and sacking, sticks and straw. He must open his eyes and see it for what it was, a grisly joke.

It had moved closer to the car, was pressed almost against the radiator grille. He wanted to scream, but no sound came from his dry throat. He threw himself back in his seat, as though recoiling from it. His hands were slippery on the wheel. Lit from below, the face half in shadow, it looked, to his appalled eyes, even more like Miss Peterson. Those, surely, were her cheekbones, that her rounded chin?

By an effort of will he made himself believe that it was impossible, that what he thought he recognized could not be. Sticks and straw, sacking, a thing that did not even scare the crows, that's what Miss Peterson had said. Just sticks and straw. Like a chant, he made it sound over and over in his head as he opened the door and stepped out into the cold, still night.

Ta-ta-t'-tap. Ta-ta-t'-tap.

There were others, tapping together at the edge of the flat field. Stark shapes in the darkness. He edged his way along the nose of the car. He had only to push her away, knock her over. *It*, his rational mind screamed at him. Make sure *it* did not scratch the paintwork. He hung on to that thought as he pushed himself away from the car and turned to meet the claiming, clawing twig hands of Miss Peterson.

Ta-ta-t'-tap. Ta-ta-t'-tap.

The others moved forward as though drawn by his cry of terror.

"I wondered if it'd still be all right to come," Hettie said, hovering just inside the kitchen, which smelled pleasantly of newly baked scones. She had the uncharacteristic look of a shy animal—a look that, in a less open person, could have appeared assumed. "I mean because of your Mr. Trope being so angry," she added.

Sue had felt nervous about this visit ever since she had issued the invitation, and thinking about Gavin's words of caution had made her more uneasy. Because of this, she replied obliquely, which was not at all like her.

"Oh? Was he?"

"Didn't he say nothing to you, then?"

"Look," said Sue, "why don't you take your coat off and sit down, and then we can talk about it?"

Hettie's face lit up.

"Well, if you're sure . . ."

"Come on, give me your coat."

"Only I don't like getting in bad with anybody, specially not neighbors," Hettie chattered as she unbuttoned her coat and handed it to Sue.

Under the coat Hettie wore a blue wool dress against which her hips strained. The dress, the heavy brown coat that Sue hung up, and the low-heeled black shoes all proclaimed that Hettie had dressed up for the occasion. Sue found that rather touching; a compliment.

"Come in," she said, leading the way into the living room.

The wood stove was burning, and Sue had arranged the tea things on a low coffee table at that end of the long room. Hettie's eyes devoured the room in greedy gulps, but whatever it was that had made her doubt her welcome remained uppermost in her mind.

"I had a word with him Saturday afternoon and I could see something had upset him, but I didn't know what it was. It weren't my fault, honest."

Sue laughed and told her to sit down. Hettie chose a corner of the settee and sat with elaborate care, as though she feared to damage it.

"Now, what exactly is all this about?" she said, smiling to cover the slight feeling of apprehension she had had ever since Hettie's arrival.

"The Sign, of course," Hettie said simply. "Didn't he tell you about it?"

"What sign?" Sue sat at the other end of the couch, her body half-turned toward her guest.

"Oh, it's just a few old twigs and a feather."

"Ah, now I'm with you," Sue said, realizing that she had completely forgotten about the manikin and at the same time remembering how it had startled Gavin. "Yes. I found it, at the bottom of the egg basket."

"I didn't know it was there, honest. Shirley put the eggs up that morning."

"It doesn't matter," Sue said, puzzled by Hettie's continuing anxiety. "I thought it was rather pretty."

"Oh, well, that is a weight off my mind. If you're sure . . ."

"Quite sure. Why did you think I'd be bothered about it?"

"Well, because of him, Mr. Trope. He didn't say nothing to you?"

"It startled him," Sue said, "but that was my fault. I stupidly put it on the breakfast tray when he was half-asleep, and he thought it was an insect or something."

"Well," Hettie said, assuming a confidential, gossipy tone, "he came up to our place—it must have been just about the time I called in here to fetch the egg basket—and he was ranting and raving about it something awful. I bumped into him on the way back, see, and he had a go at me, too, but I didn't know about it then. And, well, I thought as how you might be upset and all and I didn't know what to do. You know, whether to come today or not. But I'm ever so glad you're not mad about it," she concluded in a rush.

"Not at all," Sue said automatically. She did not want this woman who was, after all, almost a stranger, to know that Gavin had kept his feelings from her, to think that he had hurt her. If he had, she thought quickly. For Hettie might have gotten it wrong, might be exaggerating. But at the back of her mind, troubling her, was Gavin's vehemence about the Pownalls. Guiltily, she became aware of Hettie's bright blue eyes fixed on her and hoped that her thoughts had not shown on her face. "I expect it was a misunderstanding," she said. "Shall we have tea now, then I can show you round?" Sue stood up.

"Just as you like," Hettie said. "I could do with a cup, I must admit, now I've got that off my chest." Sue smiled and went toward the kitchen. "Funny, though, him not saying anything to you."

"Oh, he did mention it," Sue replied, not trusting herself to look at Hettie. "I'm afraid I didn't think it was very important so I didn't take much notice." Her hands shook a little as she filled the kettle and switched it on. She was full of questions, but her pride and Gavin's insistence that she should keep Hettie Pownall at a certain distance made her cautious. The proper person to discuss it with was Gavin, she told herself as she set out the warm scones and carried them into the sitting room. "To tell you the truth," she said, "I'd forgotten all about it. That shows you how important it was. I don't even know what happened to it."

"Oh, he brought it back," Hettie said, looking hungrily at the scones.

Sue could think of nothing safe to say so she walked back into the kitchen and spooned tea into the warmed pot.

"You said it was a sign," she called, raising her voice. "Sign of what?"

"Why, of welcome. What else?" Hettie shouted back.

How nice, Sue thought, kind. So why did Gavin—*if* he had, she corrected herself. But why hadn't he told her about seeing the Pownalls and Hettie?

"Most people think it's a daft idea," Hettie said, propping herself in the doorway. "Nobody bothers with it anymore. Well, what chance is there here, nowadays? It's an old custom, I remember my grandpa used to go on about it. It's supposed to be a little man, you see. The idea was that you didn't go bothering people when they first moved in, so you sent the Sign, see, to welcome them and bring them good luck."

"I think that's lovely," Sue said, pouring water on the tea. "Sort of like a visiting card."

"Yes, well . . . but you can see how little it happens now. Me, I come barging straight in asking about eggs."

"And very pleased I was to see you," Sue told her. "Now, I think we've got everything. Let's go and sit down."

Hettie ate with relish, exclaiming over the scones and lemon cake. Even the china won her approval. Then she referred back to the conversation Sue had hoped was finished.

"It was Ashton who did it," she said, wiping crumbs from her lips. "He likes things like that, all the old customs. He remembers 'em all."

"Ashton?" Sue inquired.

"My brother. Yes, I reckon it was him put the Sign in the egg basket."

"Tell me about your family," Sue said, glad to change the subject.

"Didn't Mr. Trope tell you about us, neither?"

Sue was stung by the way she said this. "Yes, of course he did. But I know nothing about you personally, how you live."

"Oh, there's nothing to tell. Dull, I am."

"I don't believe that. For a start you've got a brother."

"Two, Ashton and Lucas. And then there's my mum and dad. They're getting on now and retired, like."

"But you all live together, up at the farm?"

"Oh, yes," Hettie said, as though any other arrangement was unthinkable. "And Shirley—that's Lucas's wife—and their three kids . . ."

"Heavens. Don't you feel overcrowded?"

"No. There's plenty of room."

"And what do you do?"

"I just help out round the farm, do the deliveries and that, and the milking, mostly. 'Course we're mainly arable, but we keep a few cows, for our own convenience, like."

"And you enjoy that?"

"It's all right. I'm just used to it, if you know what I mean."

"You never thought of moving away?"

"No. Well, I did once, thought I might join the women's army. Quite fancied that, I did."

"So what stopped you?"

"Well, I was needed at home, see. It was the time of Ashton's accident."

"Oh, dear. What happened?"

Hettie frowned, could be seen debating with herself how much, if anything, she should tell.

"Yes," she said, nodding her head. "It's best you should know about Ash. Nothing personal, mind, don't get me wrong. It's just that, well, you don't want to go telling other people all your business, do you? Anyway, people are funny about such things. But you being such a close neighbor, yes, I think it's best."

"I really don't want to pry."

"Bless you, no. It's just, well, he's car mad, Ashton. We've got more old bangers up there than you've had hot dinners, I'll be bound. He does 'em up, you know? Ash can make anything run. Hot rods, he calls 'em. Anyway, he had an accident a few years back, damn near killed himself. In hospital months and months he was, and, well, that's why I couldn't go in the army. We was shorthanded, you see."

Sue nodded sympathetically. "But he's all right now?"

"Oh, yes. Fit as a fiddle. Only, well, he's a bit . . . there was brain damage, you see. He almost lost the top of his head. The doctor said it was like someone had sliced the top off a boiled egg." Sue winced, the image being too graphic for her taste. "It's a miracle he lived at all. And it's left him a bit, well, funny, you know? But he's harmless. I want you to understand that. He's not violent or nothing like that. He just don't connect things up too well."

"I understand. That's terrible, must be terrible for you all. Didn't you resent having to stay at home, though?"

Hettie shrugged. "Maybe. But I don't expect I'd have liked the army. Well, no, I would have liked the army, but not all that traveling about, going abroad and that."

"I think I would have resented it very much."

"Oh, well, it's different for you, isn't it?"

"How?"

"I don't know. But it must be. Farmers, see, you always have to help out when you're needed. It's like a family thing. It has to be done, and you get used to it."

"Yes. And I suppose it's difficult for you to get anyone to work for you round here."

"Oh, yes. Well, there isn't anyone. They don't want to come up here from Brooking. And then most of 'em go and work in town, see. Last help we had was, oh, years ago. In Grandpa's time. Actually, he built this old house for a laborer."

Sue felt that this was dangerous ground. She did not like the feeling that perhaps old Mr. Pownall's leaving the cottage to Gavin had contributed to Hettie's having to stay on at the farm.

"That reminds me," she said. "I noticed the other day that the village isn't completely deserted. I saw smoke from a chimney and some washing."

"That'd be old Grubber. He's a funny old chap, he is. I go and muck him out once a month or so. He's—what do they call it?—senile. Poor old beggar. Then there's Shirley's folk. They're not rightly from round here, but when she took up with Lucas they settled here. Here, what's the time?"

Sue looked at her watch.

"Ten past four."

"Oh, don't time fly when you're enjoying yourself? But could I have that look round now? I don't mean to be pushy, but I must get back for the milking."

"There's really not much else to see," Sue said. "But, yes, of course you can."

Sue felt embarrassed showing Hettie the bedroom. She did not like the feeling in herself and could not quite understand it. She was conscious, though, of hurrying her on to her room, which inevitably led to a string of questions about her work. Afraid of sounding patronizing, Sue found herself stumbling, giving vague answers until Hettie expressed a naïve amazement that "you can get paid for drawing pictures." Hettie badly wanted to see her work but Sue made automatic excuses, lied, in fact, by saying that she had not yet unpacked.

"Some other time," she said, edging Hettie out of the room.

"Oh, that'd be nice. Well, I do think it's lovely. A real little palace."

"I'm very lucky."

"And I've really enjoyed myself. I can't tell you. Thanks ever so much."

"You must come again," Sue responded, and meant it. She liked Hettie, liked her opinions and easy delight in things. And she would, in time, learn to be more relaxed with her. She fetched Hettie's coat and helped her on with it.

"And you must come and see us," Hettie said. "Meet the family, like. They'd like to meet you, really they would."

Sue remembered Gavin's caution and made a vague answer.

"Snow's all gone," Hettie remarked as she stood on the front doorstep, "but we're in for a real frost, I reckon."

"It's very cold," Sue agreed, looking beyond her guest at the twilit fields. "Oh, yes, I meant to ask you. Yesterday morning I noticed all the scarecrows had gone. I wondered why?"

"Oh, Dad'll be fixing 'em up. They take such a battering from the winds up here and the spring wheat will be through in a few weeks. He'll be patching up them as can be patched and making new ones. There's no danger from the birds when the ground's frost-hard, see."

"Oh, yes, of course."

"Well, thanks again."

"Good-bye, Hettie."

Sue watched Hettie down the path and then shut herself into the safe warmth of the cottage.

She thought about Hettie Pownall as she did the washing up and tried to imagine the woman's proscribed existence. What struck her was Hettie's cheerfulness, her openness to new experiences and people. She liked her very much, she decided, and was sorry that Gavin's reaction to the Sign had made her uncertain of her welcome. Thinking about Hettie, of course, was just a ploy to prevent her wondering why, if Gavin had been so upset about the manikin, he had not confided in her. Why he had not said that he was going to see the Pownalls, or afterward that he had seen them. Hettie was a simple soul, had probably gotten it muddled. And Sue could not imagine Gavin "ranting and raving" at them. Probably they had misunderstood, exaggerated what had taken place when relating it to Hettie. And almost certainly they must be hurt that Gavin had not understood and appreciated the little welcoming gift. She still thought it a very charming custom. She wondered what Gavin could have thought it meant. She would have to ask him about it all, get his version, as well as his explanation for not telling her about it in the first place. It just wasn't like him.

Under all this was a greater and more abiding anxiety. He had not phoned. She reminded herself that there was nothing unusual in this. When she had lived in Birmingham, several days often passed without any communication between them. It was just that here she had thought they would be more often in touch. Especially now, right at the beginning. He must know that she would want to hear that he had gotten back safely, that everything was all right. But perhaps Myra had been ill or upset. He would call tonight, after Myra had gone to bed. And if he didn't, she would ring him in the morning. Perhaps there had been an unexpected change of plan and he would come back to her before the weekend.

Sue went up to her workroom and laid out the illustrations for her book on the drawing board. But the ideas seemed frozen, unrealizable at the back of her mind. She made a few minor alterations to the most recent drawing and then wandered restlessly back downstairs. She checked the stove, added a few more logs, and put a record on the stereo. Turning the volume up loud, she went into the kitchen and opened the storeroom. Gavin had laid down a few cases of wine, and she took a bottle at random. She never drank alone but she thought possibly a glass or two would relax her, enable her to work. She opened the bottle and carried it upstairs, with a glass. The record, a recital of Tchaikovsky arias, plaintive and passionate, drifted into the room. She sipped the wine and took a fresh sheet of paper. Without planning to do so, she began to draw trees.

Ashton Pownall's room was a partitioned-off portion of the attic. It contained an old wardrobe from which much of the ornate molding was missing, a trundle bed, and a chest of drawers. Boots and soiled items of clothing, parts of an engine, tins of rust-proofer, and a paint-stained spray gun littered the floor. Three of the walls were almost entirely covered by photographs of cars taken from the various automobile magazines Hettie or Lucas collected for him each week in Brooking. He loved the cars, especially the long-finned American ones. He loved their gleaming, glossy bodies and bright colors. He loved the latent power he knew slept in them, waiting to be released. He could, and often did, spend hours looking at them, adding to this personal wallpaper.

The accident had not made him clumsy with his hands. He could still tune an engine with an artist's fingers. His lips pursed, he could clip the image of a car with absolute precision from the pages of a magazine and tack it to the wall in perfect alignment. Ashton had only a hazy memory of the accident. He remembered it as a good time, remembered going fast on a dark road, shouting out loud to himself with excitement and pleasure. After that it was just lights and doctors and nurses in blue uniforms and pain. His body had suffered very little in the crash, although the doctors said it was a miracle every bone in his body had not been fractured. His head had borne the brunt. His tow-blond hair grew thick and uneven over the bony indentation that ran right across the back of his skull from ear to ear. Sometimes the scar pained him, in a dull kind of way, but mostly he just forgot about it. Sometimes he would accidentally put his hand to the back of his head and be surprised to feel the dent. When that happened it took him a moment or two to remember what it was, how it had come about. But mostly he just forgot about it.

That night, a longing had made Ashton desert the television set downstairs around which the family clustered. It was cold in his room but, stripped to the waist, he worked up his own warmth by exercising with a chest expander, lifting parts of a heavy axle as weights. The dim, unshaded bulb in the center of the room sent his quietly panting shadow dancing on the car-bedecked walls and showed his hard, muscular body in the pitted old mirror that was screwed to the inside of the wardrobe door. When the sweat gleamed on his torso, he straightened up and admired himself, grinning.

He heard the muffled, distant sound of the television set and Hettie's laughter over it. Hettie hadn't said much at supper about the girl in the cottage down the road, especially not the things he wanted to know. He had grown impatient with Hettie's chatter about sofas and carpets and electric stoves. The girl had only an old van. But it wasn't any of that he wanted to know about. What he wanted to know he could not formulate properly. They were questions that came in the form of images, drifting through his head. Some of them made him want to giggle, while others left his mouth slack with wonder.

Ashton flexed his muscle once more, then stepped close up to the wardrobe. There was a jumble of objects piled beneath his few clothes: an odd shoe, a tin containing nuts and bolts, hinges, and other things that would come in handy one day, some scuffed and soiled paperbacks, and rags for wiping grease from his hands. This haphazard-looking mess was actually cunningly arranged to conceal a flat cardboard carton that he now lifted from the wardrobe and carried, with a combination of tenderness and stealth, to his bed.

The box contained his other magazines, the ones he got secretly on his rare trips into Nene or the city where he still had to report, twice a year, for medical checkups.

Ashton pulled the pillow from the head of his bed and placed it so that it hung over the edge. Then he lifted the lid of the box and carefully, taking his time, his lips moving wordlessly, selected a magazine. Next, he stretched himself across the bed, the pillow pressing against his lower belly and groin. He opened the magazine, stared open-mouthed at each picture for a long time, turning the pages carefully, without even a rustle. After a while, he began to flex his buttocks and to move himself gently, gently against the soft pillow. When he finished the first magazine, he selected another, twisting himself around on the bed and loosening his belt before resuming his position and giving himself up again to the images that fed his starving eyes.

By ten o'clock, Sue's head began to buzz unpleasantly from the wine and the threat of a headache. Ten was Myra's bedtime. If he was going to ring he would do so in the next half hour. She stared at the paper, now covered with trees. Why trees? The story she was illustrating had a city setting. She did not need trees. Stretching, yawning, she got up from the drawing board, tired of the trees, which she felt were only a kind of doodle. She was surprised to see that she had drunk all the wine.

She carried the empty bottle and her half-full glass downstairs, where the speakers hummed, forgotten. She switched the record player off and sat near the stove, waiting for his call. She waited until eleven and then climbed wearily, miserably up to bed.

From his attic window, Ashton, exhausted now, the longing satisfied, could see the distant, lighted windows of the cottage. He stood very still, watching the lights go out. Around him he could hear the rest of the family going to bed. His secret magazines had increased the number of things he wanted to know about the girl in the cottage. He waited until all the lights went out, until it was swallowed up by the night, then he crawled into his cold bed and lay, waiting for sleep, compulsively tracing the dent that almost severed the back of his head.

As though to make up for her wasted evening, Sue began work early. She had not really planned it that way. Like much of her best work, it just seemed to happen. It absorbed her totally. The hours passed, and at the end of them she had a finished drawing for the book and working sketches for another three drawings. She felt a mixture of elation and tiredness, her mind both charged and calm. Downstairs, as she began to prepare herself a snack lunch, she remembered that she had not called Gavin. Far from alarming her, his temporary but total expulsion from her mind was reassuring. It proved that the move to the country had not disrupted the essential rhythm of her life, not upset the balance between Gavin and work that she so needed and valued. Yesterday she had entertained some doubts, but no longer. She would telephone him after lunch, and in a much better frame of mind than she had been in last night. After that she would go for a walk, or start work on the garden. The day was cold but bright, suddenly inviting.

She did not hear the unmarked car approach, assumed that the sudden, loud knock at the front door must be Hettie. She dried her hands quickly and went to open it. A burly man in a gray suit stood there, another man hovering behind him. Surprised, Sue felt that she was being scrutinized, not altogether pleasantly.

"Yes?" she said.

The man took something from his pocket and flashed it perfunctorily before her.

"Detective-Sergeant Simmons, miss. Nene Police."

The identification wallet was returned to his pocket. Sue realized that the taller man behind him was in uniform. Aware that she was looking at him, Simmons said, "This is Constable Ricks. He's assisting me."

"Yes," Sue said. "What do you want?"

"If we could just step inside, miss." As he spoke, Simmons came forward, forcing Sue to move back. Before she could gather her wits, the two men were inside. She felt angry at these authoritative, even bullying tactics. The constable removed his hat and stationed himself just inside the door, as though acting as a guard. Simmons looked around the room. "Nice place you've got here," he said.

Sue shut the door.

"Would you mind telling me what this is about?"

"That van outside, would that be yours, miss?" Constable Ricks asked, pleasantly enough.

Sue immediately thought that she must have committed some traffic offense. Had she forgotten the insurance, the license? While she thought, Simmons prowled around the room, even looked into the open kitchen.

"Yes."

"That would be registration number . . ."

"Look, constable, it's my van. If there's anything wrong—"

"You've got the documents to prove that, have you?" Simmons cut in, planting himself before the kitchen door.

"Certainly." She took an automatic step toward the stairs, to fetch the documents.

"That won't be necessary, miss. Just checking."

She was appalled by the man's manner, expected him at any moment to run his finger along the surface to check for dust or to start prying into the cupboards.

"Well," Sue said, folding her arms, "now you've established that, perhaps you'd like to go."

Simmons gave her a cold, steady look.

"Mr. Trope here, is he?"

"Mr. Gavin Trope," the constable emphasized, as though there could be any other.

"No."

She felt the prick of alarm then, imagined car crashes, and quickly realized that she was being foolish. The police did not ask for people of whom they brought bad news.

"You're quite sure about that?"

"As sure as I am that I own the van."

"So you're here all by yourself?" Simmons said, and something happened on his face, a movement of the mouth that might almost have been a smile, an unpleasant smile. It was directed at Constable Ricks.

"Apart from you two gentlemen, yes," Sue said. The look, which she was not sure she had been meant to intercept, made her even angrier.

"Must be pretty lonely for you," Simmons commented, looking at the potted plants as though they might conceal stolen property or something illicit.

Sue decided not to treat it as a question. She walked to the large sofa near the unlit fire and sat down, crossing her legs.

"I said . . .," Simmons said, looking at her over his shoulder.

"I heard you. It's very nice of you to be concerned for my welfare, but I don't consider it any of your business."

"Just trying to break the ice, miss," Ricks said from behind her.

"What do you want?" she asked again.

"Mr. Gavin Trope," he replied, separating each word, dropping them from his lips as though she were deaf or imbecilic.

"He's not here."

"You know where he is?"

"In Higham Furze."

"You're sure of that?" he pounced.

Immediately she realized, as he had intended her to do, that she was not sure of it, could not swear to it.

"If he's not, I can't imagine where else he would be. His office would know."

"Or his wife," Simmons said, his eyes seeming to pin her to her seat.

"Yes," Sue said quickly, before the implication, which was transparent in his tone, could sting her into losing her temper.

"We've asked them," he said, turning away as though the subject no longer held any interest for him. He prowled up the room, bent a little over the stereo deck as though he had never seen a machine like it.

Sue knew that she was supposed to crack, to demand to know

why they wanted Gavin and what had happened to him, but her hostility toward Simmons and incipient fear of him made her say, "I'm afraid I can't help you, then."

"Mind if we look around?" Simmons swung about, directed his curt question at the stairs.

She jumped to her feet.

"Yes, I do."

"We can get a search warrant." Simmons's head slowly swung in her direction. His skin was very smooth, as though polished. His head, with its slightly wavy brown hair, seemed almost too delicate for his powerful, compact body.

"Please do," Sue said, and turned away.

"It would be easier, miss," the ever-reasonable constable began.

"For whom? Certainly not for me," Sue said, turning on him angrily. "If you want to search my house, you get a warrant."

"Your house?" Simmons questioned.

It was a body blow, perfectly timed, and Simmons knew it. He waited patiently, sure that he had won.

"Ask Mr. Trope for permission, then," Sue said, as calmly as she could.

"If we could do that, there'd be no need."

"Mr. Trope's missing, miss," Ricks said, his voice kindly.

"When did you last see him?" Simmons was suddenly standing too close to her, his eyes steely.

Sue began to panic. "Sunday night."

"What time?"

"Eight, eight-fifteen."

"He was here?"

"Yes. He left—"

"Where was he going?"

"Home. Higham Furze."

"How?"

"In his car."

"Navy-blue Ford Escort, registration number . . .," Ricks read out the digits from his notebook.

"Yes," Sue said, edging away from Simmons, feeling trapped and frightened. "That sounds right."

"Which route did he take?" Simmons barked.

"Th—that way." She pointed, vaguely, up the road. "I went outside. I watched him until he rounded the bend, by the farm."

"At eight? Or eight-fifteen?"

"I'm not sure. Somewhere between the two."

"What time did he get back here?"

"He didn't. I haven't—"

"Where did he go?"

"Higham—"

"After he came back here?"

"He didn't come back."

"He phoned you."

"No!"

"Oh, come on." Simmons turned away as though disgusted. Sue could only watch him walk across the room, turn with his back to the ceramic stove, as though comfortably warming himself. "Sit down, Miss Jackman," he said, his voice a little warmer.

She wanted to, badly, but she shook her head sharply. She could imagine him standing over her, leaning down, shouting into her face.

"How did you know my name?" she asked.

"It is your name, isn't it?"

"Yes. But—"

"Suzanne Felicity Jackman?"

"Yes."

"How long have you known Mr. Trope?"

"Two years."

"And what is your relationship?"

"A friend."

"He's your landlord, isn't he? You pay him rent for this place?"

"No."

"Housekeeper?"

"No. I told you."

"He lives with you?"

"No."

"But he visits?"

"Has visited," Sue burst out. "Once. We only moved in last Friday. Didn't you check on that, too?"

"On what basis did you move in here?"

"I live here now. Mr. Trope is to visit at weekends, whenever he can."

"You're his mistress, right?"

She nodded, hated herself for not being able to look at Simmons. She walked to the settee and perched on its arm. Her hands were trembling.

"And you don't know where he is?"

"I thought he was in Higham Furze."

"Thought?"

"Until you came. I was going to ring him this afternoon."

"Where?"

"At his office, in Higham Furze."

"But now you think he might be somewhere else?"

"You said . . . I don't know where he is."

"If you did, would you tell me?"

"Of course. Why not? Gavin's got nothing to hide and neither have I." She stared fully at Simmons then, knowing that she was speaking the truth. He held her eyes for what seemed like minutes then walked to the window, flapping his hand at the constable.

Ricks came forward, opened his notebook. Sue watched him, cold dread churning in her stomach.

"The thing is, miss," he said, "Mr. Trope's car was found abandoned Monday morning. It was just off the road, about twelve miles from here, in a wood called . . .," he consulted the notebook, "Ashton Wold."

"Do you know it?" Simmons snapped, staring out of the window.

"No."

"It would appear that you were the last person to see him, miss," Ricks went on. "Apart from the car, there's been no trace of him since."

"An accident?" she said, her mind refusing to take in what he said.

"No, miss. The car was undamaged. It had been driven there deliberately. And left."

"Oh, my God."

She covered her face with her hands, saw a black void, saw a world shattered like an old mirror, the shards mocking as they threw back a thousand memories.

"Are you okay, miss?" Ricks asked.

His voice reminded her that she was not alone. She did not want Simmons to see her in distress. She felt certain it would give him satisfaction.

"I'm fine," she said. "After all, it could be worse, couldn't it?"

Neither man answered. After a while, Simmons spoke, his eyes still fixed on some point, something outside the window.

"You could be hiding him."

"Why?" Sue went toward him, her hands held out. "Why should he need to hide?"

Slowly Simmons faced her.

"There could be any number of reasons."

"I know of none."

"Still, you do see how it would help us, help you, if we could just make sure."

"Go and look," she said tiredly.

At once, Ricks went through into the kitchen. Simmons climbed the stairs like a cat. Sue could not be bothered. She knew she ought to supervise them, but how could she be in two places at once? If Gavin had really disappeared, it would not matter what they did. Ricks came back.

"No sign," Simmons said, coming down the stairs.

"All clear down here, sir."

"Miss Jackman," Simmons said in a voice designed to command attention. Sue looked at him but she did not speak. "It would be an offense to conceal information about his whereabouts once there is an official police enquiry. Therefore, if he should come here, telephone, or write to you, you must immediately get in touch with me. Do you understand?"

Slowly, Sue nodded. Simmons thrust a square of card at her.

"I've made a note of my phone numbers." He opened the front

door. "*Au revoir*, Miss Jackman. Be seeing you again, no doubt."

She could only think that they did not suppose or believe him dead. They expected him to contact her.

"Thank you very much, miss."

She even managed a smile for Ricks.

Gavin was not dead. He would get in touch.

She did not go to pieces. She did not crack up and shed floods of tears. She made tea and drank several cups. She put fuel into the wood stove and fetched more logs. Most of the time she sat, watching the light change, the afternoon die away. She did not think she was in shock. People did disappear, even though it sounded impossible or crazy. She had read about cases, seen them charted on television. Sometimes people disappeared completely, never were traced. Not people like Gavin, though. Never. He had no cause, especially not now. People lost their memories. A bump on the head, an accident. There had been no accident. The car concealed in the woods. Why? All right, she told herself, if Gavin had chosen to disappear, it would be for a good reason. Simmons was right. He would contact her. That was the first thing he would do, as soon as he was able or judged it safe. But why hadn't he told her, confided in her? He would have his reasons, good reasons. She thought, in a sudden panic, of all the things she should have asked the police. Was anything taken from the car? His briefcase, for example. Were they searching the wood in case he was lying there injured or—? They did not think he was dead. But they ought to look, in case.

She jumped up, banging her shin against the coffee table. It had grown dark without her noticing. She groped, hands in front of her, toward the light switch. The light dazzled her. For a moment she could not locate the card Simmons had left. She had to contact them, make sure that they were searching. She saw it resting beside the mute telephone where Simmons or she must have placed it, and went toward it, breathing fast and shallow.

A knock at the back door made her jump. Maybe it was he. Perhaps he had come back. She ought to lower the blinds in case someone was watching the house. She closed the kitchen door behind her, snapped on the lights there. Hettie Pownall stared up at her, her expression uncertain.

"Sorry to bother you," Hettie said. Sue did not move, stood, blocking the door. "Only I wondered if you were all right."

"Yes, of course. I'm fine."

"Look, don't go thinking me nosy but I couldn't help noticing. Police usually spell trouble. I couldn't help seeing, honest. I hope it wasn't bad news. And then, thinking of you all by yourself down here."

"No, really," Sue said. "It was nothing. Just something to do with my van. No trouble, really. Only I . . . I have to make some phone calls. Please, if you'll excuse me now. I'll talk to you soon."

"Oh, yes, of course. Just so long as you're all right."

"Yes, really. Thank you."

She closed the door in Hettie's face and almost instantly regretted it. Why had she lied? It would be better if she talked about it. But then she realized that her instinct had been right. The fewer people who knew, the better. Gavin wanted to keep something secret. She must not do anything to give him away. Not even ring the police. She must wait, be ready for his call, his coming. He would depend on her to do nothing stupid. When he was ready, able, he would come back or tell her where he was, where she could meet him. He would need her help and support, and she must do nothing to jeopardize that.

She hurried around the house, pulling down the blinds. It might be a long wait. Oh, please, God, she prayed, let it not be. She must carry on as though nothing had happened. She must do nothing to cause suspicion.

They were all seated around the kitchen table.

"She knows then?"

"She said they came about her van."

"But you reckon she knows?"

" 'Course. That was just a story. Police told her, all right."

"They've been turning Ashton Wold inside out."

"Shame, damaging fine woods like that."

"They have to."

"They won't find nothing, though."

"No."

"What now, then?"

"Nothing, just wait."

"She'll be glad enough to tell me in a day or so. You'll see."

"When the waiting gets to her."

"Yes."

"Let's have the telly on then. I could do with a laugh."

They rearranged their seats and sat watching the television set, waiting.

God, how Evie hated the country! She just couldn't see the point of it. Oh, it was all right for cows and pigs, the things people needed to eat, but apart from that . . . She glanced around her fiercely as though she could wither the land with a look. There were some pretty spots, she would concede that much, but Sue certainly hadn't found herself one, not if this was anything to go by. But she was probably lost again. She traveled all over the Midlands in her work, but that was from town to town, well signposted. She'd lost her way twice already today and had to ask for help. She hated asking. People looked at her as though she were mentally subnormal. Mind you, *they* were, these country bumpkins. Most of them anyway. But this must be the right road. Sue had said, just keep going through Brooking until you come to the crossroads. That wood gave her the creeps. She wondered if that was where they'd found his car? Ashton something, something funny. She'd read about it in the *Argus*. MIDLANDS MAN MISSING. Nearly had a heart attack when she saw his name. Thank God they hadn't mentioned Sue. Not yet. And fancy Sue not calling, not sending for her, her only living relative, like any normal person would have done. But that was Sue, all right. Independent. Touchy. As usual, she'd had to do it all, ring her up, drag the details out of her.

"I'm coming," she'd announced. "Coming Saturday. How the hell do I get there?"

Well may you ask, Evie thought as the road climbed on, shrouded by trees. Sue had told her to take the main road, not the twisting back one. At the top of the hill, which did indeed run for part of its length alongside one corner of Ashton Wold, there was a crossroads. Evie stopped her sunshine-yellow mini and leaned out into the cold, damp air, inspecting the signpost. Hemming was to the right, along a dead straight, dead flat road. What a place, she thought, signaling, honking her horn. A few crows scattered from the flat fields. There was no other sign of life, nothing. Just endless fields. It was enough to make anyone want to disappear, she thought. She shivered.

Then she saw a building ahead, where the road seemed to bend, and other tumble-down buildings around it. A ghost town, she thought. It's probably haunted. But smoke rising from the chimney, visible as she drew closer, reassured her. She slowed down for the bend, a sharp right angle, and to have a good look at the place, the only human habitation she'd seen for hours—or so it seemed to her. She could see into a big old shed full of cars. A man leaning over the engine of one glanced up. Evie applied the brakes.

"Excuse me," she shouted, sticking her dyed head out of the window. The man looked up, stared at her, slack-mouthed. Slowly he came out of the shed and jumped lithely across a patch of rutted mud toward her. "Sorry to trouble you," Evie said, smiling, "but how far is it to Hemming? I keep getting lost, you see."

Her smile was dazzling. She smelled better than flowers and her face was all painted pretty colors. Ashton grinned at her.

"About a mile up the road."

"Just straight on, is it?"

Evie's eyes traveled over his torso, the cleanly built muscles outlined by a tight sweater.

"That's right."

"Thanks ever so much. Sorry to have interrupted."

"No trouble."

Evie waited a moment. She wouldn't mind chatting a bit longer, but it was his turn. A girl shouldn't have to make all the overtures. He'd got a body on him, though. She waved and let the car slide away from him. She could see, in the rearview mirror, that he stood watching her, but she had more important things to think about. What was she going to do about Sue? That was the thing. How could she make her see sense?

She overshot the cottage and backed up, sounding the horn loudly. The car jolted onto the verge. Sue appeared, pale, but waving from the doorway. God, what a dump, Evie thought. She'd go mad if she had to stay here for any length of time.

"Is it okay to leave the car here?" Evie called.

"Yes, fine."

She got out and hauled her oversized suitcase from the backseat before locking the car.

"What on earth have you got in there?" Sue asked, coming to help her.

"Just a few bits and pieces. You know me, I never travel without my war paint."

Sue caught Evie by the shoulders and kissed her cold cheek.

"How are you?" Evie asked, her eyes concerned.

"Fine. Come on, let's get inside. It's cold."

"Cold? It must be twenty below, at least."

"Don't exaggerate. Come on."

Struggling with her case, Evie followed her sister up the uncertain path and into the cottage.

"Well," she said, dumping her case just inside the door, "a pretty pickle you've got yourself into, and no mistake."

"Evie . . .," Sue warned.

"All right. But somebody's got to give you a good talking to."

"That's not what I need, not now. All right? Now let me show you to your room. It's my workroom really, but I think you'll be comfortable."

"Hey," Evie exclaimed, looking around her for the first time, "you've done all right here, our kid, haven't you? Smashing, this is."

"Yes," Sue said and turned away to hide the tears that suddenly stung her eyes.

"The only thing I know, the only thing I'm sure of is that Gavin wouldn't go off somewhere and leave me. Not now. Before, possibly—though I can't really believe that—but not now. Why he went, why he should do something like this, I don't know. It's all speculation. But he'll get in touch or come for me. I know that."

The expression on Evie's face said that she wanted to believe Sue, but that it wasn't quite so simple as that.

"I'd know if he was dead, Evie. I'd know it. Truly I would. You must believe that."

Evie considered. "Yes. I dare say you would. All right, I'll buy it. But why? Why would he do something like this?"

Sue sighed.

"I don't know. I've been over and over it in my mind. There's no point. But Gavin will have a good reason. I know that."

"Well, if he's got any idea how you feel about him, he'll be back. He's a lucky man."

"Sometimes," Sue said quietly, "I feel that I can make him come back. Do you know what I mean? Even if he's lost his memory or something, he'll know, he'll sense . . . . He'll remember I'm here and . . ." Her voice faded away.

She spoke with such intensity that Evie had no heart to argue with her. Sue needed to believe in something now, something to keep her going, and Evie didn't want to be the one to bring her down. Besides, she thought ruefully, she had no alternative to offer. She stood up, stretching.

"I'll tell you what. Let's get dressed up and I'll treat you to a good dinner somewhere. There must be a decent place around here."

"No thanks," Sue said automatically.

"Oh, come on, it'll do you good."

"I can't."

"Can't? What's to keep you here?"

"He might ring, he might turn up. I must be here."

"Yes, but you can't spend the rest of your life sitting by the phone in case."

"I can, if necessary."

"Have you been out, since the police came?" Evie said, suspicious.

"There's no need."

"Of course there's a need. You can't live like a recluse, or whatever they call it. You'll drive yourself mad."

"There's plenty of food in the freezer. Hettie Pownall from the farm let me have some fresh vegetables. We've got everything we need here."

"Sue—"

"I'm sorry, Evie, but I'm not going, and that's final."

"If you're not in, he'll call back."

"He might be desperate."

"All the more reason."

"No, Evie," she shouted.

Evie sighed and walked to the window, stood looking out at the desolate landscape. Patience, she freely admitted, was not her strong point, especially not where Sue was concerned, but she would have to try. If she could just lay her hands on that Gavin, she'd—

"Well, if we're not going out, at least I can have a drink," she said, feigning cheerfulness.

"And I'll cook something really special for supper," Sue promised. "Thanks, Evie. Thanks for coming."

After that, Evie did not even try to persuade Sue to return with her to Birmingham, which was the only plan she had been able to think of. Part of her understood and sympathized. Another part nagged that if Gavin had disappeared, then he meant it to be a total break. Otherwise he'd have taken her with him in the first place. Common sense told her that. These thoughts, and others that she preferred not to think, occupied her when she went for a solitary walk on Sunday morning. Evie was no walker, no nature girl, but she found the cottage, for all it was comfortable and warm and equipped with just about everything a person could need, claustrophobic. She had to get out. She had to get away from Sue, who seemed to conduct her entire life with one ear cocked, listening for the phone, a knock at the door. Besides, Sue had said she wanted to do some work that morning, and anything, Evie thought, that got her mind off Gavin was to be encouraged. Which left her at a loose end. Wrapped in a warm, fake-fur jacket, her trousers stuffed into the tops of low-heeled boots, she decided to explore the village.

Apart from being flat, it had few advantages as walking country. There were no twists, no tall hedges or screening trees to conceal surprises, tempt the walker from the straight and narrow road. By the time Evie reached the two open barns beside the copse, she felt dispirited. The village, which she could see now, seemed a desolate and pointless goal. If only there were a pub, she thought, a bit of conviviality. She stood looking at the barns. They were really no more than galvanized-iron sheds, open on two sides, set in a bed of cracked concrete. The sun slanted through them, accentuating shadow and glare, making a drama of the light. For want of anything better to do, she left the road and wandered around beneath the largest roof. Cobwebs hung there, rust flaked, and there were old, deserted birds' nests. She kicked her toe against a booming, empty drum—there was a row of them—which gave off the rancid smell of oil. There were also several pieces of farm machinery, the purpose of which she could not guess. She walked right through the barn and out the other side. Another field lay before her, vast, regularly tilled, and boring. She turned away, skirting the smaller structure, and walked toward the copse, where she saw a gap in the uniform and almost straight gray trees and a path, well-trodden by the look of it, winding off into the wood. The copse was larger than she had thought, swelling out into the fields, masking the village. From where she stood the path seemed to run toward the road. She could cut through there, regain the road, and walk slowly back to the cottage. Walking through the woods would give her something to talk about besides Sue, or Gavin's disappearance, when people asked if she had had a nice weekend. With any luck, her sister's name would be kept out of the papers, and she certainly wasn't going to fill people's mouths with gossip.

The path turned and wound like a meandering stream, skirting trees that otherwise blocked the way. Made by people who knew the wood instinctively, it had its own kind of logic. The trees pressed in on her but did not obstruct. Ahead, always, she could see the path winding, though not, she thought, toward the road. Still, she wasn't about to plunge into the jungle of underbrush and whipping branches. She could always follow the path back.

Thwack. Thwack. Thwack.

The sound made her heart jump, made her aware of the silence. She paused, listening to her own breathing. The sun, previously so bright, seemed unable to penetrate these trees. She looked up. The bare branches interlaced, created a fretwork of blue and sunlight, but the immediate light was gray, like the threat of rain. The absence of the sun made the air colder, and she shivered.

Thwack. Thwack. Thwack. Her city ears could not make out the direction it came from.

The path rose a little up a gentle slope. Evie followed it to the lip of a steep decline. Before her lay a great hollow, covered in dead leaves. On the opposite side she saw a pile of sticks, freshly cut and neatly stacked. That must have been the noise she heard, the cutting of sticks. She looked to her right and saw that the path wound on around the bank of this natural basin.

Crack!

She swung around, her nerves tingling, all thoughts obliterated by the knowledge that something terrible was about to happen.

He towered over her, blue eyes rolling to show the whites. His very pink, moist mouth seemed molten flesh, threatened to slide from his face altogether. His arm was raised, holding a wicked-looking cleaver like those she had seen in butcher's shops. With a scream that deafened her own ears, Evie stepped back, her arms up to protect herself. His hand shot out and fastened about her forearm, tugging her back from the edge of the hollow, as a voice rang out, harsh and commanding: "Ashton! What do you think you're playing at?"

Evie twisted against his strength, saw an elderly man, spry for his age, hurrying down the opposite slope, wading through a lake of leaves. Turning back to her assailant, Evie's frightened mind recognized the man of whom she had asked directions only yesterday. Then she had found him attractive. Now he seemed a monster, filled her with loathing.

She kicked out at him, tried to butt her head against his strong chest. His face dissolved then. The mouth tried to form a funnel for laughter. His muscular arms dropped to his sides. He hung his head like a cowed dog.

"Let go of me," Evie shouted unnecessarily, cringing back from him. "Are you mad or something?"

The older man, panting, came up the bank. He looked at Evie, half-accusing, suspicious. Then he turned to the hangdog man.

"Get those poles loaded, Ashton. Get on with your work."

"Only trying to scare her," he said pathetically. "Like on the telly the other night."

"Get on." The man jerked his head, and slowly, scuffing his feet, Ashton obeyed.

"You got a license for him?" Evie demanded, rounding on the man.

"No," the man replied steadily. "Nor do I need one. He's harmless, only having a bit of fun."

"Fun? He was going for me with that chopper thing."

"He was just playing a game." He turned around and shouted after the younger man, who was making his way across the bed of the hollow. Ashton paused, looked around uncertainly, his face creased like a disappointed child's, close to tears. "Tell the lady you're sorry. Tell her you didn't mean no harm."

Ashton's cowed blue eyes moved from the man's face to Evie's. "I'm sorry," he said. "I didn't mean no harm."

"You probably startled him," the man said, turning to Evie. "What you doing here, anyway?"

"I was just out for a walk."

"Not from round here, are you? A stranger?"

"My sister lives just up the road. I'm staying with her. I felt like a breath of fresh air. What else is there to do around here? It's not against the law, is it? Which reminds me, I could have the law on him, running amok with a cleaver."

"Come on, now. Calm yourself down. There's no harm done, is there?" The man took her elbow, squeezed it companionably. "Fine woman like you, bet you've got nerves of steel."

"Well, it gave me a hell of a turn, though."

" 'Course it did. Come on, we'll give you a ride home."

The man turned her to the left, started around the lip of the hollow.

"Hang on a minute," Evie said, pulling against his grip. "Who are you? How do I know you're not going to attack me?"

"George Pownall," he said, smiling engagingly. "And why should I attack a lovely woman like you?"

"I can think of several reasons," Evie said, unconsciously responding to the smile.

"Not at my age, you couldn't. Come on. Let's give you a ride."

"But the road's that way," she said, nodding her head in the opposite direction.

"And our tractor's in the field over yonder."

"Oh, terrific. That's just what I need, that is. A ride on a tractor. Hey, and what about Tarzan of the Apes over there? Can you keep him under control?"

"He's as gentle as a lamb." The man steered her along the path. He was old but sprightly, still had his strength.

"My name's Evie Jackman, by the way. I'm staying with my sister."

"You said. Poor lass, it must be a bad time for her."

"How do you know?"

"We get the papers, Evie, even here. And we can read."

"Oh, very funny. All right. That's put me in my place. Anyway, what are you and Tarzan doing out here?"

"His name's Ashton," the man said, obviously not amused. "He's my son. We're cutting ash poles to make scarecrows with. They grow straight, you see."

"Oh."

Ashton had disappeared through the back end of the wood, the pile of sticks slung by a rope across his back.

"This way," George Pownall said, ducking beneath a low branch and moving ahead of her.

Evie followed, panting to keep up with him. In a surprisingly short time, the wood had thinned and they were on the edge of the big field, the ruined schoolhouse to their right. A mud-spattered tractor was parked at the edge of the wood. Behind it was a flatbed trailer, half full of tightly bound bundles of ash sticks.

"How many scarecrows are you going to make?" Evie said, pushing her hair out of her face.

"Oh, not all of the poles will do," George Pownall told her. "Only the straightest and strongest, the best. The rest'll come in handy for the runner beans later on."

Ashton finished loading the bundles and stood beside the tractor, his eyes cast down.

"Help the lady up, Ash," George said, "and make sure she sits safe. It gets a bit bumpy along here," he explained to Evie.

"You ride with her," Ashton said. "I'll drive."

George looked at Evie, wanting her to say something.

"Oh, come on," she said, her good nature getting the better of her. "Forgive and forget. I'll ride with you. Only if you ever do anything like that again, I'll have your guts for garters, no matter how big and strong you are."

A slow smile dawned across Ashton's face. "You're a nice lady," he said and grasped her firmly by the waist, swinging her up, without apparent effort, onto the trailer.

There was something exciting and disturbing about his easy strength. Evie, unaccountably, found herself blushing.

"Yes, well," she said. "You're a strong fellow. I'll say that for you."

He jumped up beside her and sat with his long, powerfully muscled legs dangling over the edge of the trailer. George Pownall climbed into the cab and started the tractor's slow, noisy engine.

"Hang on tight," Ashton said, and put his arm around her.

Evie did not find his tight, sheltering grip unpleasant.

Evie's departure before sunset that evening was made more poignant for Sue since it inevitably recalled Gavin's of a week ago.

A whole week without hearing from him, seeing him. Almost a week of not knowing how or where he was. The cottage seemed doubly empty somehow, without Evie's chatter, the mingled smell of her cigarettes and perfume. Her many questions had forced Sue to think, to think back and beyond the central shock of Gavin's disappearance. Over and over again she had repeated that he seemed fine, that nothing was wrong, but slowly she had begun to recall, to think from the viewpoint of his unexplained absence. Gavin *had* been different that weekend—the business with the manikin, for example, and his anger as reported by Hettie. Usually he was a cool-tempered man, and certainly not one to start at shadows. And then there had been the nightmare, the strange, embarrassed confession about Miss Peterson. With a sense of rising panic, Sue thought that these incidents, so easily dismissed at the time, so lightly taken, could be symptoms—symptoms of disturbance, of a state of mind in which an otherwise dependable, conscientious man might do something rash, out of the ordinary.

She had felt ambivalent when Evie told her the Pownalls knew about Gavin's disappearance, but now she thought it was just as well. She was beginning to think that she should explain to Detective-Sergeant Simmons about Gavin's mental state. He could check with the Pownalls, get the details from them. And of course it would be easier for her, not having to pretend with Hettie.

But if there wasn't anything wrong with his mind, if he had decided to do this awful, nail-biting thing for his own good reasons . . . The familiar arguments closed in, circled around her again. But she had the right to assume that since he had not contacted her, he could not. She imagined him lost, lonely, frightened. It was her duty to do anything she could to help him, reach him. If she were right, he would thank her. If not, he would forgive.

Sue stood, her hand hovering over the phone, Simmons's card clutched in her left hand. Suppose he laughed at her, dismissed it all as exaggeration, meaningless incidents blown up by her anxiety? She didn't trust him, didn't like him. She felt near to tears then, tears of frustration. If only she'd discussed it all with Evie. Suddenly, she realized that she could do better than that, could do something positive that would help to clarify her mind.

Without further hesitation, she pulled on her coat and, taking a flashlight, hurried out to the van. The engine was cold, and she wasted minutes coaxing it to start. Bumping and swaying, she backed out onto the road and headed toward the farm. She would ask Lucas Pownall exactly what had happened, see if he was willing to tell his story to the police.

Superstitiously, Evie took the shorter back road into Brooking. Not that she was scared; she just didn't fancy passing that wood where Gavin Trope's car had been found. Besides, she wanted to get home as quickly as possible. She was like a fish out of water in the country, liable to do something crazy.

The truth was she felt anxious about that business in the copse, with Ashton Pownall. She had made light of it to Sue, of course, playing down the fact that she had, for a few seconds, been really frightened. Fear had melted with her anger, been overtaken by stronger feelings less easy to dismiss—sexual feelings.

Normally, she would have joked with Sue about that, but she had felt embarrassed. Not because she was attracted but because Ashton Pownall was nothing but a country yokel. Even a bit simple, she supposed, definitely not her style. It was pride. She did not want Sue to think she was getting desperate. A phrase of her mother's surfaced unbidden and uncomfortable in her head: "Anything in trousers . . ." She used to say that, referring darkly to women she considered "flighty." And there was another reason, one Evie did not want to own at all. Perhaps the fright, the moment when he had appeared to come at her with the cleaver, was all part of it, part of his strength and attraction.

She pushed the thought away. It was ugly, crazy. It just showed what the country could do to a person. From now on, she vowed, she was going to stay where she belonged, where she could keep her head together. She'd have to persuade Sue to be sensible by phone and letter. Anyway, Sue wouldn't be able to stand it herself much longer. If Gavin didn't show up soon, she'd want to get back to the city—she'd have to. She couldn't go on living there forever. She'd be climbing the walls. And if Gavin did show up, God alone knew what kind of trouble he'd be in. That'd force Sue's hand. With relief, she thought she'd have no need to go back there, ever.

She sped past the twinkling lights of Brooking and headed straight for the motorway.

Lucas saw her in the cold front parlor. He was a tall man, handsome in his way, taciturn. His wife bustled ahead of them, putting on lights and a small electric heater that was quite inadequate to dispel the damp chill of the unused room. Sue apologized again for bothering them. Shirley Pownall seemed reluctant to leave them and after a moment sat down in a stiff-backed chair, waiting. She told Sue to make herself comfortable on the hard Victorian settle. Lucas stood by the fireplace watching her, but seemingly without curiosity.

"It's difficult to know where to begin," she said, feeling that perhaps the whole thing had been a mistake. "I understand from my sister that you know about Gavin, Mr. Trope."

"Yes," Shirley said in a commiserating tone. "We read about it, didn't we, Lucas?"

"That's right."

"I expect you wondered why I didn't say anything."

"That's your business," he said, as though that closed the subject once and for all.

"Yes, well . . . anyway, I've been thinking and, look, it's not like Gavin to just disappear, and I've been wondering if he was upset about something. Hettie told me he came here that Saturday. She said he was upset. I wondered . . . to be honest with you, I think I ought to tell the police that he was upset. Only I thought I ought to check with you first, hear what you think."

"We don't hold with the police much, do we, Lucas?" Shirley asked.

"I don't want to involve you," Sue put in quickly. "It's just that if I do tell them, I can only repeat what Hettie said and, well, I mean, she wasn't here." She felt all her arguments collapsing about her, like sand castles washed by a tide of indifference and disapproval. "I'm sorry," she added, making one last attempt, "that he brought your gift back. I'm sure he didn't understand that it was meant kindly. I know he didn't mean to be rude."

"Oh, he meant it, all right," Lucas said. "It wasn't the Sign that bothered him. That were just an excuse."

"For what?" Sue asked, pleading with her eyes.

"To make it clear he didn't want nothing to do with us, didn't want you getting friendly with Hettie, neither."

"He was a cut above us, see," Shirley said, with a hint of hurt in her voice. "Too good for the likes of us."

"But that's not like—" Sue began and then stopped, the blood mounting to her face. Hadn't Gavin said virtually the same thing to her?

"You think what you like," Lucas said brusquely. "That's what he came here for. He knew what the Sign was. He'd seen enough of them when he was evacuated here during the war. He made himself clear."

"I'm sorry," Sue said, unable to think of anything else.

"It's my belief," Shirley added, "that he felt awkward about old Grandpa Pownall leaving him the cottage. But Lucas told him, fair and square, that it was his now and that was the end of it. He had no cause to bother about us."

"The only thing I will say," Lucas went on, following his own train of thought, "is that my mother and father were good to him when he stayed with us and they were hurt when he kept coming to the cottage and never came to see them. Me, I didn't give a damn, but they're getting on now and they were hurt. But I said to them—long ago, before the cottage was done up so smart and fancy—I said to them, you know how he is, how he always was. It was crazy to expect anything different from him."

"Now, then," Shirley said anxiously, looking at Sue for signs of distress or anger.

"It's all right," Sue said quickly. "I can understand how you must have felt."

"I speak my mind. I don't wish the fellow no harm and I don't speak ill of no one if I haven't got cause. All I'm saying is, he always thought he was better than us and time hasn't changed him. Well, that suits me."

"I think, I truly think," Sue said, "that he wasn't himself last weekend. I'm sure he wouldn't have—"

"When he lived here he was just the same," Lucas interrupted, obviously drawing on a well of resentment. "Always hobnobbing with that Miss Peterson. We weren't good enough for him. He never wanted to play with us kids, muck in with the rest of us. It was always Miss Peterson this, Miss Peterson that. Made you sick."

"He told me about her. He had a dream about her. It upset him," Sue said. "I didn't think anything about it at the time but now . . . You must have known her."

"She was no good," Lucas said. "Not to him nor any of us."

"But it might help me to understand if you could explain," Sue said, certain now that she had been blinded by her own happiness, that she could discover here some clue to Gavin's state of mind.

Lucas pursed his lips as though nothing would persuade him to say another word.

"Please," Sue said. "I'm desperate."

"Oh, you must be," Shirley said, looking at her husband. "The worry . . ."

"I think," she said, feeling disloyal, taking a gamble for uncertain stakes, "that he was disturbed, perhaps because of coming back here, remembering. But what did he remember?" She looked at Lucas. "Anything might help me, and I need help."

Lucas turned away. For a moment it seemed that he was going to walk out of the room. Shirley half-rose from her seat, watching him nervously.

"If it's Miss Peterson you want to know about," he said, in a thick voice, "you'd best ask my dad."

"Oh, Lucas," Shirley said, moving to him, her manner agitated. "I don't know—"

"He knew her," Lucas snapped, his mind entirely made up. "I was only a kid. Come on," he said to Sue. "He's out back. I'll take you to him."

"Thank you. Thank you very much."

Lucas took her out a side door to the old stable block in the other wing.

"Visitor for you," he said, pushing his head around the single door, and then motioning for Sue to go on in.

The door shut behind her.

The long room, lit by a gently hissing oil lamp, stretched into shadow. There was a smell of sawdust and freshly hewn wood, of mellow, sweet tobacco smoke. Ash sticks were stacked against the wall.

"I thought it might be your sister."

She turned toward the shadowed part of the room and found herself facing the body of a scarecrow, hanging from a noose. It was headless, the rope knotted about the wooden shaft of its body. For a moment, as its spiked shadow fell across her, Sue caught her breath and stepped back. An old man, still powerful, lithe, stepped around the dangling thing, making it sway. The scarecrow's shadow scuttered along the floor, bent up the walls, retreated, approached again.

"Did I startle you?" George Pownall asked, his voice kindly.

"No," Sue said, pulling herself together and walking forward to meet him. "It was your scarecrow. It's very good of you to see me so late. I'm not interrupting you?"

"No."

He turned back into the light. Sue followed him, ducking around the scarecrow. The lamp hung over a workbench, littered with whittling knives and other tools, twists of wire, balls of twine. There were curling shavings of green wood on the floor, bunches of twigs hanging from the beams.

"Sit you down," he said, indicating an old chair, once fine, now tattered and worn.

Sue hesitated. "What about you?"

A little stiffly, the old man bent and drew a three-legged stool from beneath the bench.

"This'll do me."

Sue sat down, turned toward him. The light fell softly on her face, exposing her to George Pownall's detailed but kindly scrutiny. He pulled an ancient briar pipe from his jacket pocket and began to tamp tobacco into it from a tin on the bench.

"Young Gavin's done all right for himself," he said, as though delivering a judgment. "You're better-looking than your sister."

Sue wasn't embarrassed. She liked his frankness, his low, considered voice. He, much more than Lucas, reminded her of Hettie. When young, she thought, he probably had had her fair coloring and apple cheeks. Now his hair was steel gray, cropped close to a weathered head in which pale eyes seemed to sparkle.

"There's no news of him." It was not a question. He stuck the pipe in the corner of his mouth, biting the stem while he searched his pockets for an old lighter. "You'll be worried."

"Yes," Sue agreed. "I'll come straight to the point. I came here because I know Gavin had a quarrel with your son before he disappeared. I think that may have upset him. He also had a bad dream about his old schoolteacher, Miss Peterson. When he told me about it, he said it was something to do with this place bringing back memories. I want to find out as much as I can about his state of mind. It might help the police find him. Your son said you could tell me about Miss Peterson."

He finished lighting his pipe, snapped the old lighter shut, sucked on the stem ruminatively for a while, and then removed it from his mouth, his hard, calloused hand cupped about the bowl.

"That was a long time ago," he said. "I don't see how that could have anything to do—"

"It might," Sue interrupted. "Oh, I'm no expert, but sometimes, if people are upset, they behave uncharacteristically. I know it's a long shot. Maybe I'm completely wrong, but what else can I do? And I must do something."

"Aye." He nodded slowly, sadly. "Waiting's hard. It was hard on women during the war, those whose menfolk were sent overseas. Perhaps hardest of all on the young ones, like Miss Peterson, who had no men to love and pay court to them. She was from round Birmingham, come here when her school was bombed out. Everything was topsy-turvy then. And we had the evacuees, of course, like young Gavin. He was very close to Miss Peterson. Some said, too close." He paused, looking at Sue, who nodded to show that she understood. "I don't know," he admitted. "Folks say all manner of things. Things that suit them as often as not."

"What happened to Miss Peterson? Gavin said something about his being ill and then when he went back to school, she had gone."

"Aye, that's about how it went. A bitterly cold January day it was, threatening snow. I remember old man Grubb—he still lives in the village—he came up the night afore and said that Miss Peterson was closing the school, not to send the children next day. Gavin must've slipped out early. We never did discover the truth of that, nor why. Soon as we realized, 'course we went looking for him. We had an old dog then, good old dog he was. He found him, up in Gatherings Copse, just beyond your place. He'd got his foot caught in a tree root and had twisted his ankle. He was frozen near to death and took a fever. He was that bad we had to send for his mother. I remember my old dad carried him back here through the snow. He was very fond of Gavin, my dad."

His pipe had gone out. Sue waited while he slowly went through the ritual of relighting it. He sat smoking, staring at the floor.

"And Miss Peterson?" she prompted.

"She was gone. Packed up and left that same morning. My old Mary thought Gavin was trying to follow her when he done his ankle in."

"In the wood?" Sue asked.

Goerge Pownall shrugged.

"He might've thought it was a shortcut. If you go on far enough across the fields, you do hit the Nene road eventually."

"But why would he do that?"

"Like I said, he was fond of her, very fond. My belief is her going like that near broke his heart. That was what give him the fever. That's what my dad reckoned, anyway, and not much passed him by."

Sue saw a small boy shivering in the cold, going up to the closed schoolhouse, seeing it empty, deserted, and setting off on a wild, grieving search for the beloved Miss Peterson.

The old man cleared his throat.

"But why did she go?"

"Ah, now you're asking. Some said as she got a telegram about her fiancé being killed at the front. They said it drove her demented."

"But you don't believe that?" Sue said.

"Well, if she got a telegram, it wasn't delivered by our postman, old Jonah Hobbs. I asked him myself. And I never heard talk of no fiancé. It was lack of one that was her trouble, if you ask me."

She showed me her breasts.

"Do you think . . . you said a minute ago that some people thought they were too close."

He turned aside, knocking out his pipe into an old pail beside the bench.

"Talk," he said. "Might've been some truth in it, might not. What does it matter now? Poor woman's gone. Gavin's grown up. Why drag it all over?" He fixed her with his pale eyes, pocketing his pipe.

"Is that why your son thinks she was no good for Gavin?"

"Oh," the old man chuckled, "Lucas has strong opinions. What child, even when he's grown, ever really likes his teacher, especially when they work 'em. And she was a good teacher, Miss Peterson. No one'll deny that."

Sue heard the finality in his voice like a shutter rattling down, closing the subject. She wanted to shout that it wasn't that simple, couldn't be. Perhaps not for Gavin, anyway. She stood up, pulling her coat around her.

"Thank you for talking to me."

He rose to his feet, his joints cracking.

"You don't want to go digging into the past," he said. "You've got enough on your plate as it is."

"I don't know what else to do," she admitted.

"Time'll take care of it. You'll see. Only some things is best left. We all of us can live, have to, with terrible things. You maybe don't feel that now, but you will, if you have to."

He seemed tired suddenly. Sue thought that he might be referring to Ashton's accident, offering advice from his own hard experience. She held out her hand and he took it, squeezed it gently.

"You got your car?" he asked.

"Yes."

"Then I'll walk you to it."

"I told you no good'd come of it," Shirley whispered, pressed close against Lucas's back.

"What's done's done. Go to sleep."

"Coming here, asking questions. It makes me nervous. You should never have let him."

"What can I do? The old man started it. Anyway, it's done. It'll work its way through."

"As if we hadn't got enough troubles," Shirley said.

"Go to sleep."

She was still undecided whether to ring Simmons or not. Why had Gavin behaved so rudely to the Pownalls? She could understand Lucas's animosity. And if Miss Peterson had broken his heart all those years ago, surely it had mended now? She herself had healed it. Unless there was something unsaid, perhaps unknown, that had, through association with this place, risen to haunt him. But what? Her perception and knowledge of Gavin was shifting all the time, slipping out of focus. For the first time, at last, the idea that he might have killed himself surfaced in her mind. It frightened her, made her feel intensely alone, even betrayed. The van swerved and she had to concentrate very hard on her driving, especially as she maneuvered it off the road to park it beside the cottage.

So occupied was she in doing this, in holding the possibility of Gavin's suicide at bay, that she did not notice the muffled figure of Ashton Pownall steal away from the back of the dark and unwelcoming cottage.

Simmons paced the length of the room, his eyes fixed on the rugs as though he was examining them for evidence. This time he had not brought his companion into the house, and Sue missed the tempering presence of Ricks. Her head was whirling from Simmons's machine-gun questions. How had Gavin paid for the conversion of the cottage? What did his wife think about it? How much did Sue know about Gavin's financial position? How much had the conversion cost? How had he paid for it? Why didn't she know? Had he been in touch? Had he? How did Simmons know she wasn't waiting for the heat to die down so she could skip off somewhere to meet Gavin?

"All right, Miss Jackman, I'll be straight with you." He came and sat opposite her, leaned toward her, fingertips pressed together. "This is what we think. Trope's a steady sort of chap, respectable. He's got a bad situation at home but he's a blameless, considerate husband. Until he meets you." He paused there, looking at her. He was judging her, sizing her up, like a butcher appraising a side of prime beef. Sue felt sick. "Well, it's understandable. He isn't the first man to lose his head over a pretty girl. In fact, you might say, in his case it was long overdue. He wanted to impress you, of course, make everything nice for you. This place . . ." He glanced around the room as though pricing its contents. "He earned a good enough salary, all right, and he'd saved a bit, but he's got an expensive wife. The trained nurse living in, for example, which he had to have if he was going to see you—they come expensive. It's a seller's market. Then all the special things she needs, the extras. Then he wasn't going to cut corners here. Oh, no, only the best for you. That stereo system, for example. He didn't get much change out of a thousand for that, did he?"

"Gavin is very fond of music. He wanted—"

"Anyway, he couldn't afford it. Not all of it. Something had to go. But he had a conscience, our Mr. Trope. He wouldn't ditch an invalid wife."

"I don't want to listen to this," Sue said. "I don't have to. You're not here to pass judgment. You're supposed to find Gavin."

"I'm trying, Miss Jackman. We're all trying. A bit more co-operation from you and we might—"

"I've told you all I know," she repeated, bored with saying it.

"Then hear me out. He's in debt, Miss Jackman, up to his

eyeballs. He couldn't afford you, Mrs. Trope, and this place. I won't say he fiddled the books, but they are checking. He was in deep, too deep. The only chance he had was to sell this place, but he couldn't do that, could he?"

"If he wanted to."

"And then, of course, he was getting hell at home, wasn't he? I don't know what he told you, Miss Jackman, but Mrs. Trope was not happy with his little setup, not happy at all. She was putting the pressure on."

Somehow this did not surprise or hurt Sue as she supposed Simmons wanted it to. It made her feel less guilty, made Myra a more equal adversary, more human. But it also meant that Gavin had lied to her—no, for her, to protect her. She must remember that, hang on to it.

"So, we reckon it all got a bit too much for him. The debts, the rows, the fact that he probably wouldn't be able to keep this place. Or maybe the novelty had worn off. Maybe, once you were installed here, there wasn't that much to look forward to. Eh, Miss Jackman?"

"You're an offensive pig," Sue told him.

His eyes widened and his mouth twitched. For a moment she thought he was going to smile, as though she had paid him a compliment.

"Well, anyway," he drawled, "I think, we think, that all these pressures came together as he was driving home that night. Let's face it, he wasn't going back to much. It couldn't have been any fun, leaving you all alone out here, with time on your hands. So, we reckon he may have killed himself."

"Suicide?"

"It's a possibility."

"How? Why?"

He shrugged, studied his fingernails for a moment. "Ashton Wold's a big place. We'll search it, of course, but it'll take time."

"No," Sue said. "He's not dead."

"You've heard from him?"

"No, I've told you." She shook her head, wanting Simmons to go, wanting not to consider, not ever, not for one moment, the possibility that had already occurred to her and which he made sound so much more plausible. "I would know if he were dead," she told him, fighting to keep her voice steady. "I would know because I love him, because he was a part of me."

"Oh, spare me the romantic chat, Miss Jackman," Simmons almost shouted. He got up and strode across the room, letting the silence stretch.

Through her own misery, Sue sensed that she had reached him, had won a sort of advantage.

"He's alive," she repeated in a stubborn voice. "I don't know how or where. I have no proof, but I *know* he's alive."

Simmons let out a long breath.

"There's just one other thing," he said, not looking at her. "Did he make a will?"

Sue looked at him, startled.

"I haven't the faintest idea."

"If you were a beneficiary under such a will, he'd have told you?"

"I expect so. I've never thought about it."

"I think you'd better." It sounded like an open threat. "Because if he left you this cottage, that would give you a motive, wouldn't it?"

"Motive?" Sue stood up. "You mean you think . . ."

"It has been known, Miss Jackman. But I'm only speculating. Until we can locate a will, I shall keep an open mind, of course." To her relief, he walked to the door.

"I can imagine," she said, her voice heavy with sarcasm.

"Well, you think about it. I'll be seeing you."

He closed the door behind him. She knew it was stupid to let him rile her. That's just what he wanted. It was the cornerstone of what he no doubt called his technique. She wanted to beat her fists against something, scream. He made her feel dirty. He took her life, her relationship with Gavin, and wiped his feet on it. And worst of all he put doubts in her mind, wanted to make her think that Gavin was dead. He couldn't really think that she could have possibly—she turned her face to the empty room. It offered neither answers nor comfort.

Ashton Wold was much larger than Sue had expected. Though she could not tell how far back from the road it spread, she clocked just over two miles on the van before it reached a neat boundary and gave way to grazing land. Throughout her slow drive she did not see one policeman or police vehicle. No vehicles of any kind were parked in the roadside shadow of the wood. Turning the van around, she drove back to a stretch of red tape across the entrance to a cart track, the only visible sign that they had ever been there. From there she could see up the road to the crest of the hill, the false horizon of the plateau that began at the crossroads at the corner of the wood. She drove on after a brief pause, took the right branch, and followed the wood slowly downhill to within a mile of Brooking. A five-barred gate set in the rough hedge that bordered this part of the wood was clearly marked with a no-trespassing sign. It gave onto an overgrown track, the destination, she presumed, of the one marked by the tape. She stopped the van before the wood ended and rolled down the window. There was a light wind, enough to ruffle the hair. A bird sang somewhere, soft and clear. Far away, out of sight, she could hear the purr of a tractor. The temperature had suddenly risen that day, and the wind brushing her cheek felt damp and almost springlike.

This would be a good opportunity to drive into Brooking, do some necessary shopping. She could do that and be home in half an hour by the winding back road. She listened again for the crash of searching policemen, but heard nothing. The bird sang again. A flock of sparrows whirled and chattered, battling on the wing. The tractor droned on. She looked at her watch. They would not start a search now. It would be dark in two hours, sooner in the heart of that thick wood. Checking for traffic, she made a U-turn, started back up the hill. If Simmons was having her watched and she should encounter a patrolling policeman, it would be assumed that she had made the classic return to the scene of the crime. But she had seen no one, certainly had not been followed. Let him think what he wanted, suspect what his nasty little mind chose.

She paused again at the crossroads, looking along the gray, straight road that led to the farm and home. Simmons's taunting, supercilious face rose before her. Angrily, forgetting to signal, she swung the van left and drove back to the red tape marker. She parked in the soft, muddy entrance to the track. There were signs of recent intrusion, footprints and wheel tracks, the white wounds of newly snapped branches and twigs, but for only a few square yards. Beyond that, the track looked as though it had not been used for years. Sue got out of the van. What was the track for? Tree-felling? Maintenance? Who owned the wood, this remnant of a medieval forest? Who tacked up the signs and policed its game stock? Treading carefully on the thawed, soft earth, she ducked under the red tape.

The car must have been clearly visible from the road. Why, if Gavin had really meant to disappear, had he not made a more serious attempt to conceal it? That way, he would have bought time. The ground that night would have been hard. He could have driven deep into the wood. Only a hundred yards or so ahead, the track curved, providing concealment. She began to walk along it. The ground, protected by the canopy of trees, was firm beneath her feet. She stopped suddenly. The thought of Gavin getting out of the car and walking along this track stopped her. Had he? Could she imagine it, make it fit with her knowledge of him? What was she doing here? If he had walked this way and was lying here somewhere, dead, she did not want to be the one to find him. But he wasn't dead. She made herself walk on. It was an act of faith, proving to herself, Simmons, everyone, that Gavin had not broken under the weight of debts and Myra's distress.

It was gloomy in the thick wood. Within minutes she could not see back to the road. It must always be twilight here, she thought, a perpetual, secret dusk. Evergreens grew among the naked deciduous trees. Fir cones littered the tunnellike track, gave off their sharp, resin smell when she cracked one beneath her foot. How loud the sound was, like the crack of a pistol, startling the silence. She began to avoid treading on them and the strewn dead branches that had also fallen, victims of age and wind. The track narrowed ahead of her, wound away from the gate she had seen on the Brooking road. It did not seem to lead anywhere in particular and threatened to peter out, encroached upon by trees.

The farther she went the more frequently paths joined the track, crossed it. One-man-wide paths, trodden by gamekeepers or poachers, she supposed. They were obviously used, for they were clear of the tangled underbrush that grew about the roots of the trees. She turned into one that seemed to loop back to the road. It was thickly carpeted with pine needles.

The wood calmed and soothed her. For the first time since Simmons had left, she felt relaxed. The sense of enclosure and silence was good, something to hug around her. She walked slowly, hands in her pockets, head down, following the path. It was a maze, though, an easy place to get lost in. Suddenly, she felt very close to Gavin. For days now his absence had been the dominant factor in her life. She had begun to live in a comfortless vacuum, suspended, waiting. Walking through this wood, she knew him near, knew that he had not left her. She did not try to explain this feeling, to raise it to any concrete expectations. She did not think that Gavin would suddenly appear around the next curve of the path or come crashing through the trees, calling her name, holding out his arms to her. It was enough that he was somewhere, that she could feel him reaching out to her.

Something struck her in the face. She cried out, flung up her hands. For a second she thought that she had disturbed a bird. Dry, crisp feathers brushed her face. Then her hands touched against down and softness, warm wet. Her hands set something swinging, swinging back toward her in a confused blur of black and red. A cold, clouded eye stared at her.

"Oh, my God!"

She backed off until a tree jarred against her back. Three crows were nailed to an overhanging branch. Their wings, spread as in flight, were stiffly stretched, the long feathers like splayed fingers. Their glossy necks flopped, dead and unnaturally soft. Their plumed stomachs had been slit, oozed congealing blood, gray viscera, sickly white worms of entrails.

Sue swallowed against a rush of bile, her heart beating jerkily against her ribs. The back of her right hand was smeared and stained with blood. Reaching up to touch her face, her fingertips came away red. Looking down, she saw the front of her jacket stained and spattered.

Coughing, she turned and ran. She knew it was crazy, that she should force herself to be calm, consider her route, but her legs, her fluttering stomach would not obey her. Somehow, she managed to keep to the path, not to slip or trip. She regained the track and ran faster then, the ghosts of the slaughtered crows at her back. Only when she came in sight of the van did she stop, bend to ease the stitch in her side. She coughed, gulping for air, and spat bitter-tasting saliva onto the ground. When she had caught her breath, she went on again, negotiating the churned and muddied edge of the wood, ducking under the tape. She stared at her white face in the van's mirror. The left cheek was striped with blood. A congealing clot hung in her loose hair. Panting, she got the door open and searched frantically for a box of tissues. Kneeling on the seat, feeling sick, she wadded tissues together and scrubbed at her face, blotted the clot from her hair. She wiped her hands and tossed the soiled tissues out onto the verge. She did not dare to look at herself again. Her only thought was to get home, get to the bathroom, and scour herself clean of that nailed obscenity.

The Talbot Inn in Nene was quiet, with only a scattering of early evening drinkers. Coming in from High Street, Ricks had no difficulty spotting Simmons slumped on the padded wall seat that ran from the bar to the door. Ricks nodded, and Simmons indicated his almost empty pint glass and jerked his head toward the bar. Ricks wanted to be at home. He hated drinking in uniform. There was always some joker who refused to believe you were off-duty. Above all, he didn't want to buy a drink for Simmons. But he did and carried it and his own modest half-pint to where Simmons sat. He perched a little awkwardly on a low stool opposite Simmons, drew a plain manila folder from under his left arm, and placed it beside the glasses.

"Cheers," he said, lifting his glass.

In silence, Simmons drank several long gulps that drained his first glass.

"What did Jackman say when you said she was a suspect?"

"Nothing."

"You don't reckon, then . . ."

"No, not the type. Anyway, there's no will. Not yet anyway."

"I don't follow."

"Myra Trope doesn't know of one. We've found nothing. His solicitor never made one, but there's another solicitor. There's a chance he might have drawn something up for Trope, something that might give Jackman a motive."

"You haven't seen him?"

"Out of town for a few days, on business. But we will." His eyes moved slowly to the folder. "What have you got for me?"

"That report you wanted. The other disappearance." Ricks flipped open the folder. "Nineteen forty-one, it was."

"I'll read it later."

"Fancy you remembering it, though. It was a bit before your time, after all."

"Ah, but my youth was not entirely misspent, Ricks. While everyone else was playing around, I read through the files. Things stick—" he tapped the side of his head "—up here. Any similarities?" he snapped, his mind shifting fully to the report.

"Not really. Woman, schoolteacher. No car. Well, they didn't have so many in those days, did they? Petrol rationing and all that."

"Without a trace, as I recall?"

"Yes, officially, the case is still open."

"Naturally. A woman vanishes off the face of the earth in a village you'd miss if you blinked. It stays open till it's solved. And thirty years later, a bloke does a similar vanishing act. There's got to be a connection."

"You reckon? They were quite a way apart."

"A few miles is nothing. The connection is the village and . . . you tell me. What else?"

Ricks frowned. Simmons's eyes seemed to freeze his brain.

"I can't see it," he admitted, reaching for his drink.

"They were both strangers, Ricks. Both outsiders."

"Not really. Trope had been there as a kid."

"In nineteen forty-one, yes. But he was still a stranger. Once a stranger, always a stranger."

Ricks thought about it. His stomach rumbled, distracting him. He thought of the meal waiting for him. He wanted to go home.

"Drink up. Have the other half," Simmons said, suddenly jovial.

"No thanks, chief. I must get going."

"It won't take a minute."

"No, really." Ricks drained his glass.

"Got you on a leash, has she?"

"No, it's not that."

"Oh, go on then. Piss off."

Simmons drew the folder toward him, opened it.

"Yes, well . . . I'll see you in the morning then."

"Sure," Simmons glanced up, a smile cracking his face. "Give her one for me, eh?"

Tom Carpenter was curious. He had no authority, scarcely even a legitimate excuse to go poking around. Even if he got to see Suzanne Jackman, he did not know what he should say to her. But Gavin Trope's affairs were his concern. It was he, not Trope's regular solicitor, who had arranged the secret transfer of Gatherings Cottage to Suzanne Felicity Jackman. He'd let old Meade know, of course, that he was doing a little specialized work for Trope but, as far as he knew, no one except him, Trope, and the Land Registry knew that Miss Jackman was the owner of the cottage and its contents. Keeping Meade on the edge of, if not exactly in the picture had paid off, as he had fully intended it to do. Last week, Meade had tipped him off about the police. It was only a matter of time, Tom knew, before they found out about him. Before their inevitable visit, he wanted to know where he stood. Meade and the police knew that Trope was heavily in debt. What they didn't know yet was that he, Tom Carpenter, had arranged a couple of hefty loans on Trope's behalf. It would scarcely do Carpenter's reputation much good if Trope should really turn out to be a bad risk. Trope had hinted that the cottage was always good as collateral, by which Tom had assumed he meant that, as long as the Jackman girl did not know she owned it, Trope could always rescind the gift if he should ever need bailing out. There had seemed no such risk, however, at the time.

So far he felt he was a step ahead, knew more than Meade or the police, and he wanted to keep it that way. Miss Jackman, he had decided after protracted thought, might be his best chance of doing it. If Trope had not told her about the cottage—and Carpenter really didn't think he had—then the fact that he knew it belonged to her might be a bargaining point. He would tell her, in return for what she knew about Trope's whereabouts. *If* she knew anything, he thought, acknowledging the weakest part of his impromptu plan. Of course, until Trope's fate was decided one way or another, he wasn't, strickly speaking, at liberty to tell her, but in extremity the rules often had to be bent a little. On the subject of Trope's fate he felt gloomy. The transfer of the cottage could have been an obvious piece of forward planning, an insurance policy in case his creditors moved in. No one could touch it. It was sewn up tight—Tom had seen to that. He ought to have smelled a rat, though. It was his romantic nature, he thought cheerfully. He'd liked the idea of taciturn old Trope, all quiet respectability and martyred husband, having a charming and loyal mistress whose ultimate security mattered to him. The trouble was, was the said mistress about to sell up and slip off to some sunny haven with the proceeds? If she was, his chances of saving his own skin unblemished were, to say the least, slight. So, it all boiled down to whether she knew she was the owner or not. And if she knew what had happened to Trope.

He had not ruled out suicide, of course. Indeed, that had been his first reaction when he'd read in the *Higham Furze Gazette* of the abandoned car, the missing Mr. Trope. Well, with his debts he had a right to be nervous. No one knew that better than Tom. Yet the fact remained that his creditors were not moving in, not yet. But Trope wasn't a fool. Trope had known what he was getting into, and if, as Meade had hinted, his "borrowings" were both greater and less legitimate than Tom knew . . . Add a tiff with the charming Miss Jackman, perhaps a threat of expensive divorce proceedings from Mrs. Trope, and, in his shoes, Tom could easily imagine that he might have contemplated suicide. Or running. Tom would have settled for his own strong legs, especially if he had a trusty female accomplice and a nice little bricks-and-mortar insurance policy to rely on.

Thinking of his legs reminded Tom how cramped they were. He stood two inches over six feet and the low-slung, bucket-seated sports car he drove was not generous on leg room. High on his list of personal priorities was a new car, something larger, with a more subdued proclamation of class, but that would have to wait at least until he knew if Trope's vanishing trick had put his financial future in the balance.

Just beyond the crossroads at the corner of Ashton Wold, Tom drew the car over onto the verge. The warmer weather had continued. As he got stiffly out of the car, there was even a watery sun to wage a battle with the rain clouds and a light and warmish breeze to ruffle his collar-length blond hair. He eased his cramped joints and filled his lungs with fresh country air.

"Jesus Christ!" he exclaimed, almost gagging. There was the most putrid smell. He held his breath for a moment, looking around for the source of the stench. The breeze dropped and with it the smell disappeared. Muck-spreading, he thought, though surely it was the wrong time of year? His knowledge of farming was hazy, but he thought manuring took place in the autumn or early winter. Besides, animal manure did not smell like that. Minding the mud on his highly polished shoes, he walked a little way into the nearest field, treading on the top of the furrows. The smell returned, borne on the breeze. It was sweet, rancid, a little like . . . he couldn't remember. Sharp green shoots—wheat or oats, he thought—were showing between the furrows. So there was no question of muck-spreading, not with the crop coming through. He took his handkerchief from his pocket and, holding it over his nose and mouth, turned into the breeze. There was nothing, nothing at all in the whole stretch of field that could possibly have given off that stench. He could see clear over to the farmhouse, see its black smoke drifting toward him. The only interruption was a scarecrow, a pathetic, sagging thing. Something about it, some movement, made him look again. Crows clustered around it, even perched on its shoulders, he realized. A positive flock of them. But that wasn't all. Forgetting where he was, the handkerchief still held to his face, Tom began walking toward the scarecrow.

"Hey! You! What d'you think you're doing? Get off of there. You're trampling the crops."

Tom spun around, his feet slipping in the soft, wet earth. A woman was standing by his car. A short, dumpy woman, a bicycle leaning perilously against her jutting hip. Two rabbits, freshly killed, dribbling blood, swung from the handlebars, their dead weight pulling the machine sideways. All this he saw at a glance. What fixed his gaze and held it was the barrel of a shotgun she held, held in a very workmanlike way, trained on his stomach. Tom did not hesitate. He raised his hands, the white flag of his handkerchief fluttering in the breeze. He began walking toward her, treading very carefully.

"Don't shoot," he said. "See? I'm surrendering." He waved the handkerchief and tried his most disarming smile.

"You're trespassing. I could have you for that as well as for damaging the crops. This is private land, this is."

Panting a little, Tom leaped onto the road and kept his smile fixed in place.

"I really am most terribly sorry. I didn't think."

"No. Well, mind you do."

"I've made the most awful mess of my shoes," he said, using his hurt-little-boy voice. "May I put my hands down and clean some of the mud off them?"

The woman frowned, looked at his shoes, and then slowly lowered the gun. Tom began to clean his shoes on the narrow grass verge while she slung the gun over her shoulder and straightened the bicycle.

"By the way," Tom said conversationally, "have you got a license for that thing?"

"As it happens, I have. Why?"

"Just curious." He bent and pulled tufts of damp grass from the verge to wipe his shoes. "Oh, I say, this isn't vandalism, is it? I mean, I suppose it is your grass?"

"Don't be funny," the woman said tartly. "What you doing here, anyway?"

"Well, that is rather a long story. But I'll tell it," he said quickly, seeing the determination on her face. "It was the smell, you see. Here was I, just trying to get a breath of good country air and suddenly, ugh!" He wrinkled his nose. "And while I was looking for the source of this obnoxious stench, I suddenly saw your scarecrow."

"We slaughtered a couple of pigs yesterday," the woman interrupted quickly. "They're burning off the offal and stuff. You can see the smoke."

"Oh, that explains it, then."

"I'm sorry you was offended," she said, sneering.

"There is something called the Clean Air Act," he said, teasing.

"I don't know about that. But I do know about damaging crops and trespassing."

"I won't prosecute you if you won't prosecute me," Tom offered, grinning.

"Yes, well, you just be on your way, then. And keep in your car until you get by someone else's land."

"How shall I know it isn't yours, Miss . . . ?"

"Pownall. Just stay off people's land unless it says there's a public footpath or bridleway across it."

"Yes, ma'am—Miss Pownall, I mean."

She moved away then, pushing the bicycle, setting the pedals ready to mount. Tom watched, smiling to himself. He could not resist calling after her.

"I still think your scarecrow's a bit odd."

Slowly, like a woman who had just been deeply insulted, she turned to look at him. Her naturally ruddy face was pale.

"How do you mean?"

"Well, it's not very effective. There are crows all around it, even perching on it. Look for yourself."

She did not. Her pale, narrowed eyes remained on him.

"Is that all?"

"Isn't that enough? I mean, it's not doing the function it was intended for. To put it bluntly, it is not scaring the crows."

Hettie Pownall's face relaxed a little.

"You are a great ignorant ox, aren't you?" she said. "We put a couple of handfuls of corn around it this time of year, to attract the crows. That scarecrow's been there all winter. We got to get a new one made. Birds are canny creatures. They've got used to it. So we keep 'em round it with a scattering of corn, to keep 'em off the new shoots, see?"

"Well, sort of," Tom admitted. "But aren't you rather defeating the whole object?"

"They'll be mating soon," Hettie went on, her voice heavy with sarcasm. "Then they'll be nesting and having lots more little baby crows. We feed 'em for a couple of days, protecting our crops the while, then we shoot 'em. We shoot 'em dead, so's they can't breed. See?"

"Oh, yes, that's very clever."

"Which is more than I can say for you. Now get on your way."

Again she moved away. Shaking with suppressed laughter, Tom watched her scoot along, one foot on one pedal. With a heave, she swung her broad bottom onto the saddle. The machine wobbled dangerously with the weight of the dead rabbits, making the spectacle even more comic. Once he was inside the car, he let his laughter out. She was priceless; wonderful. He wouldn't have missed that encounter for the world.

A few minutes later he overtook her, stamping the heel of his hand down hard on the horn and smiling broadly at her. She scowled back at him, her face flushed with effort and anger. If looks could kill, Tom thought, and burst out laughing again.

He behaved as though he were being watched. He drove past the cottage, giving it the briefest of glances. Then he slammed on the brakes and brought the car to a rubber-burning halt. Letting the engine idle, he twisted around, craned over his shoulder, and looked at the cottage. He drummed on the steering wheel with his fingers, the picture of a man in thought. Then, carefully, he put the car in reverse and backed up level with the cottage. He waited another thirty seconds before switching off the engine. He saw no face, no sign of movement at any of the four windows. Altering his features to those of a man who was uncertain, not quite sure that he was doing the right thing, he got out of the car and walked slowly up to the front door.

When, after a long while, Sue came to the door and stood looking up at him, he did not need to pretend. She was not at all what he had expected. And he had evidently woken her from a nap. What had he expected? Someone older, certainly, and more sophisticated.

"Yes?" She frowned; oddly, he thought, it made her look more rather than less attractive.

"Oh . . . er . . . look, I'm most frightfully sorry. I've obviously disturbed you and, well, the thing is, I just happened to be passing and I suddenly thought, *that*'s Gavin Trope's place. It must be. And, well, just on the spur of the moment, I knocked."

She stared at him, at his disarming grin, his studied embarrassment. Her mind still felt half-asleep.

"Is he about, by any chance—Gavin?"

"Who are you?" she said, instinctively closing the door a little.

"Oh, how very rude of me. I'm so sorry. Tom Carpenter." He stuck out his hand, smiling broadly at her.

Sue stared at his hand for a moment, at a loss. She was holding the door with one hand, the neck of her robe with another. It fell open as she briefly took his hand.

"And you?"

"Sue Jackman," she replied automatically, clutching her robe again.

"Oh, yes, of course. How do you do?"

Sue did not understand. How did he know her name? She felt suspicious of him.

"Look, I don't . . ."

"Gavin mentioned you. In a business connection," he added quickly.

"Business? I don't understand."

"I acted for him in a few business matters."

"Oh. Well, I'm sorry, but he's not here."

She made to close the door even farther. Tom did not exactly put his foot in it, but he moved forward slightly. His whole manner reminded Sue of a rather pushy salesman.

"Expecting him soon, are you?"

Something about his tone, his expression, struck Sue as false. "If you're a business associate of Gavin's, I'm surprised you haven't heard."

"I've been away," he said and, since she just continued to stare at him, added, "nothing bad, I hope?"

"He's disappeared," she said bluntly. "I'm afraid I don't know where he is. Now, if you'll excuse me . . ."

"Oh, no. But that's awful. I'm most terribly sorry."

"Thank you." Sue made a determined effort to close the door.

"Look, couldn't you possibly tell me a bit more? I mean, this is the most awful shock."

Sue hesitated. "Who, exactly, are you, Mr. . . . ?"

"Carpenter. I'm a solicitor, actually." Briefly he told her how he had managed to trace Gavin, inform him that he had been left the cottage. Sue remembered Gavin telling her. "After that I did one or two small personal jobs for him."

"Yes, yes, I remember." Suddenly Sue felt foolish, peering around the half-shut door at this tall, perplexed-looking young man. "You had better come in," she said.

"Thanks."

He followed her in, glancing quickly, appraisingly around the room. Sue did not ask him to sit down. Fastening her robe more securely, she told him the bare facts of Gavin's disappearance.

"Well, I'm astonished. And you really have no idea where?"

"None," Sue said firmly.

Tom believed her. The nervousness she displayed was obviously caused by him, by his barging in. She made a movement as though to throw him out. He had to think quickly.

"In that case, I'm not quite sure but . . . under the circumstances, I might be able to help you, Miss Jackman."

"Help me?"

"Yes." He waited a moment. "May I sit down?"

Sue nodded but without enthusiasm.

He sat on the edge of one of the sofas, near the ceramic stove. "Your position here . . ." he said, trying to put it delicately.

"Yes?"

"Well, I—forgive me, but if Gavin's gone —God forbid but I suppose one must consider the possibility of something . . . fatal?" He looked at Sue, an appeal for help.

"I have considered that possibility, Mr. Carpenter. I am sure that Gavin is alive and will return. However, I appear to be a minority of one."

"Naturally I hope you are right, but if not . . ."

"I don't understand what you're trying to say."

"Well, your position . . . this house."

"You mean," Sue said, feeling that she had suddenly seen through him, "that I might be made homeless and could use the services of a good solicitor."

He laughed. "Well," he said, "we aren't allowed to advertise."

"That won't be necessary," Sue said, walking to the door. "If I am required to leave this house, I shall do so. I wish you would do the same." Sue opened the door.

Slowly, looking embarrassed, Tom got up and came to the door.

"Miss Jackman, I—"

"Mr. Carpenter, I've already had two interviews with the police. I've told them everything I know. I suggest you ask them whatever you want to know and tell them anything you know that may help."

"Well, of course, certainly. Only it's a bit delicate and since Gavin's fate is undecided . . ."

"Mr. Carpenter!"

"I happen to know that Gavin borrowed money, quite a lot of money. This house would be collateral, wouldn't you think?"

"I imagine so, but I really don't know much about these things."

"No, obviously," he said, smiling again. "Well, thanks so much."

"Good-bye, Mr. Carpenter."

Still smiling, he stepped into the garden. He did not expect Sue to close the door in his face, but she did, immediately and firmly. Good for you, Miss Jackman, he thought and went jovially down the path to his car.

Hettie Pownall lowered her binoculars as the sports car drew away from the front of the cottage.

"It must be the police," Shirley said again.

"I tell you he's not. He doesn't look like a cop, and doesn't talk like one either."

"Then who is he?"

Hettie slipped the glasses into their case, thinking. "You know what I reckon? I reckon he might be a reporter, from one of the papers."

"Oh, God, and him poking around."

"I didn't say he *was*. Anyway, he didn't see nothing."

"Well," Shirley said coldly, "you'd just better get up there and find out, hadn't you?"

As the days dragged by, Sue found it difficult to sleep. It wasn't the strange noises in the house at night or the howling winds that ushered in a stormy February. It was a sort of tension, an expectant watchfulness, a certainty that Gavin was close, coming closer. Sometimes she wandered around the house at night, talking to him. She made shopping lists that included all his favorite foods and, on one occasion, she actually bought them. Fridays were the worst. She felt certain that he would appear on a Friday. It had a sort of rightness about it, a symmetry that would appeal to Gavin. Sometimes on Fridays she could not stay still. Once she began to prepare a meal for two, for him.

Nothing else in her solitary life seemed important. Lacking sleep, she began to doze off over her work and she didn't feel guilty about that, didn't mind. She did her best to discourage or avoid Hettie Pownall's solicitous visits. Once she pretended to be out when the woman knocked and knocked at the door. She often claimed to be busy, just about to have a bath. In her own way she became an easy liar. Anything, she thought, was justified to preserve her readiness, her solitude, which he alone could dispel. She was glad that Simmons had not returned. Of Tom Carpenter, she did not think at all. Only for Evie would she rouse herself. Evie posed a threat. Her frequent telephone calls were all on the same theme: Sue's immediate return to Birmingham, to "civilization." She forced herself to sound alert, cheerful, in order to keep Evie happy and off her back.

She was neither cheerful nor alert. She seemed frozen, like a beetle in amber, an automaton Sleeping Beauty who could be woken only by the lover's kiss. She remembered how she had thought that Gavin must be the lover who came from nowhere, whose existence began and ended with her. Now it was literally true. She smiled when she thought this.

The days passed, punctuated only by the almost unbearable tension of Fridays. The weather changed, brought days of springlike freshness with white clouds scudding against a dazzling blue sky. The wind was chill but light, sighing across the flat land. Uniform rows of bright green shoots colored the black earth. Scarecrows appeared in all the fields, seemed to watch the cottage, back and front. The wind tugged at their remnant clothes and sometimes, especially at night, made their wooden bodies creak. Seated at her drawing board or standing at the living-room windows, Sue watched them. They were her friends, guarding her. She stared at the unkempt, growing garden and felt a pang of sadness for the bulbs she and Gavin had never ordered, never put in. The fence at the sides of the house sagged even more. Sometimes she heard a tapping sound that told her another board had come loose, was blowing in the wind.

She liked the wind, liked the feel of it on her face. On most days, though never on Fridays, she walked. She walked slowly along the straight roads, never much caring which direction she took. The monotony of the landscape suited her mood. One shining afternoon, walking toward the village without definite purpose, she left the road just beyond Gatherings Copse and went up to the tumbledown schoolhouse. Its windows were cobwebbed and laced with dust. Even scrubbing at them with her gloved fingers did not enable her to see more than shadows within. She circled the building, trying to imagine Gavin as a boy, playing here, learning. Why had she never asked him if he had any photographs of himself as a child? She would, she promised herself, picking her way over fallen masonry. The back wall of the schoolhouse was damp, vivid green with moss trailed in patterns of running water. The guttering was rusted and broken away. She imagined dainty curtains at the window, yellow and white gingham check—had Gavin told her that?—in Miss Peterson's day. Miss Peterson, who opened her blouse and offered her breasts to a small, wondering boy; Miss Peterson, who had run away demented. The forlorn building, disused, untenanted, seemed a fitting memorial to that woman long gone who haunted the dreams of Sue's absent lover.

She wandered around the other side, past the big, cracked windows of the schoolroom itself. There were no ghostly singing voices, no bell ringing, no clatter and chatter of the end of the school day. No innocent pictures of houses, square and symmetrical, tacked to the wall. No smell of chalk. Only the wind, blustering around the corner as Sue moved into shadow.

The old man stood at the side of the road, watching her. He was small and arthritically bent. He leaned on a stick, moving his stooped, skeleton head like a tortoise, following her movements. He did not startle her.

"School's not out yet," he said as she drew close to him. "Not till quarter to."

"The school's shut," Sue said. He didn't seem to hear. "Fine day," she said, raising her voice.

His milky eyes moved vaguely toward the sky, then returned to her face as though defeated by the effort.

"Whose girl are you, then?"

"My name's Jackman. I live in the cottage up there."

"Don't know no Jacksons. No Jacksons round here. Only Pownalls and Hobbs, and us Grubbs."

"You must be Mr. Grubb," she said.

"That's me, Bill Grubb. I know who I am."

Sue smiled, nodded.

"They won't be out yet, if you're waiting," he said, nodding at the schoolhouse.

"No, it's all right," Sue said.

"Used to be four o'clock until she came," he said accusingly.

"Oh, yes?"

"Fancy ways. Afraid of a day's work. Flibbertigibbet."

"Who's that?" she asked, her attention sparked, engaged.

"Her," he said, rolling his eyes toward the school.

"Miss Peterson?" she suggested, expecting him to laugh at her as though she was mad.

"Aye."

"You remember Miss Peterson?" He looked blank, cupped an old, twisted hand behind his left ear. Sue bent toward him. "I said, do you remember Miss Peterson?"

"Oh, yes." He nodded sagely. "Before your time, though, she was."

"I know, a long time ago."

"Back in the war."

"Can you tell me what happened to Miss Peterson?"

His eyes moved, seemed to slide away from her as though searching for something.

"Don't know no Petersons. Pownalls now, and Hobbs."

"Miss Peterson the teacher. What happened to her?"

"Happened to her?" His gaze returned to Sue, held steady. "What kind of question is that?"

"I wondered if you could tell me. I'm interested."

He snorted and, slowly, moving his stick, shuffled around and took a few unsteady steps toward the village.

"Miss Peterson," he muttered.

"Can I help you? Would you like to lean on my arm, Mr. Grubb?" Sue asked, walking on his good side, her mouth close to his ear.

"Don't need no help," he said, grumbling.

Sue stopped, watched him toddle a few more paces. His independence was admirable, she thought. Then he stopped, twisted his body from the hips toward her.

"What happened to Miss Peterson," he said and chuckled, a rheumy, unhealthy sound. "You're pulling my leg."

"No, truly not. It was like you said—before my time."

"Yes. Yes." He drew a breath, let it out. "Gatherer got her, of course." He sounded cross, set his frail legs in motion again.

"Sorry? Who?" Sue called.

"The Gatherer," he said, quite distinctly but in a tone that unmistakably said he had come to the end of his patience.

Sue shook her head. Poor old man. He seemed to have forgotten her, or to have let her gladly slip from his awareness. Sue watched his slow, uncertain progress along the road. He did not look back. After a while, satisfied that he could manage, she turned back toward her cottage. The Gatherer? Poor old man. Crazy old man, as Hettie Pownall had said.

He was leaning against the front door, an enormous bouquet of daffodils and irises clutched to his chest.

"For you," Tom said, presenting them to her with a little bow. "A peace offering."

Sue stared at the flowers. They were so perfect, so fresh, so full of life that she felt near to tears. She took them.

"Thank you. But there was no need."

"I'm afraid there was. You see, I didn't exactly tell you the truth last time I saw you."

She looked away from him, her expression vague, uninterested, he thought. There was no mistaking the change in her. Something vital had dimmed, perhaps gone out altogether. Tom was both touched and concerned. "Are you all right?" he inquired.

It was evidently the wrong thing to say. She stiffened, met his eyes coldly.

"Perfectly. Only I am very busy, rather tired, and in no mood for visitors, so if you'll please—"

"You've got to let me explain," he interrupted. "An apology without explanations . . ."

"These," Sue said, indicating the flowers, "are apology and explanation enough. You're forgiven, exonerated—whatever you want." She turned to the door. He barred her way with his arm A flush of anger spread across her cheeks. "You've got a damned nerve," she told him. He did not remove his arm.

"I must tell you something."

"I'm listening."

"You own this cottage and everything in it."

She hesitated just a second, searching his face. He seemed

completely serious but she didn't, couldn't, trust him. By his own admission he was a liar.

"Please get out of my way."

He removed his arm but only to pull a flat, official-looking envelope from his inside pocket. Sue, crushing some of the flowers in her haste, got the door open.

"Here are the deeds, a copy of the document of transfer."

He waved the envelope at her. Sue got inside, shouldered the door until he pushed against it with his hand.

"I'm no longer in a position to hold onto these, Miss Jackman. They are your property. And I don't want to have to turn them over to the police without your authority."

He was serious. Her mind raced. If he was telling the truth, then she would be in the clear with Simmons. Even he could not imagine her killing for something she already owned.

"All right," she said, moving away from the door. "But if this is a trick, *I* shall telephone the police."

"Look for yourself," he said, offering the envelope.

Sue dropped the flowers on a table and, with shaking hands, opened the envelope. At first the print, then the legalese blurred before her eyes. She saw her name in full, saw the date stamps, the signatures of witnesses, Gavin's painfully familiar signature.

"This is dated almost a year ago," she said, unable to take it in.

"He didn't want you to know. Strictly speaking, I shouldn't be telling you now, but under the circumstances . . ."

"You said something about the police—turning them over to the police?"

"I had a visit from Detective-Sergeant Simmons. I showed him the deeds but not the transfer. I stalled. I've been avoiding him, but I can't much longer."

Sue's legs suddenly felt weak. She sat down quickly, the stiff documents clutched in her hands.

"Why not?" she asked in a small, frightened voice.

"I didn't think it was his business. Anyway, I've no authority. I don't act for you, and legally those documents are yours. Besides, I don't like Simmons's manner."

"He asked me if there was a will."

"There isn't. Only this. Everything else will go—"

"He implied that I might have . . . that if the cottage was . . . could be mine, it would be a motive." She looked up at Tom, her eyes wide, her lower lip trembling.

"Well, this proves that you had no such motive, and I can vouch for that."

She did not appear to be listening. Her eyes returned to the document.

"He did this for me?" she asked, wonderingly. "A year ago? And never said. Oh, God."

The papers fell to the floor as she covered her face with her hands. She wept silently, the tears trickling between her fingers. Tom watched helplessly. He wanted to comfort her, to touch her, but he knew that would be an intrusion. He turned away, went to the window, and stood staring out miserably. There was a scarecrow in the field opposite. The wind tugged at its ragged scraps of clothing.

"Excuse me," Sue gasped, as she got up and ran across the room. Tom turned around in time to see her hurrying up the stairs.

He stood quite still, listening. He heard her muffled footsteps overhead, then silence. No sobs, no wails. He looked around the room, not knowing what to do. His eyes lighted on the flowers. He picked them up and went into the kitchen, where he began a systematic search of the cupboards for a vase. In one he found a matching pair of brown vases; he set to work trimming the stems, putting them in water. He had no skill as a flower arranger, but he was quite pleased with the effect. He carried the vases into the sitting room and placed them, one on a coffee table, the other in one of the windows. Back in the kitchen, clearing up the leaves and bits of stalk, he thought she could probably use a cup of tea. He knew he could. The kettle was singing when he heard her go into the bathroom, heard water running.

She looked young and almost painfully vulnerable with her face scrubbed, shining, a slight red swelling around her eyes.

"I'm sorry," she said, moving to pick up the fallen documents. "I don't usually do that."

"I had meant to tell you more gently."

"I'm sorry—really, I owe *you* an apology."

"Let's not go on apologizing to each other. I'm making some tea, all right?"

"Lovely."

She sat down, scanned the documents again. He brought the tea, neatly laid on a tray.

"You're very domesticated," Sue said, acknowledging the flowers and the tray with her eyes.

"Just well trained. Will you pour? Milk, no sugar for me."

Sue put the documents aside, let the tea steep, and then poured.

"You said you would vouch for me to the police. . . ."

"Just a minute. I said I *could*. But I have a question. Then, perhaps, we can do a deal."

"A deal? I don't understand."

"Please—" he held up his hand "—What I'm going to say isn't very pleasant, but I have to ask. Is it possible that Gavin made the cottage over to you because he knew, one day, he would have to disappear?"

"Of course not. Why should he?"

"So that," Tom answered levelly, "if ever he got so deeply into debt that he would be effectively bankrupt, he would have this place—which must, at the most conservative estimate, be worth a lot of money—as a sort of insurance policy."

He watched her carefully. She took it very well, he thought, biting back the denial that inevitably rose to her lips and thinking about it.

"You mean, so that I could sell it and take the money to him?"

"It's the sort of thing that crosses one's mind, yes."

"I don't know. But if that is what he wants, that is exactly what I will do."

She stared at him defiantly.

"But the idea is new to you?"

"Completely. I don't care whether you—"

"I do believe you. Now will you promise me something?"

"I don't know."

"If Gavin contacts you, for whatever reason, will you tell me before you tell the police?"

"Why should I?"

"Because, as I told you, I arranged certain loans for him. A default on his part could damage my reputation with some very influential people. I want to protect myself as best I can."

"And you wouldn't tell the police?"

"Not until and if it became absolutely necessary."

"And in return?"

"I will swear that you did not know that you were the owner of this cottage until today, until *I* told you."

"All right," Sue said, then suddenly turned pale. "But . . . wait a minute . . . That won't help at all. Since I *didn't* know, from Simmons's point of view I still had a motive to . . . get rid of Gavin."

"Oh," said Tom. "That I had rather overlooked . . ."

"What can I do now?"

"Wait a minute. Let's try and work it out. If you think there is a chance that Gavin may contact you and ask you to sell up, then it's obviously in your interest to keep very quiet about the cottage. Let Simmons go on thinking Gavin owns it until the truth absolutely has to come out. He might try and get you on withholding material information, but I can prove that you didn't . . . . Or not for long, anyway," he finished lamely.

"Supposing I tell him the truth now?" Sue suggested.

"It would put you in a good light, of course. But it wouldn't allay Simmons's suspicions. If you did want to make a run for it, for whatever reason, he'd follow you wherever you went."

Sue did not know what to do or say. She felt herself in a trap, the arms of some awful pincerlike machine closing in on her. She shook her head.

"I don't know. I just don't know. I can't think straight."

Tom leaned forward.

"Two heads are usually better than one. Let's discuss it over dinner. There's a very good restaurant in Nene."

"No, thank you, I'd rather not."

"Oh, dear." He slumped back in his seat.

"What?"

"Well, that does rather put me in a fix. I'd banked on your agreeing."

"I don't understand."

"My car's in Nene. I have no way of getting back, unless you drive me."

Sue did not believe him. She got up and went to the window, looking for his car.

"How did you get here?" she asked.

"I hitched a ride."

"Here? From Nene?"

"With Miss Pownall. A very obliging lady—as long as you don't tread on her crops."

"Perhaps she can run you back," Sue suggested.

"I'd hate to impose."

"Then I can call you a taxi."

"But you wouldn't."

She hesitated, watching his smile, contrite but coaxing.

"All right."

"Marvelous." He leapt up.

"I'll run you in, but no dinner."

"I shall do my best to persuade you."

"Do you want to go now?"

"I don't really want to go at all, unless you're prepared to dine with me."

"I'll just lock up and get my coat," Sue said, walking past him.

Ashton Pownall watched the van disappear into the early evening dusk. He waited impatiently for night to close over the unlit cottage, then he stole out of the farmhouse, leaving his bedroom light on.

This, his second nocturnal visit to the cottage, was rewarded with success. It had been a fine day and Sue had hung a line of washing in the backyard. Furthermore, she had forgotten to take it in before driving off with Tom Carpenter. Ashton's wet smile wreathed his face as he played a flashlight briefly along the line. Killing the light, he relied upon touch, sampling the textures of the articles that attracted him. He wanted all three of them, but some remnant of caution made him take only one. One might not be missed, might have blown away in the night. He chose the one that excited his fingers most, unpegged it from the line, and pushed it swiftly into his pocket. He was breathing heavily, scarcely able to control the longing that pounded in his blood. He melted away into the night, his boots pounding eerily on the deserted, silent road.

Sue could not concentrate on Tom's "confession," as he called it. Apart from driving on unfamiliar roads, her head buzzed with the question of whether or not she should tell Simmons about the cottage. The thought of contacting him was in itself repugnant, but she pushed that objection aside, knowing it to be irrelevant. Tom's idea seemed so unlike Gavin. She could not imagine him phoning her from somewhere, asking her to sell the cottage and join him. But then the whole situation was not like Gavin and she was beginning to wonder if she had ever really known him. But if that was what he wanted, had schemed for, she would do it. If he really wanted a chance to start a new life with her . . . the phrase had a chilly, familiar ring. It was what she had thought that morning when she left Birmingham. No one, she felt absolutely sure, was ever given that chance twice.

"I fear my eloquence, on which I do rather pride myself, is wasted on you," Tom said, breaking into her thoughts.

"I'm sorry," Sue said automatically. "I'm still trying to decide what I ought to do. What were you saying?"

"Nothing of moment; just trying to draw attention to myself."

"You do rather a lot of that, don't you?"

"That was below the belt. Please, can't we call a truce? Sue?"

"I'm sorry," Sue said again. "I didn't really mean to snap at you."

"Snap at you, Tom," he coaxed.

"All right."

"Prove you didn't mean it, by having dinner with me."

"No, I've told you. Besides, I'm not in the least bit hungry."

"A drink, then. Just one small drink. Is that so much to ask when a chap's gone to so much trouble to apologize and explain and, dare I say, help a little?"

"You also went to a lot of trouble to trap me into having dinner with you. I don't like that sort of maneuvering."

"A drink would be a compromise. No loss of face on either side."

"All right," Sue said, not very graciously. "One drink, but that's all."

"Terrific. Go straight up the High Street. The Talbot's on your left."

He did not attempt to conceal the smugness in his voice, Sue thought. But he had been kind, had tried to help her. His confirmation that she had not known about the cottage might be essential. That thought made her depressed again.

She felt conspicuously out of place in the pub, in old jeans, a quilted jacket, her hair uncombed. While Tom was fetching the drinks she considered going to the ladies' room to tidy up and then guessed that Tom would take that as an intention to stay. She unzipped her jacket and ran her fingers through her hair, realizing that she really didn't care what people thought of her appearance anyway. As soon as Tom joined her, she asked, "What do *you* think I ought to do?"

"Seriously?"

"Yes."

"My professional opinion?"

"If you like."

"I'd have to advise you to go to the police, tell them."

"And is that what you really think?"

He sipped his neat scotch before replying. "If you're really in the clear, really don't know where Gavin is, yes."

"You said you believed me."

"I do. But you mustn't take that for granted, not with everyone."

"When you love someone very much," Sue said, suddenly needing to make him understand, "you don't question them. You don't ask where every penny comes from. Our time together was always limited, rushed. Oh, I don't know."

"It's all right," he said gently. "But it's a cynical world, full of cynical people. Your sort of trust—faith, I suppose, is a better word—is very rare. We're not used to it."

Sue stared into her drink, lost in thought, until a shadow fell across her.

"Well, well, well," Simmons drawled, an unpleasant smile stretching his mouth. "I didn't know you two knew each other."

Sue started, spilling her drink. Tom laid his hand on her arm.

"And there I was thinking you knew everything, Sergeant," Tom said, easing himself back into his seat.

"I suppose I should have guessed," Simmons said, his eyes fixed on Sue.

"We do have certain obvious interests in common that should not have been beyond your powers of deduction," Tom agreed smoothly.

"Like a lack of cooperation; like insolence and withholding information?" Simmons suggested.

Sue stood up, shaking off Tom's hand, jarring her legs against the table.

"Thanks very much, Tom," she said. "Good night."

"Hey, wait," Tom said.

She ignored him, ran out of the bar, ran because she could not stand it any longer. Being seen with Tom would convince Simmons, she knew, that anything she told him was a lie. She cursed herself for ever having let Tom wheedle her into having a drink. Most of all, she cursed Tom.

Simmons swiveled, watching her leave. Tom maneuvered his long legs around the table, and brushed against Simmons, who grabbed his arm in a very tight grip.

"Take some advice from your elders and betters, sonny. Let her go."

"Get your hands off me," Tom said through gritted teeth.

Simmons waited, watched the blood rise to Tom's face and then, just in time, let his hand fall.

Tom raced out, shouting Sue's name, but the van was already moving away. He stopped at the curb and swore. Should he follow her? His car was in the parking lot at the other end of High

Street, but he could easily overtake her. Would she stop? Would it help or only alarm her more?

"Was it something I said?" Simmons appeared at his shoulder, flexing his hands in a pair of new leather gloves.

"No, just the smell," Tom snarled.

"Now, listen here, Carpenter."

"No. You listen," Tom shouted, rounding on the policeman, who stared at him coldly. "You leave her alone, okay? Just stick to your job. Find Trope or his body, but leave her alone."

Tom glared at the policeman, his fists bunched, his chest heaving. Simmons turned up the collar of his overcoat.

"I see. Like that, is it? Well, I can't say I blame you, but it does put a different complexion on things. Yes, indeed."

Simmons turned on his heel and walked away. Tom swore again. He'd played straight into the man's greasy hands. There was no point in following Sue now, he knew. She would justifiably be furious with him. And Simmons would make capital out of it in any way he could. Tom walked up the street, toward his car. Damn his temper. Damn Simmons. Damn these stupid, unfounded feelings for a girl who—all of a sudden he realized that he had to find Gavin Trope. The thought hit him like a blow, taking his breath away. He had to find him. He'd done it before and by God he'd do it again.

"Hello. Have a nice time last night, did you? Here, I brought your washing in. It looks like rain. And six eggs like you asked me for."

Hettie bustled around, uninvited, as though the kitchen were her own. Sue watched, lacking the energy to stop her.

"Here, you feeling all right? You look proper done in to me." The look of concern left her face, nudged aside by a roguish smile. "Late night, was it? Paying for it today, are you?"

Something stirred and surfaced in Sue's mind.

"Did you give him a lift from Nene yesterday?" she asked.

"That Mr. Carpenter? Yes. Why?" Hettie looked at her with a rather defensive expression. Or perhaps it was apprehensive, Sue thought. "I hope I didn't do wrong," Hettie said, fiddling with the belt of her stained and elderly raincoat.

"No, it's your business," Sue said, turning to the kettle, which had begun to spout steam.

"Well, not really. I wouldn't go giving lifts to no strange men. It was only on your account and him asking so nicely and everything."

"He asked you for a lift?"

"Well, of course. What's he been telling you?"

"Nothing, actually," Sue said. "Do you want a cup?" She gestured toward the jar of instant coffee.

"Oh, never say no, me. It's getting chilly out there, too."

She began to undo her coat. Sue made the coffee, adding a generous amount of sugar to Hettie's mug.

"Well, I was in Nene, yesterday being market day. I usually go in to do a bit of shopping. Anyway, he suddenly comes up to me with this great bunch of flowers. I've never seen so many. Like something off the telly it was. And he says can he cadge a lift because the clutch's gone on his car and he's bought the flowers for you and the car won't be mended before nightfall." Hettie paused, not to draw breath but to slurp coffee noisily. "Oh, that's a treat, that is. So, what could I say? He was ever so polite, and since I knew he was a friend of yours . . ."

"How did you know?"

"Well, I've seen him before, haven't I? That's how he knew me. I gave him a right telling off, I can tell you. He was trampling all over our early wheat, that first time he came to see you." Hettie stopped, frowned suspiciously. "He is a friend of yours, isn't he?"

"No. He did some business for Gavin."

"Oh."

"He's rather a nuisance, actually."

"Still, you did go out with him last night. Go somewhere posh, did you?"

"Hettie, I just drove him into Nene."

"Oh, what a shame. And I was only saying to Shirley how it would do you good to get out more. You ought to, you know. It'd do you good."

"Oh, stop it, Hettie," Sue said. "You sound just like my sister."

She pushed past Hettie, went into the sitting room, and sat down, nursing her coffee mug on her knee.

"Excuse me, I'm sure," Hettie said stiffly from the doorway. "I was only being neighborly, only thinking of you. Still, a nod's as good as a wink."

"I'm sorry." Sue twisted around to look at her, tried to smile. "I know you meant well. It's just . . ." She shrugged, turned away again, her eyes fixed on the empty room. Hettie came to stand in front of her.

"It's getting you down, isn't it? Not knowing?"

"Something like that, yes."

"D'you want to talk about it? It helps, you know. A trouble shared . . ."

"There's nothing to say, Hettie. You know it all. It's just . . . oh, God, what am I going to do?"

"Well, what you mustn't do is take on so. You'll make yourself ill. Come on, now."

Awkwardly, Hettie set her mug down and sat beside Sue, putting her arm around her. Sue rested her head gratefully against her shoulder. She so badly needed comfort and reassurance, and Hettie seemed so safe, so sensible, and above all so simply kind. She poured out her heart to her. Hettie held her tight, rocking her from time to time, but keeping unusually silent.

"Well," she said, when Sue had finished, "if it was me I wouldn't say nothing to the police. What they want to know they'll find out. That's what my dad always says. That's what they're paid for. But they must be mad to think as how you'd do anything to him."

"Thanks, Hettie," Sue said, sitting up and pushing the hair out of her face. "I needed somebody to tell me that."

"It stands to reason. You loved him."

"I still do."

"Well, of course."

"I can't get it out of my head, you see, that he will come back, come for me."

"And he will. 'Course he will." Hettie reached around Sue, picked up her tepid coffee, and finished it.

"You don't know how good it is to hear you say that." Sue's eyes shone. There was a touch of color in her cheeks.

"I can guess, though. You poor thing. Why didn't you say something to me before?"

"I don't know. I wish I had, truly I do."

"Well, you know where I am, any time you want me." She stood up.

"Must you go?"

"Well, I ought. It's my day for seeing to old Grubb."

"Can you come back? Please? This evening. Come to supper," Sue asked anxiously.

A slow smile lit Hettie's plump, kindly face.

"Well, of course I will. You only have to ask."

"Oh, thank you, Hettie. Thank you."

"Don't be silly."

Sue got up and walked her through into the kitchen.

"About seven?" she suggested.

"All right. And we'll have a good old chin-wag. Take your mind off things."

"Oh, Hettie." Spontaneously, Sue embraced her, hugged her close.

"There, there. All this for a bit of neighborly kindness? Now, look, I promised to be at old Grubb's."

"Yes. Yes." Sue sniffed back her tears of gratitude and relief.

"Only he gets so bothered if he thinks you're letting him down or anything."

"Yes, I can imagine. I bumped into him the other day."

"I bet you didn't get no sense out of him," Hettie laughed, belting her raincoat.

"I asked him about Miss Peterson, you know, the school-teacher?"

Hettie nodded.

"He remembered her."

"Oh, he's not all daft," she agreed. "Just gets things muddled up like."

"Anyway, he said—when I asked him what happened to her—he said the Gatherer got her. What did he mean?"

"Why, silly old fool, how does he know?"

"But what is the Gatherer?"

"Death," Hettie said simply. "The Reaper, they call him in some parts."

"Oh, yes. How stupid of me. I'd just never heard that term before."

"They always used to use it round here. Old so-and-so's been gathered, they'd say. Well, sounds nicer than dead, doesn't it? And I'll get worse than gathering if I don't get a move on," she said, opening the back door.

"But was she—is she dead?" Sue asked, delaying her for a moment longer.

"Search me. Old Grubber don't know, that's for sure. But she must be getting on by now. It's likely. See you later then."

"Yes," Sue said, closing the door behind her.

The Gatherer, she thought. She liked it. Hettie was right. It did sound better and more comforting, like Hettie herself. Gathered to Abraham's bosom, she supposed, would be the source and derivation. Gathered unto one's maker. Yes, it had a gentle sound to it, was less bleak and final than dead.

The phone shrilled, startling her.

Tom leaned back in his swivel chair, listened to the breathless, anxious way she said hello.

"I didn't dare call you last night, though I wanted to. Please don't hang up."

"It wasn't really your fault," she sighed. "It was him, Simmons, knowing what he'd think."

"I'm afraid I rather made that worse."

"Worse?"

"I lost my temper. Told him to lay off you, or words to that effect. I'm afraid he jumped to certain conclusions. But I have tried to make amends."

She waited, not saying anything.

"The only way out of this, to satisfy Simmons, you, everyone, is to find Gavin. I've had a word with an acquaintance, someone in the Chief Constable's office."

"And?"

"I suggested they might try a bit harder, make a proper search of the Wold, put his picture in the papers, on TV. You know the sort of thing. I can't guarantee anything, of course."

"I see."

"I'm afraid it will mean publicity."

"Isn't that the idea?"

"I mean for you. I think you ought to go away for a while, just a few days."

"No."

"It might be unpleasant for you."

"That won't be anything new," she said.

"I'm very sorry."

"Please, just make sure Simmons knows there's nothing between us."

"I'll try, of course, Sue."

The line purred at him. She had hung up.

Hettie's enjoyment was infectious. She enthused over everything —the meal, which she approached with typical English suspicion, and her first taste of "real" wine, promising to bring Sue a bottle of Shirley's homemade parsnip next time she called. During the evening, Sue felt herself relaxing, coming out of her shell. Hettie, she realized, was the first person she had felt comfortable with since Gavin's disappearance. Her guest, too, became mellower, more thoughtful.

Sipping wine after supper, Hettie sighed and said, "I envy you. I know it's a terrible thing to say, but I do."

"I can't think why," Sue said, remembering the hollow at the center of her life.

"All you've got, all you know. Oh, I know you aren't married and that, but at least you've got something to show for your life."

"Why did you never marry?" Sue asked, feeling there were no constraints between them now.

Hettie chuckled and shrugged. "Who'd marry me?"

"Lots of people, given the chance."

"Ah, well, chance'd be a fine thing. No," she paused, twisting her wineglass against the firelight. "There's no one round here, no chance. And I never had the time or the money to get myself dressed up and go looking for a husband."

"It's not too late," Sue said. "It's never too late, not if that's what you really want."

"Yes, well, I don't know that it is what I want. I look at my sister-in-law sometimes and I'm really glad I'm not her. Tied to a man, three kids round her day and night. I don't know. I sometimes think I'm not so badly off."

"But marriage isn't the only alternative," Sue pointed out. "Not even the first, necessarily."

"Not if you're clever. Not if you know something. But me, what do I know? How to milk a cow and raise a few hens."

"You're not stupid. You could learn."

"Me? I can barely write my own name. Besides, I never had the patience for studying. And I'm too old to change my ways now."

"So what would you like?" Sue asked, changing tack.

"Oh, nothing much, a place of my own, nice things. Bit of money put by. Boring, isn't it?" She laughed, mocking herself.

"No. That's all most of us want. Independence, our own space, the chance to choose."

"Yes, well, it sounds better put that way but it's all pie-in-the-sky for me. You have to make the best of what you've got and get on with it."

"Yes," Sue said, reflecting. "That's what I keep telling myself but I don't know. It doesn't seem to help much."

Hettie was silent for a while, watching her.

"What are you going to do? In the long term, like."

Sue shook her head.

"I can't imagine it. I can't think beyond tomorrow."

"You'll have to one day," Hettie said, sounding very sure of herself.

"It'll be easy when Gavin comes back."

Hettie opened her mouth to speak, then closed it. Sue, who had been staring into the fire saw this and looked at her fully, waiting. Hettie flushed a little.

"You think I'm fooling myself, don't you? You think I ought to act as though he was . . . as though he had been gathered?"

"I never said anything of the sort. I think you should think what you want to think."

"But if I'm wrong?"

"You'll find out and you'll think accordingly. Time'll sort it out, Sue, not anything I say or you think."

Sue turned back to the fire. There was a crumb of comfort in Hettie's voice.

"I was thinking," Hettie went on. "It was you asking me about the Gatherer that set me off—you know how they always say things were so bad in the old days, especially for women? Well, I know they were. I know it's better now in lots of ways, but they were better off in others, I reckon. They had more comfort. Oh, I don't mean in their homes and that but like, well, like in your situation."

"I don't follow," Sue said, looking at her.

"Well, they believed things. They had charms and things. I'm not saying they did any good but they must have been a comfort to them."

"What sort of charms?" Sue asked, her interest aroused.

"Oh, bless me, I don't know. They're all forgotten now. But I've always remembered a tale my mum told me about when she was a girl. She was in service over at Ashton Hall before she married my dad, and the parlor maid there, Alice, I think her name was, she got it real bad for one of the stable boys. Of course he strung her along but all the time he was engaged to another girl, back home where he came from. Anyway, according to my mum, he broke off with this Alice and was all set to marry the other girl, see, but Alice, she wasn't beat that easily. So, d'you know what she did?" Sue shook her head. "She did this charm and she put a spell on him. It took three weeks and then he comes to her and says he's sorry and he wants Alice to marry him."

"And did she?" Sue asked as a log shifted in the fire and flared up brightly.

"I can't remember."

"And do you believe it?"

"My mum does, Alice did—that's the point."

"All right, but how did she do it? How did she put this spell on him?"

"Search me, I don't know. Bless me if I know why I started on all that anyway."

"You were talking about things that were a comfort to women in those days."

"Oh, yes, that's right. It must have given them hope, see. Like there were some who reckoned they could call people back when they'd gone away, some even when they were dead."

"That," Sue said, getting up and fetching the wine bottle, "I do not believe." She made to freshen Hettie's glass but Hettie put her hand over it.

"Oh, no more. You'll make me tiddly."

"And you believe that, do you?" Sue asked, filling her own glass.

"No, 'course not. But I still say it made it easier for people."

"I see your point," Sue admitted. "Maybe we have become too practical, too cynical. It's like religion, like losing faith."

"It was a comfort," Hettie insisted, pursing her lips.

Sue said nothing. Her thoughts fluttered back to Gavin again, to the emptiness she felt. The wind gusted suddenly, blustering outside.

Ta-ta-t'-tap. Ta-ta-t'-tap.

Sue glanced toward the window. Hettie stood up.

"I must be going," she said.

"I must do something about that fence. The wind rattles the loose boards," Sue said. "Oh, sorry, Hettie. Must you really go?"

"If I'm to be up in time to do the early milking, I must."

"It's been lovely. Thank you ever so much for coming."

"Oh, it was a real treat for me, I can tell you."

"I'll come a little way with you."

"You'll do no such thing. That's an east wind blowing, and there's no sense in both of us getting cold." Sue gave in, helped Hettie into her best coat, and embraced her. Pulling a flashlight from her pocket, Hettie opened the front door.

"You take care of yourself now. And thanks again."

"Good night, Hettie. Go carefully."

Sue remained for a moment in the doorway. She shivered. Hettie was right; the wind, which seemed to be increasing every moment, was bitterly cold. She closed and bolted the door. Hettie had insisted on washing up after their supper, so there was nothing to do but clear away the wineglasses. Sue took them into the kitchen and then noticed the bundle of clean washing Hettie had brought in earlier that day. Methodically she began to sort it into two piles, items that needed ironing and those which could be put straight away. She had washed three pairs of panties, she was sure. She looked around, wondering if one pair had fallen somewhere.

Ta-ta-t'-tap.

The wind howled.

The green nylon ones. She remembered distinctly. Perhaps Hettie had dropped them in the garden. Sue went to the back door and opened it. The light from the door and kitchen window would be sufficient. She stepped out into the wind.

Ta-ta-t'-tap.

Something moved. Some*one*. She turned into the darkness, her heart racing. The fence rattled insistently. She saw something moving away in the darkness. It had a swinging, lumbering gait.

"Gavin?" she whispered. Then louder, "Gavin?"

Ta-ta-t'-tap. Ta-ta-t'-tap.

Nothing. The wind flattened her clothes against her. Peering into the darkness she could see nothing, no movement. The wind rose, sang. She turned sadly back into the cottage. It must have been a trick of the wind, her imagination.

Ta-ta-t'-tap.

Gavin Trope's face appeared on television throughout the country. The press made the usual appeals for anyone who had seen him to contact his local police station. The search of Ashton Wold began in earnest and, at the weekend, the police were augmented by civilian volunteers. A trickle of cars passed slowly by "the remote weekend cottage," as Sue's home had been described. Toward noon, Tom Carpenter's sports car drew onto the verge outside. Wearing Wellington boots, old jeans, and a ski jacket, he knocked at the front door. Sue, who had seen his approach, did not want to let him in, hoped he would go away. At his third knock she went to the window and unlatched it.

"I've been helping with the search," he said, when she ignored his greeting. "There's nothing. I brought a hamper with me. I wondered if you'd like to have an impromptu picnic."

"That's all it is to you, isn't it?" she said bitterly. "A day out in the country, a nice picnic."

He flinched from the accusation, the roughness in her voice.

"Look," he said, barely controlling his own anger, "I'm seriously worried about you."

"Don't be," she said.

"Do you realize you're becoming completely antisocial?"

"You don't know anything about me. You don't know what I'm becoming."

"I can see the change in you. I can see that you're making yourself ill, shut up here."

"When I want a doctor," Sue snapped, "I'll get a real one."

She slammed the window so hard the glass rattled. It was all Tom could do to prevent himself banging against it with his clenched fist. Furiously, he turned away and went back to the car, which he started with an ostentatious roar. It had been an act of bravado to join the search. He wanted to show Simmons that he was not afraid, had nothing damaging to hide. He had lied to himself about Sue, had almost convinced himself that he only wanted to check that she was all right, was not being pestered by reporters or sightseers, when the truth was that he wanted to be with her, wanted for her to like him a little. And this thought led naturally to the next admission. He did not want Gavin Trope to be found—at least, not alive. The thought appalled him, made his hands tremble on the steering wheel. But it would not go away, could not be denied. With a suddenness that made him feel confused, made him doubt his own feelings, Trope had become a rival. He eased up on the accelerator and slowed down. What he felt, hoped, was crazy. Crazy enough to make him wish a man dead. But he could not let her go on as she was, living there alone, brooding, dying from within. She was driving herself mad, he thought, remembering the moist, haunted eyes that had stared at him through the window. Eyes that had grown too large for her face. Cheeks pale as parchment, drawn tight, hollowed. Her hair without luster as though dried and sprinkled with dust. He had to do something about her, had to get through to her somehow, simply because he cared and could not blot her out of his mind.

He had no stomach for lunch, or to return to the search. He turned the car toward home, thinking that he would get roaring drunk and pass into oblivion.

Gently, Sue touched the purplish-black crescents beneath her eyes. It was the dreams, she thought, as she stared at her face in the bedroom mirror, dreams that lingered over into the days, which sometimes became muddled with the uneventful reality. She dreamed of conversations with Miss Peterson, who wore long, trailing Edwardian clothes and a hat decorated with dead crows whose blood seeped in red puddles, dripped unnoticed onto her very pale hands. The worst dream and the most frequent concerned herself, alone in the cottage. She would be lying in bed or sitting at her drawing board. Everything would be normal, quiet. Then she would hear Gavin's voice calling to her softly, calling her name. She could not move. No matter how desperately she tried, she could not get up, could not go to him. He was calling to her, wanting to come in, and she was doomed to remain motionless, to endure the agony of hearing his voice fade, go away.

When she woke from this dream there was never anything but the tapping of the board fence in the wind. No matter how she searched, how loudly she called into the cold nights or pallid dawns, there was never any answering voice, nothing. Nothing but the stark scarecrows in the fields, which seemed to change their position every day. She thought of taking down the fence altogether, making a bonfire of it, but she lacked the energy. The March winds would stop soon and the rattling that disturbed her exhausted sleep would cease with them.

So what if she looked hollow-eyed and washed out? Who was there to see? She had no one to please with her appearance. It was her own damn business.

Huddled in front of the television set, she forced herself to watch the six o'clock news bulletin. The search of Ashton Wold was complete, the result negative. The routine appeals were repeated. The police were following up every supposed sighting, no matter how remote, how unlikely.

"Oh, please, Gavin, please," she whispered. "Please, if you saw that, get in touch with me. I know you're out there somewhere. I know you can't have forgotten me. There's no risk, Gavin. No risk at all. Just telephone me. Let me know, just let me know that you're all right. Please."

Without knowing how she got there, Sue found herself at the

window, her hands pressed to the cold glass. The moon had risen, a full moon, riding low among silver clouds. Behind her, hymns sounded from the television set.

"Please," she sobbed, letting her head rest against the glass. "Please."

Simmons was not in the least disappointed that the search had yielded nothing. He had been against it from the first. It was a waste of time and money. The intervention from above had infuriated him, but he had kept a cold grip on his temper. The whole charade might work to his advantage in the end. Now that it was all over he was content to lie low for a few days, let those who knew what had happened to Gavin Trope think he'd lost interest. That way they were more likely to make a mistake. It was a cat-and-mouse game now, and that was how Simmons liked it.

Making a show of being the responsible officer in charge, he was the last to leave Ashton Wold. He smoked a cheroot, leaning on the hood of his car, and watched the moon rise. He toyed with the idea, turning it lasciviously over in his mind, of paying little Miss Jackman a call. He had plenty of excuses. But pleasant and tempting though the thought was, he let it go. He wasn't quite certain of her yet. She remained his long shot. He wanted her to stew in her own juice, too. It wouldn't be long now until somebody made a move. The cracking time was coming; he could feel it. It made the short hairs on the back of his neck prickle in a pleasant, almost sexual way. Stamping the red-glowing butt of his cheroot under foot, he got into his car. Still, it wouldn't hurt to stop off at the pub in Brooking, sink a pint or two with the locals, pick up the gossip of the years.

Ashton Pownall laughed until the tears stood in his eyes. He kept pounding his knee with his fist and rocking back and forth, until Shirley's temper snapped.

"Shut up, you great fool," she said, getting up from her chair and switching off the television set.

Ashton's childish, out-of-control laughter died as though operated by the same switch.

"Don't you speak to him like that," Hettie said. "You've no call."

"I want the hymns," Mary Pownall grumbled. "Put it back on. You know I like the hymns."

Shirley ignored her. They all ignored her. Shirley stood in front of Lucas, her head bent down toward him.

"That's that then," she said, "isn't it?"

Mary fussed with the crocheted blanket spread over her knees. Hettie and her father stared at Lucas, waiting for his reply.

"Isn't it?" Shirley said again, her voice cracking with tension.

"They don't find nothing. I told you they don't find nothing," Ashton burbled. His laughter threatened again.

"Sh," Hettie told him. "Be quiet now." She touched his arm to still him.

"Looks like it," Lucas said at last.

"Is that all you can say? With them on our doorstep, poking round? How do you know they won't come back? What d'you think they're going to do now? Answer me," Shirley shouted.

"Calm yourself," George Pownall said, rising stiffly from his seat. "They're gone. Now let's put the hymns on for Mother."

"You just don't care, do you? None of you. You just don't care. You've no thought for me and my kids." She rounded suddenly on the old man who was stooped over the controls of the television set. "You should have stopped this years ago," she told him.

He straightened up, easing his back. A hymn drifted into the room.

"That's enough," Lucas said. "Go and get supper on. Go on."

Shirley stared at them all—at Mary straining toward the warming television set, impatient for the picture; at Ashton, who grinned back at her, the laughter still bubbling in him; at Hettie's face, closed, secretive.

"I shan't tell you again," Lucas said, very quietly.

Shirley whirled around and ran out of the back parlor, slamming the door behind her. George Pownall sighed, pulled out his pipe, and stuck it into his mouth.

"Got a bit of work to do," he said. "Got to make a few finishing touches."

Lucas grunted, fixed his eyes on the television screen.

"I'd best go and see Sue," Hettie said. "See if everything's all right?"

Ashton snickered, his thoughts moving off into forbidden, secret places.

"Lucas?" Hettie said, prompting him, raising her voice over the crescendo of the hymn.

"Get your supper first," he said. "There's no hurry."

Mary Pownall smiled at the screen, nodded her head in vague time to the music.

"I don't like all this singing," Ashton grumbled.

"Go upstairs for a bit," Hettie suggested. "I'll call you when supper's ready. Let Mum enjoy her hymns in peace."

"No need to ask if you watched the news," Hettie said.

Sue had been curled up in the dark, the fire burned down to embers. Her face was swollen and ugly from weeping. The light hurt her eyes. Hettie switched off one of the lamps and knelt at the grate, sweeping up fallen ash, then fetched dry kindling from the kitchen storeroom. When she had a fresh blaze crackling, she stood up, dusting her hands together.

"I thought you might like someone to sit with you tonight," she said. "Shall I make us a nice cup of tea?"

Sue shook her head.

"Some cocoa, then? Very soothing, that is."

"There's some wine."

She glanced at a part-full, recorked bottle on the bar. Hettie went toward it.

"You ought to go easy on this stuff," she said, warning.

"It helps me to sleep. You have some."

"Just one small one, then, to keep you company."

Hettie Pownall poured the drinks and settled opposite Sue.

"Do you want to talk about it?" she asked.

Sue shook her head again, but immediately began to talk.

"Don't you see, Hettie, this proves I'm right? Oh, I never thought they'd find anything there. It's like I've always said. He's alive somewhere. I know he is."

"If that's what you think," Hettie said carefully, "why have you been upsetting yourself so?"

"Oh, I don't know. Relief, I suppose. You know," she hurried on between rapid sips of the wine, "the other night I saw something moving outside and I was sure it was Gavin. And then I thought maybe he'd lost his memory. I kept thinking about him wandering around somewhere, lost, not knowing who he was or where he belonged."

"If that was the case they'd have picked him up by now."

"Right," Sue agreed excitedly. "Then I thought, but suppose it's not like that at all? Suppose he's perfectly capable of looking after himself, getting a job, somewhere to live. Gavin's a very practical man. If he did lose his memory through worry or something, I'm sure that's how he would be. He wouldn't become a tramp or anything. He'd make some sort of life for himself, wait until his memory came back."

"Let's hope he saw the television, then," Hettie said.

"Yes." The excitement, the animation went out of Sue.

"Somebody'll be bound to recognize him," Hettie said.

"Yes." She got up and went across the room to slop more wine into her glass. "You're absolutely right, of course."

"So?"

Sue frowned, seemed reluctant to answer. She looked at her glass for a moment, then took a large gulp. "Well, just in case nobody does recognize him, or he doesn't bother to read the papers or something—I mean, I'm sure he will, but just in case, as a *comfort*, you know?"

Her eyes were bright, almost feverish, pleading with Hettie.

"Yes? What?"

"Oh, Hettie, you remember what you said." She came to Hettie's side, squatted down, her hand resting on the woman's knee. "About those charms that could bring people back. I know you said there was nothing in it, but if the person believed . . ."

Hettie stared at her in disbelief, then she threw back her head and laughed. Sue stood up immediately and walked away from her.

"Don't laugh at me," she said.

"I'm sorry." Hettie became serious, watched Sue pace up and down. "I didn't mean . . . I didn't think you were serious."

"Well, I am. Deadly serious. I don't care what you believe, but you've got to help me. Please, Hettie?"

"How can I help you?" Hettie said uncomfortably. "I don't know any old charms."

Sue stopped pacing.

"I think you do. I think you're only pretending."

"Are you calling me a liar?" Hettie asked sharply.

"No. No, I didn't mean . . . I just thought you could help me if you wanted. If you really thought about it, I'm sure you'd be able to remember something."

"Well . . . ," she said, not committing herself.

"Oh, please, Hettie. Listen, since I've been living here, have gotten to know you, I realize how much more simple and natural and good things are. Somebody said to me the other day that it's a cynical world. But it isn't here. It's fresh and natural, simple. I can't express it, but there's a power here, in the country, a kind of magic. The seasons, growing things, the cycle of the seasons. I can feel it, Hettie. And I want to be a part of it. I know it can help me, if I only trust it enough. If only you'll help me."

"You want to be a part of it, you say?" Hettie asked quietly.

"Yes. I want to belong."

She weighed this for a time, while Sue looked on nervously.

"It's funny stuff what you're thinking of playing with. Do you realize that?"

"I'm not going to play with it, Hettie. I believe. I shall do it with respect, reverence."

"I don't know. I think you should think some more about it."

"I have thought, Hettie. Truly I have. You can help me? Tell me that you can."

"I can ask. There's people, like my old mum, I can ask about it. But I'm not promising anything, mind."

"Oh, thank you, Hettie, thank—"

"I'm not sure as it's right," Hettie interrupted. "There's some things we have no call to go dabbling in."

"A *comfort*, Hettie. That's what you said. That's all I'm asking. God, can't you see that I need something?"

Her voice rose suddenly to a shout. Hettie stared at her, her expression slowly softening to pity as the tears started from Sue's eyes.

"Come on," she said, standing up. "You've had enough of that, my girl." She took Sue's glass from her. "It's bad for you. You're all worked up."

"Please, Hettie, please," she sobbed.

"All right," the other woman relented. "I'll do what I can. But only on the condition that you get off to bed."

Sue nodded, whispered her thanks through her tears.

"Come on, then. And no more nonsense tonight. You go on while I tidy up down here. Then I'll bring you a nice glass of hot milk and make sure you're comfortable. Go on now."

Sue obeyed. She suddenly felt very tired. Her muscles ached for the relief of bed, for sleep.

Hettie watched her go, then set a pan of milk to heat on the stove.

In making the perfect house, wanting in nothing, Gavin Trope had forgotten one thing: an upstairs telephone extension. It seemed to Evie that she had been listening to that maddening burr-burr, burr-burr for hours. Pictures flashed into her mind, each one bringing its own burden of dread, as if she wasn't already upset enough.

"What the hell's going on there?" she shouted as soon as Sue picked up. "Where were you? I've been hanging on for ages."

"Asleep," Sue said. Her voice sounded distant and fuzzy, as though muffled.

"Asleep? What time is it?"

"I don't know," Sue said faintly.

"You haven't taken something, have you?" Evie said, angry fear squeezing the concern out of her voice.

"What?" Sue said.

"Pills. You haven't taken an overdose, have you?"

There was a sound at the other end of the line, a sound Evie could not immediately identify.

"No," Sue laughed. "I haven't even got any."

"It's not funny. You had me worried sick."

"I'm sorry. I had an early night. The news . . ."

"Yes, well, I was going to ring you anyway. Who's this Tom Carpenter bloke?"

"Who?"

"Tom Carpenter?"

"How do you know about him?" Sue's voice suddenly became sharper.

"I know about him because he rang me. He said he was worried about you. Said you were behaving funny and looked dreadful."

"Jesus Christ, has he got a nerve!" Sue exploded. "I hope you told him to—"

"I couldn't tell him anything, could I? *I* don't know how you are. You haven't rung me up in days."

Evie's aggrieved petulant tone quelled some of Sue's anger.

"I'm sorry. I haven't been sleeping too well, but I am all right, really."

"You don't sound it."

"I'm half asleep, for heaven's sake. If Tom Carpenter kept his nose out of my business . . ."

"All right, all right, Don't shout. Who is he, anyway?"

"Some solicitor acquaintance of Gavin's. He did some work for him."

"So why's he worried about you?"

"I don't know. He's a bloody nuisance. He keeps on coming here, trying to get me to go out with him."

"Oh, I see. Like that, is it? He certainly sounded very concerned."

"How did he find you?"

"The phone book, he said. I don't know. I was that worried."

"I'm sorry, Evie, but I'm fine. If he calls again, do me a favor and tell him to mind his own business."

"He was only trying to help. Anyway, what did you think about the news tonight?"

"It was what I expected. I told you. He's not dead."

"Oh, Sue."

"I believe it, Evie. I have to."

"I don't know. Look, why don't you come up here for a few days?"

"Was that Carpenter's idea, too?"

"No, it wasn't. He said that I ought to go down to you. But I can't. I've got a hell of a week coming. . . ."

"I don't need anyone. I just want to get some sleep."

Evie absorbed this, keeping a tight hold on her temper.

"I'll be down as soon as I can fix it," she announced. "I don't care what you say. Probably not before the weekend."

"Evie!"

"I'm not arguing with you, Sue. I'm coming. And when I get there, your bags had better be packed, ready to come back here with me."

Evie surprised herself by slamming the receiver down before Sue could say anything. She fumbled a cigarette into her mouth and lit it. Her immediate impulse was to pick the phone up again, and apologize, but she thought better of it. Sue would only try to talk her out of it. Let her think about what Evie had said. Perhaps that way she'd see some sense. It had gone on long enough, this moping and mooning about that godforsaken place. Any sane person could see that. And she had to face the fact that Gavin Trope was either dead and buried or didn't want to know about Sue anymore. It was time someone knocked some sense into her, and Evie felt completely equal to the task.

The scarecrows were all different, with personalities of their own. It was all right to walk on the little strips of unplowed grass that marked the historical boundaries of the fields. The Pownall brothers always left those. It was a tradition, a sign of respect, roots, a sense of continuity. These were the things Sue admired and envied, to which she wanted to belong. The presence of these little paths turned the landscape into a vast green-and-brown checkerboard, a grid system that led nowhere. Sue walked it, looking at the scarecrows. She called it "visiting" the scarecrows.

She was not quite sure when she had first noticed their individuality, probably the morning she had found three pressed against the fence at the back of the house. It wasn't just that they were sexually differentiated. They also possessed little quirks of expression, marks of individuality. They reminded Sue of crude embryos or mummies. She concluded that in making them George Pownall practiced an ancient rural art. Her imagination had taken flight. She wanted to draw them, could imagine them being exhibited at a County Show, perhaps even in the folklore section of a museum. The carved African mask, the totem animals of other cultures were now prized and accepted as art; why not these scarecrows?

When Ashton had come by later in the morning, to set them up in the field, she had asked him about them, how they were made, why such care was taken to give each its own personality. He had smiled at her, his eyes moving restlessly over her body, and said that she'd have to ask his father about that. Him, he preferred shooting the crows, a bit of sport. They didn't come near their own dead anyway. Sue remembered the ones she had seen in Ashton Wold and shuddered at the memory. This was the best time, Ashton went heedlessly on, when they were getting ready for mating and nesting. Sue did not want to hear any more, made an excuse, and left him to get on with his work.

Later, she walked to the farm and found old Mr. Pownall seated outside his workroom in a patch of mild spring sunshine, sorting twigs and tying them into bunches. She learned from him that the basic craft was handed down, father to son, but that each maker had his own idiosyncrasies, his trademarks, as it were. Once the Pownalls had made scarecrows for the whole county, but now there was no demand. Modern farmers had mechanical scarers, guns and robots. He doubted that Lucas would follow after him. Nor was it just a matter of the craftsman's personal pride to make them different. Crows weren't stupid and soon lost their fear of a standing, familiar object. That's why they kept moving the scarecrows around, why they made each one different, so that the crows would never completely lose their fear. Yes, she could draw them, if she'd a mind to. He told her how to use the little paths, to ask Ashton if a scarecrow was moved before she had finished studying it.

She had begun in the field immediately behind the cottage, annotating her sketches with penciled questions: How was this suggestion of a cheekbone achieved? Why did this one have the belly of a Falstaff? And now she had worked her way across behind Gatherings Copse to where a solitary scarecrow stood aloof. It was a male, wearing a faded blue denim shirt, with epaulettes and button-down pockets. Her heart froze, seemed to shrivel and clench inside her.

Gavin, selecting a shirt that evening before he left her. She had turned away, drawing a plastic bag over his business suit which he would hang in the rear of the car. When she next looked at him he was buttoning the cuffs of a denim shirt, with epaulettes and button-down pockets. She could still feel the texture of it, the warmth of his body as she laid her hand briefly against his chest.

"Gavin?" she whispered.

The scarecrow was set in the middle of the great field, inaccessible unless she broke the rules and risked trampling the crops. For a moment her head whirled. How could she, at a time like this, allow rules to stand in her way? Her sketchpad slipped from her fingers unnoticed. A gust of wind bellied the blue shirt.

Ta-ta-t'-tap.

The figure swayed a little. She stepped into the field, her shoes sinking into the soft, deep earth.

"Gavin?" she whispered again.

A cloud, moving fast, passed across the sun. She saw its shadow reach across the field, envelop the waiting scarecrow, engulf her. It acted like a cold shower. She stopped, looked down at her feet, at the mashed green seedlings protruding from the soles of her shoes. She was trembling. Blood mounted to her face. She looked back at her fallen sketchpad. She was crazy, crazy. She turned and, biting her lower lip, carefully retraced her steps, placing her feet in the track she had already impressed upon the soil. Embarrassment flooded her. She looked around, afraid of being observed, and quickly picked up her pad. She followed the green path, almost running, without looking back. It led her to the rear of the ruined schoolhouse. Out of breath, shivering with fear of herself, Sue leaned against the lichen-green wall, the pad hugged to her breasts. She did not want to admit what she had almost done, did not want to acknowledge that, for a moment, she had mistaken a thing of straw and sticks for a man. She had to get a grip on herself, control her mind before fancy carried her over the brink.

She pushed away from the wall, shaking her head as though to clear it of cobwebs, of nonsense. She walked briskly, a determined woman, perfectly in control, around the building and onto the road. She had frightened herself badly. Her mind had slipped momentarily out of control. It would not happen again. She would be vigilant.

As she approached the copse, she paused for a moment and looked back into the field where the scarecrow stood. She caught her breath. Her heart tripped, then fluttered too fast. The scarecrow had turned around, was now facing the schoolhouse, its arms outstretched as though yearning for something lost.

On Thursday, Evie came down with the flu. Her throat felt raw and tight. Pain pounded in her temples and every muscle in her body seemed to clench and ache. Her temperature soared and, exhausted, sweating, she crawled into her bed, pulling the covers over her head. Sue would have to look out for herself. Evie was good for nothing.

"You're having me on," Hettie said, her fresh face crinkled with laughter.

"No," Sue protested. "I told you. It was definitely facing toward the schoolhouse. Before it had been—"

"Scarecrows can't move," Hettie interrupted, her voice high with scorn. "At least not without our Ashton to lift and carry them, they can't."

"It frightened me," Sue said simply.

"It must've been Ashton, playing his crazy tricks."

"I'd have seen or heard him."

Sue saw the look, suspicious, pitying, apprehensive, settle on Hettie's plump features.

"You think I'm mad," she said, wanting it brought out into the open, discussed and dismissed.

"I never said . . ."

"Well, I'm not. I've been working. Look." She pointed to a flat package, already wrapped and addressed. "I've finished the illustrations for that book. I'm going into Nene this afternoon to post them. I'm going to keep myself busy. I've even had an idea for a book of my own."

"That's good," Hettie said. "Yes, that's best. And it'll do you good to go into town."

"I know. You see, I'm perfectly in control."

" 'Course you are."

"Just as long as that's clear," Sue said briskly, lifting the package and moving it unnecessarily from one part of the kitchen to another.

Hettie watched her, her eyes veiled.

"You won't want to be bothering with that other stuff, then," she commented.

"Stuff, what stuff?"

"Charms and such."

Sue turned slowly toward her, two bright spots of color flushing her cheeks. "You've found something for me?"

"Maybe," Hettie said cautiously. "If you're really interested, that is."

"You know I am."

"After what you've just told me . . ."

"That was a trick of the imagination; all right? This is something I'm interested in. I just want to know. Oh, I probably won't even attempt to do it. You're right. I'm sure it's all nonsense, but I would like to know."

"Very well, then. I'll come by and explain it to you, if you're sure."

"Yes."

"All right, then."

She turned to the door, pulled it open.

"When?" Sue said sharply, anxiety grating in her voice.

"Soon," Hettie replied carefully. "There's things to be got first. You want it all right and proper, don't you?"

"Yes," Sue agreed, realizing that she must not appear too eager.

"Then I'll let you know," Hettie said, closing the subject. "You have a nice time in Nene now. Give yourself a proper break."

"I will. Thank you."

Sue stood in the doorway, feeling the warm sun on her body, and watched Hettie go.

There were only two scarecrows in the field now. Ashton must have removed one. Funny, she hadn't heard his tractor or seen him from the windows. She must really have been engrossed in her book, which was a good sign, she thought. A very good sign indeed.

He watched her from the shadows of the old Corn Exchange, which played host on Thursdays to itinerant stall-holders who bellowed their wares at the heart of the market. He saw her come out of the post office and hesitate for a moment, as though abashed by the crowds; then she turned toward him and began to walk slowly along the pavement, window shopping. He kept his eyes on her, easily detaching himself from the bustle and chatter of the market crowds. He drew back a little when, for a moment, she glanced across the street, toward the stalls, but she did not see him. Her attention turned to the bay window of a boutique, Francesca's, which offered a range of expensive and trendy clothes to the well-heeled wives of Brooking and Nene itself. After inspecting the window, she went in, and he slid from the shadows, pushing his way through the crowd to idle at a corner of the shop window.

He could see her inside, moving around the shop, inspecting garments, smiling briefly at the sales assistant. She was much taken by a dusky pink sweater. It was made of some kind of fuzzy wool, in a loose, fancy stitch. The color would complement her, he thought, watching her hand feel the texture of the garment. He imagined it stretched across her loose breasts, flattering her natural shape. She glanced at the price tag and immediately moved away from the sweater, a look of regret on her face. He could not help smiling to himself and, for a brief, weak moment, thought that he would like to buy it for her. He pushed the absurd idea away and moved along the window as she came to the shop door and opened it.

"Well, well, what a pleasant surprise," he said, looking down into her startled face. "The very person."

"Hello, Mr. Simmons," Sue said, trying to keep her tone neutral.

"You've saved me a journey, Miss Jackman," he said, taking hold of her elbow. "You can spare me a few minutes?"

"Why?" she said, trying to pull away from his grip. But he held on, steering her down the street. "Where are you taking me?"

"Not to the police station, never fear."

"But you wouldn't have any reason, would you?" Sue responded, at last snatching her arm free.

Simmons did not answer this. Instead, he pointed across the street to a double-fronted café, the Copper Kettle.

"A cup of tea?" he said. "Or would you prefer coffee?"

"Either," Sue answered, and walked to the edge of the pavement, waiting for a gap in the traffic.

He escorted her across the street and held the door of the café for her with elaborate courtesy. All the time Sue felt that he was patronizing her, even laughing at her deep down inside. He ordered tea for them both.

"You're sure you can spare the time?" he asked.

She didn't reply.

"You're not meeting anyone?"

"No."

"I thought perhaps Mr. Carpenter?"

"Sorry to disappoint you, but I am not in the habit of meeting Mr. Carpenter, nor is it one I intend to acquire," Sue said. "Now, what did you want to see me about?"

He looked at her, deliberately letting the silence stretch. His eyes were openly lascivious and that made her feel embarrassed, at a disadvantage.

"What a pity we have to talk business—such unpleasant business, too."

The tea arrived and they waited in silence until the waitress had gone.

He poured the tea and she took her cup before he could hand it to her. She rested the saucer in her left hand, held it and the cup a little above the table so that he could see that she was quite steady.

"I know Trope signed the cottage away some time ago," he said flatly, his voice grating a little.

"He signed it over to me."

"I thought as much."

It was almost a relief to her that he knew. "Yes," she said. "I only just found out myself. Tom Carpenter told me, the day you saw us in the pub. I've got the documents at home."

"Why didn't you tell me before?"

"I didn't think it was any of your business. Besides, since I didn't know, I daresay I thought it would only confirm your theory that I murdered Gavin."

"Oh, come now, Miss Jackman. Murder is only a little speculation, not a theory." He sat back in his chair, pulled a packet of cheroots from his pocket and slowly unwrapped one, crushing the crackling cellophane into the ashtray. "No, it's much more likely that he'll get in touch with you, ask you to sell and take the proceeds to him. And I think it is probably true that he kept you in the dark. A very wise move, I should say."

"Indeed? Why is that?"

"So you wouldn't have to lie. You're not very good at it, I should guess. And you'd be more likely to do as he asks when you're worried and so relieved to know that he's all right that you'd do anything, no matter how foolish."

"I see."

"So what are your plans now?"

"I have none. I'm just going to wait and see."

"And if my theory is right?"

Sue set her cup down, looked him straight in the eyes.

"We'll both have to wait and see, won't we?"

Simmons chuckled then. He sounded, for once, genuinely amused.

"Oh, but I can't wait, Miss Jackman. I really look forward to the day you put that cottage on the market." He leaned forward suddenly, all trace of humor leaving him. "Do you know why? Because that's the day I'll get you, Miss Jackman. I'll get you and Trope."

"Is that a threat?" she asked, feeling the familiar rush of fear he always seemed able to start in her.

"No, Miss Jackman, that's a promise."

He held her eyes for a long moment, searching them. When his gaze finally released her, Sue stood up.

"Thanks for the tea," she said.

"Oh, please, you haven't finished." He half rose from his chair, all courtesy again.

"We've nothing more to discuss, Mr. Simmons. I'd like to get on with my shopping now."

She walked around the table, moved quickly to the door. Simmons forced himself not to look around. Slowly, he lit his cheroot and blew a cloud of smoke toward her empty chair, his mind turning over, remembering the pink sweater, the way she had touched it, how she would have looked in it.

Simmons had taken the shine off her day. Probably, she thought as she laced her way through the shoppers, that was what he had intended to do. She felt relief, though, that he knew about the cottage. The man himself never ceased to astonish and anger her. How did a man get to be like that and how could he bear to live with himself? There was a predatory crudeness about him that was entirely reductive, she thought. He narrowed the possibilities of human contact to a bleak inevitability. There was no richness, no grace about him. She was glad that she had not allowed him to intimidate her. Thank God, she thought as she turned into the parking lot, she had never known another man like him. She felt better suddenly, remembering what Simmons had told her.

It's much more likely that he'll get in touch with you . . . get in touch with you . . . get in touch with you.

Oh, yes. She believed that too. And surely he wouldn't say that if he didn't have reason? It was his job to find out. He must know much more than he said. Her heart thrilled at what seemed to be the certainty of it. She could not wait now to get home, to take up her place by the telephone, to wait and watch for Gavin. In a way, she actually felt grateful to Simmons, for he had reinforced her hope.

"I'll fetch the milk over straight after evening milking," Hettie said.

Sue nodded absently as Hettie let herself out. Stretched on the flat of her hand, cushioned by a bed of tissue paper, was a little twig-and-feather manikin. It seemed to her identical in every way to the one she had found at the bottom of the egg basket, the one that had frightened Gavin. Now it was to be the instrument of his recall. The manikin, she realized, was like a miniature scarecrow, tattered clothing cunningly suggested by the single feather. But what a cheap kind of magic this was that used a single artifact for both greeting and conjuring. She felt a laugh burn in her and set the thing aside on the kitchen counter. She had not, after all, inspected the other one as closely. There might very well be differences, subtle, apparent only to the practiced eye.

Hettie had also brought a plastic bag. Sue knew what it contained but she untwisted the wire fastener at the neck and dug her hand into the soft contents. Feathers. White and gray-speckled chicken feathers plucked from freshly slaughtered birds —while they were still warm, Hettie had said. Sue held a fistful of feathers. Several escaped from her clenched hand, disturbed by her shallow breathing. She watched them drift, like little coracles on an invisible sea, to the kitchen floor. Sighing, she released the rest of the feathers back into the bag and fastened it.

She felt somewhat as she had that last morning in Birmingham when she had been conscious of being poised between two lives. Now, as she walked into the sitting room, she knew that a clear moment of choice was approaching. She felt almost as though she stood a little back from herself, and that the part of herself that stood back was a level-headed young woman fighting off panic—the panic of loneliness and rejection. She was a product of the second half of the twentieth century and knew that only detection and search located the missing and the dead, not tricks and mumbo jumbo. This young woman did not believe in magic, saw ahead beyond the contemplated ritual to disappointment, failure.

This rational woman watched another, a woman in the grip of a mind fever, who kept her shoulders hunched and her head bent, whose brain darted and trembled, circled around upon itself. Her bright but sunken eyes, the unnatural flush of her pallid cheeks, betrayed the turmoil and the obsession within. She moved in fits and starts, began gestures that remained unfinished. It seemed at any minute that she might moan aloud, or throw herself down on the floor, wailing.

It should have been possible to keep these two women separate, to choose clearly and definitely between them. But they had one crucial thing in common that made choice irrelevant, if not impossible. They were connected by grief. Even as she saw this, Sue was no longer an onlooker. Back in the prison of her own body, looking from the fixed perspective of her own eyes, she saw and accepted the umbilical cord of grief. Grief for the absent lover, for the left-behind self. Grief for the empty house, symbol of the empty life. Grief for his body lying in a ditch somewhere, unshriven and unmourned. Grief for herself, betrayed and rejected, occupying no corner of his mind.

She clasped her arms across her chest, digging her fingers painfully into the soft flesh of her upper arms. She would not think that way, dare not. Those were the small and nasty thoughts of a Simmons, of a Tom Carpenter, who saw everything in terms of chicanery and defection, who simply could not believe that a man could be good and caring and loyal—especially not a man who took a younger mistress and installed her in the cottage of his dreams. How desolate and sad those dreams looked now, the polished surfaces filmed over with dust.

As soon as she saw the room as it was, Sue began to clean up. She paused when she found a letter, unopened, forgotten. She had no idea when it had come. The postmark was smudged, indecipherable, the return address written in an unfamiliar hand. She tore open the envelope. The letter was shakily signed by Myra Trope. It had been dictated to her nurse.

> If you know where my husband is, if you have any means of contacting him, I beg of you to let me know. I feel that I can no longer support this awful not knowing.

A trick, she thought, dreamed up by Simmons, in which Myra naturally enough colluded. Then she felt ashamed and, rereading the letter, heard the authentic voice of a grieving woman, as frightened and alone as she was herself. A woman already diminished by illness, perhaps Myra was the only other person who could understand. The cleaning forgotten, Sue now turned to the manikin and bag of feathers, the ritual of consolation and of nightmare.

The milking machine hummed and droned with comforting familiarity as Hettie led one slightly bemused cow into a seldom used stall and tethered her close to the feeding rack. George Pownall and his two sons moved to block the open end of the stall. The old man handed Hettie his three-legged stool. She nodded her head as she took and placed it, with soothing words, beside the cow. She maneuvered the bucket into place, clasped between her plump knees, and bent over, reaching for the swollen teats. A snicker of laughter escaped Ashton as gently, gently, she squeezed and pulled, and the first long squirt of milk rang against the pail. Lucas nudged him with his elbow, cutting off his laughter. Ashton drew away from his brother and gave himself up to his imagination, imagined his own hands moving on breasts as large as the cow's udder, imagined himself suckling there, nearly suffocated by warm and scented flesh. He let his fancy roam, stirred by the sight of Hettie's competent hands, the smell of the warm milk, until the wound at the back of his head began to throb dangerously.

The milk fizzed into the bucket, setting bubbles to float on its slightly steaming surface. Lucas went to check the milking machine and to fetch the can in which Hettie would carry the milk to the cottage down the road.

The pain tightened across the back of Ashton's skull. His normally loose face became tight-clenched. His fingers moved absently back and forth across the indented wound in his skull, catching his father's weary attention. The old man moved toward him, knowing it was going to be a bitter night.

Sue watched as, tongue between her teeth, Hettie carefully poured the tepid milk into a burnished copper pan. She felt superfluous, shut out from the mystery with which this woman seemed so familiar, even comfortable.

"There," Hettie said, setting the Charming Pan aside and covering it with a stretch of white muslin weighted with glass beads that tinged and rattled against the metal. "Let that stand till you're good and ready. Don't go messing with it." She looked around her, checking. "Is the hearth swept clean, as I told you?" She darted past Sue into the living room and saw that it was. Nervously—or so it seemed to Sue, who followed after her—she tightened the belt of her old raincoat. "That's that, then."

"When should I . . . ?"

"At sunset, while the moon's rising. It'll be a full moon tonight and good clear skies. Cold, too, I'll be bound."

"Won't you stay a while?"

"No. No, thanks." She moved toward the door. Sue blocked her way.

"What is it, Hettie? What's wrong?"

"Nothing. I . . . oh, well, are you sure you want to go on with this?"

"Of course." Sue smiled, hoping that was all that was bothering her.

"Then I'll be on my way, if you don't mind."

"Surely you're not afraid?" Sue said incredulously, stepping back to let her pass.

"It's not for me to be afraid," she said pointedly.

"You think I should be?" A thought struck Sue as she followed after Hettie into the narrow kitchen. "Do you know more about this than you've told me?"

" 'Course not," Hettie answered sharply. "I've told you all I know."

"Then why are you so—?"

"Because I don't hold with meddling in things you know nothing about. I've told you so before. Some things don't seem right."

"What on earth do you think can happen?" Sue asked, laughing a little yet feeling an unpleasant tingle of nervousness.

"What do *you*?"

"I don't know," Sue began but stopped immediately because she knew that she was lying unnecessarily. "I believe that if the charm works he will hear and remember. He'll remember me. Is that so bad?"

Hettie stood at the back door, her hand on the knob, and did not turn to Sue as she said, in a shaking voice, "And what if he's dead?"

Sue caught her breath. The question seemed brutal, tactless. Perhaps Hettie thought so too, for she opened the door and stepped out into the cold, still dusk.

"Then it won't work, will it?" Sue said carefully, holding herself back from the abyss Hettie's question had opened, dark and forbidding, before her.

"I hope not, for your sake," Hettie said and closed the door behind her.

Hettie shut herself in her room, shivering. She fought a childish desire to crawl into her bed and pull the covers up over her head. It was done now. She washed her hands of it, wanted no part in it. Downstairs she could hear them moving about, doors closing.

Shirley shushing the children, getting them ready for bed. She heard the clatter of sticks, the sounds of preparation. The moon was a pale, dissolving disk in the sky as she pulled the curtains close across her window to shut it out, all of it.

She was unaware as she did so that Ashton crouched in the embrasure of his attic window, the soiled green panties pressed to his naked groin as the blood pumped and thundered in his head, maddening him.

Sue's hands were quite steady, her mind fiercely concentrated as she carried the Charming Pan to the hearth and placed it on the stones before the grate. It had been brushed with twigs and scoured with bunches of sharp-smelling grass, according to custom. Sue settled back on her heels and watched the milk sway and settle in the pan. The light in the room was dark gray and thick with shifting shadows. The match she struck flared brightly. She touched the flame to the heap of feathers in the grate, then dropped the charring, twisting matchstick into them. The feathers seemed not to burn but to melt, to collapse in on themselves, until there shot up a thread of black and oily-looking smoke. It rose steadily, straight up the chimney, as though drawn by a string.

Quietly, as though afraid to disturb something sleeping, Sue moved back and lifted the manikin from its tissue cocoon. She held it between the tip of her thumb and forefinger so that it was silhouetted against the milk.

"Come, my love," she whispered. "Come, my love, to a maid heart-sore."

Next, in a single, unbroken gesture, she raised the tiny twig-and-feather model to her lips and lightly kissed it. After a moment's pause, she placed the manikin on the surface of the milk in such a way that its feather garment rose clear of the liquid. It floated lightly and easily, face down, like a drowned man. Quickly now, for speed was important, she struck another match and lit the feather. It caught at once, burned green, then flared bright yellow, sending up a wisp of acrid smoke. As the feather burned down, the manikin began to move. She watched it, holding her breath as it traversed the pan. Then, as the flames began to lick along the twigs, it began to scutter and circle. Charred motes of the burned feather lay on the rippling surface of the milk. The flames struggled for possession of the dry twig against the rising moisture of the milk, sending up bright, brief sparks. Sue leaned across the pan, as she had been instructed, and emptied the remainder of the feathers onto the smouldering ash pile in the grate. They flared up at once, startling her, making her recoil. This brisk flare lit the surface of the pan where the last defeated flame flickered. Immediately after it had gone out, she snatched the blackened and warm manikin from the milk and dropped it among the burning feathers. There was a hissing sound and then a new flame rose up in the center of the others—a pale, translucent blue in the midst of yellow. Concentrating on her wish, her heart's desire, she watched this flame until it died down, until curls of feather ash began to rise up the chimney and the only sign of burning was the first thread of smoke, black and straight, rising again from a red glow in the grate.

This gave her just enough light to see that the soots and motes on the surface of the milk had formed themselves into a recognizable shape, a known configuration. Holding her breath so as not to disturb their precious patterning, she leaned over the pan and saw a stark black *G* inscribed upon the white surface of the milk.

Having decided on the spur of the moment to visit Sue, Tom was careful to keep his hopes down. She probably wouldn't even let him in. But he would see her, hear the sound of her voice, and she would know, whether she wanted to or not, that he cared. And since he planned to make many more such calls, she would gradually begin to understand how much he cared and perhaps would grow to like him a little. He would bring no more flowers, make no attempts to corner her into having dinner or going out with him. He would state his case simply, without pressure. He thought about her, and wanted to see her, know that she was all right.

He began to hum, thinking what a perfect night it was for a romantic excursion. The moon was low but full, a sulfurous yellow shading to silver, a mysterious rainbow-colored aureole around it. Already it shed a clear but soft light across the countryside. Diamondlike points of glitter, the first signs of a hard frost, showed in his headlights as he sped on. He would almost be able to drive back without headlights. When the moon was at its zenith there would be enough light to see the road by.

The moon was rising quickly now, stark and sharp against the cloudless sky. It flooded the great flat plain of Hemming with its mysterious light, casting shadows impenetrably black and sharp, as though drawn with geometrical instruments. The plowed fields were barred and striped, the new plants washed to silver insignificance. The scarecrows that dotted the plain cast their shadows like second selves, black mirror images that seemed embossed upon the land.

The moon was reflected in the blank front windows of the cottage, each small imperfection in the glass spoiling the completeness of the sphere so that it took on a wavering, underwater appearance. The light inside the cottage was gray, dusty. Sue sat with her back to the windows, waiting. The silence buzzed against her ears. No breath of wind. No sound within. She sat on the very edge of her seat, ready to leap up. She stiffened when she heard it, a thudding sound, irregular, yet repeated, coming closer. Her hands broke out in a damp sweat. The sound was not exactly that of footsteps, yet she could put no other name to it. It was an irregular, limping gait, each foot placed heavily, awkwardly, with a rest between each pace. Her heart jumped at the thought of injury, and she rose fearfully from her chair, turned toward the silvered windows. For a while she did not dare to move, but stood in full moonlight, visible to anyone outside. The thudding sound came again, and she fancied she heard a kind of creaking as of a branch bent intolerably by a gale-force wind. But there was no wind to cause such a sound.

Ta-ta-t'-tap.

Just as there was no wind to rattle the boards of the neglected fence.

Ta-ta-t'-tap.

It was more insistent, this familiar sound, as though calling to her, demanding a response. Her breath hissing, her body bumping against unseen furniture, she went to the window, then pressed against the wall at the side of it, out of the full light of the high moon.

Ta-ta-t'-tap. Ta-ta-t'-tap.

He came out of the moonlight, a black shape, moving steadily toward the window. She caught her breath, a cry of joy and recognition clogged in her throat. But there was something wrong, something badly wrong. He could not walk properly. His progress was slow, as though one or both legs were stiff at the joints, had to be swung out from the hip in order to gain ground. She pressed forward, her breath misting the cold window so that she could not see. The black bulk of his shape, pressed against the window, obliterated the light. She moved back, intending to open the door, throw herself into his arms, but a scrabbling, scratching noise at the window stopped her. That sound, that insistent raking at the glass was not, could not be human. She felt for the lamp beside her, almost knocking it over. The bulb was of low wattage, the shade thick, but when she stepped away from it, sufficient light hit the window to show her what knocked and tapped and scrabbled for admittance. At first they had the appearance of fingers, bone-thin and spiky, but then she recognized the stiffness of twigs, the wooden bone of the stiff wrist.

"No," she shouted and fell back against one of the sofas.

The thing wore a blue denim shirt. She saw the open cuff flapping about the gnarled wrist as the raking bunch of twigs jabbed and clawed continuously at the impeding glass. She wanted to scream, to close her eyes, but was powerless to do either. Then, for just a moment, the whole room seemed to explode with light. She saw half a ghastly skeletal face, eye-socket and slack jaw covered with sacking. The light settled. There was a cry, and then her window was blank, a yellow square of fixed light.

Tom did not know what the hell it was. Later, he was to think that he had first become aware of it as his car raced from the shadows of Gatherings Copse and he got a clear sight of the cottage, its façade bright and two-dimensional in the moonlight. But what was it? A sort of rag, flapping at the window? A web perhaps, or a blown curtain? As he drew closer and began to slow down, he swung the car instinctively across the road so that his headlights swept across the house. For a second he saw something humanly inhuman. He halted with a screech of tires and threw open the door. By the time he had extricated his long legs from the car, the creature was already moving away. Beyond the reach of his lights, it was lumbering with surprising speed, mere movement in the dark shadows cast by the house. He yelled at it—at *him*—and gave chase. His big stride carried him swiftly forward, across the uneven patch of grass that fronted the house. He shouted again, uncertain now as to where the thing, the intruder, was. Then something caught his ankle, drove hard into his knee, and with an involuntary cry of fear he pitched forward, his hands sliding against splintering wood. With a loud crash, the tumbledown fence gave beneath the full force of his weight. He and the sagging fence fell to the ground and he rolled over, the breath driven from his body.

He lay there on his back, feeling sick and dizzy, unable to catch his wind. Light flooded the garden and he felt the approach of timid steps. The beam of a flashlight crept up his body, blinded his eyes.

"You," she said, her voice shocked and trembling.

He put his hand up against the beam to shield his eyes. She saw that the back of it was grazed, the skin scraped free, blood beading the strong, thick fingers. Wincing, panting, he managed to sit up. He was surrounded by splintered wood, his legs entangled in it.

"What are you doing here? What were you doing at my window?" Sue cried, shrinking back from him.

"It wasn't me—for God's sake! But I saw it, saw something."

She watched, not sure that she could believe him, as he tried awkwardly to lever himself out of the mess of the fence.

"Please," he said. "I swear it wasn't me. If you'll just help me . . ."

Relenting, Sue pushed some of the wood away with her foot and took hold of his outstretched arm. He managed to get shakily to his feet, then bent over, coughing, clutching his stomach.

"You'd better come inside," she said.

He did not answer or move. She stood near him, uncertain what to do, while his breathing gradually settled.

"Park my car," he said, straightening a little, but still panting. "It's all over the road."

She turned and saw the car, its engine still running, diagonally blocking the road.

"I can manage," he grunted as she turned back to him, and to prove it he took a few, staggering steps toward the house.

Sue used the flashlight to find a safe path across the uneven ground. She had never driven a sports car, but after a quick inspection of the unfamiliar controls, she put it cautiously into reverse. Once she had straightened the car, it was an easy matter to drive it up onto the verge before the house, where she parked it. Light spilled from the open door and uncurtained windows of the cottage, lighting her way back.

Where had the intruder gone? She looked nervously toward the dark side of the house and felt panic catch at her throat.

Inside, Tom was stretched along one of the big settees, his pale trousers streaked with grass and mud, his hands bleeding a little. His breathing was shallow and obviously painful. Sue pushed the door shut, grateful to be inside, and went toward him, a frown of anxiety on her face.

"Hello," he grinned, wincing a little. "Sorry about the dramatic entrance. I'd planned it otherwise."

As she bathed his hands in disinfectant and removed the worst of the splinters with a pair of tweezers, Sue was glad of his presence. The scrabbling horror at the window seemed to recede, to belong to another night, another time. Tom's being there enabled her to get it all into some kind of perspective. Anticipating the inevitable questions he would ask helped to distract her mind from what had happened. Perhaps she had imagined the whole thing. A trick of the wind; her own, overstimulated imagination. The act of bathing and drying Tom's scratches, and applying salve and strips of sticking plaster to them, was soothing. Her mind gradually seemed to right itself again, become steady. Apart from an occasional wince of pain, Tom was silent throughout, as though he knew that she needed time to recover her composure.

Sue carried the bowl of sharp-smelling, cloudy water into the kitchen, emptied and rinsed it. She dried her hands slowly, feeling suddenly drained of all energy.

"I expect you'd like a drink," she said, coming back into the brightly lit sitting room.

"It would be a lifesaver. You look as though you could use one, too."

"Yes," she said vaguely, pushing her tumbled hair out of her face. "What would you like?"

"Brandy?"

She nodded and went to the bar and poured two generous shots.

"Can you manage?" she asked as, awkwardly, he took the glass.

"Yes, fine. Thank you." He raised the glass toward her in a half salute, and then sipped gratefully.

Watching him, Sue also drank, feeling the sharp warmth of the brandy burn her throat, then spread comfortably across her chest.

"Well," he said, leaning back against the sofa.

"Yes." She moved away, sat on the other sofa, at the far end.

"I meant, well, what on earth was all that about?"

"I don't know."

"You didn't see anything at your window?"

"I'm sorry I thought it was you. No, I really didn't see anything clearly. Did you?"

"But you must have," he said, his voice rising on a note of incredulity.

"I was upstairs," she lied, not wanting to mention the foolishness of the charm. She hurried on: "I heard a noise, a sort of scratching. I couldn't find the light switch. By the time I got the lamp on, you'd arrived. Your lights confused me."

He seemed satisfied with this, at least for the moment. He looked down at his brandy, thoughtfully.

"It's probably just as well," he said.

"So, what was it?" she asked, tensing herself for the answer. "What did you see?"

"I'm not sure. Look, I don't want to alarm you, but there was definitely someone out there."

"Some*one*?" she asked, lifting her eyes to his.

"Well . . . I suppose. Hell, what else could it have been?"

"I don't know." She felt him looking at her curiously. "Of course you're right," she said quickly.

"You sound remarkably calm about it."

"It was all so sudden. . . . Anyway, it's over now. No harm done." To her own ears her voice sounded overbright, but Tom did not appear to notice.

"Has anything like this happened before?"

"No."

He was silent for a while, swirling the brandy around his glass.

"You really shouldn't be here by yourself. You must see that now. And you must report this to the police."

"What could I say?"

"That someone was trying to get in through your window. It looked to me as though he was lunging at the glass, trying to break it."

She twisted around, over her shoulder, to look at the window. "It's not broken."

"It was all so quick. I never got a good look at him. Just a shape, you know? Dark movement."

"Please," she said, getting up suddenly. "I'd rather not go on talking about it."

"Sorry, I should have realized. I didn't mean to upset you."

"I don't know what to do about your clothes," she said quickly, changing the subject. "Those stains."

"Don't worry about that."

"I feel responsible."

"Nonsense. Anyway, they're only clothes—replaceable."

"How do your hands feel?"

"Smarting a bit. You make a good nurse."

"It was kind of you to chase him off."

"Reflex," he said. "If I'd thought, I might have remembered the fence."

She laughed a little, not easily but with warmth. She was beginning to like this lanky young man.

"I've been meaning to pull it down anyway."

"I've rather saved you the bother," he said, smiling.

"Yes. More brandy?"

"Just a drop, if I may. I didn't mean to intrude on you."

"But you were coming to see me?" she asked, her back to him as she freshened his drink.

"Yes, I was."

"For any special reason."

"No, just to say hello, how are you."

She brought his glass back to him.

"You telephoned my sister. I wish you hadn't."

He ducked his head like a boy caught in some naughtiness. The gesture she saw was not feigned.

"I'm sorry. I was worried about you—I think, after tonight, with some justification, don't you?"

"That won't happen again," she said definitely. "You needn't worry."

"You don't know that. You can't be sure."

"Oh, yes, yes."

"May I ask—" He stopped as her expression changed, became veiled and hostile. "Did your sister come to stay?" he asked instead. Her relief was instant and obvious.

"No. She got the flu."

"I'm sorry. I shouldn't have rung her."

"No."

"But, really, it's not safe for you to stay here alone. You must see that now."

"Not safe? That's nonsense."

"There was somebody at your window," he said, his voice tightening with anger.

"You didn't really see anyone, though, did you? Moonlight plays strange tricks."

"I saw something. You know I did. *You* saw it, too. It's written all over you. But you're not going to tell me so."

He held her eyes, willing her to contradict him. After a while she said, "You're in no condition to drive. You'd better stay the night."

"Thank you. I'd like that."

"I'll make up the spare bed." She put down her glass.

"No, please, don't do that."

She looked at him, waiting.

"I'll be perfectly comfortable here, really. And I'd like to be downstairs in case your mysterious visitor returns."

"Oh, I see. Well, if you're sure, I'll fetch some blankets and pillows."

"Fine."

As she went upstairs, Tom stood up and stretched his legs. He walked to the window and peered out. The moon floated high, already seemed to be losing its brilliance. As he turned back into the room, his eye fell upon the hearth. Curious, he went to it and stooped over the copper dish of milk in which little black flecks floated. There was the lingering, slightly acrid smell of burned feathers. He reached down and tested the ash in the grate with the tip of his finger. It disintegrated at once, fell away into a dust. He started up guiltily when he heard her step on the stairs. He watched her descend, his back to the hearth.

"There you are," she said, dumping pillows and blankets onto the couch.

"Thanks."

"I think I'll—"

"What's this?" He stepped aside so that she could see the ashy grate, the bowl of ash-sprinkled milk.

"Oh, I'd forgotten all about—I'll clear it away."

She hurried forward, squatted, lifted the pan in her hands.

"What were you doing?"

She hesitated. Her hand shook. The milk slopped against the shallow side of the pan.

"I was trying out a recipe. An old one. You have to warm the milk very gently over an open flame. I got it all wrong, got soot in it, as you can see." She stood up, the bowl pressed against her.

"A recipe for what?"

"Oh, cheese, a sort of curd cheese."

"Sue, if there's something you can tell me . . ."

"Of course," she said brightly, and carried the bowl into the kitchen. "I'll do better than that," she called. "When I've made some, you can try it."

He did not answer. He listened to the milk being poured away, the rattle of the pan. She came slowly back into the room and closed the door behind her.

"I'd like to go to bed now," she said. "Help yourself to anything you want."

"Sue, I came here tonight to see how you were. I was planning to tell you how much I care about how you are. I won't go into that now, but I do know that you cannot stay here. Even if there's no physical danger from whatever was out there, I don't think—I mean mentally, this place, all that you've suffered here, the isolation, it's no good for you."

He half expected her to be angry, but to his relief she remained calm.

"Perhaps you're right, but that's all over now. Things are going to be different. I realize that now. And it's really very nice of you to be so concerned. Good night, Tom."

He could not stop himself moving toward her. He caught her hand on the banister rail. She let it lie passively under his, but did not look down at him. The words froze in his throat.

"Good night," he said, and let her go.

And if Tom had not come? Sue lay wide-eyed in the dark and considered it. Would she have opened the window or the door to the scarecrow? There was an extraordinary relief in naming what she had seen. She thought, in all honesty, that if Tom had not come, she might have been crazy enough to let it in. The easily recalled sight of the twig hand at the window, the brief glimpse of the skeletal face still had the power to make her recoil. Her flesh cringed at the imagined touch of that dry wood hand scratching and scraping. It was like an electric shock, jolting her back to normality. She had been mad, she realized, had allowed herself to give way to something dark and unfathomable. She had heard of people unhinged by grief, but hesitated to explain her own behavior thus. She felt responsible for it. After all, she had chosen. What had been at the window was the scarecrow she had seen in the field behind the schoolhouse, the one she had mistaken for Gavin, the one that had moved while her back was briefly turned. How this was possible she did not know. The mere idea scared her. And perhaps that was all it was, an idea. Perhaps it was all rooted in her and she was in the process of discovering what other dupes and self-deluders had discovered before her—the true definition of magic. It is in the mind of whoever wants it. The mind works magic. But there were other explanations. There had to be. After all, scarecrows could not move without Ashton Pownall to lift and carry them. Hettie had said so firmly enough. Hettie, she vowed, had some straight talking to do.

Below, she heard Tom shifting on the couch, trying to settle himself comfortably, and again thought: What if he had not come? His presence in the cottage was comforting and made sleep possible.

But not for Tom. In part this was because just being under the same roof as she was excited him and made him feel very alive. But more important was his increasing sense of anxiety. This anxiety was centered upon, and caused by Sue, not by the highly unlikely possibility that the intruder might return. He did not believe Sue's story about making cheese and was certain that she had seen more at the window than she would admit. Perhaps she even knew who it was and felt able to handle the situation alone? What the dish of milk and the burned feathers meant he had no idea, nor could he form any meaningful connection between them and what he had seen. What tied them together in his mind was her manner, her transparent lying. When she spoke of either, she wore the same air of someone inventing, covering up, improvising. Therefore he had to consider the possibility that he had interrupted some surreptitious visit from Trope. That, more than any other theory, would explain her behavior. The trouble was, what he had seen was not Trope, was not wholly or simply human. To that he would swear. How to describe it, then? he challenged himself, but the challenge went unanswered. It was human and yet not human. His mind collided with the blank wall of it and turned to Sue instead. Her calm was unnatural. The balance in her seemed precarious. He concluded where he had begun: the greatest danger to her was in isolation, from her own mind.

He got up at first light and watched the dawn creep in from the east. At sunrise, a red threat that set the frosty world shining, he let himself quietly out onto the whitened grass, filling his lungs with raspingly cold air. Then, taking his time, shivering against the biting cold for which he was not properly dressed, he inspected the area beneath the window for footprints, tracks. There had been no frost yesterday. The soil would have been soft and tacky. He found no mark of foot or shoe, only a series of widely spaced square indentations and a little scattering of twiglets. He examined these and the marks carefully. An absurd idea flitted through his mind and was quickly dismissed. Standing from his crouched position in front of the window, he saw Sue coming down the stairs, her face bleary with sleep. He would not mention any of this to her. He would go to see Simmons instead. He considered leaving straight away, without speaking to her, but that proved impossible. He let himself back into the warm house and joined her in the kitchen. She smiled and said she was making coffee. "Did you sleep?" she asked.

"I'd like to spend the rest of my life doing this," he replied, and took the coffeepot from her warm fingers to set it upon the stove.

"That's very astute of you, Mr. Carpenter," Simmons said with only a trace of a smirk. Since he regarded his office as his sanctuary, his very private territory, he had descended to the ground floor of the ugly modern Nene Police Station and closeted himself with Tom in a barren little interview room. He stood, or rather lounged, against the wall while Tom occupied the only chair. Thus he loomed over the taller man. "The point is, can you keep it to yourself?"

"Whom would I tell?" Tom asked innocently.

"Sue Jackman, for one."

"No, that would only make her—" Tom paused, realizing his error. Telling her, really frightening her might be just the thing to make her leave the cottage.

"Quite," Simmons said drily. "The perfect way to get her out. Only I don't want her out, not yet."

"Then you must protect her," Tom said. "Round the clock, twenty-four hours a day."

"No way." The policeman shook his head.

"But you must," Tom insisted. "If you won't, I'll go over your head."

"Like you did before when you brought the Chief Constable into it?" Simmons watched Tom through narrowed eyes, enjoying the slight flush of embarrassment, but decided to let him off the hook, turning his attention to his own grubby fingernails. "You can try it if you like; it won't do you any good."

Tom made a face signifying that he was prepared to call Simmons's bluff.

"Oh, come on, man, use your head," Simmons exploded. "How could we keep a watch on her there? Everyone would know. You can see for bloody miles."

"There's the copse," Tom aruged, reluctant to admit that Simmons was right.

"And the Pownalls are in and out of it all day long. They know every inch of the place. We'd be spotted in hours." He heaved himself away from the wall and twisted around, slid one buttock onto the square table, forcing Tom to move back in his chair. "Look," he said conversationally, "we already have a car going through there twice a day. If I can get the manpower and a regular change of vehicles, I'll increase the frequency. But no promises."

"All right," Tom said. "Then it's up to me."

"No. You could put them off."

"But you can't just leave her there, without any kind of protection."

"I don't have any choice. You can make the odd social call, but I don't want you hanging about. This is a waiting game, Carpenter. I've been waiting for weeks. I'm not going to let anyone blow this one."

"Even if you have to risk Sue?" he challenged.

"The risk is minimal. Now be a good chap and say you'll cooperate."

"How long?"

The policeman shrugged, inspected his nails again. It was his belief that the case was about to break, that the waiting had become intolerable, but he didn't intend to tell that to Carpenter.

"What about her sister, then?" Tom said. "You couldn't object to her sister visiting."

"As long as she doesn't know what's going on, no."

"All right. That's a deal."

"Not a word; nothing. And I don't want you playing amateur detective, either."

"I wouldn't know how to begin," Tom said, standing up.

Simmons ignored this. "We can't prove anything," he said fiercely. "But we'll get proof if everybody—and that means you especially—keeps very still. Understand?"

"Perfectly." Tom moved to the door. "You know," he said, turning back to face the detective-sergeant, "I'm amazed. I thought you'd say I'm crazy."

"Great minds, Mr. Carpenter; great minds."

Simmons actually smiled.

It did not surprise Sue in the least that Hettie seemed to be avoiding her. The milk was delivered early, long before she was up, and she did not doubt that this was deliberate. In a way she was grateful. It gave her time to collect her thoughts. When she was good and ready, she walked to the farm, determined to say her piece. She saw no one en route. The yard and farmhouse had a deserted, somnolent feeling, but Shirley, looking preoccupied, eventually answered her knock. She did not ask Sue in but stepped out into the yard, drawing the door closed behind her.

"She's gone over to Brooking," she said of Hettie. "I can't rightly say when she'll be back."

"Perhaps your husband's around, then?"

"No, he's over in the west meadow." Shirley jerked her head vaguely toward the westerly horizon. "I could give him a message."

"No, thanks. I'll have a word with old Mr. Pownall. It's all right," Sue added, starting off before Shirley could stop or forbid her. "I know the way."

Sue felt the woman's eyes on her until she turned the corner of the house. The top half of the double stable door was open and she could smell George Pownall's tobacco. She called to him, leaning into the dark interior of his workroom. There was no reply. She looked around to see if Shirley had followed her, but the yard was quite empty. She made up her mind immediately, reached over the door, and slid back the bolt that held the lower half. The hinges were well oiled, and the door opened soundlessly. She slipped inside, closed it behind her, then stood still for a moment, letting her eyes adjust to the dimness within. Her heart was beating fast and loudly. She did not know what she was looking for, what had even prompted her to act on this impulse, but she moved away from the door into the long, narrow room.

Where on her previous visit a recognizable scarecrow had hung from the ceiling, now there was only the crude armature of another, without clothes or features. It hung like a great primitive cross, dividing the room in half. She ducked under its rigid, outstretched arm and approached the bench. There was a small dusty and cobwebbed window opposite, admitting some dusklike light. The intended hands of the scarecrow lay on the top of the bench. Staring at them, Sue told herself that they were only bunches of twigs bound together with loops of red bailing twine. She went to the bench and looked more closely at them. They were very cunningly made, the whole comprising five smaller bundles, bound together at what would be the wrist. They were of different lengths and thicknesses, the thumb and little finger clearly distinguishable as such. It was no wonder, Sue thought, that she had, for a moment, taken the twigs scratching at her window for an actual hand. The memory of those few seconds still made her shudder, but at least this closer inspection bore out her theory and strengthened her resolve to have it out with the Pownalls.

She passed along the bench, looking for anything else of interest. The far end of the room lay in deep shadow. As far as she could see it contained nothing but stacks of wood, straight ash poles bearing white wounds where they had been recently trimmed, and a sagging cardboard box of old clothes, presumably intended to dress new scarecrows. She walked toward this box and was just about to search through it, when a hand fell on her shoulder—a strong hand that gripped tight to the bone and spun her effortlessly around.

Letting out a cry of surprise and fear, she stepped backward, her heel disturbing some of the stacked poles, making them rattle with a familiar tapping sound.

Ashton Pownall released her, let out a high-pitched giggle that did little to still her jumping nerves.

"You startled me," she said.

"It's no more than you deserve," he said, his head cocked on one side, appraising her, "poking round in other folks' things. You're trespassing," he added with an attempt at solemnity that he could not sustain. His moist lips slipped into a smile.

"I was looking for your father," Sue said, taking a step toward him. He did not move.

"Thought he was hiding back here, did you?" He laughed.

"All right. I was looking around. Idle curiosity."

"Yes. You're interested in scarecrows, aren't you? I remember you going on about them." He turned to the bench, stood looking down at the hands.

Sue edged forward wondering if she could dodge past him, under the skeletal scarecrow, and out into the yard. As she drew level with him, he spun around, an explosion of fleetness and energy.

"Not so fast," he said and thrust out his arm. In his hand he held one of the bunches of twigs. He pointed it at her.

"Don't do that," Sue said. "I only wanted to see Mr. Pownall."

"I'm Mr. Pownall," he said, a note of pride in his voice.

"I meant your father."

"Well, you're out of luck then, aren't you? Hettie took him over to Brooking to see a man about a scarecrow." He laughed again, the sound bubbling in his throat, as though he had made an irresistibly funny joke.

"I'll call back then," Sue said. All she had to do, she told herself, was to walk firmly and purposely to the door.

As though he could read her mind, Ashton thrust the twig hand forward so that the sharp splinters of wood touched her cheek. Sue twisted her head away. This only made him laugh. Backing away from him, she found herself pressed up against the wall. Keeping the twigs extended toward her, Ashton moved closer, his smile slowly fading.

"Please, don't do that," Sue said.

"Pretty," he murmured and gently touched her cheek again with the twigs. Again she ducked her head aside. The twigs caught in her hair as Ashton maneuvered the twig hand in a clumsy smoothing, stroking gesture.

"Please," Sue repeated.

"It's all right, won't hurt you. What are you scared of a few old twigs for?"

"Don't you know?" Sue said, snapping her head around to face him. "It was you, wasn't it?"

The twigs lay on her shoulder, touching her face. He held them quite still.

"Don't know what you're talking about."

"They can't move, can they, unless you lift them about? Two nights ago? At my window?"

She watched his face carefully. He looked confused as though he had forgotten where he was.

"Don't know what you're talking about," he repeated and let his arm fall, the twigs still loosely grasped in his hand.

Sue pushed away from the wall. Ashton seemed to have lost interest in her. He turned away, tossed the bundle of twigs onto the bench. Sue walked quickly toward the hanging scarecrow.

"Don't go," Ashton said, hurrying after her. "I was only having a bit of fun."

"Tell your father I'll call again," she said, almost running now.

"You shouldn't go poking around . . . ," he said lamely.

Sue threw her weight at the lower door and almost fell out into the yard. She was breathing heavily and her heart was thudding. Only when she got to the corner of the house did she look back. Ashton stood in the doorway watching her with the expression of a disappointed child.

Evie's voice was still thick with cold.

"What *is* going on down there? I've had another call from that Carpenter."

"I'm sorry, Evie. I told him he shouldn't ring you. How's your flu?"

"Better than it was, but I still don't feel right."
"You won't, not yet. It takes time. Do you feel very depressed?"
"Well, yes, I do a bit. And then being worried out of my mind . . ."
"I'm all right, Evie. Honestly. Nothing to worry about at all."
"That's not what he said."
"Who are you going to believe, me or him?"
"Neither. I'm coming down to see for myself."
"Fine. A change'll do you good. When can you come?"
Evie hesitated, surprised by Sue's apparent willingness.
"Well, can I let you know? I don't feel up to a long drive yet. A couple of days, say?"
"That's fine by me."
"You seeing a lot of this Carpenter chap?"
"No, and it's nothing like that. I told you."
"Well, he's very concerned about you."
"I expect he's a very caring man, but I can look after myself."
Could she? After Sue had put the phone down she asked herself that question. She had not felt very confident with Ashton Pownall. In fact, she had been badly scared. Looking back on the incident now it seemed almost trivial. After all, she knew that he was simpleminded and probably, to him, the whole thing had seemed a harmless joke. The point was she had been frightened and had not known how to handle the situation. She still could not be sure that she knew what Ashton had wanted or intended, and, she reminded herself, some jokes were known to misfire. She also could not quite forget that he was strong, much stronger than she.

She was happy to admit that she would be glad of Evie's company. Ever since that night she had felt the isolation of her loneliness differently. It was no longer her friend, her protector. That role seemed to have been assumed by Tom Carpenter, and she really did not know how she felt about that at all. She was annoyed that he kept on pestering Evie, and yet his timely arrival that night had left her with a residue of gratitude toward him that was not easily dismissed. Tom Carpenter, like so much else in her present life, confused her. She felt like someone emerging from the dark; it would take a while for her to become accustomed again to the light.

With Evie coming she decided to clean the house from top to bottom. It was long overdue, anyway, and she would be glad to lose herself in mind-numbing physical work. She set about it cheerfully.

"You'll have to go and see her," Shirley nagged. "It'll look funny if you don't."

"She asked for Dad, not me."

"She asked for you first, Hettie."

"Well, I can't and that's all there is to it."

"Somebody's got to."

"Then make Dad go. I won't. It's not my trouble; never was."

"You're right," Shirley said bitterly. "The old man should've seen to it years ago."

"You tell him then, not me."

Shirley's expression hardened with determination.

The windows stood wide open to air the house. He waited outside unnoticed, listening to her singing lightly as she worked, then drew close to the window before calling her name.

"Oh, Mr. Pownall," she said, surprised.

"I heard you wanted to see me," he said, regarding her coolly without expression.

Sue opened the front door.

"Please come in. I'm sorry the place is in such a mess."

He made a little noise of dismissal and came into the cottage.

"Actually," Sue said, "you or any member of your family would have done. I get the impression they're avoiding me."

"And why would they do that?" he asked.

"That's what I wanted to talk about. Do sit down."

He nodded his thanks and took a seat, stretching his left leg out in front of him as though it was stiff and painful.

"A touch of rheumatism," he said, tapping the knee lightly.

Sue closed the windows.

"It's not too cold for you?"

"No."

She perched on the arm of one sofa, looking at him.

"The other night," she said, "somebody came to that window there and tapped on the glass. It frightened me. I don't know why anyone should want to do that. Perhaps they thought it was a joke. I just want to make it clear that I don't find it funny and I want you to make sure it doesn't happen again."

"Who came to your window?" he asked, folding his large, calloused hands.

"It appeared to be a scarecrow," Sue announced, daring him to laugh.

He did not. Instead he looked at her very carefully for a moment, then let his eyes drift about the room.

"In that case I don't see as how I can help you," he said simply.

"Oh, don't be so ridiculous," Sue said angrily. "Of course it wasn't a scarecrow. That's just what somebody wanted me to think. Look, I can't prove it but I think it was your son playing a stupid trick."

"My son?"

"Ashton."

He looked hurt, then a tight frown settled on his face.

"You know about Ashton? Hettie told you?"

"Yes, but that's got—"

"Oh, yes. That's the way folk are. Once they know there's something wrong with a bloke's head, even though it's not his fault, they're quick to blame. Any little thing. It must be the village idiot." He spat the words out, bitterly.

"Now hang on a minute," Sue said, the color rushing to her face. "I never said or thought anything of the kind."

"Then what did you think? What are you saying?"

"That somebody scared me badly—I think deliberately—and I don't want it to happen again."

"But it was Ashton came into your mind."

"Yes, because of what happened yesterday." Briefly she told him about the incident in his workroom.

"He means no harm. He wouldn't hurt you for anything. It's a game to him."

"I believe you. All I'm saying is, it's got to stop."

He was silent, searched through his pocket for his pipe, which he stuck unlit into his mouth, chewing at the stem.

"Would that be the night you worked the charm?"

Sue had been expecting this, though she had dared to hope that perhaps Hettie had not told her family. She did not want to talk about it even though she knew it was important.

"Yes," she admitted.

"That's different, then, isn't it?"

"I don't see how." She waited, watching his face. His silence goaded her. "All right. I was a fool to try anything so stupid. I think I was a little crazy myself. But I didn't imagine someone out there, scratching at my window. A friend of mine saw it too. Whoever it was ran off when he arrived."

"Lucky for you," he said mysteriously. Suddenly his eyes hardened. He looked at her with a kind of fervor. "You've changed. Last time we talked you were more accepting, not so angry."

"I've come to my senses," Sue snapped.

"Ah, is that it?"

Sue got up, crossed her arms. She could feel her temper simmering and she did not want to lose it.

"Look, Mr. Pownall, I don't want to quarrel about this. I just wanted you all to know that I'm not completely stupid. I have a pretty good idea what happened the other night. You knew I was going to do the charm and you thought you'd play a trick on me. I asked for it and now I've learned my lesson. Hettie did her best to warn me. But it was a cruel trick and I was badly frightened."

"I'm sorry for that," he said.

"Well, let's leave it there."

"Just as you want." He got up stiffly favoring his left leg. "But I can promise you this much. Whoever or whatever was out there that night, it wasn't Ashton."

"Then who was it?" she challenged him.

"Well, now, I'm not sure as you'd believe me if I told you."

"Try me."

"Let me ask you something first."

"All right."

"Did you never think the charm might've worked?"

Sue started to laugh but from his face she saw that he was absolutely serious. The laughter died. She felt as though an icy hand had brushed her skin.

"No," she said. Her voice sounded weak.

"Hettie was right to warn you," he said, half-sighing. "You shouldn't meddle with what you don't understand." He shook his head and hobbled over to the door.

"I shan't do anything like that again," Sue said. "I can promise you that."

"Sometimes once is enough."

"What do you mean?" She followed after him, trying to see his face, but he kept it averted.

"Folks round here would say that was the Gatherer at your window and they'd advise you to go careful, very careful."

"The Gatherer?"

It was as though a cold wind had entered the house, yet it was a still, mild day. George Pownall stood in the doorway, staring out across his flat fields.

"That's nonsense," Sue said, more to reassure herself than to argue with him.

"That's the stupidity of it," he said harshly, turning to look at her. His blue eyes were very bright, burning into her. "People like you think they can believe a part of it and not the rest. Well, it's not that way, missy. You meddled and perhaps you succeeded better than you bargained for. You can't pick and choose what you will have and what you won't. You may learn that. And that don't give you no right to go accusing innocent folk. Whatever was done was your doing."

Without another word he marched off, his gait clumsy but surprisingly strong and fast. Sue opened her mouth to call after him, but she realized that she did not know what to say. She closed the door and locked it with trembling hands.

She forced herself to return to the cleaning, but for the rest of the day it was a mechanical process, performed without zest.

The Gatherer was death. Hettie had told her. She remembered clearly.

Of course she did not believe a word of it. Such things did not, could not happen. Besides, she had been trying to reach Gavin, not—Had she believed? How could she ever have thought . . . been so stupid?

Making up Evie's bed in her workroom, Sue fought off a panicky impulse to call her sister, to beg her to come at once. She found a brief comfort in imagining Evie's expression if she should be so foolish as to tell her. Evie would have her certified in twenty-four hours flat.

The old man was just trying to frighten her because she had been clumsy and tactless about Ashton. He was understandably protective of his damaged son. Maybe she had jumped too quickly to a false conclusion, and it was not necessarily Ashton but perhaps somebody who wanted to teach her a lesson. Hettie? Perhaps jealous of all she had? Perhaps she, in a careless, self-absorbed moment, had patronized or offended the other woman. In any case, she ought to be grateful to whoever it was, cruel as the trick had been, for it had shocked her out of her madness. So why did the old man need to go on punishing her?

She could ring Tom Carpenter. He would come over. She did not know his number but could easily find it; it would be on the correspondence concerning the cottage. But she would not ring Tom Carpenter, would not encourage him to think . . . There was nothing, after all, to be afraid of, except the fancies of her own mind.

She straightened the bed, plumped the pillows. The house was now clean and shining, ready for Evie's visit.

There had been no scarecrow at her window. A scarecrow could not move and tap. A scarecrow cunningly decked out to have a fleeting, superficial resemblance to Gavin. Did they want her to think then that Gavin was the Gatherer, was death? She had caught them out there; yes, definitely.

Then anger flared in her, anger directed against Gavin. He had gotten her into this ridiculous situation. She went downstairs and hurled logs into the ceramic stove. Oh, Gavin, Gavin. The longing returned. Her anger melted to grief and loss, and she poured herself a drink, admitting that she was afraid of the approaching night.

She had found the idea of the Gatherer comforting. Now . . . She carried her drink to the window and stood there, looking out. The horizon was misty as evening crept in. She reached up and pulled the scarf from her head, shaking her hair free. She needed a bath, a good relaxing bath.

There was no such thing as the Gatherer. No one wished her any harm. She was not going to die.

A car. She heard a car and almost shouted out loud for joy. She twisted her neck, straining to see it. It began to slow. Her heart shrank with disappointment. It was not Tom's car, not Evie's. A plain, black car slowed, dawdled past the house. There were two men in it. The men looked at the house, stared. Then the car increased speed, went away. She listened until the sound of its engine became absorbed into the silence.

It was dark and she did not know how she was going to get through the night alone. Check the windows, the doors. She hurried about, testing every catch and lock, drawing the blinds, pouring herself another drink.

It was all nonsense, all in the mind. The old man was just being wicked, playing with her. Now that he knew she was on to their silly game, nothing else would happen, nothing at all. She was just frightening herself.

She heard a noise at the back of the house and froze, wide-eyed, staring into the darkened kitchen.

The silence hummed.

Nothing would happen. Nothing could happen.

Snug under the comforter in Sue's pretty pink workroom, Evie listened in disbelief to the dawn chorus. The nearest she had ever come to it was the raucous chatter of evening starlings around Birmingham Town Hall. And people said there was nothing like the country for peace and quiet! Evie didn't see how anyone could sleep through that racket. Her head was still heavy with cold and her nose badly needed blowing, but she felt better. The drive yesterday had tired her, but the warmth of Sue's welcome had made it worthwhile. Lying there, watching the light grow and creep around the edges of the blind, Evie knew that she felt better because a major anxiety had been removed. Sue really was all right. More than that, she had changed. She wasn't exactly the old Sue—whoever that might have been—but was certainly more familiar than she had seemed for a long time. But she was different, too. There was a sort of nervous anticipation about her that, under other circumstances, Evie might have regarded with suspicion. Since she felt welcome, because Sue was obviously pleased to see her, she was inclined to see everything in a positive light. On her last visit Sue had seemed dreary, lifeless, stubbornly set in her own peculiar ways. Evie knew and admitted that Sue had had reason, but that could not detract from the relief and pleasure of seeing her sister lively and friendly, full of energy again. *And* she was beginning to talk sense. Last night, over a hot toddy designed to ease Evie's stuffed nose and chest, she had talked about coming out of something she could only describe as the dark. She had even spoken obliquely of setting her life in order. Evie had not pushed her. It was enough that finally, after these many weeks, Sue was beginning to think about the future. She dared to hope that it was even becoming obvious to her sister that she could not hang on here forever, waiting for a vanished man. Some people never turned up. There were cases of people who disappeared without trace forever. Facts had to be faced.

Evie also felt better now that she knew Sue owned the cottage. Gavin had played fair by her; she had to give him that. One of her biggest worries had been Sue's financial situation. No matter what she said, drawing work was hard to come by and didn't pay that much, and with nothing regular coming in, well, it made Evie anxious sometimes just to think of it. But if she sold this place, she'd be worth a bit, would not come out of this whole fiasco empty-handed as well as brokenhearted. And Evie didn't care if that was cynical. These things mattered. She knew. She remembered how tight things had been at home before Sue was born and how much worse they got after their father died. She'd seen her mother scrimp and save, had herself gone without, and she didn't want to see that happen to Sue. Of course, this business of the police keeping her under suspicion, saying Gavin might get in touch and want the proceeds of selling the cottage, was a blasted nuisance, but common sense told her they couldn't keep that up forever. And, as she'd said to Sue last night, she could always rent the place, especially with the summer coming on. She hadn't said it very enthusiastically, though. Try as she might, she couldn't imagine anyone wanting to live in this bleak and desolate place. It was scarcely a holiday resort, although the cottage itself was nicely appointed and you never knew. All in all, Evie thought things were definitely on the upswing. She pushed herself up out of the nest of her pillows and blew her nose loudly. That felt better. Now she was wide awake. On impulse, she swung her feet to the floor and gingerly let up the blind. It was a gray morning, without much promise to it. Perhaps it would cheer up later. She tried to look on the bright side. It was that damn flat view that depressed her, nothing to see for miles except a few old scarecrows, and they gave her the creeps.

Turning away from the window, her arm brushed against Sue's drawing board, scattering a pile of drawings torn from a sketch pad. Cursing, Evie bent and gathered them together. She'd even been drawing the damn things. What on earth could she see in an ugly old scarecrow? They were good drawings though, almost lifelike, which was a crazy way of putting it, she admitted to herself, when they were only sticks and straw. But they had more than that, a kind of feature, personality. Leafing through the sheaf of drawings, Evie did not know what to call it. Then her stomach contracted and she thrust them hastily away from her. One, with a shirt billowing in the wind, looked exactly like Gavin Trope.

Sue slept on through the singing birds and Evie's early morning coughing. It was the first night since George Pownall's visit that she had been able to sleep soundly. Evie's presence comforted and reassured her. Alone, she had lain awake, listening and, in her haunted ear, hearing the scrabble of dry wooden hands at the cottage window. She knew that she was spooking herself, but no amount of reasonable self-lecturing could drive the fear away. When sleep came, it was thick with dreams that gave disturbing visual shape to her imaginings. She fled through the house as dead hands beat and clamored at the doors and windows, demanding to be let in. There was no hiding place. She started awake, her heart bounding, her hair sticking to her scalp with a cold sweat of dread. It took a long while to calm herself again, and then the familiar worries and fears would start, as often as not sparked by some inexplicable sound outside.

She had mentioned none of this to Evie and never would. Indeed, the moment Evie was installed in the house her fears faded, became foolish phantasms. A weight had been lifted from her spirits. That night, before drifting into longed-for sleep, she had been able to touch her fears and smile at them. She relegated them to the dark, to the time when she had allowed herself to believe in the charm, had consciously welcomed the idea of giving herself up to something ancient and beyond reason. Evie's cough and hoarse voice, her familiar accent and dry common sense put all the ghosts to flight. She giggled to herself at the thought of what Evie would say if she should ever confess what she had been afraid of. For all their differences, all Evie's faults, she loved her. Evie was, after all, her own flesh and blood, and dependable. As sleep crept soothingly through her body, she vowed that she would remember that, whatever happened, whatever turn her life might take.

Tom prowled around the house that afternoon. He had knocked and called, had even tried the doors, only to find them securely locked. He reasoned with himself against the panic that rose in him. If the van had not been there, parked at the side of the house, he would automatically have assumed that she had driven into Brooking or Nene. She had obviously gone for a walk, and would not be long. He would wait. He got into his car and sat there, fingers drumming impatiently on the steering wheel. He felt cramped, enclosed. He got out of the car and paced a little way up the road. The loneliness of the place hit him with full force for the first time. The only sound was the distant drone of an engine. What good was it to be able to see for miles when there was nothing to be seen? If she was out walking, surely he ought to be able to see her, a dot, a figure moving against the horizon? His panic threatened to return again. The sound of the engine had grown louder, he realized, and he knew now that it was coming from the direction of the copse. He began to walk toward it, with no particular purpose in mind. Before he had gone more than a few yards, a yellow tractor bumped onto the road from the disused barns that stood beside the copse. Behind it, clattering and bouncing, was a flatbed trailer on which something was covered by a green tarpaulin. Tom turned back to his car and watched the steady approach of the tractor. The road was narrow. Nervously, he checked that there was room for the tractor to pass without scraping his paintwork. He estimated that there was, but positioned himself by the hood of the car to make sure there was no accident. As the tractor drew close, he waved it down.

A man leaned from the cab, his tow-colored hair almost covered by a knitted gray cap. He looked suspicious, slightly amused. His wet lips were moving as though in some often repeated song, lost in the sound of the tractor. Tom had to shout.

"Do you know Sue Jackman? The lady who lives in the cottage?"

Ashton answered, but Tom could not catch the words. He understood the accompanying nod of assent, though.

"Have you seen her anywhere? I think she must have gone for a walk."

By fiddling with the dashboard, Ashton Pownall succeeded in lowering the sound of the engine appreciably.

"What say?"

"Have you seen her? I think she's out walking."

"No."

Tom did not like the appraising way the man's eyes scanned him or the lopsided smirk that settled on his lips.

"She yours?"

For a moment Tom was completely taken by surprise. He did not know whether to laugh or be angry. Then, just in time, he saw that Ashton meant his car. He was staring at it greedily, with a kind of mute longing.

"Yes," Tom admitted. "She's mine, all right."

"Nice. How much she do?"

"You can get a ton out of her under the right conditions. She's past her prime now, though."

"I used to drive fast. Hot rods, fuel-injected, stock cars. Raced and all."

"Oh? Did you enjoy that?"

"It was great, best thing . . ." His eyes seemed to mist over, his features crumpled. Ashton shook his head and put the tractor into gear. With the utmost care, he edged past Tom's car.

Still shaken by the abruptness with which the conversation had ended, Tom stepped back as the trailer rolled past him. A wooden arm in a black sleeve jutted from the green tarpaulin. He stepped back to avoid being brushed by the spiky-fingered hand. And as he turned to watch the trailer recede up the road, he could have sworn that the tarpaulin had covered everything when he had first seen it. So the load had shifted, he told himself. The thing was bouncing around enough. It was utter madness to think, as for a moment he had, that the scarecrow had reached for him. Utter madness.

It was only his mind playing tricks. He acknowledged that he was already feeling edgy. He watched the tractor and trailer become smaller, heard the sound of the engine fade to a hum. The landscape was responsible for his jumpiness, too. Its lack of distraction turned one inward. He felt, with a warm rush of sympathy, that he could understand a little of how these last long weeks must have been for Sue. His mind balked at the idea of spending days on end here, alone, with nothing to look at but the swirling sky and those bloody scarecrows.

Ta-ta-t'-tap.

A cold shiver ran down his back. Catching his breath, he swung around. There was nothing there, nothing but an ancient-looking scarecrow wearing a porkpie hat in the field opposite the house. The wind must have rattled it. Yet he had not felt any wind. He looked to the left and to the right, straining his ears for the sound again. Beyond the farm, on the long stretch of road that led toward Ashton Wold, he caught a glimpse of movement, a car, traveling quite fast. The sight was amazingly reassuring. It was still too distant for him to hear its engine, and this silence made it look more than ever like a child's toy car, pushed along by some giant, invisible hand. For seconds he was carried back into his own childhood, to the hours he had spent on hands and knees, pushing toy cars across the sitting room carpet or, in summer, up the long stretch of the flagstone garden path. He could still hear the noise he used to make—broom! vroom!—as he imitated an engine's roar. How he had loved his toy cars, how clearly he could remember them.

The memory misted and vanished as the real car disappeared behind the farmhouse and then reappeared, having slowed to take the right-angle bend. He could hear it now, make out its color. He wondered if it might be one of Simmons's promised patrol cars and if it was, if he should stop it and tell the police that Sue was not at home and not to be seen anywhere in the landscape. But he saw that that would not be necessary. The yellow mini was already slowing, veering in toward the verge. With relief, he saw Sue behind the wheel, and she was smiling at him.

A sallow-faced woman leaned out of the passenger-side window. "Hello, I'm Evie. I'm glad to set eyes on you at last."

He smiled and went forward. Now he would get another blast from Sue, he supposed, but his relief was such that he did not care.

"I said to her there was no way I was going in that old wreck of hers. I've got my pride. But she had to drive. I had enough of that yesterday. Oh, this flu does bring you down."

"How are you?" Tom inquired, putting down the bags of groceries he had carried in from the car.

Evie began to cough, making the question redundant.

"Would you like some tea?" Sue asked, coming in through the front door with a third bag.

"Lovely."

"Oh, can't we have something a bit stronger?" Evie said. "Tom must be frozen standing out there."

"It's a bit early," Sue said.

"Tea would be fine, really," Tom said.

"All right, tea it is. I can't drink alone."

"Of course you can," Sue said, carrying the shopping bags to the kitchen. "It would probably be good for your cold."

"That's just what I was thinking. Oh, all right. After all, I am recuperating. A small gin and tonic."

"Let me," Tom said, walking toward the bar.

"Thanks." Dropping her coat on the couch, Evie tottered on high-heels to the kitchen door and said, "It's all right, Sue. You put the kettle on. Tom's fixing the poor old invalid her drink." Then she went to stand close by Tom and asked in a low voice, "Were you checking up on her?"

"I'm afraid so."

"Don't be. I'm glad and grateful. Listen, I want to tell you something before you leave. Just follow my lead, okay?" She moved away quickly as Sue came back into the room.

"Kettle's on," Sue said.

"Where did I put my bag, Sue? I'm dying for a cigarette. I make it a rule not to smoke in the car while my chest's bad," she added for Tom's benefit.

"You shouldn't smoke at all with that cold," Sue lectured, finding Evie's bag and handing it to her. "This is a perfect opportunity to give up altogether."

"I know, and I shouldn't drink gin at four in the afternoon, and there's a lot of other things I shouldn't do besides that I can't mention in mixed company, so shut up and let me kill myself in peace."

Tom brought her drink and received a flashing smile.

"Sue never told me you looked like Robert Redford with muscles."

Tom laughed. Glancing at Sue, he said, "I don't think she noticed."

"No. She always was dead slow on the uptake, that one. Sit down."

"You just happened to be passing," Sue said, softening her words a little with a smile.

"I did have some business in Nene," he said apologetically.

"Then you're the very man," Evie said, lighting a cigarette. "Are there any decent restaurants there? I'm determined to get my sister into a frock and to have us a night on the town."

"Now she tells me," Sue played along. "Just when we've bought enough food to last a month."

"Feed a cold, starve a fever," Evie said. "Go and make that tea. Tom's gasping."

Sue left them. She could see that Tom liked Evie, and although she was fairly certain that her sister would come on to him like a practiced matchmaker, she found to her surprise that she did not mind. She let the tea brew and finished unpacking the groceries. It might be quite a nice idea to ask Tom to stay to dinner, she thought. When she carried the tea tray in, Evie was holding forth. Sue poured tea for Tom and herself, then freshened Evie's drink, aware of Tom's eyes following her. It made her feel slightly self-conscious, but she didn't mind. It was so very different from the way Simmons or Ashton looked at her. She suppressed a shudder. Unaware that she was doing so, she stood staring at Tom, not listening to Evie's chatter. He did not look a bit like Robert Redford, she thought.

"Didn't anyone ever tell you it was rude to stare?" Evie said, cutting in on her thoughts.

Sue felt herself flush.

"Sorry. I was miles away."

"I've always bored her," Evie confided to Tom.

"I don't believe that for a moment," he said.

"Actually," said Sue, "I was wondering if Tom would like to stay for dinner? If you're free, that is," she added, looking into his eyes.

"Ah, well, you're too late," Evie said. "That subject's already explored and he can't. But we're all going to— What's that name again?" she interrupted herself, turning to Tom.

"The Feathers. Just outside Nene. It's very good."

Sue felt a pang of disappointment and, more familiarly, resentment at Evie. She did wish her sister wouldn't try so blatantly to run her life for her.

"I'm afraid I ought to be going," Tom said. "Thank you anyway, Sue. Some other time?"

"Of course."

"And we'll see you Friday," Evie said, getting up.

"Yes," Tom agreed. He turned to Sue. "Good-bye. And thanks for the tea."

She looked puzzled. What had Evie done to get rid of him so quickly?

"Hang on," Evie said. "Just let me get my coat."

"What for?" Sue asked, surprised.

"I promised to take a look at Evie's car," Tom said, helping Evie into her heavy coat.

"Why? There's nothing—"

"See, I knew she hadn't noticed. Not surprising, really, when you think what she drives. We won't be a second."

Sue watched, completely unable to stop Evie as she took Tom's arm and bustled him out of the house. The poor man looked thoroughly embarrassed, too, she thought as they passed the window. Evie was leaning on him like an old friend. Sue began to clear away the teacups.

Outside, Tom opened the hood of the mini.

Evie spoke. "Like I said, she's definitely better. She's beginning to think about some sort of life for herself. The only thing is . . . it's probably not important now, but I wanted to tell you, since it shows how right you were to be worried and how far gone she was."

"What?" Tom said, alarmed.

"Keep looking at the engine. Fiddle with something. She's got eyes like a hawk, my sister."

Tom bent over the engine block, checking that the spark plugs were correctly positioned.

"There's a whole lot of drawings she's made," Evie said, keeping her back firmly turned to the window, "of scarecrows. And one of them, well, it gave me a real turn, I can tell you. One of them looks just like Gavin Trope."

"What?"

"It does. It's him to a tee, but like a scarecrow."

"Oh, my God," Tom said.

"Well, that proves how all this has got to her, doesn't it?"

Tom was silent, white-faced. He stood with his hand frozen on the hood, ready to slam it closed. His mind raced. It was there, like the missing piece of a jigsaw puzzle, seen so often but completely overlooked. Of course. Now it all made a terrible kind of sense.

"Whatever is it?" Evie asked, touching his arm.

He could not say anything. He wanted to but he dared not. After all, he had no proof. He slammed the hood of the car down.

"What's got into you?"

"Evie, look, I can't explain. I must go now. I've just remembered something." He was already moving toward his own car, the keys in his hand.

"See you Friday," Evie called.

"Or sooner, yes. I'll ring, anyway."

"Mind how you go."

She felt cold, despite her thick coat. Unsteadily, she returned to the house. The sound of his car, accelerating away, reached her before she had closed the front door.

"And what," Sue asked, "was all that about?"

"I don't know," Evie said and then remembered herself. She shut the door and locked it. "He remembered something important, he said. He was off in a hurry."

"I meant," said Sue, "about your car."

"It has got a knock in it, honest. I heard it all the way back."

"I didn't."

Evie looked at Sue and saw the hurt and distrust on her face.

"Oh, come on, Sue," she said. "I wasn't making a date with your young man, if that's what you're thinking."

"I don't know what you're talking about," Sue said, turning on her heel. "And frankly, I couldn't care less."

"Not much, my lady," Evie said under her breath. "It's written all over you."

She tugged off her coat and let it fall on the sofa. What was it about Sue drawing Gavin as a scarecrow that so upset Tom? Not just jealousy, she was sure. Whatever it was made her feel distinctly uncomfortable.

Everything about that day had been wrong. First, the birds woke Evie even earlier than usual, although her unpracticed ear detected nothing changed in their clamor. Others heard it, though, their heads twisting on restless pillows, or lifted to the sky, listening. It was as though the birds had been startled, disturbed in their perched and huddled slumbers. They shrilled an uneasy warning as the day broke.

The world had closed in. A mist, damp and cloying, hung like a curtain across the great fields, creating another false horizon. The trees in Gatherings Copse dripped with a still, invisible rain, rags of mist looped in their bare and sullen branches. And the roads shone moistly under a universal, pearly light.

Raising her blind, squinting, Evie thought that it was like looking into the mother-of-pearl innards of a vast shell. The mist made her shudder. It pressed so close that she felt claustrophobic. The strange light lent a sickly sheen to her skin as she inspected her face in the bathroom mirror. A pervasive damp seemed to have entered the house, making her bones ache and her flesh recoil from the chill. She applied more makeup than usual, built a large fire and huddled over it, her hands clasped around a steaming mug of coffee. The silence, after the birds fled, was intolerable.

Sick at heart, Shirley Pownall grimly prepared the children's breakfast while Lucas sat dumb at the hearth, feeding the fire. Hettie and Ashton shared Lucas's chores between them, the one white-faced and nervous, the other jumpy and clumsy with excitement. They did not speak or look at each other, not even to comment on the restlessness of the cows or the fact that the chickens had not laid that morning.

Old Bill Grubb surveyed the world from his dusty window and checked that his doors were bolted. His breath misted in the damp air as he raked the dead ashes over. The coal bucket was almost empty but he dared not venture out to fill it. He climbed gratefully back into his bed, already piled heavy with extra blankets and old coats, and huddled down. He would open his door to no man, no thing that day. He would be deaf and dumb and blind, as though he did not exist.

When Sue came down, yawning, feeling almost hung over from the depth of her sleep, Evie was talking quietly and rapidly into the telephone. Sue went into the kitchen and began to make herself coffee. She stared blankly through the window. The mist seemed a reflection of her own muzziness. A single scarecrow loomed from it, close to her fence. The mist eradicated its individual features so that it appeared no more than a silhouetted cross in the opaque swirl of light.

Evie startled her.

"I don't know what's happened to the weather. I thought spring had come," she said. "Listen, do you fancy a run into Nene? I've been speaking to a garage there. They can service my car as long as I get it in before ten. It's well overdue and I don't want it to break down on me."

"I'm not really awake yet," Sue apologized. "Anyway, it looks horrible out."

Evie was both relieved and surprised that her nervousness was not obvious. She could not put a name to its source or explain it. The awful weather and the light made her restless or, as she put it to herself, gave her the creeps. Sipping her coffee, she had thought about the car. She *had* heard a knock in it. Suddenly it had been very important to her not to be stranded there, without transport. She had even thought of leaving, but had pushed the thought aside. To have the car serviced provided a compromise. She had a longing for the sound of anonymous voices, crowds, streets, and reassuring buildings.

"I'd really like to get it done," she said. "This is a good opportunity."

"You'd better get a move on, then," Sue said, pouring coffee.

"You'll be all right?"

"Of course, don't be silly."

"I'll be back as soon as I can."

"It's bound to take a while." Sue roused herself a little. "You can have a good look round the shops. Take your time."

Evie smiled gratefully.

"All right, then. I'll go and get ready. Can I get you anything?"

"No, we're fine. But put a warm scarf on or something. This damp mist will be bad for your chest."

Evie dressed quickly for the outdoors. She folded a silk square across her chest beneath her coat, pulled a woolen hat over her bleached hair, and added an outer scarf of matching beige wool. Maybe she would be able to visit the hairdresser while she was waiting for the car. She wanted to look her best for Friday night. She and Sue had not mentioned Tom Carpenter again since he had left in such a rush, and Evie felt slightly uneasy about that. She wasn't sure that Sue had believed her, was certain that her sister did not yet understand her own feelings. In fact, it was probably because Sue was still examining those feelings that she had seemed withdrawn again. She was friendly and relaxed enough on the surface—they had had no quarrel—but Evie sensed that Sue was less open, was holding something back. There was no time to worry about that now. Evie felt almost excited at the prospect of a day in town, albeit a small and poky one. The need to be doing something was a sure sign that she was getting better. She'd never been one for sitting and doing nothing and, unlike Sue, she could never settle into a book.

"Ugh! I don't envy you," Sue said, coming with her to the door and peeping out into the white day.

"I'll be warm and cozy in the car," Evie said, suppressing a shiver as the damp air brushed her cheeks. "I must remember to take it easy, though. I don't want to break down on the way."

"You'd better get going, then."

"Right you are. See you later."

Sue watched her hurry across the wet grass and then shut the door gratefully and hurried back to the fire.

Ta-ta-t'-tap.

Evie glanced up nervously as she was inserting her key into the car door. The sound came again, closer, louder. She could see nothing moving. Visibility was down to about a hundred yards, although the mist was patchy, shifting in a slight breeze. She climbed into the car, shivering, her clothes beaded with moisture from the air. The engine grumbled and growled, turned over once, then died. Evie cursed. It was cold, that was all. She tried again, nursing the engine along, giving it time to warm up. At the fourth attempt its uncertain noise caught and held to the proper rhythm. Evie heaved a sigh and revved the motor steadily before gently easing the car out onto the road. She put the headlights on low beam, more so that she could be seen than because they increased her visibility. The road stretched ahead of her, straight and glistening, like a corridor through the pressing mist.

She eased the car up to thirty miles per hour and at once heard the knock. It was much louder than before, and more insistent. It alarmed her so much that she immediately wondered if she could make it into Nene. She reduced her speed, but that did not seem to make any improvement. The car jerked suddenly, threatened to stall. Evie increased speed again as she drew level with the shrouded farmhouse. She took the right-angled bend too fast. An explosion behind her rocked the car. Loud as a gunshot, it belched black smoke from the exhaust, and the engine died on her. The car coasted to a halt and stopped with a shudder.

"Oh, God," Evie groaned.

She did not know what to do. Her impulse was to put her head down on the steering wheel and weep. Then she wanted to get out and kick the unreliable machine. She did get out, and, with a gesture of futility, opened the hood. She stared balefully at the engine. Everything looked all right. Maybe if she was very careful . . . She knew it was useless. Well, at least she was within walking distance of the cottage. She would have to phone the garage, get the bloody thing towed away.

"Having trouble?"

"Oh!" Evie's heart leaped and fluttered. He appeared silently, on the other side of the car, startling her. "You damn near gave me a heart attack," she said.

"Ground's soft." He looked down at his Wellington boots. "What's the trouble?"

"God alone knows. I was just taking it in for servicing. I heard a knock the other day. It just seemed to explode on me."

"I heard it." He grinned and put his hands on the car, leaning over the engine.

Evie waited, watched, stamping her feet against the insidious cold.

"Can you see anything?" she asked.

"Not sure. I might have to strip her down. Mind you, I'm not saying I can fix it."

"If you could just get it going, just so I could get into the garage."

"I reckon. Best get her into the yard, though."

"Do you think we could push it?"

"Hang on." He thrust his large hand into the confusing mass of metal. Evie had no idea what he was doing. "You get in and when I say so, start her up gently."

"Okay, thanks," Evie said, obeying him.

At the third signal Ashton gave her, the engine started. It made a sound as though every moving part were dry, grating one against another. The steering column vibrated beneath her hands. Ashton tapped on the passenger window, motioning her to wind it down.

"Back her gently up to the yard and then take her to the other side of that old barn. Take it easy, though. Don't force her."

"Would you like to do it? I don't feel . . ."

The idea seemed to excite him, then he looked nervously over his shoulder and shook his head.

"No, I'm not used to them minis. You do it. It'll be all right if you don't force her."

Tongue between her teeth, Evie backed the car gingerly along the road. Ashton kept easy pace with her, ran ahead when she came to the bend, and guided her around with clear and expert signals. Funny chap, Evie thought and briefly remembered the ease with which he had lifted her, how strange she had felt. She was glad that the need to maneuver the car, give it all her attention, forced that memory to fade quickly. She backed beyond the farm entrance and carefully eased the gears. Coughing, the car bumped into the farm driveway. With a laugh of relief and achievement Evie brought it level with the hole knocked in the wall of the stone barn.

"You're a genius," she told Ashton as she got out.

"I'm good with motors. I'll have a go."

He strode past her into the barn. She heard the rattle of tools.

"I'll pay you, of course," she shouted. "I hope you can spare the time."

He came out again, carrying a scratched metal toolbox, a bundle of rags in his other hand.

"I said I'd make it worth your while," Evie said and almost immediately wished she had not.

He froze in the act of putting down the toolbox. He was stooping a little, his broad shoulders bulging beneath his shabby clothes. His eyes were dancing, burning as they locked onto hers. His smile was slow and predatory, a little one-sided. She saw that his lips were very moist. It was as though he had become a different person. The concentration, the efficiency with which he had inspected the car, guided and instructed her, had completely gone. There was a wordless animal communication between them that Evie could not deny or turn aside with a joke or a laugh. She felt herself entirely in his power. The blood drained from her face. Her stomach felt tight, as though clenched, and she could not tear her eyes away from his. They were rather large, blue eyes, and she read in them things that made her feel sick and dizzy, as though her body had taken on a life, a desire independent of her will.

Slowly, Ashton straightened up. His eyes slid from hers, to her chest, and Evie was able to move. She stepped backward, involuntarily, and twisted away from him. She was panting slightly and her flesh prickled with a kind of ugly heat.

"We'll see about that," he said quietly, almost caressingly, "when I've fixed her." He laughed suddenly, as though at some private, unspoken joke in his head.

"I meant money," Evie said quickly, her cheeks burning.

"I'll have to get underneath. Be quicker if you stay here and help me. Hand me the tools, like."

The box, a series of interfolding trays, was a model of neatness, each tool aligned in its designated place. He lifted out a wrench.

"But I'd better go and ring the garage. They're expecting me," Evie said feebly.

He squatted down, his back to the car.

"If I can fix her it'll only take a few minutes," he said, stretching himself on the damp earth and wriggling his torso beneath the car. "You stay and help me."

"You'll catch your death," Evie exclaimed, squatting beside him. She could not make out what he said. "You'll get all wet and muddy."

"Second shelf on the right-hand side, third tool along," he called, his voice muffled.

Evie leaned over his legs, located the instrument, and placed it in his outstretched hand. He grunted. The tool disappeared. Evie was almost touching his legs. His thighs swelled with muscles thrusting against the tautly stretched cloth of his stained trousers. Evie looked away, backed off. He crooked one leg to give himself leverage and her eyes strayed back to him. He said something about oil that she did not catch, turned over onto one hip, sliding himself along the ground. His shirt had worked free of his trousers. She saw the sharp angle of his hipbone, his flat, pale belly, the deeply indented, smooth navel.

"I've got to go," she said, hearing the note of tight hysteria in her own voice.

"Give me a rag," he said, "quick."

Startled, confused, Evie stepped over his body and snatched a cloth from the loose pile he had dropped on the ground beside the box. He flipped over onto his back again, one hand up toward her. She was standing astride his legs, her mind whirling. She thrust the cloth at him, feeling that she had lost all control. The cloth, bunched in her hand, blotted out the sight of his groin. She let it fall. He fumbled for the cloth, and just as his fingers found it and pulled it out of sight, she recognized it.

Last November it would have been, or early December, she remembered. She and Sue had met in the center of town, had had a cup of coffee before braving the crowds to do their Christmas shopping. Evie had a list a mile long, as usual, but Sue was set on something very special for Gavin. She had sought Evie's help. And late that afternoon, when Evie's feet were beginning to throb, after Sue had rejected suggestion after suggestion, they had found it. The perfect gift, a shirt of palest gray, made of finest Egyptian cotton, monogrammed on the single left-hand pocket in a darker shade of gray with a cursive flowing *G. G* for Gavin.

"What's up?"

The noise and bustle, the dry heat of the overcrowded store in the center of Birmingham faded. Evie was standing again in the chill, damp farmyard, beside her car. Ashton Pownall was sitting on the ground at her feet, his back resting against the door of the car. He was staring at her with the look of a confused boy. The cloth, streaked with dirt and oil, lay across his thighs.

"You all right?"

Evie reached down and snatched the cloth from his body. She shook it out like a banner. A gray shirt. The gray shirt. She stared at the monogram.

"Where did you get this?" Her voice was shrill. She seized the collar, twisting it down to expose the neatly woven black and gold store label. It was unmistakable, completely familiar to her. Many of her own clothes came from that very store. And it was Gavin's size. "Where?" She almost screamed, flapping the shirt at him. "Where did you get this?"

"I don't know." He seemed indifferent, quite calm. He reached into the toolbox, replacing the piece she had handed to him. Carefully, taking his time, he selected another.

"Tell me," Evie shouted. "Look, it's important." She squatted down beside him, holding the shirt out. He glanced at it.

"I don't remember. There's always old bits and pieces lying around, for the scarecrows mostly."

"Oh, my God." Evie clutched the shirt to her.

"I just help myself." He held a heavy wrench in his hand, looking at her.

Evie stood up. The backs of her legs were trembling. Her throat was dry, making it difficult for her to speak.

"You think you can fix it, then?" Her voice was a cracked whisper now as she backed away. She was afraid of him, wanted to thrust the telltale shirt out of sight behind her back.

"I reckon." He shifted his body, preparing to slide under the car again. "Here, where you going?"

"Nowhere, I've—"

"Give me that rag, then," he said, stretching his hand out for it.

"No." She snatched it behind her back. "No, I've got—"

"Give it to me. I need it."

"No."

Evie did not think. She turned and ran, bunching the shirt in her hands, holding it fast. She had not even reached the yard entrance when he overtook her, seized her arm, and swung her around.

"Let me go," she said.

"Give me that. You don't want to go messing with that."

"No, leave me alone." Evie held the shirt tight in both hands, pressed against his chest.

"You'll be all right. I'll get the car fixed." He spoke reassuringly, but Evie watched the strange and horrible transformation come over him again. His mouth loosened. She felt his hands tight on her back, pressing her against him. He ducked his head toward her, mouth wetly open. His arms tightened about her, holding her fast in a terrible intimacy, his groin hard against her belly.

"No," she said, twisting her head.

"Ashton!"

The word was like a whiplash, cracking through the air. As

though he had lost his strength, Ashton's arms fell from her. His eyes darted, rolled nervously. He stepped back from her. Evie was shaking so much she scarcely felt able to stand.

Lucas Pownall stood black and scowling near the car, absolutely still. Ashton hunched his shoulders and turned away. Evie stared at Lucas, fear singing in her ears. His eyes were fixed on the shirt.

"Leave that," he said. "You got no right to take that."

Evie hurled the cloth from her. It fluttered feebly to the ground, the monogrammed *G* staring up at them.

With a little sob, she turned and ran toward the road.

She heard the sound of an approaching vehicle over the sound of her own rasping breath and turned instinctively toward it. She could run no longer anyway. She was ill and out of condition. Her chest felt tight, her lungs constricted, unable to take in enough oxygen. Her head buzzed with the effort and panic while her legs ached as she had never known them to do before.

She stood at the side of the road, doubled up. The mist appeared to be thicker, to have lost its opalescent quality. It had become a gray mask. The lights of a vehicle pierced the mist like two laser beams. It reared up at her, a yellow tractor, out of the mist. Behind the windshield of the high cab she saw Ashton Pownall's face, and he was laughing. She turned and forced her legs to move. The tractor came on, brushed against her, making a tight arc. It was heading her off. Evie realized this even as she plunged into the mist, her feet sinking into the soft earth of the field. Again it droned near. Automatically, she began to run. When she stopped, feeling unable to go any farther, it came on behind her, driving her forward. She veered to the left, telling herself that she must not lose her sense of direction. If she kept going, she must reach the back of the cottage.

Ta-ta-t'-tap.

Before she could react to the sound she had stumbled against a scarecrow. It swung around on some mechanical pivot of its own.

Ta-ta-t'-tap.

Evie grabbed it, hung on to it. Its arms swirled in a full circle and dealt her a sharp blow just above the left ear. She cried out, lost her balance by throwing up her arm to clutch her head, and fell awkwardly onto her backside. Whimpering, she watched the thing circling, swaying above her. It wore a crazy stovepipe hat, an old pipe stuck into its soft, toothless mouth. Even as she stared at it, the tractor approached on its flank. She sat in its path. Hands and feet slipping in the fine tilth, she managed to stagger upright. The tractor swerved, its roar deafening her, goading her on.

She ran then, arms flailing, feet slipping. The mist became patchy. She passed from thick, concealing clouds into comparatively clear air. Once she even caught a glimpse of the cottage. To her excited eyes it shimmered and shifted like a mirage. The tractor swept close, slowing. Then it traveled a little to her left and behind her. When she veered toward the cottage it accelerated and would have knocked her down had she not straightened her frantic run. The tractor slowed again, remained poised to intercept and cut her off. Looking up, Evie saw Ashton's face laughing down at her. If only she had the strength to dodge and weave. As it was she could barely manage a stumbling walk.

Bent over her drawing board, Sue heard the tractor in the field at the back of the house. Its sound irritated her, intruded on the mood of deep concentration she had created. Without looking up, she reached her hand out to the volume control of the cassette recorder at her side. The "Dies Irae" of the Verdi *Requiem* thundered out at almost full volume. Hunching her left shoulder, she added more deft strokes to the strange, semi-human stick figures that would become the main creatures in her book.

The sound of triumph and fear rolled around the house, easily drowning out the inadequate but persistent shrill of the telephone downstairs. When the music subsided, the telephone was silent.

Sue went on with her work, totally absorbed.

Tom Carpenter had a lunch appointment with the two men who had lent Gavin Trope large and apparently unreclaimable sums of money. It was important. It was own-up time and there was no way he could postpone or cancel the meeting. His mind was already preoccupied with the meeting as he replaced the receiver in the cradle. His watch reminded him that he should leave now. His secretary was gesturing to him through the glass door of his office. Sue would have gone out, he reassured himself, Evie would have insisted. In Higham Furze it was a lovely, sun-filled day. There was nothing to be anxious about. Evie would look after her. It was the best thing they could have done. A nice drive, perhaps, lunch at some charming rustic pub.

"All right. All right, I'm going," he told his secretary as she opened the door.

He grabbed his briefcase and hurried out. Now what the hell was he going to tell these chaps? Could he save his own hide, at the very least?

The tractor seemed to lose interest in her once she found the strength to run toward the copse. The copse offered sanctuary. The tractor could not follow her there, and if Ashton should continue the pursuit on foot, she might at least have a chance to elude him among the trees. She summoned the last of her strength and ran for it. The tractor stood off, playing a sentinel role. She threw herself into the copse, heard dry twigs and low branches crack beneath her weight. An unnoticed briar snagged at her coat as she fell, full-length, onto the dried leaves and soft loam beneath the trees.

She was too tired to cry. Every breath hurt her. She lay where she had fallen, coughing every now and again, desperately trying to fill her clogged lungs. The sounds she made blotted out the drone of the waiting, watching tractor. He could have followed her easily, crept up on her, but she did not think of that. Her whole body ached, was perilously close to failing her altogether. Besides, she was too afraid to think. Afraid and exhausted. When she closed her eyes, the world swam dizzyingly. Propping herself up, she dribbled bile from her gasping mouth. She had never known such pain. It would not go away. She must adjust to it. But even as she did so, giving herself over to its nagging claws, she knew that she was helpless. Schemes rattled through her head.

She could cut across the corner of the woods, to where the old barns stood, and leg it to the house. She could fight her way through the copse, regain the road. But they weren't realistic possibilities anymore. Her legs would not carry her. With every inadequate breath her lungs threatened to burst or collapse. A jagged pain started in the region of her skipping heart. She thought that she was going to pass out, briefly welcomed the idea; but it was this new pain, which swelled in intensity with every hard-won breath, that kept her on the daylight side of consciousness. It was in an attempt to ease this pain that she struggled into a sitting position, her back resting against a spindly gray tree. This brought some relief. The tractor passed up and down the field. She tried to make her breathing steady, tried to fit the swelling and diminishing of the pain to the receding, returning hum of the tractor.

The game was over, then. He had not followed her. She was safe? Hysterically, she began to shake. Her left hand pressed to the ugly pain in her side. She remembered the shirt, Gavin's shirt. There was only one way, only one, that they could have gotten it. And now that she knew about it they would stop at nothing to silence her. They could not afford to stop at anything less. Why was he waiting, why postpone it? She twisted her head toward the field from which she was barely concealed. Why didn't he come and finish it now? She clapped her hand over her mouth to prevent herself from shouting to him. She wasn't mad, not yet. Her mind had not failed her. Instinctively, she crawled deeper into the wood. Every slithering movement brought new shock waves of pain, but instinct drove her on. As long as she had her mind she would try to live. She settled herself against a larger tree and slowly drew her knees up, then let her head hang down, between her knees, to ease the surge of nausea that threatened her.

Slowly, slowly it passed. The pain in her side slackened to a stitch. The sweat of her efforts chilled her body. She brought her head up, teeth chattering, and began to chafe her arms through her ruined coat. She knew that she had to get moving, had to keep her circulation going. Her head swam as she hauled herself, with the aid of a low-hanging branch, to her feet. She tottered, putting all her weight on the branch, but eventually, miraculously, she found her balance and her legs held. If she had possessed the energy she would have laughed to encourage herself. There was life in the old girl yet.

She had crawled into the thick part of the copse, where the trees grew close together and the going was rough, cluttered with underbrush. But there were paths. She knew that from her previous visit. She had to get to one of them. Lurching from tree to tree, she made toward a clearer part and rested upright, willing her legs to stop shaking. The barns were somewhere behind her. She needed to find the path she had taken that first time. It must be possible to find it; it could not be far away. She set off again, heading always for clearer ground, looking about her for a discernible track through the trees, pushing and shuffling her feet through the leaves, still clinging to branches and trunks to give her balance and support.

It was during one of her frequent rest periods that she missed the regular drone of the tractor. No sooner had she realized this than she caught another sound, a cracking of undergrowth, the crackle of dead leaves. She cried out, a sort of animal whimper, and pushed away in panic from the trunk that supported her. The ground sloped a little and gave her an unbalanced impetus. Weaving, staggering, her legs threatening to collapse under her at any moment, Evie covered a few yards. Her feet found clear ground. Breathless, holding her side, she rested. Only slowly did she realize that she had found a path. The ground beneath her feet was clear of leaves, packed hard, worn smooth. It must be *the* path. Swaying, she turned to her right. Yes, thank God, the path curved to the right, would lead her to the barns, must—

But she did not move along the path. Any hope it offered that might have given her fresh energy, was broken off by the sight that met her appalled eyes.

It was tall and black and it straddled the path only yards from her like an immovable obstacle. If only it had been immovable. If only. Even as she looked, her breath caught as though her lungs had become ossified, it moved toward her, its clumsy wooden legs moving one at a time in a swaying, ugly gait. Its great outstretched arms brushed against the trees, snapping twigs, scraping against branches. Its square footless stumps pounded the earth, seemed to root there, only to be wrenched up again, to come on toward her.

Some part of Evie's brain knew that it was useless to scream, was a waste of her failing energy, but she could not help it. The terrible scream was torn from her when her lungs began to work again and demanded that her breath be expelled. As she screamed she began to move, backward. Her head swung from side to side, denying her own eyes, the evidence of all her merciless senses.

It was a scarecrow, bigger than any she had seen, and it could move. It expelled clouds of visible breath into the damp air. It had eyes that glittered through slits in its sacking face. It even had arms, a second pair of arms that swung out from its rigid, stick shoulders and reached toward her.

Evie screamed and screamed again. Prompted by the impulse to survive, she turned around and ran, ran blindly. The instinct to survive blotted out everything, even the pain of her protesting body. A branch whipped her face, lashing the corner of her eye so that it began to water and close. A briar clawed her hand into bright beads of blood. She blundered on, half-blind, with only one thought: to survive, to get away from the scarecrow that meant to kill her.

She screamed again when she lost her footing at the edge of the great leaf-filled hollow and went tumbling down. But her scream was cut off, all breath driven from her body, as she somersaulted, rolled, like an already inanimate, will-less object, and came to rest on her side.

The scarecrow paused on the lip of the hollow, knowing that it had her now, could take its time, relish her gathering.

Still Evie did not give up. Without considering her position, her fingers clenched upon the soft soil beneath the dead leaves. She dragged herself along, her mouth open in a silent cry, her eyes rolling in terror as the thing, in two giant strides, swung down the slope toward her. Her congested lungs whistled shrilly as she wriggled and tried hopelessly to shift away from the scarecrow. It reached her, stood over her; numb with fear and exhaustion, she could only stare at it.

She thought it was a trick of her almost petrified mind when the thing seemed to split apart. The great wooden legs fell away. The body seemed to detach itself from the stiff and terrible sticks that gave it form and kept it upright. It fell upon her with a grunt of all too human breath. She saw eyes roll wildly behind the slits. She saw features molded by a hood of sacking and, ugly and terrifying as this sight was, it gave her a final desperate moment of courage. If it was human it could be fought. With her last strength she lashed out at it. Time and movement slowed as it struck back at her. She saw a bloodless hand beneath cuffs of stiff twigs. The hands were bound with barbed wire. She saw this clearly before she felt the thudding impact of that hand that snapped her head to the side, driving one cheek into the ground.

He tore his barbed hand free, snagging gouts of flesh from her cheek, the blood spattering him and her chest. He wished she would scream. He liked to hear the screams. She was too mute, too passive. He let out a wordless roar of frustration as his clumsy, deadly hands tore at her clothing. The silk scarf beneath her open coat shredded under his hands. But the roll neck of her thick sweater still hid her throat from him. Pausing, working carefully, aware of the feeble twitch of her legs imprisoned by his body, he inserted his barbed fingers between the sweater and her throat. One sharp barb punctured the white skin, causing her to flinch. Her face bled where he had struck it. The wool tore under his maniacal grip. He grunted again as he pulled his hand free, the wool caught in the barbs, unraveling. Then he tore and clawed at her again and again until the sweater parted unevenly and she lay almost naked beneath him.

Silently, he reached for her small breasts, cupped in white cotton. He caressed them, dragging his spiked hands gently at first and then with more and more passion across their thin concealment. The cotton shredded, her pale flesh showed red weals that bloomed droplets of blood. He mashed her breasts hard in his gripping palms, feeling her body jerk beneath him, and bore down on her with his full weight, driving the last breath from her body. It escaped her as a sigh that he chose to hear as satisfaction, pleasure. It was replaced at once by a terrible gurgling deep in her throat. He dragged his hands down her body, causing the blood to well and flow. Then and only then, when he had spoiled her breasts, torn them to an unrecognizable, shredded bloody pulp, did he reach for her throat and lay it open with his blood-soaked, wire-tangled hands.

Sue had skipped lunch. In fact, she had forgotten all about it. It was mid-afternoon when she went downstairs and ate some cheese and celery. She felt that special combination of pleasant tiredness and mind-racing excitement that comes from a sustained, successful period of creative work. The book had begun, quite suddenly, to take shape in her mind. All those stray, half-formed ideas that had occurred to her over the past weeks had coalesced unexpectedly, and the drawings she had made that day gave the whole project a coherent form.

She badly wanted to tell someone about it. Evie would be pleased, interested. She wished Evie would hurry up. Surely she would not be long now. Sue went to the window, as if by watching she could hurry her sister's return. The mist seemed to have receded and thinned, so that should not delay Evie. Then she noticed something else, something that caused her to step back, startled. Then she was angry.

Three scarecrows stood in her garden, implacably facing the house.

What the hell did they think they were playing at? That was her land. She was at the front door, impatiently fumbling with the deadlock, when dread awoke in her. Quickly, she relocked the door and stepped away from it, her hands shaking. She stood there for a good while, trying to reason it out. They were trying to frighten her. Nothing could happen to her if she remained calm and, above all, stayed inside. Evie would be back in a minute. Sue walked purposefully into the kitchen, avoiding the windows, and locked the back door.

There was only one scarecrow in the back garden, but another three were ranged along the field fence, all facing the house.

Sue resisted the impulse to stare at them, to panic. Instead, she made herself go back into the living room and close the kitchen door. Then, steeling herself, she walked to the window and lowered the first blind quickly, blotting out the staring figures. At the second window she paused just long enough to see that one scarecrow, the central of the three, was closer to the house, as though it had sensed her first impulse to open the front door.

"They can't sense anything," she said aloud and pulled the blind down tight.

If it was not some trick of her eyes, the already uncertain light, then she knew that somebody must be out there with the scarecrows. They could not move by themselves. She knew that. Somebody was out there, watching the house, maneuvering the scarecrows like giant, threatening puppets.

She ran lightly up the stairs and into her workroom. From a filing cabinet she snatched the documents relating to the house and quickly found Tom Carpenter's office number. Downstairs again, slightly out of breath, she dialed the number carefully, trying to control the tremble in her fingers. After a series of clicks the number rang and was immediately answered.

"Tom Carpenter, please," Sue interrupted before the receptionist had finished identifying the firm.

"One moment please."

The line went silent for a moment. Sue tapped her foot impatiently, looking at the covered windows.

"Can I help you?" Another female voice.

"I want to speak to Tom Carpenter."

"I'm sorry, Mr. Carpenter is out of the office at present. This is his secretary speaking. May I take a message?"

"When are you expecting him back?"

"I really couldn't say."

"You *are* expecting him back?"

"I'm sorry, Mr. Carpenter didn't say."

"Look, this is urgent. I absolutely must speak to him."

"I'm very sorry, but Mr. Carpenter didn't leave a number where he could be reached. If you'll leave a message I'll get it to him just as—"

"Yes, please, tell him Sue Jackman called. Tell him, please, that I must speak to him urgently."

The line suddenly hissed and then became silent, dead.

"Damn," Sue said and put her finger on the receiver rest, jiggled it anxiously. "Oh, come on," she pleaded. There was no dial tone, nothing. Slowly, with a feeling of helpless nausea, she put the receiver down.

Ta-ta-t'-tap.

The sound came from the window, at the front.

Ta-ta-t'-tap. Ta-ta-t'-tap.

The lunch had been long and less acrimonious than Tom had feared. As he waited for his credit card to be returned to him, he felt pretty certain that it was so because of the quantities of alcohol he had poured down his guests. They had left already, rather red-faced, smiling and pumping his arm with temporary bonhomie—at least he thought it was temporary, but hoped it would last because the lunch had cost him a small fortune.

The receptionist slid his card over the counter top and, on impulse, he asked, "Is there a telephone?"

"You can use this one." She smiled and moved the telephone toward him, bending to free the tangled wire.

It was too late to go back to the office. The hotel was some fifteen miles out of Higham Furze, fifteen miles closer to Hemming. Anyway, he'd promised Evie he would call.

The line was busy.

The receptionist smiled at him.

"No luck?"

"Busy. I'll try again in a moment."

"Can I get you something?"

He realized that his head was pounding a little from the claret and the cognac. The hotel was quiet and sleepy, poised between lunchtime and the dinner-hour rush.

"I'd like some more coffee," he said, returning her smile. "Black."

She pointed to a group of easy chairs arranged around a circular coffee table.

"I'll bring it there."

"Thanks."

He turned back to the telephone, waited until the girl had written his order on a slip of paper and had carried it through a door behind the counter. He dialed again. The line was still busy. Evie, he supposed, chattering to her friends in Birmingham. Well, at least everything was all right. He crossed the reception area and sat down, waiting for his coffee.

Ta-ta-ta-Ta ta. Ta-ta-T'-taptaptap. Ta-ta-ta-taptaptap. Ta-ta-t'-tap tap tap. Ta-ta-t'. Ta-ta-t'-tap tap tap.

"Stop it," Sue screamed and covered her ears with her hands.

The tapping did not let up at all now, at the door, both windows, back and front of the cottage. The sound grated at her nerves.

Ta-ta-t'tap. Tap. Tap. Ta-ta-ta-ta-t'-taptaptap.

How many must there be now? She imagined the house surrounded, imagined them pressing, a solid wall of wood, against the house, demanding to be let in. The constant sound, moving around the house, first this window, then that, the door, made it impossible to tell how many there were. She twisted her head, following the sound, unable to block it out.

"Go away," she yelled. "Go away."

Hands fastened over her ears, she ran up the stairs. In the darkened bedroom she closed the door and leaned against it. The window showed her only darkness, the drift of mist. She groped her way toward the bed and sat down, shivering. The sound was audible but muffled. With an effort of will it could be pushed into the background. If she put a pillow over her head . . . but where was Evie? The car must have been serviced hours ago. If she had gone to a pub or something, Sue vowed she would kill her. Twisting toward the window, reaching for a pillow, Sue froze. A shape loomed at the window, black against black. There was a terrible screeching noise emanating from the glass, a sound like chalk scraping on a blackboard. She could make out movement, a sort of stroking motion against the lower right-hand pane.

How big must it be to reach . . . With a cry, Sue seized the pillow and hurled it against the window. Then she got up and ran. Out in the corridor the tapping became unbearable again. It sounded everywhere at once now, faster, more demanding.

"No," she moaned, and moved away from the stairs.

In her workroom the first thing she did was lower the blind. She leaned over the drawing board, her arms braced against its sides. It could not be so tall. She would be safe here. Oh, God, where was Evie? How long would this terrible thing last?

Tom woke with a start, his mouth dry. For a moment or two he was disoriented. A little silver pot of coffee stood before him, the cup unused. He caught the watchful eye of a man behind the counter. Loud voices announced the arrival of the first guests for dinner. The receptionist must have gone off duty. Tom felt like a fool. He saw from the glowing lamps and darkened window that it was already night. And his mouth felt as though he had just finished a long march on a hot day without water. Straightening his tie nervously, he hurried past the counter and down the thickly carpeted corridor to the men's room. Inside he cupped water in his hands and drank thirstily. When his throat seemed to be working again, he splashed water on his face. It was horrible, but it made him feel better. God, he would never drink at lunchtime again. Well, not so much, anyway.

He returned to the desk and asked to pay for the coffee he had not drunk. As he waited for the man to make change, he noticed the telephone. Without asking, he picked it up and dialed Sue's number. Somebody was still talking on the line.

Screek. Screek. Screek.

It was an unearthly, percussive symphony. The sound of the tapping and beating downstairs lapped and overlapped in a complex, inhuman rhythm. It gave a kind of amusical support to the nerve-jangling scratching at the window.

The moment it had started, Sue had moved away from the window. Now she was pressed against the far wall, trying to block out the noise with her fingers. But the scratching continued, as though there was all the time in the world, as though the very glass could be worn thin, worn away. But she knew that her nerves would give first. She could stand it no longer, would do anything to stop it.

Sue began to sing, as loud as her uneven breath would allow, half-remembered songs. Then she began the soaring tunes of Verdi's *Requiem*, willing herself to keep her back pressed against the wall.

Suddenly, there was silence. Her voice, surprisingly loud, screamed in her own ears. She stopped in mid-phrase and felt the silence come tumbling in on her.

The window cracked, split at the second mighty blow. Glass fell, tinkling. Wood splintered. A single white hand shredded the flapping blind in two, leaving it in ragged and useless tatters.

Tom did not want to go home. He sat behind the wheel of his car, dawdling. The prospect of his empty, cheerless apartment was daunting.

That decided it. He started the car and sent gravel spurting from its back wheels in a clattering shower as he roared down the hotel driveway and onto the road. It was a clear night, with little traffic. He liked driving fast. It was just his luck to fall for a girl who seemed singularly unimpressed by fast sports cars, not to mention his other assets. At lease Evie had seemed to notice.

Sue never told me you looked like Robert Redford with muscles.

Evie couldn't have been on the phone all that time. It was a physical impossibility for anyone, even someone as naturally garrulous as Evie Jackman. Perhaps the line was out of order. He had, he realized, provided himself with a perfect excuse to make an unannounced call. He eased the pedal closer to the floor, enjoying the thrust of power at his back, the good-tempered, well-tuned song of the engine. He pushed the car, the adrenaline beginning to flow, sharpening his reactions.

But he reduced speed as he approached Brooking. Cars were drawing up to the pub. He swung past it, taking the shorter back road. As the ground began to rise, the road twisting and turning, flags of mist drifted across the road. Nothing serious, he thought, but it was thickening. He switched his headlights to full. Visibility decreased to about a hundred yards by the time he reached the plain proper. The village, such as it was, looked more than usually forlorn. As he flashed by the few houses he saw no lights. Well, on a night like this, what was there to do in Hemming except go to bed? The schoolhouse hung for a moment in his lights, then fell back into darkness. Ahead the mist was white. It condensed on his windshield. His lights raked the gray trees of the copse as the road kinked a little before settling on its dead straight course. Nearly there, in record time.

"Jesus Christ!" Tom said.

He would never know, as long as he lived, what counterimpulse overrode, in those split seconds, all the carefully trained and practiced reactions of the good driver. Something, something for which he was ever to be grateful, prevented him from hitting the brake. Instead, his teeth set, his head pushed back against the headrest, he drove straight at the scarecrow.

He shut his eyes a split second before the impact. He heard the crack of tortured wood. Something thudded against the windshield and slid from the hood into the road. He sensed, rather than saw, something tossed into the air, over the roof of the car. He had gotten through. That was the important thing. He did not look back but concentrated on holding the racing car steady. Then he began to reduce speed.

He saw movement around the cottage, shadows breaking away from its absolute darkness, as though plucked by the mist. He stopped the car and scrambled out in one uninterrupted gesture.

Tom lashed out blindly at the shape that threatened him. His elbow thudded against wood, and with a clatter, the scarecrow toppled. He ran toward the house, shouting for Sue. The scarecrows were everywhere, all shapes and sizes. They stood and leaned against the house, like so many sinister totems. Tom felt a momentary repugnance as his hands touched sackcloth and damp straw. Roaring her name, he hauled the things away from the house, tossing them aside, kicking out with his feet when they tangled in his legs. They lay on the grass like the untidy makings of a bonfire.

"Sue, Sue. It's me. Tom. For God's sake, Sue. Open up."

He beat on the door, bruising his hands. He even thrust his shoulder against it. Remembering all the movies he had ever seen, he took a step back, and aimed one good kick at the door. The impact jarred through his body, but the door held.

The window, he thought. The window.

Like a dervish now, he began another onslaught on the scarecrows, pulling them away from the window, hurling them to the ground. He must cover his hand before breaking the glass. Or use his elbow.

"Tom?"

"Sue."

"Is it really you?"

He stumbled back to the door, shouting her name over and over again. He heard the heavy deadlock turn and he pushed against the door. Her face was a white oval in the darkness. He reached in, grabbing her.

"Tom?"

"Come on, quickly."

"Wait. I—"

He pulled her out. She shrank away from the fallen scarecrows. Tom made himself deaf. He did not care if she was hurt. He had to get her out. Every nerve in his body ordered him to get her away.

He all but flung her against the car, reached into its lighted interior to release the catch on the passenger door.

"Get in. Come on, get in."

"Tom."

Her voice was very faint. Pulling his head out of the car he saw her, apparently petrified, her back pressed against the car, staring toward the house. He did not hesitate, but pushed her, would have slapped her if there had been time.

"Get in the other side. Get in. Get in."

To his relief she began to move. She was whimpering. Her legs seemed uncoordinated, but she was moving, sliding blindly around the back of the car.

"Don't look," he shouted and swung around to see for himself what it was that held her almost mesmerized.

It was coming from the back of the house, steadily, unstoppable, unbelievably tall. He could make out only the vague silhouette of the head against the misty sky. It was its movement, its awkward, rolling, but seemingly inevitable progress that made it terrifying.

He turned away from it.

"Get in. Quickly, for God's sake."

He threw himself into the car, banging his knees, and leaned across, throwing her door open. Her hand was ice cold. He seized it and pulled with all his strength. His touch, the force with which he pulled her, seemed to act like a countercharm. She began to cry, but stooped and fumbled her way into the car, then shut the door. Tom slammed his own door and gunned the engine. The wheels spun, slipping on the damp grass. Sue covered her face with her hands. The tires bit and the car shot forward, rocking onto the road.

"All right now. It's all right now."

Then his heart suddenly froze in him.

"Christ! Where's Evie?"

He turned to look at Sue, slowing automatically.

"Sue? Evie, where is she?"

"I don't know." She shook her head.

"She's not back there?"

"No. Keep going, Tom, please. She went into Nene. She's all right."

He knew, anyway, that he could not go back. He accelerated again, forcing the car along the road, lights blazing. He began to slow as the right-angle bend at the farm raced toward them, even though his nerves cried out for speed. He eased back.

"Oh, God," she said, a sort of hopeless moan. "There's another of them."

His lights caught the scarecrow, planted at the side of the road, as though to guard the bend, its arms pointing in both directions. Tom reached out, felt her hair. He pulled her face down to his shoulder.

"Don't look," he said. "Keep down."

But the scarecrow did not move. He took the bend too fast, swinging the wheel wildly. The straight road opened up ahead.

The tail wind of the car racing by lifted the woolen scarf that dangled around the scarecrow's set shoulders. It ruffled the few stray, dyed curls that escaped the woolen hat to which dead leaves clung. The scarecrow hung there limp on the wooden crosstree, the eyes staring open, lifeless, as the car was swallowed up by the misty night.

In the early hours of the morning, Simmons had the Pownalls, all except old Mary, whom he had allowed to stay behind with the children, file through the main entrance of the Nene Police Station. It would have been easier, as was customary, to take them around the back, but he knew that Sue Jackman was waiting in the lobby and he wanted to see what would happen when they were brought face to face with her.

The old man, George Pownall, went first, walking stiffly, his head high. Simmons might have been mistaken but he thought that somewhere, deep down, the man was glad. A terrible anxiety had been relieved in him.

As soon as George Pownall got through the door, Sue Jackman turned away. Simmons noticed the eagerness with which Tom Carpenter's arms went around her. He felt cheated.

Lucas came next, a blanket draped around his shivering body. His wife walked by his side, distanced, not touching him. Carpenter cradled the back of Sue's head, warning her to keep her face turned.

Ashton, Simmons thought, looked like an imbecile, arms dangling, mouth slackly open, his eyes fixed on the floor. Hettie held him lightly by the arm, and it was she who turned toward

Sue Jackman. Her face was a picture of confusion. Her lips parted as though she were going to call out, but she bit hard into her lower lip to prevent herself. Her face became red, hot with embarrassment—or was it anger, Simmons wondered? Hettie set her back against Sue while the formalities were completed. Finally they were over.

"It's all right now," Tom said gently. "They've gone."

He felt Sue's tense muscles give a little as she pulled free of his arm. "All of them?" she asked, glancing toward the desk.

"Yes."

"What now?" Sue spoke sharply. She did not want to hear about the Pownalls, not yet.

"I'll ask."

Tom left her and went to the desk, spoke in a low voice to the sergeant on duty.

"We're to wait," he told her. "Simmons won't be long."

"Why bring them all in?" Sue asked, unable, in spite of her feelings of fear and repugnance, to leave the subject alone.

"Questioning, I suppose. They all must have been involved to some extent."

"Even old Mrs. Pownall?"

"I don't know. Does it matter?"

She shook her head.

"Come and sit down," Tom said. "Please."

She sat slumped forward, her hair shielding her face. "Hettie, too," she said miserably.

"Leave it."

"Why, Tom? Why?"

She turned her pale face to him. Her eyes begged answers. He took her hand, felt it flinch, then grasp his loosely.

A swinging door beside the desk sighed open, swung back with a long, hydraulic hiss. Simmons's shoes squeaked on the linoleum. He stood before Sue, looking down at her.

"We recovered a body." Her head snapped up to meet his eyes. "I'm afraid so," he said, answering the question he read there.

Tom gripped her hand tighter, twisted his body around to face her.

"It's my duty," Simmons went on, "to ask you to identify the body." Tom felt Sue tense, begin to shake. He half rose from his seat.

"Let me. It'll be too distressing for her. I can do it," he told Simmons.

"No." She snatched her hand free of Tom's. "I'll do it." She stood up, holding herself upright, as though already braced for the shock.

"Very well, if you'll follow me."

"Let me come," Tom said.

"No. Thank you," she added, after a pause.

"I'll wait," he called as she ducked under Simmons's outstretched arm and walked through the swinging door.

The door hissed closed behind them, leaving Tom feeling terribly alone.

There might almost have been nothing under the sheet. She wished that it might be so, just a white sheet over a white table in a white-tiled room.

"You realize we've had no time to clean her up?" asked a man in a white coat.

Simmons nodded brusquely, leaned over the table, and lifted the sheet, drawing it back barely to the shoulders.

"Yes," Sue said. "Yes, that's Evie."

She could tell by the eyes and the hair, the stray curls. The whole side of her face was macerated, bruised, and bloodied. Simmons went to cover the face.

"No," Sue said, her voice ringing loud in the chill, fluorescent-lit room.

She placed her left hand on the sheet, beside Simmons, nudging his arm away with her elbow. He let go and moved swiftly around the table so that he could see her face. She pulled the sheet down to Evie's waist with one fierce, angry gesture.

At first the torn clothing, the dried clots of blood, the exposed, pink streaks of flesh did not make sense, would not arrange themselves into a coherent picture. When at last they did so, she felt her cheeks burn with outrage and horror.

"Why?" she demanded, looking straight at Simmons.

Her eyes were large and terrible, seemed to bore into his, into the dark places of his mind. He looked down at Evie, at her ripped and flayed breasts.

"I don't know," he said, and jerked the sheet up over her. "Probably we never will know."

"Why do that? Why? Why to her breasts?" Sue shouted. She leaned toward him, across the body, gripping the edge of the white table so hard that it shook.

"I don't know," he repeated. Then, under the intensity of her gaze, he fumbled for explanations. "Look, some men . . . they can't . . . perhaps he couldn't . . ." He felt sick suddenly. His stomach urged him out of the place, away from the girl's ugly, accusing eyes.

"Some men," she echoed him. "All of you. My God, what hope is there for us, when things like this happen?" She looked at Simmons, her eyes blazing.

For a moment, Simmons thought she was going to spit in his face. He tensed, ready to feel her hatred wet on his cheek, but it never came. She turned on her heel and hurried out through the door. Anger suddenly exploded in Simmons. It had been there all night, fed by the ugliness of his job, by her, by Carpenter's arms and hands all over her. He crashed through the door and in two strides caught up with her. His powerful hand closed about her arm. He swung her around against the wall with enough force to jar her shoulder.

"All right, you've had your say," he said, his red face inches from hers. "Now you hear me. I don't care what you think of me. The only thing I care about is that the guilty party doesn't get away with it. I want to nail him. I want to see him hang."

"An eye for an eye," Sue said, with a tinge of hysteria in her voice. "That fits. Now it's Ashton's turn to hang."

Simmons's anger turned to surprise. He let go of her arm. "Ashton Pownall? What are you talking about? Ashton's a bloody animated cabbage. It's Lucas I'm charging."

It had all begun to go wrong when the toffee-nosed townie, the evacuee kid, came to live with them. Lucas hated the idea of it before he had ever set eyes on Gavin Trope. It wasn't right. It wasn't fair. Up until then he'd been special, his grandpa's favorite, weaned on the old man's fantastical stories. He had spent hours in the old stables, huddled close, listening, watching. In his child's mind the scarecrows took on personalities, became lifelike. Above all, he loved the tales of the Gatherer, the giant scarecrow who stalked the land, gathering up sinners to their graves. Telling only his grandpa, enlisting his secret aid, he had made the first pair of wooden stilts and the clumsy harness that, over the long, rancorous years, he had improved and refined. He had fashioned the hood of sacking and, when all was ready, had stalked out into the fields, the very personification of the Gatherer.

They had all watched amazed, and laughed. They laughed because he was special, his grandpa's favorite, the eldest son, secure in his position, his rightful inheritance. Hettie didn't count at all, being only a baby and, besides, a girl. And Ashton was at best only the second son, the afterthought. Anyway, Ashton had no interest in his grandpa's tales. Ashton didn't care about the scarecrows at all.

Then when the war began and they started to talk about the evacuee children and listened to the news about them, gathered around the old battery-operated radio, things began to change. He wasn't supposed to hear, so he affected not to hear the arguments between George and Mary, his parents, and the old man. They said that he was getting too old to play crazy games, that the old man had turned the child's head with his nonsense. Scarecrows, indeed. What did an almost-grown boy want to play at scarecrows for? Weren't there enough of the damn things cluttering the place up as it was, without Lucas forever stomping about, shouting that he was the Gatherer? Folk in the village were beginning to talk, and who could blame them? Mary Pownall didn't like the way folk looked at her these days. It had to stop. The old man was becoming a bad influence.

One morning, just before Gavin Trope arrived, he had found his precious stilts sawed into short lengths for burning on the kitchen fire. His grandpa had wiped his bitter tears and led him, finger pressed to his mouth, into the workshop and there, under a shroud of sacking, had shown him the new ones, bigger and better, more solid. But he must never breathe a word. It was their secret. The old man had laughed and ruffled his hair. How did he think they could go on without the Gatherer to keep the world free of sinners and fornicators? He only had to trust his grandfather to contrive a time and place where he could practice. He'd fix it, never fear. The copse would be a grand place, as good a place as any.

And so it was. So it always would have been if Gavin Trope hadn't come there to play the cuckoo in his nest. Until then, Lucas had been first and best. First with his grandfather, best at school. To his amazement and everlasting pain, Grandpa soon favored the townie lad. He said Gavin made him laugh, he had such a quaint way of saying and doing things. And the new teacher, smelling of flowers and something unknown and intimate, who turned his flesh to a tingling jelly every time she stooped over him in order to correct his work, she favored Gavin, too. Miss Peterson let it be known that Gavin was better than he, cleverer. Lucas, like the others, would do well to model himself on Gavin, his manners and cleanliness, his neat writing and regular columns of correctly added figures. Well, Lucas was damned if he would. He had no need to follow anyone. He was a Pownall, the eldest son. One day he would own it all and when he had sons of his own, he would make the scarecrows himself and be just like his grandfather, a respected man.

It was pride and anger, not his grandpa's rejection, that kept him out of the old stables that long winter. It was love and a new, mysterious, frightening feeling in his body that made him hang on Miss Peterson's every word and follow her with his dumb, wondering eyes. None of the village girls appealed to him, ripe though several of them were for experimentation. And he would sooner cut it off than go near those stuck-up evacuee girls. He was glad when they went.

The only pleasure he knew that long, soulless winter was playing the Gatherer on his stilts in the copse. The copse that shielded him from prying eyes. The stilts made him tall enough to see way beyond his years. He observed the trottings to and fro of

Gavin Trope, the good little boy, the teacher's pet who got invited to sit with her of an evening, who was privileged to enter her magical world.

It was his stilts that gave him his first glimpse of her naked. He never knew what gave him the idea to try it. It was after he had seen Gavin Trope trot goody-goody home with Miss Peterson waving to him from the golden light of her forbidden door. His chin just reached to the windowsill of her bedroom when he was on his stilts. There was a chink in the curtains, an unnoticed corner caught up on something. Just big enough for a hungry eye it was, just big enough to show her to him as she moved in the golden lamplight, unleashing the marvel of her hair and turning at last full onto him as she released the terrible wonder of her great breasts and touched them with the awful ache of a woman alone.

Night after night he searched for that same chink, but never again did he find it. It was desperation, want of her, the sight and smell of her that drove him onto his own legs to spy on her and Gavin Trope. He had to know what she saw in Gavin. For her he would ape the boy, become him if that was what she wanted. For many nights he remained in ignorance, the checked curtains closed tight against the bitter nights that froze him. But at last, like Grandpa said, patience was rewarded. It sickened him. It sickened him to a frenzy to see her unfasten the buttons of her silk blouse and hold out to Gavin the treasure he had seen first and must be possessed of or die. It crazed him. It carried him to the very borderline of insanity. And then it had made him crafty. He told. He sought adult justice. He told what he had seen, and his heart rejoiced as he heard the rumors fly. He waited until the decision was made that his father should speak to Miss Peterson and suggest, nicely, that Gavin should not spend so much time with her, seeing as how it caused bad feelings and worse comment in the village.

He hid in the lavatory after school and waited until they had all gone, thinking that he with his strong legs had raced on ahead. Then, his heart thumping, his blood throbbing through his body, he had crept back into the schoolroom. She had just finished building up the stove for the night. A stray tress of hair lay against her cheek, which was bathed in a rosy glow from the fire. One button of her blouse had come undone. As she twisted, startled, toward him, the gap made by the button widened to show the swelling hillock of one breast, its soft and perfect whiteness stained pink by the fire glow.

"What do you want, Lucas? Shouldn't you be at home, helping your father on the farm?"

She stood up, pushing the tress of hair out of her face, her breasts uplifted as she tucked it neatly into her daytime bun. But he knew how she could look, how she looked at night, when all but Gavin Trope were gone. He could not speak.

"What is it? What do you want?"

It was like walking into heaven, that long moment as he steadily approached her and put out his hand. Buttons popped from her blouse as he wormed and squirmed his hand inside and, for a moment so brief it could never quite be recaptured, felt the warmth and softness of her.

Evil, she called him. A dirty, snotnosed country bumpkin. An animal. She hit him and chased him out, her screams of revenge following him.

"You haven't heard the last of this. I shall report you. I'll have you punished."

And he had begun to hate her then for the snobby, stuck-up, secretive whore she was. She wasn't fit to live. She was ugly. And the ugliest thing about her were those great flopping tits that she was so proud of. He'd seen better on a cow at milking time.

It was the school caretaker old Bill Grubb who came with the news, after supper, after Gavin had gone to bed. The school would be closed tomorrow. Miss Peterson was in shock. She had asked to see the school board. She was making a formal complaint against Lucas. She was placing the matter before a higher authority. Until it was settled, she refused to teach. She had been vilely assaulted. She was too distressed to eat or sleep or think.

He did not deny or defend himself. He certainly did not confess. He stood there and, no matter what they said to him, no matter how they threatened, he would only repeat what he had seen, what she had done with Gavin Trope.

And there it might have taken its own course, out of all their hands if he hadn't wakened in time to see Gavin Trope skipping along the road to visit her at the crack of dawn. He knew then that there would never be any rest for him unless he dealt with it himself. The old ways were best. His grandfather had taught him that, always. They needed no School Board, no police. This was a job for the Gatherer, for she was a condemned sinner.

With the long passage of the years it became vague in his mind. He remembered putting on the thick, thorn-proof gloves and, in a moment of inspiration, winding some old, rusty barbed wire around them. He remembered getting up on the stilts, fixing the harness, and setting off for the schoolhouse. But he didn't remember much else until she lay beneath him, squealing out her terror like a stuck sow as he scraped and tore her breasts to a bleeding tatter.

And all the time his father was beating him, he thought that it was worth it, knew in his sore bones that he had reached the end too soon, that nothing to come in his life would be as good, as satisfying, as beautiful as what he had experienced that morning as he straddled Miss Peterson and gathered her.

He knew that they had covered up for him. Everyone said so now. Well, he was only a lad. What else could a family do? Gavin Trope was ill, he remembered, and he was glad enough of that. Mrs. Trope came to visit Gavin and from that day till the day he died, Lucas's grandfather never spoke to him again. But that was not the punishment it would once have been, since Grandpa had already betrayed him for the evacuee boy.

It surprised a lot of people now how quickly it was put aside, how easily life returned to normal. But it didn't surprise Lucas. How else could it have been? He grew up. The war ended. And still, in secret—though he always suspected that Grandpa knew—he would put on the stilts in the copse and stalk the land for an hour or two. How it made him feel, what memories it awoke he would never tell anybody, even if he had the words.

People began to move away from the village, tempted into the new factories and the big cities where money was plentiful and more easily earned. Soon there weren't enough children in the village to keep the school open. That reminded Lucas of his duty as the eldest son. He was no longer all that young, but that didn't matter. He began to look around for a woman. That caused a stir in the family, that did. No sooner had he set his eye on Shirley Yates than they had him bundled up the aisle of Brooking Church. As though he would ever do anything to her—she was the mother of his children, the woman who helped him do his duty as the eldest son.

Then there was Ashton's accident. That was the time he became a real loner, keeping the farm going while they all went back and forth to the hospital. He used the stilts a lot at that time, added many refinements to the harness, and made himself several pairs of gloves, more effective than the crude things with which he had caressed Miss Peterson. Ashton's misfortune diverted their attention from him and gave him greater freedom.

That freedom was complete when the old man died. He was neither sorry nor glad; just relieved. Of course he knew that by this death he would not inherit the farm. That would come to him in due course, at the right time, not from Grandpa but from his father. But he had set his heart on the old cottage. He was a married man now, the eldest son, with children of his own. He had a right to a place of his own. He wasn't even surprised when Gavin Trope got it. Gavin Trope had always gotten everything.

He bottled up his anger, even when Gavin had the cheek to write and offer to sell it back to them. His rage broke only when he learned that Gavin Trope had installed his mistress in there. It was a sign, as clear as daylight, that wherever he went Gavin Trope brought with him sin and bad women. And then, of course, as they had all been quick to say in the first flush of anxiety, he would never be completely safe while Gavin Trope lived.

Gathering Trope had been a different kind of pleasure. Afterward, he had been at peace with himself. He'd taken only a few clothes from the back of the car to dress the scarecrow. How was he to know that woman would come snooping around and that Ashton, who helped him now because he liked to play games, would be so crazy as to go using his shirt for a rag? He had to kill her then, to shut her up, though doing so had never been any part of his plan. The other one, the sister, Gavin Trope's young trollop, had been the one he intended. For she was only Miss Peterson all over again, giving and withholding according to some fickle idea of justice that shamed all decent men.

Well, there was always some good to be found in any situation, his grandpa had always said. Sitting, waiting for his trial, Lucas Pownall never for one moment doubted that the Gatherer would get Sue Jackman one day. It was a great comfort to him. A great comfort.

The trial, dubbed the "Scarecrow Murders" by the popular press, lasted three weeks and contained enough bizarre elements to fire even the most jaded imagination. A focal point for reporters and public alike during the first day was the display of exhibits arranged on a special table before the Judge. Exhibit A: a photograph of the skull of Miss Andrea Jane Peterson. Exhibit B: a photograph of the almost complete skeleton of Gavin Trope. Exhibit C: the obscene accoutrements of the murder—a pair of stilts equipped with a leather shoulder harness, the sacking hood with tiny eye-slits, the stout gloves, wound about with vicious, blood-stained barbed wire and almost covered by two great cuffs of twigs.

A gasp of shock went around the court when Detective-Sergeant Simmons of the Nene constabulary confirmed that the skull and the skeleton had been found in the fields around Gatherings Farm, not buried, but serving as parts of scarecrows. Similarly, the body of Evelyn Florence Jackman had been discovered hanging on the rough wooden armature of a scarecrow.

After the macabre and the shocking had run their course, the press mined the rich store of human interest offered by the case. There was the young mistress who sat every day in court and gave her evidence in a clear, light voice, showing emotion only when describing the last time she had seen her sister. She was variously described as "beautiful," "attractive," "pretty," "stunning," and "pallid." Photographs of Evie were obtained from friends and published in all the papers. She was described as the "attractive, fun-loving victim of the Scarecrow Murderer."

The murderer's wife came in for her share of attention, too. Dark, gypsyish, the woman betrayed no emotion. It was widely rumored that she had escaped prosecution herself as an accessory by only a whisker. Before the case had ended, she had been approached by one Sunday newspaper for her story: "My Years of Fear with the Man Who Wanted to Be a Scarecrow."

But it was in the last week, as the trial wound toward its climax, that the press had a field day. The presence in court of Myra Trope, rug-wrapped in a wheelchair, attended by a uniformed nurse, brought outbursts of speculation and fancy to the front pages of the tabloids. How must she feel, seated in the same courtroom as the young, able-bodied girl who had stolen her husband and narrowly escaped a brutal death in a remote love nest?

The truth of the matter was that the bulk of the evidence was dull—forensic reports, psychiatric testimony as to the sanity and insanity of the accused, the power of childhood fantasies, of role-playing and sibling rivalry. Sue's account of her hours in the besieged cottage, heard with rapt attention and a few sharp questions about the failure of police surveillance—ably fielded by an unruffled Simmons—caused a momentary stir.

The only really newsworthy evidence was that given by Thomas Paul Carpenter. His description of the smell of Gavin Trope's rotting corpse and his later realization that the scarecrow Hettie Pownall had prevented him from investigating was indeed Gavin Trope, set pens and pencils flying. The thing he had seen at Sue's window and the marks—now clearly identified as coming from a pair of stilts—all provided color and drama. The climax of evidence was reached when Carpenter recounted his last conversation with Evie and told how her mention of Sue having drawn Gavin Trope as a scarecrow enabled him to see how the murder could have been concealed. Simmons's failure to act then, even though he accepted Tom's theory, brought forth more criticism from the bench along with a commendation for Tom.

The sentences, when at last they came, were almost a foregone conclusion. Life imprisonment for Lucas Pownall in a maximum-security prison for the criminally insane; twenty years for Ashton Pownall, as his accessory, with provision for periodic review subject to psychiatric reports; fifteen years for Hettie Pownall for conspiring to murder Suzanne Jackman. George Pownall received a suspended sentence. The court took into consideration his age and health and accepted that he had acted out of a misguided love for his sons. Only Hettie Pownall broke down when she was sentenced and was seen to look across the courtroom at Sue and shake her head in denial.

They were led from the dock. It was over.

Sue waited in the courtyard at the back of the court where the reporters were not allowed. She felt nothing but exhaustion, the desire to get away. Too late, she recognized the sound of rubber wheels on the temporary ramp set over one side of the steps leading to the courthouse and turned, embarrassed. The nurse, her eyes cast down, stopped Myra Trope's chair beside her. Myra's head was bent to the right and shook a little. Her right arm twitched. It was impossible to tell how she had looked before the illness had twisted her muscles and puffed her flesh. With apparent difficulty, she said, "I don't know what to say to you." Sue nodded. She felt the same. "Yet I felt I must . . . say something."

"It was brave of you to come," Sue said.

"I felt I had to. I wanted to show you that I was wrong ever to have thought that there was some sort of . . . what do they call it? . . . conspiracy? . . . between you and Ga—my husband."

"He told you—I think he told you the truth about us. All of it. I believe he did, anyway."

"Oh, yes, yes. Gavin was a man of his word. Always."

"Yes."

"Did you really love him?" Her head suddenly became still as she held Sue's eyes with her own.

"Yes. Very much."

"So did I."

"I know."

"That must make us friends, then," she said and stiffly, unable to conceal her emotional pain, she held out her left hand to Sue.

Sue took it clumsily and held it. After a moment, she felt the weak fingers press hers and she returned the pressure, smiling.

Tom's car accelerated away, leaving the newspaper photographers scattered across the road, their flashbulbs popping in vain.

"Are you all right?" he asked.

She knew that he was referring to her brief meeting with Myra Trope, which he had observed with alarm.

"Yes, fine. Better than I ever expected."

Tom did not know what to say. He felt and accepted that whatever had passed between the two women in Gavin Trope's life was private. He drove in silence toward Evie's apartment, where Sue had been living for the past months. He could not ask about Myra and he felt it would be wrong to raise again the only topic that really interested him. So, it was Sue who broke the long and awkward silence.

"Thank you, Tom. Thank you for everything. You've been marvelous these last weeks."

"I wanted to do it. You know that."

"I just wanted you to know that I do appreciate it, that my decision isn't . . . has nothing to do with you."

"That doesn't make me feel any better about it."

"I'm sorry."

Tom sighed. "I can't believe you're really going."

"Well, I am," she said, making her voice sound cheerful. "First thing tomorrow morning."

"I'll drive you to the station."

"No. Thanks, Tom, but I've already booked a taxi."

"This is it, then. This is where I get my marching orders."

"If you want to see it that way."

"What other way is there? You know I love you. I want to be with you, and you—"

"I have to make a life of my own. Can't you see that? I've drifted and relied on other people too long. Gavin wasn't the answer, not for me. I see that now."

"I'm not Gavin."

"No. But just now I can't . . . I've got to see how I make out on my own. It's really so very simple."

"I want to look after you."

"*I* want to look after me. That's what you won't understand. I want to take care of myself. I never have. Now it's something I've got to do."

"And I?"

"Oh, Tom, you can look after yourself. You've proved that. You were trained for it. I've got to learn."

"And that means no men in your life?" He sounded bitter.

"For the time being, yes. I know it won't be easy, but I think it will be worth it in the end. If I hand myself over to you now, what will I ever be?"

"Happy, I promise. And secure."

"But I think I can make myself happy, provide my own security. I don't want to take things ready-made from you. That's what I was doing with Gavin."

"You never had a chance. The Pownalls saw to that."

"And, in an odd way, they gave me another chance. Please don't spoil it for me, Tom."

The car came to a stop a few houses down from Evie's apartment. Sue opened the door at once.

"Thanks again for everything. I'll write."

"Can't I come in?"

"We've got to start somewhere, Tom. Both of us."

"I love you, Sue."

"I owe you my life. Don't begrudge my using it, making something of it. You didn't save it all for yourself, now did you?"

"Of course not. Don't be so—"

"Then let me go, Tom, and wish me luck."

She closed the car door before he could answer. He watched her walk up the street. Frustration made him clumsy. He ground the gears of the car. Damn it, he thought, it's time I traded in this young man's toy. He looked up and returned Sue's wave with a smile.